The Web of Humanity

A Novel

Maria Turchin

Aesculapius Books

This book is a work of fiction. Any references to historical events, real people, or real places are used fictitiously. Other names, characters, places, and events are products of the author's imagination, and any resemblance to actual events or places or persons, living or dead, is entirely coincidental.

Copyright © 2018 by Maria Tourtchaninova
ISBN: 978-0-9675868-9-2

All rights reserved.

No parts of this book may be reproduced or transmitted in any format or by any means, electronic or mechanical, including photocopying, scanning, recording, or by any information storage and retrieval system, without permission in writing from the author.

Photographs courtesy of the author & public domain.

Published in the United States by Aesculapius Books

Cover design by Andrew Klimov

For Us

Table of Contents

Preface

The creation of art is often shrouded in mystery and sometimes affected by mystical elements—this is what I experienced with the writing of this book. I was always fascinated with words and languages, but I never identified myself as a writer. Several years ago, I heard an author's interview on NPR. The author repeated a quote that resonated with what had been blocking me for so many years. It went something like this: "It doesn't matter how good a writer is with language and words; the only thing that matters is the actual story, which makes readers think after they have finished a book." I couldn't agree more, but in a sense, the revelation did not matter because I did not have the right kind of story.

Shortly after, my family and I embarked on a road trip throughout Greece. We visited all the archaeological sites of antiquity under my father's frantic passion, who, although a physician, is an avid historian. One of our key stops was the town of Delphi, home of Apollo's temple and sanctuary. Within this world-famous temple, the Delphic Oracle, Pythia, made her predictions to ancient world leaders and those lucky enough to gain access. The accuracy of Pythia's predictions was astonishing.

For centuries, one of the customs was washing one's head and face in the sacred Castalian Spring used by pilgrims for purification before stepping foot into the Sanctuary of Apollo. Many artists, including

Lord Byron, did this to glean inspiration through Apollo's muses. After we finished exploring the sanctuary, we all washed our heads in the refreshingly cold waters of the Castalian Spring that still flows today. As I did this, I asked Pythia the question endemic to the course of a lifetime: What should I do with my life?

Back at the hotel that evening, I watched the sunset over Delphi and journaled. At 3:00 a.m., I awoke to the hissing sound of a woman's voice saying, "Write the book, write the book..." I sat up in bed and looked at my parents, who were sound asleep. I tried to meditate to see if I could hear the voice again but got nowhere.

When we returned to the U.S., I still could not decipher what that voice had been talking about—w*hat book?* I spent months trying to think of ideas that went nowhere until I realized the story you are about to read had surrounded me the entire time. If you ever make it to Delphi, be sure to donate to Apollo's Temple and wash your head in the Castalian Spring. You never know what inspiration may be waiting for you there.

—Maria Turchin

BOOK I

THE WEB OF MEMORIES

Chapter 1

History is just the stories of our ancestors, our families, and us. Some people live their entire lives without knowing where they came from or what they believe in. But that's no longer me, thought Anna Venu. Not after last year.

Anna's gray eyes battled the sun as she looked out onto the caramel desert stretches of Phoenix, Arizona, from Sky Harbor International Airport. Her cell phone vibrated and pulled her out of her reverie. Her flight to the Dominican Republic had been delayed.

Maybe it was the sweet smell of espresso from Cartel Coffee Lab, or maybe it was the distinct German seductively whispered between two traveling lovers. Still, whatever it was, something made Anna yearn to revisit her grandfather's memoir.

The Memoir of Navy Lieutenant John Venu

It was the end of the 19th century in New York. Like the stories of many Americans, my parents were immigrants; Sicilians hoping to escape poverty and life under mafia rule. However, fate intervened and weaved unwanted irony into their expectations, turning their American dream into just another impoverished neighborhood centered around Elizabeth Street in Manhattan—a district now affectionately dubbed Little Italy. During my parents' era, there were no quaint souvenir shops and gelato cafés; just slums, survival, and, yet again, the ruthless control of the Italian Mafia.

On the corner of Elizabeth and Hester Street, a tiny pastry shop emerged from my parents' endless work and perseverance. Our Vennuci family secret cannoli recipe earned the shop its reputation. The innocent dessert became the particular favorite of a not-so-innocent man Joe Masseria, better known as Joe the Boss, head of one of the largest New York gangs. My father was expected to pay him *respect* each morning with a delivery of ten fresh cannolis.

In 1901, my older brother, Lorenzo, was born, which all of Elizabeth Street celebrated. He was a newborn in America, destined for greatness. Each penny was saved. He was going to be a doctor; he was going to make something of himself; he was going to take every scrap the American dream claimed to offer. My parents were to watch it all unfold—justification for coming here and for their continued suffering and hard work. And maybe they would have been, if the Masseria Gang did not exist, or if Lorenzo did not have a temper easily seduced by power, but it did, and he was.

By the age of 17, he was already a street soldier of the Masseria Gang, the cancer that metastasized throughout our neighborhood, preying on the lives of young men. Street freedom, easy money, and easier girls trumped working at the bakery with immigrant, foreign-speaking parents. And so, he looked past the tears of my mother and the painful silence of my father; he simply ignored them.

By the time I came into this world in 1922, Lorenzo was out of the house completely. The first shots of the famous 1930s Castellammarese War were fired around my eighth birthday. The bloodshed between the Masseria and Maranzano gangs skillfully orchestrated by Charles "Lucky" Luciano, spread like wildfire throughout New York

City. My brother was one of its first victims and so, too, was our American dream.

Devastated, my parents turned their focus to me, to make sure I would not follow in my brother's footsteps. They did not have to try hard. I hated the Mafia as much as they did. I was not given the freedom Lorenzo had, so instead, I read about it.

Books about traveling and seafaring adventures filled my lungs with the aspiration and hope that one day, I too would see distant lands. My copies of *Captain Blood* and *Moby-Dick* were worn from use. I imagined myself pulling lines on a ship while kneading dough at the bakery. Every moment I could get to the docks, I was there. The stronger the wind, the heavier the rain, the more vividly I could see myself at the mast of a ship, a real seaman.

When World War II began in 1939, I was nearly eighteen and ready to enroll in the navy but was rejected—to my parents' relief. A childhood fracture had caused my right leg to be slightly shorter than my left. It was hardly noticeable but unacceptable to navy physicians. I felt cheated, my dream taken from me by something I had no control over, but I persisted. There just had to be another way, and I found it when I applied to the U.S. Maritime Training Station, in Sheepshead Bay, Brooklyn. I started my training as an apprentice seaman and graduated as a merchant marine in the rank of ordinary seamen.

The *Connecticut,* a steam merchant ship, was the first realization of my long-awaited vision. The ship sailed between South America and New York, importing coffee, sugar and exporting cars and heavy machinery for South American factories. This first trip was more thrilling than I had ever dreamed. Tropical flora; exotic ports humid dense air with every particle carrying the deep scent of coffee and cacao beans. Nothing like the street life of my New York City childhood.

Intoxicated with joy, I looked to the future with the certainty and conviction that I was following my destiny. It was on the *Connecticut* that I met James, my best friend.

On my first day on the docks, I walked alongside the ship, looking for the captain to introduce myself. The *Connecticut* looked like a massive sea monster groaning with delight as the port cranes' giant arms fed it different pieces of heavy machinery. Crate after crate disappeared one after another into the beast. Obediently, provisions stood along the dock waiting for their turn to be swallowed up into the ship's steel belly.

In front of me, a group of sailors and port workers were gathered in silence, hanging on someone's every word. Straightening my uniform, I made my way swiftly in their direction, hoping to catch the last of whatever instruction was being given to the crew. I joined the semicircle just as a roar of laughter erupted. To my astonishment, the center of attention was nothing more than a young sailor only a couple of years older than myself. The look on my face must have expressed such surprise that it caught his attention. He locked his sharp eyes onto mine, ceasing his laughter abruptly.

"So, who are ya anyway?" he asked me.

Caught off guard, I stared at him wide-eyed.

"Oh, my lads, I think the lady needs an introduction," he continued to taunt me. Everyone's attention was focused on me, watching as redness splashed across my face.

"Oooh no! We got ourselves another shy one!" The sailor snickered, fanning himself in a bashful exaggerated motion. The crowd once again erupted in laughter, while I attempted to look like I was in on the joke. To my relief, with their last laughs, the crowd dispersed. Still having no instruction, I was about to pick a direction to self-assuredly walk to when the sailor grabbed my shoulder.

"Don't be upset, lad. We were just having a bit of fun. I'm James," he said to me. James began to tell me a story with his arm draped around my shoulder as if we had been buddies for years.

"Two days ago, it was Mikie's birthday and now, whachya gotta know about Mikie is....the kid runs his mouth about messing with dames all the time. Thinks he's Clark Gable. So, I figure, okay, I'll take him to the cathouse, see how suave he really is! So, we're togged to the bricks, looking real sharp, except Mikie's trousers are too big, but it's the best pair he's got from his old man." James stretches his hands to show the width of Mikie compared to the trousers.

"When we get inside the joint, Mikie starts looking like a mess of nerves."

James imitated Mikie trying to keep his cool.

"We're facing the room of girls now; they're all winking, you know, pretending like they're crazy about us. And as I'm chatting up this one broad, I look to my right and Mikie is frozen staring at a blonde who's stroking his chest. All the hairs on this kid shot straight up like a damned cat. The girl glances at me because the kid looks stupefied. I mean, *not moving* stupefied, as if he's just seen a ghost. I shrug my shoulders and say that it's nerves. So, the dame gets this sly look on her face, says she knows just how to change that. Suddenly, she's shoving Mikie's head between her breasts and he starts shaking uncontrollably. We start cheering him on, not expecting that all the shaking would wriggle his pants straight to the floor! Poor Mikie feels it and starts waving his arms around, but the broad doesn't notice and thinks we're all laughing along with Mikie's good time! The idiot steps back and trips over his own pants and falls backward! So, there's Mikie on his arse, beaming red like a Christmas light in front of a room of laughing dames!"

James is laughing so hard he can barely finish the next sentence.

"And then," he says, trying to keep his words straight, "we see his underpants wet right where it counts, the poor devil!" James's laughter turns into tears, making me dissolve into hysterics right alongside him.

"And then *you* walk up with that petrified look, just like Mikie... Oh, I'm sorry, lad, but I couldn't help myself."

James composes himself and wipes his face. He then asks me where I'm from and what crew I will be a part of. He gets a bit more serious and says, "Kid, listen, we're your family now, so don't think for a second that you can't rely on any of us like you would on your own brother."

Shaking his hand, I smirked at the irony in his sentence; I wouldn't have trusted my brother with anything.

James was about 5'8" and, even though I towered over him at 6'1", I still felt like I was the one looking up at him. His jawline was strong and the features on his face were prominent all at once, giving him the appearance of somehow being bigger than he was and more mature than he was. Knowing James meant knowing an incredible storyteller with a sense of humor so great it heightened your own. With a strong willingness to help, a sense of camaraderie, and the Irish ability to drink himself sober, James was loved by every crewmember from the captain to the wiper. The only treasured possession James carried was a stone cross that hung from a thick leather string between his collarbones. A well-known priest gifted it to him when he was just a boy, days before his family emigrated to America. Even though his Irish roots should have rendered him my enemy, they brought me closer than my Italian blood had to my own brother. Being a few years older than me, but already ranking as able seaman, James took on the responsibility my older brother never did. We became inseparable.

On December 7, 1941, Japan attacked Pearl Harbor. A day, which will live in infamy, had turned our lives upside down. Four days later, Germany declared war on the United States, and overnight sailing became a life-threatening ordeal. German submarines arranged themselves into wolf packs ravaging our transatlantic communication lines. Those of us who sailed between South America and the United States didn't experience U-boat encounters. Yet hearing the stories of other seamen who'd survived the brutal attacks in the Atlantic and were miraculously rescued by merchant or naval ships kept our eyes constantly scanning the seas.

The situation changed dramatically by 1942. U-boats increased the range of their operations and now started to hunt us along the Atlantic coast and between the Caribbean Islands leading to more and more sunken merchant ships. In response, the U.S. Navy began forming convoys of merchant ships, which they guarded with destroyers. The problem was there were never enough destroyers to cover all the transatlantic and South American routes. Many ships had to risk sailing alone since the eastern industrial centers desperately needed bauxite ore from Trinidad for steel production and fuel from the Gulf.

By 1943, two things had changed: The U.S. Navy learned how to deal with U-boats, turning the tide of the Battle for the Atlantic in favor of the Allies, and both James and I started sailing on the turbine tanker the *Esso Gettysburg*. The ship belonged to the Standard Oil Co. of New Jersey and transported crude oil from the Gulf to the upper east coast. The *Gettysburg* changed my life, and I always keep a photograph of her on my desk.

Esso Gettysburg

Peder A. Johnson was our captain and James swore with 100% assurance that he was a descendant of bloodthirsty Vikings.

"His ancestors sailed 'round the world for generations," James would declare.

Captain Johnson was in fact of Scandinavian descent and an incredible leader with seasoned wartime experience on the *Josiah Macy* and *Esso Providence* tankers. We held onto his career successes like a comfort blanket. Johnson was a tall, well-built man who projected authority, confidence, and composure. Always clean-shaven and without a wrinkle on his uniform, he ran our crew with an iron fist, but always remained fair and calm.

Captain Peder A. Johnson

The *Esso Gettysburg* was a new ship launched in 1942. Onboard, we had a mercantile crew of forty-five officers and sailors, and twenty-seven U.S. Navy personnel who served as gun crew including one officer. We sailed from Atreco near Port Arthur, Texas, on June 6, 1943, carrying more than 120,000 barrels of crude oil destined for Philadelphia. The weather was great, and the trip promised to be an easy one, aside from the looming threat of potential German U-boat attacks. Captain Johnson warned us to be extremely vigilant since we were sailing unescorted with five Navy anti-aircraft gun crews on board as our only defense. They would need time to react to a torpedo or U-boat attack.

The Florida Strait and the Atlantic coast between Florida and Virginia were our two significant challenges on this voyage. Captain Johnson assigned two sailors with binoculars as watchmen on each open side of the bridge. One constantly scanned the ocean from bow to bridge, while the other scanned the ocean from the bridge to the stern and the waters behind the ship. If a watchman could report an approaching torpedo from a far enough distance, it gave the captain enough time to maneuver the ship away from the hit and for anti-aircraft guns to destroy the approaching torpedo. Depending on the model, U-boats carried fifteen to twenty-five torpedoes; if they had been on duty for a while, there was a good chance they only had a limited number of torpedoes left.

On June 10, we were approximately 100 miles southeast of Savannah, Georgia, when at 0100 hours Captain Johnson received a coded message that an aggressive U-boat patrolled the sector we were passing through. Within the last two weeks, it had managed to sink one British merchant ship and severely damage another U.S. tanker. Captain Johnson immediately put the entire ship into alarm mode. He ordered maximum speed and changed the course to a short zigzag to make it more difficult for a torpedo to target us.

James and I had the watch on the port side of the bridge. The night was peaceful, the ocean calm, and the moonlight gave the water a mercurial appearance. In this sort of weather, we were sitting ducks for a U-boat, but it also gave us a chance to see the torpedo's trail from afar.

At Approximately 0340 hours, James shouted with all his might, "Torpedo on the port side directed to the bow! We are on a colliding course!"

My chest contracted with sharp intensity. Without even locating the torpedo's trail, Captain Johnson ordered full reverse while throwing our ship as far to the left as possible. We froze in terror because the torpedo's trail was now clearly visible, even without binoculars. Our gun crews started to fire at the approaching torpedo and toward the approximate location of the U-boat.

The torpedo was getting closer and closer. Despite the full reverse, our ship's momentum continued to push us toward disaster. The torpedo was headed straight for our bow. I remember everything in slow motion: the white silverfish torpedo trail, the ship dipping to the far left as it tried to avoid collision, and my clenched fists around the rails expecting the deafening blow of impact.

Instead, cheers rang into my ears. My eyes burst open; the torpedo had missed our bow by a couple of feet. Everyone jumped from joy below me, and I was about to yell in triumph, but my voice immediately cracked. The trail of a second torpedo suddenly became visible as it snaked toward us.

I screamed in a high-pitched voice, "Torpedo on the port side directed toward the bridge!"

Our ship began to pull in reverse. The captain called for continued full speed as the torpedo grew closer. We prayed for our lives and then, it happened. It hit us mid-ship, somewhere between tanks #6 and #7. I don't remember the moment of impact because I was thrown overboard by a powerful explosion, which disabled our steering gear.

What happened later, I only know from the way James described it to me. The explosion threw him against the wall of the bridge and, for a second, he was disoriented. When he got up, he saw a 25-foot hole in the deck and oil spilling into the ocean. He didn't see me anywhere until he looked at the waters below. I was floating facedown in the water motionless. Without thinking twice, he immediately dove into the ocean. Somehow, he was able to turn me on my side, drain my lungs, and force me to breathe. I started to cough and spit out the rest of the water. I was disoriented and only able to frantically squeeze James's shoulder. He began to talk to me. "You are okay! You are okay!"

As soon as I heard his voice, I began to calm down. We floated close to the ship as I tried to get myself together. Suddenly, James grabbed me by my life jacket and paddled us away from the ship. Simultaneously, I felt a wave hit me; it looked like a huge shark had passed by me.

"Oh, my God! A third torpedo!"

A burst of fire erupted into the sky. The torpedo had hit the ship's engine room. The explosion ignited a fire that ate greedily at the oil that gushed out of the damaged tank. Our ship was engulfed in flames, quickly becoming a floating torch. My chest tightened. She was burning and sinking and I couldn't do anything about it. With every sound of steel splitting and glass shattering, we heard her cry out to us.

A firestorm rose 100 feet into the air, lighting the entire sky with an unnatural red-orange haze. The steel surrounding the hole in the deck glowed red from the heat generated by the burning oil. Scorching waves of steam distorted our vision; it was hell in its most dramatic personification. Amazingly, the *Gettysburg* kept fighting as she died. The gun crew was still shooting in the U-boat's direction up until the damage forced them to abandon their posts.

Suddenly, James's completely calm, deep voice broke my fixation. "Can you swim fast?"

I turned to him, with a silent question in my eyes. He pointed behind our backs and I immediately understood how grave our situation was. The entire ocean was on fire from the oil burning on its surface, creating a surreal image of burning water. We floated facing the ship's port side close to the stern, and on our right the burning oil continued to leak from the tanker. It was spreading around us, pushed by new oil, wind, and current. A burning snake trying to encircle its victims against an already flaming ship. If it happened, we were going to be burned alive.

"Yes!" I shouted.

Quickly, we deflated our "Mae West" life jackets and began swimming in the direction of the stern to escape a fiery death. I never swam so hard in my life, and the concussion I most likely had, began to take a toll on me. I felt myself slowing down more and more until my swimming finally became useless paddling. I was out of breath and dizzy to the point of vomiting. I simply didn't have the strength to continue onward.

James grabbed my collar and pulled me forward to help me swim. The burning oil was getting closer, and around us, the water and air were growing unbearably hot.

I screamed for him to leave me alone and save himself. His wet head turned, his face blurry from my pounding headache, but his words rang clear. Every single curse word I had ever heard combined themselves into one powerful vulgar sentence that shot out of James's mouth. Somehow it gave me a final boost of energy to make it through the narrow strip of clear hot water between the wall of fire on the left and the burning ship on the right.

It was a victory, but my heart was pounding so hard that I barely acknowledged the win. We caught our breath, and James inflated our life vests to take a break. He pointed to the stern of the ship. "Johnny, listen, we need to do one more swim, okay? Are ya with me?" he asked between fast, shallow breaths.

I nodded, spitting out water.

"We need to swim around the stern to the starboard side of the ship. The crew must've launched lifeboats there because the fire is on our side of the ship."

I tried to focus on James to keep my head from spinning. My legs kicked automatically. My brain knew it had to keep going, but my body didn't cooperate. After a couple of minutes of floating to regain some strength, we started to swim again. Suddenly, we heard a deafening explosion from the starboard side of the ship. We stopped and stared up at the *Gettysburg*. She had taken in much water and began to settle by the stern and roll towards us. James cursed and spat into the water. "Damn it! Johnny, swim away from the ship or the whirlpool will suck us in when she goes down!"

The ship continued to sink while we tried to get away as fast as we could. Once at a safe distance, we stopped and floated, completely exhausted. James thanked God we were alive and without burns.

The ship sank slowly with its stern first, a fiercely violent event. Like a demonic being, the black ocean tore apart the steel insides of the helpless *Gettysburg*. The sounds of snapping cables rang through our ears like gunshots from ghostly shooters. The low creaking noise of pressure building up within the vessel, the deafening noise of tearing metal accompanied by the sound of raging fire created a gut-wrenching soundtrack to the devastating visual. The air finally pushed out of the ship as she sank with a final groan as if a giant living creature was drowning in front of us.

Deep sadness emerged from my core as I watched her go. A final realization that this was it. Our home, our protection was gone, and we were left alone, vulnerable to the elements, and unsure of what to do.

Only burning oil and various debris on the ocean's surface were left after she went down. The fire eventually exhausted itself and the early morning hours allowed us to look around, but we didn't see any lifeboats. James started to paddle. My eyes followed his gaze until I saw a partly burned large buffet from the officer's dining room floating a few feet to the left of us. We swam to it and I immediately understood how lucky we were. Just the day before, the steward, with the help of two sailors, took the buffet onto the deck to clean the mold he found growing on the back of the furniture. Now, this cabinet became our savior.

"Look at that, Johnny," James knocked on the wooden buffet. "Looks more like a tree trunk shaped into a buffet than a buffet made out of a tree, it's so thick. We have come up on some luck, kid. This will be our raft to get us out of the water for a bit."

When James got on the buffet, it partially sank. The two of us were too heavy for it, so we took turns. Our only food and water source were the kitchen's apples that bobbed among the debris, little spots of red salvation.

As I floated on our newfound raft, the guilt hit me: It was all my fault. The scene replayed in my head: the first torpedo, my fear, my eyes closing, the hoorahs that made me forget about my post. I had abandoned my duty of watching my sector for another possible torpedo. When I did finally see it, it was too late. Too late to make any changes in the ship's course, too late to save my crewmates, too late to stop our ship—our world, ourselves—from drowning. And now, where were we? In the middle of an ocean that had already tasted drowned men. Hot tears rolled from my eyes, soothing the burn of saltwater.

I started to weep uncontrollably, and James stared at me. "What the hell's wrong?" his voice rose to concern.

"It is my fault, James, don't you see? I missed the second torpedo. I shouldn't have stopped looking; I'm so sorry... I'm so sorry... James, please forgive me."

I was hysterical now, barely making sentences.

"We are going to die here.... It's all my fault."

James tried to calm me down, but I was inconsolable. I cried for my crew, for James, and for myself. He started to shake me.

"Get a grip of yourself, lad! This isn't anyone's fault; we are in a goddamn war, for Christ's sake! There's people dying everywhere."

I wasn't hearing him until *bam!* The left side of my cheek throbbed, and the taste of blood got into my mouth. James had punched me. It shocked me at first, but my hysteria attack stopped. I looked at him. He wasn't sure if I was going to punch him back or cry again.

"Thanks..." I said slowly, rubbing the left side of my face.

"You gotta hold it together, Johnny. Nobody's going to die out here. At least I'm not planning on it," James assured me.

"I know for sure that our radioman sent out an SOS signal after we were hit and any passing merchant ships, the Hooligan Navy, or the navy will sooner or later show up and pull us out of the water. We just need to survive twenty-four, forty-eight hours to give them time to get to us. Okay?"

I nodded. I had completely surrendered myself to James and was immediately sure that this was exactly what would happen. We continued to float on the buffet, each of us holding onto it for an hour or so at a time.

It was James's turn to climb onto our raft when he suddenly grabbed my hand and calmly said, "Look to your left."

I turned, and we momentarily froze. Less than 100 feet away, a periscope looked at us from above the surface of the calm ocean.

"Oh my God! It's the U-boat that hit us!" I said in disbelief.

"Really?" barked James. "And I thought it was Captain Nemo comin' to save us."

James's sarcasm annoyed me, but it worked at diffusing the tension and fear for a few seconds. The periscope started to move forward slowly, and James gave it the finger.

"Are you fucking crazy? They'll kill us!" I hissed.

"To do that, the bastards gotta surface first, and they aren't dumb enough to risk it while a navy ship can pass by at any moment," he finished.

Slowly, the periscope disappeared back under the water's surface.

"Why are they still here?" I asked.

"It's a trick. Our ship sent out a distress signal. U-boats hang around waiting for another ship to show up to rescue survivors. Then they make their next kill," James explained with disgust.

"Ruthless cowards," I said.

"Damn right they are. Any navy ship or submarine that sinks another ship and abandons its crew in the middle of the ocean aren't seamen; they are damned war criminals," James spat in the periscope's direction.

"Do you think we're the only survivors?" I asked.

James immediately felt the pain in my voice. "John, where's your logic? It was forty-five of us crew and how many of the gun crew did we have?" he asked.

"Maybe twenty-seven?"

"So it was seventy-two souls and the ship didn't sink quickly. I bet some got hurt, but they had enough time to launch lifeboats and abandon the ship from the starboard side. Remember how the gun crew continued to fire at that damned U-boat when we were in the water? We got separated from them by the burning ship and, after she sank, the current dragged us apart. They're safe and we'll see 'em as soon as we get to shore."

What James said made sense and I started to feel better, but it didn't improve our current situation, which began to get more and more desperate.

I could tell it was around 0630 hours by the way the sun hung over the horizon, illuminating nothing in the distance aside from occasional debris.

"Here we go again!" James uttered.

"What do you mean *again*?" I asked.

James pointed to my left and I saw the periscope for a second time. It slowly rotated and, after a couple minutes, it once again went under.

"If we were closer, I'd break that thing!" James weakly punched the water with the little strength he had left.

That was what I was thinking, too.

"What should we do to warn other ships about the U-boat?" I asked.

Just before James tried to answer my question, we heard a strange noise and suddenly the water started to swirl around us. Approximately 300 feet from us, the German U-boat began to emerge from the ocean. The bridge appeared first, a steel gray shark fin gliding through low waves. The nose followed, and then the submarine's massive body shot upward from the depths picking up and slamming down onto the surface with a loud blast. It rolled side to side on its own waves, waiting to stabilize itself. An eerie roaring cartoon lion head with the number "66" inside a black rhomb was drawn onto the side of its conning tower as if this killing machine was a mere toy.

"Listen," James whispered to me, "we need to surrender and offer ourselves as POWs. The Germans will take us on board and we'll live."

"But won't someone eventually show up to rescue us?" I asked him nervously.

"John, don't be an idiot! Everyone on the bridge saw me dive into burning oil. They're gonna assume us dead and as soon as the lifeboats make it to shore, the rescue search will stop. Nobody will look for us!" he blurted out. "This is our chance to get outta here alive!"

"James, but you just told me—"

"Forget what I told ya and follow me," he interrupted.

A scraping sound disrupted the panic building inside of me. The hatch on the top of the conning tower opened and a young boatman materialized; he briefly looked at us and carefully scanned the ocean with his binoculars. He said something into the conning tower and, a minute later, the captain appeared. A trimmed beard partially covered his pallid face, and a white scarf tied around his neck. Both men looked at us expressionlessly.

James asked me to stabilize the buffet. He had managed to sit upon his knees and started to wave, trying to explain that we were merchant sailors and needed their help. He also told me to push him closer to the U-boat slowly. The Germans were silent for a couple of minutes; then the captain said something to the boatman, and he shouted at us in a powerful German accent. "Name your ship, tonnage, and your route!"

"*Esso Gettysburg,* a hundred and twenty tons, we were sailing from Atreco, Texas, to New Jersey with crude oil," James answered officially.

The boatmen looked to the captain, but he remained silent until a sickly cough broke the tension. By now, we had come very close to the U-boat, thanks to my slow paddling. James continued to plead for help, talking very slowly. The captain said something to the boatmen who disappeared into the hatch. We remained in the ocean next to the submarine while the captain stared at us from atop the conning tower. Finally, he moved, and I saw something flash in his right hand. I realized that he was pointing a gun at us only after James started to shout: "Don't shoot! Don't shoot!"

Bang! It was too late. I heard the shot, but the pain didn't come. I saw James start to fall back on the buffet. It was James! He was shot! My breath stopped. With all my strength, I steadied James on the makeshift raft. Blood covered his face; I held his head only to see that his right temple was gone. He was dead. My soul ripped open.

I looked at the German at the top of the U-boat desperately; pleading for him to turn the clock of time back, but instead the gun was now pointed at me. I looked into the shaft; a small black hole responsible for the demise of both my brothers. Peace suddenly engulfed me. I didn't care. Let it come; I wanted this tragedy to end.

Suddenly, an alarm sounded inside the U-boat, causing the German captain to hesitate for a second before lowering the gun. He looked at me with cold hard eyes; a thin smile spread on his face. He closed the hatch and the U-boat immediately started to submerge, disappearing in several minutes. A nightmare vanishing with the morning sun.

James was on his stomach with his head turned to the left. He looked asleep—or at least that's what I needed to believe. Panic was making me nauseous. I couldn't see him dead. I started talking to him like he was still alive.

"My God, James, we almost died!" I understood that I was talking crazy, but I ignored my common sense.

"James, it's okay. I'm going to take charge now. You said yourself that no one is dying here.... Just leave it up to me, okay?"

I slapped myself in the face hard while the ocean calmly stroked me. I started to think about what to do next.

"If the ocean gets rough, James, I'm going to have a hard time keeping you on the buffet."

I tore his pants into long strips of fabric using my teeth and tied them together, securing James onto the buffet. I took the life jacket off James and inflated it to the max. Then I placed it into the buffet, which gave it more stability. My energy faded; I chewed on an apple—salty skin with sweet juice underneath.

The sun was getting higher, the stress of the last few hours took its toll on me and I slowly drifted into a semiconscious state. I dreamt I was walking with my father along a cool forest road in the Catskill Mountains where we had rented a small cabin for the weekend. Suddenly my dream was interrupted by a sense of bitter loss to the point of physical discomfort. I woke up and I realized to my horror that I was floating utterly alone in the middle of the ocean. I started to panic and called for James, but I had drifted away from him.

With adrenaline fueling what was left of my lucid mind, I identified that I was floating up to my chin and saw everything on the water's level. I needed to lift myself above the surface to look around. I fumbled to take my life jacket off and tried to jump out of the water, but I lost all my strength after two attempts.

After several unsuccessful tries, I put my fully inflated life jacket under my knees and rose above the water.

Carefully scanning the horizon, I noticed a dark spot directly against the sun. With great relief, I realized it was James. I tied the life jacket around my shoulder and swam in the direction of the sun, taking short rest stops to float on the jacket trailing behind me. I don't know how long it took me to get to him, but it felt like hours. When I finally reached the buffet, I attempted to speak through a parched mouth.

"Please, James... Please don't ever leave me alone here. We almost lost each other!"

Only bits of the sentence came out. I was mostly mumbling. Using the remains of the fabric, I tied myself to the buffet. An entire day passed, and I constantly talked with James, trying to keep his spirits up and inform him of any changes. My only goal was to get him ashore. I no longer cared for my own life.

Exhaustion ate at me, my mouth swelled with salt, and my eyes lost themselves in the identical waves surrounding me. The endless sky, the feeling of constant suspension, my mind was in a state of hypnosis and I blacked out more frequently. We floated between the heavens above and the hell below, lost souls unable to find peace.

I think it was midafternoon the following day when I hallucinated a boat approaching. I felt myself being pulled from the water, but I was sure it was only the waves toying with me. I heard myself yelling not to forget James but didn't know who I was talking to. Only when I hit the deck of the ship did I realize we'd been rescued.

Our savior was the private yacht *Gloria*, belonging to the Hooligan Navy, who patrolled the Atlantic coast's waters for possible U-boat and survivor sightings. The crew realized James was dead after he was pulled on board. I didn't listen to them and kept repeating that they must put us in the same cabin. They didn't argue, and, in several hours, we docked in the Savannah port.

I was rushed to the hospital but aside from complete exhaustion, dehydration, and an intense sunburn on my face, I was okay. I soon learned that only fifteen crewmen from the *Gettysburg* aside from myself survived the U-boat attack. They were saved by the U.S. Navy's *George Washington* and were in Charleston.

The guilt I felt for James and the crew's deaths was devastating, and this time I did not have James to punch it out of me. It set in firmly, plastered into my chest. *What right did I have to live?* A deep depression overtook me, and I was transferred to the psych ward.

My days felt pointless. I wasted them away drawing pictures of the U-boat and its goddamn commander who had pointed his gun at me only to do worse and murder James. The detailed graphic drawings that I left blanketing the floor around my bed got the nurses' attention, the doctors', and for some odd reason, Navy Intelligence.

My doctor notified me that Lieutenant Commander Kramer from the U.S. Navy had requested to visit me, hear my story, and ask me some questions. I obliged and, the following day, a tall thin man with a crooked nose and a forehead that hung heavy with the type of lines carved by stresses that far surpassed any ordinary man, stepped into my room.

He patiently sat on the edge of my bed while I told him the detailed play-by-play of what had happened to me, James, and the *Gettysburg.* He took notes and carefully studied my drawings. When I finished, he said that he had never heard of a German captain shooting survivors in the ocean. If he hadn't talked with the crew of the *Gloria,* he simply would not have believed that what I was telling him had actually happened.

He pulled out many photographs of U-boat captains and asked me to identify James's murderer, but I failed to. All I could remember was his icy, lifeless stare.

Disappointed, Lt. Commander Kramer returned to my drawings. "These are inaccurate, you know. U-boats of this type have only one periscope, not two."

I closed my eyes to inspect the image in my head.

"The sun was in my eyes that day and the captain was on the top of the conning tower, so I couldn't see him clearly, but I remember that damned steel shark. My drawings are accurate."

For a second, annoyance flashed on his face. I did not care if he believed me or not. He thanked me for my time and left.

Two days later, he returned with another officer and a navy psychologist; they wanted to test my memory. Now I was the one irritated; first, they didn't believe me and now they considered me insane?

By the day's end, I had passed all tests and was wished a speedy recovery by the three men. Before Lt. Commander Kramer left, he gave me his contact information in case I remembered anything else. He added that if I ever wanted to enlist with the navy, he would find me a position at the Norfolk base in Virginia, where he was stationed.

Only later did I find out why my account had caused such a commotion. I was the first to report witnessing the new VIIC 41 U-boat, the first model equipped with two periscopes. It was later confirmed by the French Resistance agents who saw the new VIIC 41 leaving the Saint-Nazaire base in France for Atlantic patrol.

After leaving the hospital, I tried to snap myself out of my new reality and back into the life that had *not* been taken from me. Figuring I would start where things had ended, I traveled to Charleston to see my remaining crewmembers from the *Gettysburg*.

My nerves got the best of me as I geared up for their anger and blame for failing to spot that second torpedo. Instead, they rejoiced at my arrival.

Thomas, our second mate, pulled me into a firm embrace, "Johnny! I can't believe you're here! We were sure you had died."

"I felt like I had died myself," I replied. The joy I felt made me realize I would be able to keep on living. Everyone thought highly of my actions and were shocked by the circumstances of James's tragic death. I wanted to know what had happened to the rest of our crew.

The men around me sobered and Clyde broke the silence to speak. "After the second torpedo hit, we all panicked, but Captain Johnson, God rest his soul, remained so damn calm directing rescue efforts amidst the firestorm coming from our gunners that all of us fell into line. Immediately, we began lowering lifeboats and, for a moment, we thought we'd be okay." Clyde wiped his face but continued talking. "And then the entire starboard exploded and the *Gettysburg* quickly sank, taking the lives of the captain, thirty-seven crewmen and twenty armed guards.

"Two lifeboats made it to the water and most of us dove overboard, but not Ensign John Arnold." Victor grimly took over the tragedy, "Burning oil sprayed his face and neck, but he continued to direct the gun crew to keep shooting until they too had to dive overboard. He's going to receive the Navy Cross for his heroism."

"Fifteen of us had made it to the lifeboats.... We didn't see you, Johnny, and we didn't see James. We floated through sunrise and much of the next day. Down to our last flare gun, it miraculously signaled the *SS George Washington*."

What a tragedy. We were grown men, but we wept like children. That night, we saluted our crew and Captain Johnson, true heroes taken by the sea.

With a heart full of dread, I visited James's family in Boston. I felt deep guilt that I was there instead of their son but James's parents hugged me and gave me his stone cross. I wear it to this day—it is my most precious possession.

With Lt. Commander Kramer's help, I joined Navy Intelligence, mastered German language courses, and quickly rose in the ranks. After D-Day, I was transferred to Army Intelligence and stationed in France throughout the war's end. For that, I thank God each day because in Paris I met my wife, Helga.

After World War II, I was convinced people wouldn't let such atrocity happen again. Still, as I watched wars unfold in Korea, Vietnam, Afghanistan, the Balkans, Somalia, Iraq, and Sudan, I realized how susceptible we are to violence. When our inner values and beliefs are manipulated by power-hungry leaders, we too become victims of war.

This madness must stop within each family first and as I have heard it said, it is better to have ten years of negotiations than to have one day of war.

> *This memoir is dedicated to the bravery of the 9,300 merchant seamen who died in the Atlantic Ocean, maintaining the U.S. economy and supplying a lifeline to the Red Army with weapons, ammunition, and food rations. Survivors returned to a nation that denied them veteran status and any benefits of the G.I. Bill for four decades, the majority of their remaining lives.*
>
> *—Lieutenant John R. Venu, USN, 1995*

Anna sat staring at her cell phone, her grandfather's photograph stared back at her; his eyes focused with the keen intellect that helped him survive the war. Though she'd read his memoir before, this was the first time that its greater meaning—and its impact on her family—finally hit her. Anna's mind began stretching back to the beginning, which started with the end of her grandmother's life

John R. Venu

Chapter 2

The end of Grandmother's life came with as little warning as a midnight earthquake scraping beneath families in dormant sleep. Helga had held everyone together; a conglomerate of the entire family was enclosed within her. She had blue-gray eyes that smiled through wet stares. Her lids seemed to hold back a sea wanting to splash forward and down her once-soft facial features that had hollowed with age. She had been a woman of average height and delicate build but projected the aura of a six-foot-tall queen. Grandmother was unlike any woman Anna had ever met. She had keen intuition, which she had used resourcefully playing stocks in the 1960s and pulled out of the same market shortly before the internet bubble burst.

By the time Anna appeared in the world, her grandmother had filled her days teaching French, Austrian, and Russian. Her knack for language acquisition was no coincidence; her father, a local doctor in a small Austrian town, knew very well the promise of education. This talent would twist and lead her every second of her life.

Grandmother starred in Anna's memories like a central figure in a film noir. Cast amidst the black and white undertones of a mystery surrounding the entire first half of Grandmother's life. Grandmother had simply refused to talk about it. On the edge of seventeen, Anna had gathered a rough outline of Grandmother's youth, from what her grandfather and father knew, which in itself was not much.

Against her parents' wishes, Grandmother had run away to Berlin to marry a young German officer at the start of World War II. Shortly thereafter, he was killed on the Eastern Front during Germany's push into the Soviet Union. She survived Berlin's occupation, secured work as a translator for the Allied forces, and was transferred to Paris, where fate kindly took her hand and joined it with a young Naval Intelligence Officer, Anna's grandfather. Once settled in the United States, her grandfather offered to help Grandmother search for remaining relatives back in Austria. Grandmother met his proposals with cold blank stares until her grandfather stopped offering.

Anna's family understood that the tragedy and devastation of World War II had caused Grandmother to completely disassociate herself from Germany and Austria to the point of obsession. As a child, Grandmother had soaked in her father's disgust with his countrymen who betrayed Austria. She recalled seeing swarms of people line the streets of Vienna and hysterically cheer as "that monster rode in an open car holding his hand in that stupid salute."

Her parents' chanced deaths from a collision with a German Army truck reinforced her hatred. What the Nazi regime had done—to the world, to her, to her family—was unforgivable. She chose to purge her life of any associations of that time and place.

This was why, as Anna matured, she seldom asked her grandmother to recall something that evoked such tragedy until, one day, her curiosity overtook any sense of right and wrong.

Preparing herself for Grandmother's usual vagueness, Anna was stunned when Grandmother met her eyes and then, looking beyond them, started speaking.

"When I was a girl, I was fascinated with exotic animals—especially the zebras and giraffes. It must have been their colors and patterns...they mesmerized me. I moved to Berlin young and the world-famous Berlin Zoo became my safe haven. That all changed when the first Allied bombings and Russian artillery devastated the city. There was no precise aim, so everything got hit, including the zoo. A tragedy in itself that is never mentioned....

"It was one of those rare moments when, early in the morning, quiet fell on the city while Soviet artillery took a break. The shells had silenced everything—no birds singing, and no people chattering or riding their bikes as they had when I'd first arrived. I walked through rubble, in a state of stupefied exhaustion. My dear friend had been killed the day before and I didn't think I could feel any more pain. Shattered Berlin was now my only companion, and, in my grief, I breathed heavy for the dying city. I felt closer to it than I ever had before. I was completely alone and the hope of perseverance had left me. The shells did not matter anymore; nothing did. I aimlessly walked by crumbled buildings struggling to keep themselves upright, and through glass-littered streets that sparkled ironically in the dim light. Spring fog was mixing with city dust, turning the air an opaque white.

"Suddenly, my ears picked up a noise that I couldn't place—a low nicker. I walked toward the sound with caution—and black stripes stepped out of the fog. Zebra.

"I stood there, staring in awe, trying to comprehend the surreal image before me, set in stark contrast against the backdrop of a ruined city. Still exhausted and in a state of shock, my mind and body struggled to sync what it saw with comprehension. *How could this be?* I was ready for tanks, bombs, and agony, not this image that seemed pulled from a dream.

"We met eye to eye at a short distance with no barrier between us. Slowly, we walked toward each other. I tried to think of what I would do once we met, what I would say. My hand hit a stale piece of bread in my coat pocket and I curled my fingers around it: the perfect offering.

"There, in the silence, in the presence of this wondrous creature, eyes big and black, staring at me, I felt a soft set of lips carefully engulf the bread. My hand was sticky and wet. I felt the hot air escaping its massive nostrils; black eyes still focused on my face."

"My body again was shocked by the flood of a long-lost emotion, joy, that filled me like a helium balloon. Time froze for those few moments, and the world somehow made sense again.

The zebra waited and watched me. I said I had no more bread and that I was sorry. As if the zebra understood, it turned and started to walk away slowly."

"Then my memory stops. The next thing I recall is severe deafness, succeeded by intense pressure and pain, and being pinned against what must have been the street. My eyes slowly were able to focus through a hammering in my skull; disembodied hands tried to lift me."

"Later, I learned an artillery shell had landed several feet away from me. The zebra had died. Its body took the impact of the blast, sparing me. Amid artillery fire, my neighbors pulled me from underneath the dead animal and into a shelter. I owe my life to the sacrifice that creature made for me. It gave me the strength to survive all that followed."

Anna felt her face streaked with salty tears, and, as she wiped her cheeks, Grandmother briskly left the room. She resisted the urge to ask anything more but replayed the story until it had etched itself verbatim in her mind. Grandmother was left alone to keep her remaining secrets until her death sealed them away forever.

The day Grandmother died was calm, touched by a warm, soft breeze potent with the Sonoran Desert's sweet smell. Grandfather was first to sense something was wrong and shouted to call an ambulance. Anna was unable to believe it until the paramedics announced that her Grandmother had passed.

Anna and her parents worried for Grandfather; whose entire world had revolved around his wife. His love for her surpassed that of even his own life—how would he go on? Therefore, they were dumbfounded when he seemed to be taking it the best out of all of them. Perhaps, they thought, age and his own traumas had prepared him for loss.

However, after a month elapsed, the emotions that had been dormant within Grandfather went through him like an electric shock, numbing him to the world. Grandfather no longer said much; in fact, he seemed to disappear altogether. Locked in his book-lined study for days amidst famous words and still, even among them, he could not find his own words to express the sorrow he felt.

Instead of coming together, her family retreated into themselves, leaving Anna to find consolation among the mountain trails of Dreamy Draw Park.

Chapter 3

The mountain trails of Dreamy Draw Park led Anna farther and farther skyward. The clouds hung low; they were oversized heaps of snow that floated with bright blue bottoms close to the earth. Anna reached her favorite peak, from which she could see the whole of Phoenix spread out before her, a topographic map. She had always flourished there, amidst the mountains that took turns rising between buildings and suburban housing developments.

Grandfather had wanted Anna to see all of America, and she did. She lost and found herself in New York, soaked in colonial history in Boston, and ran through Oklahoma's fields. Curiously she peered into the geysers of Wyoming and roamed freely with the buffalo across Montana's stretches. Mysticism enveloped her at the foggy beaches of Oregon, and the Washington rains soaked her till she felt herself blossom with every drop. Along the California coast, she turned into a fish and then a bird when she marveled at the redwoods whose roots reached the ocean shore.

But Arizona never stopped being home. Each time she looked to the horizon where sunsets and sunrises spilled hot red hues across the desert sky and the strong red giants of earth rose to meet the blaring sun, she felt her spirit soar as if the vastness of it all could carry her upward until she became one with the atmosphere.

Anna pondered life as she often did in the solitude of the mountains.

Grandmother, you've been gone for a year now...

Grandmother had been Anna's closest companion throughout her father's disciplinary focus on education. Through her, Anna learned about the workings of the world and developed a love for the piano; a talent passed on to Anna from her grandmother and great-grandmother, a woman Anna knew nothing about but felt connected to through music. Grandmother had died before Anna had graduated from Arizona State University.

Whether by her father's suggestions or by her own choice—it was hard to differentiate the two—Anna decided to apply to law school.

Anna's thoughts now shifted to her father and the anger she had been trying, but failing, to subdue all morning. Earlier in the week, he had gone behind her back and arranged for her to interview for a summer internship with Richard Crane, a corporate executive from his arsenal of law school buddies.

She inhaled the smell of wet earth and pushed away the anger to not ruin her chance at solitude before being forced to act fascinated by Richard Crane's world of contract law. She looked to the sky.

I miss you, Anna said to herself—to the sky, to her grandmother who she hoped was listening.

Anna took her time walking back down the freshly rain-stained trail, winding between the boulders and cacti. Her new white Audi TT Coupe—the graduation present from her father—glistened out of place against the natural world.

She drove down Scottsdale Road and slowed down in the far-left lane as she approached Frank Lloyd Wright Boulevard's intersection. The light was about to turn red. She felt herself getting impatient. Her car's radio was speaking nonsense, which only irritated her further. Her index finger mindlessly pushed scan, bouncing between stations.

Anna's eyes flashed to her right, briefly resting on the woman behind the wheel in the neighboring lane. The woman's hands gripped the wheel tightly, exposing blue veins twisting around her knuckles. Anna's finger continued to push onward, clicking past stations until her peripheral vision noticed the opposing traffic light change to yellow. Right after Anna's finger pushed the scan button one more time, and before her foot was able to push down on the accelerator, Anna's entire body felt a deep vibration radiate through her. A remarkably powerful and haunting sequence of notes emerged from her surround-sound system at piercing volume.

The station she had landed on was in the midst of the 2nd 4-bar motif of Ludwig von Beethoven's Fifth Symphony on its seventeen-second mark. *Dun dun dun duuuunn...* These mere four seconds caused Anna to lose her senses, the light flashed green, and the woman in the car to her right peeled into the intersection.

The melody started to gain momentum, speeding up Anna's heart rate and disorienting her mind from the tremble of the music. Her hand was unsuccessfully fumbling for the volume knob as the driver in the car behind her slammed a palm on their horn. Still at the light, Anna was about to shift gears when her eyes momentarily caught a gleam of metal coming from the right at an alarming speed—and running through the red light in front of it. The music ascended, growing louder and higher into the heavens, faster and faster.

Instantly, the hard metal shell of a dark blue truck crushed quickly into the right side of the car next to her at the thirty-two-second mark of the symphony. The car spun around, dismantling itself with every turn as the song reached its peak at thirty-eight seconds into the first movement.

Anna's eyes were wide, her pupils dilated, and her fingers turned white from the pressure of being pinned into the steering wheel. The powerful notes enclosed Anna within a capsule of raw human alertness. Anna could see the woman's body jerk from side to side beneath her seatbelt every time the car spun, skidding on tearing wheels. Her eyes witnessed a life on the brink of destruction. She did not feel the hot tears blur her vision, but her heart felt the sting of despair as the symphony slowed with the introduction of the trumpets at forty-one seconds. The wrecked cars finally came to a mangled halt.

At forty-four seconds, the symphony's trumpets seemed to calm her, stroke her, like angels blocking her journey to the other side. They told her things had to be this way—it was not her time yet, but someone else's. The music then got busy, once again taking speed, an ironic dance. She could not understand why the symphony suddenly sounded so joyous. Then it came once more, that warning: *Dun dun dun duuuuun...* Anna sat staring, still at the light, her foot frozen on her brake pedal.

Around her, people ran out of their cars amidst the disaster of crunched metal and steam. The notes were blurring now, yelling at her, making her nervous and overcome with grief. At six minutes fifty-eight seconds, Beethoven's masterwork went silent. Anna slowly lifted her head from the steering wheel and returned to the physical world.

It had only taken minutes for the ambulance to arrive; traffic was getting redirected around the catastrophe. Anna pulled her car away from the accident and onto a side street. Shivering, she parked it as her body attempted to relax.

That woman's face kept flashing inside Anna's mind. It was a face that had left everything up to God but was terrified to do so. Anna got out of her car and felt the heat of the desert hit her face.

What the hell was that? She asked herself, bewildered. *That could have been me. If I had not heard those notes... I would have sped forward...*

The music had called her to attention like her own personal mynah bird out of Huxley's literary world. If not for the music, she could have driven into the middle of the intersection first; the truck would have hit her instead. Her stereo was set to an average volume, but the Fifth Symphony had deafened her. That was the odd part. An eerie chill came over her.

"I couldn't even find the damn volume knob!" she said aloud to herself, recalling the intensity with which the notes had affected her in the most usual way.

It was as if I was conversing with the music, but I have no idea what was said.

Anna replayed the events in her head: *I was driving to... The interview!*

Suddenly, it dawned on her. Memories of the past several years twirled around her, yet this moment of clarity came with a sense of dread trailing behind it.

Whose life have I even been living?

Anna pulled out her cell phone and texted her father about the accident and missing the interview. She started the engine and pulled onto Bell Road to head home.

The familiarity of her room returned a sense of solace. The sheer gold curtains engulfed everything in the warmth of the setting sun like they did every evening. While the comfort nagged at Anna, her mind rearranged itself—it was used to snapping back into focus. She did not like the strangeness of the day's events. Everything had some sort of meaning, and she needed to find it.

Anna opened her MacBook and stared at the Google search screen.

"Alright, Beethoven, just like anyone who has interfered with my life, the first thing I'm going to do is Google you."

She typed "Symphony 5 Beethoven" into the search. Wikipedia came up first, and Anna scrolled through the history and score breakdown. With temptation, she considered replaying the song.

Anna lowered the volume to decrease the impact. As before, the first notes trembled through her. The entire event at the intersection began to replay in front of her. The woman's screams echoed through Anna's mind before coming to a lifeless end. Anna tried to push her imagination out of the way and scrolled through the rest of the Wikipedia entry:

"Written between 1804 and 1808..."

Beethoven was thirty and losing his hearing then. How in the world did he compose such music while being half deaf? Incredible!

Anna's eyes quickly scanned over the section labeled Fate motif. Anna read it over casually until a sense of eerie vitality came over her. She kept reading:

"... symbolic significance as a representation of Fate knocking at the door."

Right here, right in front of her, was evidence supporting her premonition. Fate was knocking on the door—her door. Anna laughed into her empty room.

Are you kidding me right now? I have what? Beethoven telling me to chase the unknown?

Anna's fingers massaged her temples. The sound of the front door opening caused Anna to sprint to her bed. The last thing she wanted was another parent lecture; she was sure that would be saved for early the next morning.

Chapter 4

Early the next morning, Anna awoke with new eyes to face her own world—one she had somehow missed for the past several years. She washed her face in the bathroom and curiously observed her reflection. The same fox-like face, ashen hair, and her grandmother's deep-set gray eyes. Yet something was different. The room surrounding her was vivid and her skin tingled with sensation.

"Everything is illuminated," she whispered to her reflection, "and what I want...is to leave."

With a smile, she turned and walked out the front door. Carefully, she pulled out of the driveway, knowing exactly where she was headed. Anna rolled down the window and felt the warm desert wind on her face.

After twenty minutes of driving west on the 101 freeway, Anna eagerly took the familiar 51st Avenue exit and descended into a large housing community situated on the edges of a sprawling man-made lake complete with fishing boats and trout. It was an oasis of sorts in the middle of the typical desert sprawl.

She parked and walked to the large glossy wooden door of her grandparents' exquisitely constructed home. Anna let herself in and started making her way toward the back patio, which opened pleasantly onto the big lake. She quickly spotted the back of her grandfather's head of white hair, which glowed in the sun like a patch of new snow.

"Grandpa!" Anna threw her keys on the countertop and slid open the screen door.

"Anna!" John turned around, put down his coffee, and hugged his granddaughter.

"Every time I see you, Anna, you are even more beautiful." John took his granddaughter's hand and softly twirled her around.

John was a tall man and had always taken measures to be physically and mentally fit. After Grandmother's death, his frame began to sag under the weight of grief. His mind, however, was still sharp, even though he had entered his tenth decade.

"So, what brings my favorite granddaughter today?"

"I'm your *only* granddaughter," mocked Anna.

"But still my favorite."

"Grandpa, I got into a car accident—well, almost."

Instant worry hit John's face as she began to replay the series of events leading up to the crash. She detailed the moment of clarity, one of confusion, and the persistent feeling of exploration.

John listened intensely. Every word was carefully considered; each detail evaluated separately and then once again as a whole.

"Listen, Anna," John began, "it is peculiar to me that this epiphany happened to you at this exact moment in time."

Anna gazed questioningly. His comment was unexpected.

"Let us first get out of the sun, so we can talk."

John led the way to his study; a room Anna knew well, due to her years exploring it as a child. International maps covering the walls, a floor globe the size of the world to her when she was little, and shelves of thick, sturdy books provided a calming atmosphere. Various knick-knacks peeked out provocatively between navy ship models. They both sunk into suede chairs facing John's oak desk.

"I know you, Anna, better than I think your father does—or I should say, better than he will admit to knowing you. I have seen you succeed in everything you have ever wanted or were told that you wanted. I know you will travel to wherever you feel you need to venture."

"Yes, there are a couple of research fellowships I want to apply for—"

"Anna," John cut in, "though I admire your strategy, it won't be necessary." She shut her mouth, feeling rather dismissed.

"Your grandmother left you a considerable amount of money in her will accessible to you after graduate school. However, considering the circumstances, I am giving you access now."

"Grandpa are you serious?!" she exclaimed.

"Anna, listen for a minute," he said solemnly, putting Anna's excitement on pause. "There is a condition to this funding."

"Of course! What is it?"

"I have a personal favor I need to ask of you," he began. "Do you know how your grandmother and I met?"

Anna nodded. "Yes, you saved her from that street gang in Paris after the war..."

"Correct." John's gaze fell for a moment, his eyes gathering within themselves the ability to travel back to the movie of his own past.

"There is, of course, a much longer version," he said.

"It was late April of nineteen forty-six. I was walking back from one of the bars where the boys and I were celebrating our buddy's return home to the U.S. His demobilization papers had come in a few days prior. I remember walking through the city at night and noticing how especially dark the streets were. Paris was known as the City of Lights, but the war had cloaked it in gloom. In the shadows of the city and the war, hooligans and street gangs would convene every night, looking for ways to act on the trouble around them.

"I was making my way down Rue Dupetit-Thouars, my eyes constantly scanning my surroundings. They landed on a teenager standing on the corner of a darkened side street Cité Dupetit-Thouars. He was taking short quick puffs from his cigarette. He noticed me as I drew closer and started to fidget, showing nervousness. He was trying to play it cool but was failing at it miserably. I could sense his eyes following my every step from underneath the brim of his flat cap.

"My gun was always on me, and I gripped its handle tightly as I walked past the guy, listening for any sounds or footsteps. I doubted he was alone. By now, I had reached almost the middle of the side street when my peripheral vision caught a glimpse of what seemed to be a bare female chest glowing white in the light of a full moon; darker shadows enclosed her.

"The woman appeared to be pushed up against the wall of a building with men surrounding her. By the time I reached the opposite side of the street, I already knew my plan of action. The war had trained my brain to quickly find optimal solutions for problems and situations I would need to get out of.

"My first thought was to verify that this was indeed assault and not a prostitute dealing with her clients. I made my gait unstable and unbuttoned part of my uniform to appear careless and drunk. I turned around sloppily and made my way back across the street toward the kid with the cigarette. This time I focused my vision to cut through the shadows. It was obvious this woman was in real trouble.

"As soon as the kid saw me walking toward him, he started to panic. I didn't want him to do anything stupid, so I quickly smiled from a distance and pulled out a cigarette from my pack, motioning for a light. The kid relaxed, smiled, and gave me his lit cigarette.

"Using his cigarette, I slowly lit my own and simultaneously moved to the kid's left side pretending to protect the burning butt from the wind. As soon as I got behind the corner, with one sweeping motion, I clinched the kid's neck into a headlock, pushing my forearm firmly under his throat. And I pulled the kid into the front doorway of the neighboring building. I stuck my gun into his face and told him that I would shoot it off if he made a sound. He started to whimper from pain, and I tied his hands to the rails with my belt and stuffed my handkerchief down his throat. I told him that if he remained quiet, I would let him go; otherwise, I would arrest him and hand him over to the police for prosecution. He nodded convulsively that he understood.

"I unbuttoned more of my uniform jacket and untucked my shirt, making myself look even more like a drunkard. I walked into the side street and assessed the situation. Five young men between the ages of sixteen and eighteen surrounded a beautiful young woman. Two of the men had her arms pinned against the building while one slightly older man, who seemed to be the gang leader, stood in front of her, fondling her breasts and saying something, which made the other guys laugh.

"What was unusual was the woman's reaction to her desperate situation. Her face was completely detached, full of confidence. It was as if this was a mild irritation brought onto her by these pathetic scums. She looked directly into the leader's eyes and showed such annoyance, boredom, and even superiority that the leader was clearly irritated. The gang was so caught up in the drama that no one noticed my approach until I came very close. In a drunken voice, using English instead of French, I said, 'Good evening, everyone! What a pretty fish you caught here, my friends!' The entire gang turned to me, stunned as if I were a ghost.

"Perfect, I thought to myself. I had caught them off guard. After a moment of silence, one of the younger guys came up to me and started to speak to me in French; his words carried the smell of cheap beer. He told me that I should go home because it was their French business and this girl was a whore who had slept with Nazis. I pretended I didn't understand a thing and lightly punched his shoulder in a playful manner with a broad, stupid smile on my face.

"The entire gang looked at me and then to their leader, who finally left the young woman and walked over to me. That was exactly what I wanted. His face wore a smirk that was half-hidden by a big crooked nose. It made him look both menacing and comical. His eyes glowed with the type of confidence fed only by the fears of others. The belt that held up his pants bore an American Army seal. It looked stupid, shining against his dirty trousers, and, frankly, it pissed me off. A heavy, oversized brown leather jacket gave him the impression of being a much bigger man.

"He knew some basic English with which he started to tell me the same story, but with exaggerated motions and gestures to entertain his watchful crew. I got closer to him, pretending that I was trying to understand his English, pulled out my gun, and stuck it under his chin. Several seconds of complete silence followed until I heard the young woman's voice calmly saying in almost perfect English, 'Behind you...'

"Immediately, I realized I was in a vulnerable position and quickly recalculated my course of action. I slightly turned the muzzle of my gun to the right and pulled the trigger.

"The sound of the shot was deafening, shattering the night, which hung low in between the buildings of the alley. The leader fell to the ground and everyone in his gang assumed him mortally wounded. The guy behind me started to make a run for it along with the rest of the crew who scampered like wolves to save their own hides. I squatted near the gang leader who was in a state of shock.

"'*Tu m'as tué ! Tu m'as tué!*' he screamed as blood streamed over the right side of his face.

"I responded in French, 'I didn't kill you, you little piece of shit, but if I ever see you again, I promise you I will finish the job. You are in luck because today I only shot off part of your right ear.'

"He began to cry and curled himself into a fetal position, cupping the damaged cartilage. I turned around to see what had happened to the young woman. And there she was, standing in the shadows looking at me. I stepped over the crying idiot and I then saw her; I mean, *truly* saw her. She stood out against the night backdrop like an angel. Only when she blinked did her stare leave mine.

"Her eyes sparkled like ice against the moon. Her nose sloped softly down to a plush set of lips. Wisps of pale hair caught the corners of her mouth where her red lipstick had been smudged, and all I wanted was to brush them away. She was the only woman who had made me lose my bearings. Pulling myself together, I asked if I could escort her to her home and she silently nodded yes.

"As soon as we started walking, she grabbed my arm and squeezed it tightly. Her hands were small and delicate, but I could feel her strength in them. We walked back onto the Rue Dupetit-Thouars, where I still needed to free the boy I had tied to the rails, but she would not let me go. So, we went together and set him free.

"I didn't want to pressure her with any questions, so I started to tell her a bit about myself. When she stopped in front of her apartment, I looked at her and realized she had cried while we'd been walking. It was a heart-wrenching picture, tears pouring from those gray eyes down her cheekbones. Her makeup's streaks created a pattern of rivers while she remained completely silent, her face motionless. Not a single sob escaped her lips.

"Instinctively, I wrapped her in my arms. It felt as if some part of her had always been with me, but only now did she exist in flesh and blood. She breathed life's meaning back into my chest and I knew I would never let her go. Never again did I see your grandmother cry like that. Every second of my life, I miss her, Anna. Every second."

"Grandpa, I feel so awful she had to live with that memory."

"Anna, your grandmother, survived the Battle of Berlin; I am sure she had gone through worse things than that. I bring this up because I have come to the belief that even though we had an unmatched love and devotion to one another, your grandmother kept certain things from me."

Anna's attention quickly returned to the present. "What do you mean?"

"I found something strange when I finally packed up her belongings for donation. It has erased the peace I thought I had finally gained after her passing."

John walked over to his oak desk, which stood with authority over their conversation. He picked up a yellowed piece of paper and handed it to Anna. On it was a drawing of a tulip shaded with red pencil surrounded by foreign words. Anna only understood the word "Helga." Curiously enough, the tulip was drawn exceptionally well, but the writing was in a child's hand with the letters messy and disproportioned to one another.

Anna tried to make sense of this random item in front of her. "Grandpa, what does it say?"

"Alles Gute zum Geburtstag Helga! Meaning, Happy Birthday, Helga!" John paused for a second and said, "It is in German."

Anna immediately understood what was at stake. She knew that her grandmother had cut out everything and everyone from Germany, yet here was this birthday card.

"I don't think that Grandmother was keeping things from you," Anna quickly asserted. "It could be anything, really. She had probably kept it from the war."

John reclaimed his seat in his armchair and faced Anna. His expression conveyed the workings of his mind, which turned and ticked with the precision of a Swiss-made watch.

"Anna, we are both aware of your grandmother's photograph as a child with her mother—the one that sat on her nightstand. It was the only photograph she said she was able to save from the war when she was trying to salvage her belongings during the Battle of Berlin. She told both of us it was the only item she cherished from her life in Austria and Germany."

Automatically, Anna's eyes drifted to that same photograph that now sat on her grandfather's desk. In it, Grandmother was a little girl; her hair tied back with a big white bow. Her mother, Karin, an elegant woman, hugged the child close to her side. Karin's left arm was linked with a man's—her husband and Anna's great-grandfather Kurt. Anna had never seen Kurt's face before due to damage from a fire the photograph had suffered, which singed out his figure. Grandmother had permanently sealed the photograph to prevent further deterioration.

"I know that Grandpa, but you know how she hated recalling those days. The drawing could be from one of her friend's children," Anna challenged.

"Okay, Anna," he said in a calm tone, "please flip over the drawing of the happy birthday flower."

Anna looked at the back of the paper that showed several areas with brown faded dots on the lower right side, forming a pattern.

"Grandpa, what is this? Are these letters?"

"The child's drawing was sent to your grandmother by someone very close to her from Germany sometime back in the nineteen fifties."

"Wait, what?" Anna exclaimed. "How in the world do you know that?"

"I first studied the back of the drawing with a magnifying glass, which convinced me that those dots were imprints of letters. When I brought it up to a mirror, it was even more obvious that they were pieces of words within sentences."

"The letters are backward because the drawing was folded and placed in between the pages of a letter written with an ink fountain pen. The ink didn't fully dry before the letter was put into the envelope, leaving the ink's imprints. Upon realizing this, I decided to take it a step further and examine the paper scientifically. A friend of mine, a colleague, heads the California Criminalistics Institute or CCI, in Sacramento, one of the country's best labs. They have helped me numerous times in my criminal cases, and I could send it over on short notice.

"CCI confirmed that the marks on the drawing were imprints from ink-written characters. The paper was at least fifty to sixty years old and was produced in Europe. They were also able to recreate several of the partially imprinted words which were German."

John walked over to his computer, pulled up an image file, and double-clicked the mouse, which created blue lines connecting the dots to form completed letter characters. Another mouse click made four red boxes appear on the screen that encased a grouping of connected letters.

"These red boxes highlight the parts in which more than one letter was clearly identified, making it possible for the lab to partially reconstruct the actual word. They estimated how many letters were missing from each word by calculating the distance between each of the letters and words. The results were: 'Bes r', 'Ade r', 'Gel ' , ' ance.'

"I immediately contacted Professor Easterly at Arizona State University to help me find the missing letters and reconstruct the words from the back of the drawing. He's an expert in Germanic studies and the German language. We concluded that the most logical meaning of the German words were: *besser, Adenauer, geld, chance.* Translated, they mean: 'better', 'Adenauer', 'money', 'chance'."

"Hmm, but what does Adenauer mean?" Anna asked, completely baffled by the chain of logic.

"Well, that is the word we had the most difficulty trying to decipher. It wasn't until my brain woke up and put together two things: the paper's age and the historical events happening during that time in Germany. A popular chancellor led West Germany by the name of Konrad Adenauer. When I matched him to the paper's age, the professor agreed this was a very viable guess. Adenauer was the head of West Germany between forty-nine and sixty-three."

"Wait— You and Grandmother were in America by then," Anna said partially to herself, "which means the letter could not have been in her possession before...she had to have received it here."

"Exactly right, Anna. If Adenauer had not been mentioned, I would have no evidence the letter was mailed to her, which means," John continued looking into Anna's dilated eyes, "we now know that at some point during the nineteen fifties, your grandmother was in communication with someone in Germany. That someone must have informed her of the inner politics going on in West Germany. The subject of money was also mentioned, and, on top of all that, we have a child's 'Happy Birthday, Helga' drawing. As you know, Grandmother hated everything, German. She even refused to return to Austria to look for any remaining relatives. Do you not find it the least bit strange that I found this note?"

John's eyes narrowed, focusing in on Anna's face so he could pick up on the slightest change in reaction.

"For all we know..." his voice fell with the weight of the sentence he knew he was about to say next, "the child who drew that picture could be your aunt or uncle. It could even be my step-child."

Anna looked at her grandfather. *My God*, she thought, *he has encased himself so much in these mysteries that his logic was getting the best of him.*

A strange sense of rage wrapped itself around Anna. To examine the drawing was one thing, but to accuse Grandmother, *her* grandmother, of being anything else but utterly selfless to everyone and everything around her was insulting.

"Are you insane?!"

The respect Anna had always directed toward her elders was lost in the disbelief of what she heard from her grandfather's proposal.

John's eyes widened with curiosity at Anna's reaction.

"Your theory might look good on paper, Grandpa, but it doesn't hold up on the basis of character. How could you even think that about Grandmother? Do you seriously think that she had had a child in Germany and left it there for all these years just to marry you? By the way, if it was her child, the card would read Mom or Mother, but not Helga. Your theory is insulting."

"Look, Anna," John's voice rose to the occasion of being tested on the premise of his case. "I was a criminal lawyer for many years, and my job was to piece together evidence without dismissing a possibility because of an emotion. You cannot tell me without a doubt that the child who drew this picture is not Helga's offspring. I met Helga in Paris in nineteen forty-six and, at that point, she had been working for the Allies for almost seven months. She could have left the child with relatives or friends, and if the child was small enough at the time the letter was mailed, he or she would have only known her as Helga. She could have given it up for adoption."

Anna saw the hurt that John had let into his mind.

"I think you are wrong," she spoke smoothly and calmly. "The truth is, we don't know the truth, but when I find it, it will prove to you that I was right."

Half a smile made its way onto John's lips either in sympathetic doubt or hopeful relief that he no longer carried this mystery alone.

"Exactly right. This is why I need you to make a stop in Austria during your travels. Find out as much as you can about Grandmother's family. It should not be too difficult since we know her maiden name, the town she was born in, and her parents' full names. I am sure there were survivors from the war or maybe some records on file."

Anna's plan to travel abroad now carried significant importance. Fate had knocked on her door, to uncover a past that had to still exist in Austria; a past that would eradicate the demons eating away at her grandfather.

She knew this would be kept between Grandfather and herself.

"I am sure I will be able to find some answers Grandpa."

"You better take this with you," John handed Anna the photograph of her grandmother as a little girl.

Anna stood up to go when a thought came to her. She mulled it over in her mind before finally giving into the strong urge to say it out loud.

"Grandpa, there is one more thing: I don't think it's relevant or anything like that... It's more supernatural than anything,"

John narrowed his eyes in concentration. "Go on, Anna."

"Since last year, I keep having the same dream about Grandmother."

His expression instantly piqued with attention.

"I am riding on a bus in New York along Fifth Avenue. It is raining, and I see people walking along the street, but all their backs are to me. No one ever walks toward me, so I am only able to see their backs and umbrellas. Then someone in the crowd turns to face me and I clearly see that it is Grandmother. I think she is crying, but I can't tell because of the rain on the bus window. The bus keeps moving and she disappears."

John briskly walked over to his desk and picked up a notepad.

"Did Grandmother say anything, or make any gestures?"

"No, she was just looking through the window at me."

"How frequently do you have this dream, Anna?"

"Umm, pretty often. At least two or three times a month."

John stopped writing and looked up at Anna. An expression of surprise showed clearly on his face.

"When did you start to have this dream?" He spoke more cautiously now.

"About a month after she died, I think."

John's arms dropped forward as if the pen and notepad had suddenly become twenty pounds heavier. Seeing the shift in her grandfather's calm demeanor to one of shock made Anna lose her patience.

"What? What does that all mean? Grandpa, you are making me nervous! What is it?"

John regained his senses and held up his finger, indicating to hold on a minute. He walked over to the bookshelves lining the wall surrounding an oval mirror. He withdrew a small black paperback book and handed it to Anna with an air of importance.

Looking down at the book, she read: *Man and His Symbols* by Carl Jung.

"Anna, I need you to read this and come back to me as soon as you finish it."

Anna wanted to know what her dream had sparked in her grandfather immediately, but the tension he exuded silenced her questions.

"Fine. I'll be back tomorrow," Anna stated. "And I expect all my questions to be answered!"

She made her way to the door, menacingly waving Carl Jung's book.

Chapter 5

Carl Jung's book was on her lap and she greedily read through it the entire day. He was one of the fathers of psychoanalysis and a close associate of Sigmund Freud. Anna recalled the short review of twentieth-century psychoanalysis theories from an introductory psychology class she'd taken. Psychoanalysis was portrayed as an outdated attempt to explain human behavior from the view of suppressed sexuality and violence.

But Jung's book did not fit into the shallow one-sided explanation Anna had been taught. This frustrated her because she hated being deprived of information and would have preferred to come to her own conclusions.

Each page of *Man and His Symbols* materialized a complex world of the human mind that Jung analogized to a dark mansion filled with dangerous labyrinths, secret rooms, and corridors leading somewhere—or nowhere at all. This was where the unconscious stored our personal experiences and those of previous generations whose marks have been left on us through our DNA.

The conscious mind is represented by a well-lit attic, the floor of which has a small opening leading into the lower levels of a dark mansion and back to our unconscious. During the night, this door opens, allowing the unconscious and conscious to communicate through dreams and intuition. If Freud and Jung were right, then the unconscious tries to warn us, guide us, or change our behavior, but the messages we receive come in symbolic form, making them difficult to interpret.

Anna reached for her laptop and began researching psychoanalysis. Toward the bottom of page one, an entry titled "Who Was Sabina Spielrein?" caught Anna's eye. Sabina was Jung's famous patient and lover who had proven to him the clinical effects of psychoanalysis. The page showed a photograph of Jung, Sabina, and Freud.

Karl Jung, Sabina Spielrein, & Sigmund Freud

Anna was surprised to find a movie on the topic, *A Dangerous Method*, starring Keira Knightley. She could stream it online in one convenient click. Excitedly, Anna called her grandfather.

"Anna! Finished already?" John's voice boomed with surprise.

"Hi Grandpa! I'd like to propose an indoor movie date tomorrow—just you and I. Expect Carl Jung to be present," she said cheekily.

"You have got an old man intrigued, my dear. I will see you then."

At 12:00 p.m. sharp, Anna opened the door, let herself in, and hugged her grandfather hello in the living room.

"So, what is the surprise?" asked John, eyeing the copy of *Man and His Symbols* that Anna carried under her right arm. John's anticipation was endearingly obvious.

A few minutes later, *A Dangerous Method* submerged Anna and her grandfather into the Austro-Hungarian Empire at the beginning of the twentieth century and into the complex relations between Freud, Jung, and Sabina Spielrein.

After ninety-nine minutes, the credits started to roll, and John looked at his granddaughter.

"That was a great find, Anna. Ironic that you discovered it now, considering the circumstances."

"I know... For the past few days, I have felt that my life has been filled with strange coincidences," said Anna, almost talking to herself.

"Our date continues, Grandpa. Now, we are off to lunch."

They drove forty minutes, crossing the desert into Scottsdale, a city brimming with fine restaurants, designer stores, desert gardens, luxurious apartments, and an ever-growing nightlife.

They walked to an outside table that sat cozily on the edge of the Scottsdale Waterfront. After ordering drinks, Anna's thoughts drifted away from the laziness of the warm sun to Carl Jung and his book sitting quietly in her purse.

"Grandpa, may I ask you why you left psychology to pursue law?" John was silent for a moment as he gathered his thoughts. "After the war, I served with the U.S. Army Intelligence, hunting war criminals and SS officers among the POW camps. What struck me most was how ordinary these people were. They were loving sons, devoted husbands, and loyal friends who had committed unthinkable atrocities. Most troubling were the many horrible things perpetrated by ordinary citizens who weren't even part of the military.

"Analyzing my own war experiences and the events around me, I realized how right Freud's and Jung's ideas were. There is something much deeper governing our behavior if masses of people can suddenly act with such hatred and unstoppable desire to harm those they think are different.

"When I returned home, I enrolled at Clark University. However, the more I studied psychology, the more I realized that it no longer reflected my expectations. At the beginning of its development, cognitive psychology was becoming mainstream, and it focused on modifying human behavior without recognizing the critical role played by our subconscious and unconscious.

Initially, Psychoanalysis became a threat to these new theories, and the existence of an unconscious was pushed to the side. And yet, a subtle force continued to govern human behavior, so cognitive psychology introduced terms like subliminal processing and implicit memory; concepts ironically based on Freud's and Jung's theory of the unconscious.

"But grandpa, cognitive psychology continues to help people; I imagine psychoanalysis won't work for everyone."

"Anna, there is a critical point that most of us miss: Cognitive psychology can help you ease anxiety or get over a divorce, but it cannot explain the complete degradation of morals and the brutal mass violence that was carried out not only by the German military but by ordinary citizens. It cannot explain why French citizens hunted their Jewish neighbors to send them to concentration camps or how Croatians burned Serbian villages.

"Our culture is based on the premise that evil is foreign to us, but the seeds of hate and violence are within us and are either hidden or just suppressed by society until the right moment presents itself."

"So, what is the solution?" Anna remarked.

"People must be educated on the impact their unconsciousness has on their behavior from a very young age. If we acknowledge the presence of a violent force within us, then the well-lit attic of our consciousness would better control the events in the dark maze below."

"I see what you mean," said Anna, "so, you gave me Jung's book to read because I had this weird dream about Grandmother, right?"

John nodded in response. "Specifically, it was because the dream was recurring. The majority of dreams develop as a result of daily activity or the accumulation of sensory information, but, according to Jung, recurring dreams or motifs are what the therapist must pay attention to."

John slowly sipped his ice water. Anna noticed his hesitation. He looked thoughtfully into Anna's eyes and said, "I think that your unconsciousness made a decision for you and delivered it to you in the form of your dreams. And my advice is to always follow your dreams."

The coy play on words reminded Anna of Grandfather's charming philosophical wit.

"There is another strange coincidence," he said after a short pause. "You said that

you started to see this dream with Helga approximately a month after she died. Am I correct?"

"Yes."

"Do you remember how worried everyone was about me when I became depressed a month following Helga's death?"

"Yes. Dad even tried to get you to live with us. He was afraid that you would do something harmful..."

"I know. The real truth was that right after her death, every night, Helga visited me. My life turned upside down. I was in a dream-like state during the daytime, not paying much attention to anything in my life, acting like a robot as I waited for the night to come so I could fall asleep and spend time with her. I tried to sleep during the day, but it didn't work; she was with me only at night."

"You had the same dream every night?" Anna stared at him wide-eyed.

"I did. I would be on our porch practicing my closing arguments for an upcoming case while Helga laid on her favorite swing sofa and listened to me as she had always done."

"Would she say anything?"

"No, she would simply listen, but I felt that she was agitated, and I didn't know if it was because my speech was bad or for some other reason."

"Did you analyze your dream?"

"Yes, I tried, but I could not decode it; I did not know what my unconsciousness was trying to tell me to do. Suddenly, the dream stopped. I was devastated, and that was when the depression hit me."

"When did the dream stop?"

John took a long pause; he looked at Anna. With an emphasis on each word he spoke the following sentence: "One month after her death."

Shivers ran down Anna's spine. "Grandpa, but... that is exactly when I started to see my dream about Grandmother! That *is* an eerie coincidence. What do you think it means?"

In a fraction of a second, she realized the amount of discomfort emanating from the confident man before her, who was troubled by the very same question.

He took his time to answer her. "I have no explanation, Anna. Let us leave it to the world of spirituality and the unknown." He tried to smile, but instead showed a grimace of pain.

I know why, Anna said to herself. *Grandmother is reaching out—there is something unfinished.*

Grandfather's eyes seemed to look off into the distance. She knew he would never return to normal until his questions were answered.

Anna drove Grandfather home in silence. Just before saying good-bye, John kissed Anna on the cheek and handed her a black cardholder. Questioningly, her hands accepted the smooth leather rectangle that held a single silver bank card and account statement.

"I told you before about the trust your grandmother left you. I know you will use the money wisely and when necessary."

Anna sat stunned by the amount and did not notice John leaving the car until the shutting door startled her back into the present.

Her eyes followed his walk to the front door; it had become slow and labored; Atlas holding the world on weakened shoulders. Anna pulled out of the driveway, burdened by her grandfather's troubles.

Chapter 6

Her grandfather's troubles motivated Anna to focus on her destination: Grandmother's hometown of Sankt Gilgen, whose 3,784 inhabitants lived in the Salzkammergut mountains on the stunning Wolfgang Sea. British Airways Flight 288 would leave Phoenix, connect in London, and arrive in Salzburg, Austria's second-largest city and Wolfgang Amadeus Mozart's birthplace.

Landing in Austria did not hit until she picked up the unfamiliar scents of her surroundings. She made her way down the stairs of the plane and breathed in the chill of spring. Her feet touched the nation that had always been such a mystery. It felt wrong for her to be there. *Had Grandmother been alive, she would have stood in the way of this trip entirely.*

The Sound of Music posters covered the windows of the airport shops. The movie was filmed in Salzburg, and the city had been using it as a tourist attraction ever since. She loved the movie; it was the only Austrian thing Grandmother could tolerate.

The Hauptbahnhof, the central train station, was smaller than she expected, but it gleamed white in the face of heavy construction. Her poofy Calvin Klein suitcase fell onto its stomach from the weight of the contents of its heavy front pockets.

"Calvin, behave yourself," Anna said under her breath as she heaved the suitcase back up with an annoyed look as if it were a careless child.

I just named my suitcase.

She shook her head and wondered if this would turn into a *Cast Away* / Wilson type of adventure. The possibility was high.

Anna boarded Bus 150, which would take her to Grandmother's hometown of Sankt Gilgen in a mere hour. There, she would find public records of the town's residents and ask everyone she met if the name Helga Eckert was familiar to them. Most importantly, she hoped to uncover a truth that would negate her grandfather's ridiculous theory and restore his image of Grandmother.

Outside her window, a wonderland started to unfold before her. Hills covered by spring vegetation rose like waves from the countryside only to then melt into blooming pastures that stretched and rolled till the next hilltop. Half-timbered houses sprung up in the valleys in blues, reds, yellows, and whites, and goats grazed by them basking in the sunlight.

Bus 150 climbed higher until the atmosphere radically changed and the sunlit towns she had passed were now hidden by peaks that cast shadows on little Sankt Gilgen.

Anna dragged Calvin off the bus and admired the sloping rooftops of a still-hibernating city. The air was wet and hung heavy. An eerie sensation made Anna look back only to see the wispy arms of fog stretch toward her like snakes trying to escape the narrow streets behind her. She sped up her pace. Whatever secrets Sankt Gilgen had, they seemed to want to remain hidden.

The crooked streets guided her to Johann Pichler Platz, where the yellow-and-green three-story Hotel Kendler awaited her arrival. Upon entering the warm interior, she was relieved to find life within its walls and a modest room, which she quickly settled into.

The following day, Anna stepped into the stillness of late morning. This day's fog felt lighter, whisking itself up from the shores of the Wolfgang Sea. She had hardly walked a minute before reaching the eggshell-colored three-story building that was the Town Hall.

Hopefully, someone is here on a Saturday.

Dark green panes outlined each of the eight windows. A small fountain out front depicted Mozart as a child playing the violin; his little body bent to his instrument's melody. Anna knocked hard on the front door but received no answer. A few more knocks brought forth a petite woman in a dark purple sweater and black slacks.

"Guten tag!" said the woman, looking at Anna with a big question mark for a facial expression.

"Entschuldigung?" Anna managed to sound out, "English, please?"

"English... English." the woman repeated to herself as if hoping to reprogram her mind. "Umm... Little little bit." She squeezed the measure of her English capability between two fingers. Anna was grateful.

"Ich heissen Anna," Anna said warmly.

"Frau Hoffmann," the woman said as she gently shook Anna's hand. "Tourism yes? Vee close today. Monday okay." She began to close the door.

"Wait, Frau Hoffmann! My grandmother was born here," Anna said. "I came to Sankt Gilgen to find her relatives to tell them that she died last year."

Frau Hoffmann starred at Anna but said nothing.

Unsure if she was understood, Anna continued, "I am looking for any information or family records for the last name Eckert. Do you know anyone with that name?"

Suddenly Frau Hoffmann's indifferent smile burst into sporadic laughter. Her unexpected reaction made Anna uneasy.

"I am sorry...Anna," Frau Hoffmann managed to say between ongoing chuckles. "Here, Eckert name all around." Frau Hoffmann pointed to the left and right. "I vas Eckert before marriage. Eckert old, old name."

"Then, do you know of a Helga Eckert who moved to Berlin and then America?" Anna asked excitedly.

"Helga Eckert in America...America," Frau Hoffmann again repeated several times. "*Nein,* Anna. No Helga from America."

Frau Hoffmann continued thinking until an idea presented itself on her face. "Inna Berger! Inna Berger know everyone in Sankt Gilgen. Che owns bed-and-breakfast here and shpeaks English okay. Walk straight to Mondsee Strasse, house forty-five."

Far from the center of town, the houses spread out more generously. Small green pathways wove in between parked cars and moss-covered fences leading off into unknown directions. Forty-five Mondsee Strasse could have been a small mansion if it had not been for the slanted cottage roof. Each of the house's four stories were draped in green foliage that stretched and covered every shingle. The effect was that of a living organism.

Before Anna could knock on the front door, it opened to reveal the stare of a young boy of maybe six.

"Oh, hiiiii there!" Anna tried to coo. The door shut in her face.

A promising start. She sighed.

Anna gave the door a firm knock, and once again, the child met her gaze but quickly ran away laughing. A cough and footsteps were making their way toward the door. Through the opening, Anna could see a large woman shuffling closer with a lopsided gait. A loose cream sweater clung around the places on her body that protrude outward from age. The top of her head was a mess of short, dyed auburn hair, white at the roots. The expression on her face was full of vigor, alert and questioning. Inna Berger came closer and leaned her weight onto the doorknob of the front door.

"Guten tagen," she spoke, forming the phrase into more of a question directed at Anna's smiling face.

"Guten tagen, Frau Berger," she said carefully. "My name is Anna." She pointed to herself. "Frau Hoffmann, at the town hall, told me to come see you."

"Slower! I'm old!" Inna barked.

"She said that you know—" Anna paused for effect, "a lot about the people from Sankt Gilgen."

"*Ja*... I lived here whole life," Inna said with critical importance. "Vat are you searching vor?"

"Can you tell me about families that have lived here before nineteen forty-one?"

Inna reacted unexpectedly, a red blush spread over her face and neck. "Vhy? Vat your agenda?"

Confused, Anna shook her head. "I don't have an agenda. I am a descendant of this town. My grandmother grew up here, and I hope to find relatives, but Frau Hoffmann told me half the town has her last name—Eckert," Anna finished.

Inna eyed her with a newfound interest.

"My grandmother's first name was Helga.... She moved to America after World War Two...."

Inna's intrigued expression suddenly went into a blank stare.

"Helga Eckert..." Anna repeated.

Suddenly, Inna's eyebrows arched with such tension that her entire face looked five years younger.

"Helga Eckert... America? Vrom Sankt Gilgen?!"

"Yes." Anna started to tense, feeling the excitement from Inna's massive frame.

"She passed away last year, but did you know her? Did you know my grandmother?"

Inna stared at her with bulging eyes until suddenly her movements became quick, forceful, and exaggerated. Her big body, forgetting its circumference, was in the process of knocking over the umbrella stand to the right of the door. Inna let it fall, her hands clasping themselves over her mouth.

"Oh, das good Gott...." Inna's large arms reached out and pulled Anna into a tight embrace.

She smelled of sunflower oil.

"My lost shparrow! Helga's granddaughter in my house...avter many years..."

Anna was hurled into a pot of Inna's emotions, which she didn't quite understand.

"Komme herein! Dear Anna, come in!"

Anna entered into a paneled center room with excitement and confusion where four hallways led off to different parts of the house.

"I vas not nice earlier, don't mind zat.... Vollow me, dear."

With newfound agility, Inna led the way into an intricately decorated room filled with several antique grandfather clocks, mantle clocks, and cuckoo clocks that hung from the walls, anxiously awaiting their cue to chime.

Inna and Anna sat facing each other on two green floral-print sofas. The clocks ticked in a calming yet eerie unison with one another.

"Frau Berger," Anna started as calmly as she could, "what do you know about my grandmother?"

"Anna, you shtill not understand, and, please, call me Inna. You are our vamily, dear! I am your grandmother's virst cousin!"

"What? Are you serious?" Anna's voice emitted genuine disbelief that slightly tore into Inna's old wounds.

"I see Helga didn't tell you about her big vamily in Austria." Bitterness tainted Inna's tone and Anna felt this as she shook her head in a silent "no."

The hands of the clocks ticked, and Anna counted the seconds before Inna spoke again. "My mother and I alvays hoped she vould return someday and vorgive us, but she never did. It's hard to undershtand, but she had every right to anger."

"I'm really sorry, but I don't have the slightest idea of what you're talking about. Forgive what?" Anna asked.

With a foreboding air, Inna stood up. "I have shpecial place to show you." Anna followed her to a door down a short hallway.

They entered into a dark room fragrant with the scent of roses. Inna flipped the light switch, sparking a crystal chandelier in the middle of the ceiling. Immediately, a wave of golden shimmer illuminated the room.

As Anna's eyes adjusted, she saw that she was standing between walls blanketed with thousands of small golden picture frames that reflected the chandelier's light off one another in a beautiful golden dance.

"Frau Inna, this is breathtaking!"

Inna glowed pink at the compliment but waited silently for Anna to understand what she was looking at. Anna walked to the room's center, past a burgundy antique upholstered high-back sofa, its wooden legs carved into animal paws.

In amazement, Anna scanned the room's sage green walls. Copper painted spirals twisted like branches connecting the picture frames that held individual photographs of men, women, and children. Some frames displayed painted portraits or only pieces of paper bearing single names. Miniature international flags were pinned above each photograph. The entire room was a family tree.

"Is this all your family?" Anna asked with hesitation.

"Not just my family, dear, *our* family!"

The sheer magnitude of the faces shocked Anna. "My family? But... How could you have collected all of this?"

"Zis is my life's vork," Inna explained. "It began vith my mother, vor us to do togezer. Ve searched zrough family, church records, everyzing! Our family live in nineteen countries now; relatives send me photographs of their marriages and children. Ven children grow up, I ask for adult photographs, too."

Anna continued to scan the photographs but didn't see the face she was looking for.

"Inna, did you meet my grandmother?"

"*Nein*. I vas born after das var, but my mozer knew her very vell... She vould have given so much to see you, bless her."

Inna's voice faded as her eyes traced the generations along the walls. A melancholy fell onto the room, and they stood in stillness until Inna's voice cracked open the stream of conversation once more. "*Gott* has given me chance to reunite vith lost past. Now I remember how many, many years have gone by."

"I am sorry to bring this back up...."

Inna snapped out of her trance, "Anna! You here is miracle for me. I just have moments.... Ah, stupid goat! I forgot da tea. You see? I vill be back."

Anna was left alone, surrounded by hundreds of relatives from the past, the present, and the children who would grow up to be future generations. It felt unreal. Back home, hardly anyone knew their relatives past their great-grandparents, yet here she was looking at over a century of shared DNA scattered worldwide.

Inna came back carrying a silver tray with a ceramic tea set and a plate of cookies.

"I vill show you everyzing, but first drink, eat."

Anna bit into a soft butter cookie, at which point questions came spilling out of Inna's mouth like crumbs.

"Vhere did Helga live? Vat did she do in... vhere vas it? Arizona? A desert? Did she marry? Vas she happy? Vhy did she never tell you about us?"

Anna answered the last question, embarrassed. "I do not know."

Inna sighed heavily.

"That is why I came here," said Anna. "Grandmother never said much about her past."

Inna nodded. "Das var caused many memories to stay silent." She then laid her thick hands on Anna's slim shoulders and guided her to a specific wall section. "And zis is vat you came here for."

Anna faced the portraits of three young men and one woman. "Zis is my mother." Inna pointed to the curly-haired woman. "And zese are her three brozers. Your great-grandfazer, Kurt— Helga's father, is on das right."

Tall and well built, Kurt had a square face with boyish features and brilliant eyes. The grin on his face made him look mischievous, as though he had just committed a prank.

Inna's voice interrupted. "Kurt married Karin Bauer in nineteen twenty." Inna traced her fingertip to the left where a young woman with a round face sat smiling through a grayed wedding photograph. She wore a white bridal hat decorated with beaded flowers and a long-sleeved white dress. Behind her stood Kurt, dressed in a suit and bowtie with neatly parted hair.

"And zis is zeir child, your grandmozer, Helga, ven she vas two years old."

Anna eyed the little girl whose hair was pulled back and tied with a big white bow. Her eyes were wide open as if scared to see what the camera would actually do. Anna smiled to herself as she thought her grandmother must have been such a serious child.

"Are there any of Grandmother when she was older?"

"Nein," replied Inna. "I don't have any ozer photographs of your side of family. They vere lost in das var like many other zings."

"Frau Inna, earlier you said something about my grandmother's forgiveness.... What did you mean by that?"

"Our family's roots are German, and the idea of merging Austria vith Germany under great Adolf, he vas Austrian, you know, vas exciting for everyone in our family, but not for Uncle Kurt. He said it vould lead to das var and Austria's destruction. Eventually, entire family cut ties vith him. Mother tried to keep togezer, but it vas already sour relationship."

"Zese pictures—" Inna pointed to the wall above her, "Dey are from happier times vhen vee vere all togezer." Inna exhaled and smoothed back her unkempt hair.

"Right before Hitler invaded Soviet Union, Helga ran to Berlin to a German lieutenant. She vas maybe eighteen. I don't zink she ever found him. She vrote zat she vas going to school for nurses in Berlin, to help das vounded.

A nurse? Anna thought. *That was how she must have survived the Battle of Berlin.*

"Tragically, Kurt and Karin vere killed in a car crash vith German army truck. Vhen poor Helga came back to Sankt Gilgen to bury her parents, only family zere at funeral vas my mother. She begged Helga to stay vith her, but Helga said zis vas not her home anymore. She felt everyone turn zeir back on her, she vas all alone."

"What happened afterward?" Anna asked impatiently.

"Vell," continued Inna, "Helga returned to Berlin...das var..." Inna's voice cracked as she recalled the past "...killed half our family. Vee vere beaten by each death. The tousand-year reich under great Adolf now looked stupid. Everyone said Uncle Kurt, rest his soul, had been right. Austria vas destroyed, vee vere destroyed.

"After var ended, my mother searched for Helga, contacting Red Cross many times. She finally got news zat Helga vas alive somevere in Paris."

Anna immediately thought of the strange birthday card Grandfather had discovered. "Did your mother ever send any letters or cards to Helga in Paris?"

"*Nein*, dear. Vee vere unable to trace Helga to any address."

Anna sighed out disappointment, the card would remain a mystery for now.

All of a sudden Inna clapped her big palms loudly down on her thighs. "And now, look at you! Here in my house! I tell you, right ven I zink I have seen it all, *Gott* surprises me again! Tonight, I invite you for dinner. You meet rest of the family!"

Chapter 7

The rest of the family awaiting Anna for dinner awoke her appetite for both sustenance and information. Yards from the front door, she could already hear numerous voices waiting to greet her—the lost relative who had sought to make peace with the forgotten family.

She rang the doorbell and was met with a *pleasant ding-dong* sound. Instantly, with the warmth of the opened door, her body was being moved around the room without her control. It was being hugged; her hands were being shaken, and her cheeks pressed against other cheeks.

My God, who are all these people? There have to be at least thirty of them.

Names were thrown at her in German, in English, and then in both simultaneously. It was overwhelming. She even saw Frau Hoffman, who now greeted her as a relative instead of another tourist. *Why did Grandmother hide from all these people for all these years?*

They all sat down at a long oval table connected to another by a white lace tablecloth, and the questions started quickly. The Austrians wanted to know about her, her life in Arizona. What was she doing? (just graduated college); what was Phoenix like? (a modern city in the sprawling desert); why didn't she know German? (Grandmother did not teach her); would she learn it? (Yes).

"Grandmother *did* teach me the piano!" Anna added with enthusiasm, expecting the stories of Grandmother's concertos to circulate the table.

Inna looked surprised. "Zat must be somezing. Helga learn music in Germany. Good on her!"

Folks around the table nodded in agreement. A few chimed in that they, too, had wanted to learn the instrument, but no one in the family was musically inclined. Anna knotted her brows.

Braised pork reached the table. Chewing substituted her relatives' words, which fell onto Anna's plate with an unpleasant flavor.

Grandmother had not shared much with Anna regarding her past, this was true. Yet, the stories Grandmother did share were of learning the piano at a very young age from her mother. There were several such stories. The piano was an intergenerational bond between Anna, her grandmother, and the great-grandmother she would never meet, but now these people, her relatives, were saying the opposite.

Anna pushed potatoes around her plate, smiling and nodding in between forkfuls that never made it to her lips. She needed to speak with Inna, alone.

At 9:15 p.m., while helping Inna stack dishes in the kitchen, the chance she was looking for finally presented itself. "I wonder where Grandmother learned to play the piano..." Anna began. "She was rather good."

Anna watched as Inna nodded along, cleaning food scraps off each plate.

"Maybe Karin taught her?" Anna pried.

Inna replied casually, "As I know, Karin did not play music, but maybe Helga vanted to learn. I do not know. It vas before my time."

Anna mulled this over. She brought Grandmother's photograph to surprise Inna, and it was now burning for attention inside her purse.

"Inna…" she started, masking the neediness in her voice, "I want to show you this photograph Grandmother had, and I was wondering if this was Karin when she was older?"

Having retrieved the frame from her purse, Anna handed it to Inna's thick pink hands. Inna pulled the picture closer and then farther away.

"Nein," murmured Inna. "Zis not Karin. According to my mother, Karin vas kind but simple. Voman here looks too fashionable, too rich and too skinny, like rail. I am sure she is not Karin."

Inna's hands rested on where her hips used to be. The skeptical expression that had adorned Inna's face when they had first met each other returned.

Anna dismissed the photograph quickly. "I had never seen it before, but recently found it in an old box of things," she heard herself say.

Inna's eyebrows wrinkled and then released. She looked tired, physically and emotionally. The day had been long.

"Inna, can I see the photographs of my relatives again? It was just so comforting being among their portraits," Anna said innocently.

Once again, Inna lit up at the thought of her family tree. "Ov course, dear. You know vere das room is. I vill pack you leftovers for tomorrow."

Anna left the kitchen and quickened her steps as soon as she was out of Inna's sight. Inside the family tree room, she made her way directly to Kurt and Karin's wedding photograph. She then removed her own photo from the purse and put the two side by side. In her picture, Karin had a long slim figure, full lips that smiled softly above an angular chin, pulled-back hair tucked neatly underneath a fashionable hat whose short veil ended at the top of her cheekbones, hiding her eyes. Her nose held a gentle straight slope.

The Karin in the wedding photograph was heavier set with a full face and the same gently sloped nose. She looked happy. Anna started to relax. Inna just didn't recognize the older Karin in her photograph.

After a few more glances, Anna noticed a detail that she had paid no attention to before: Karin's hands. Karin had thick short fingers with almost non-existent nails in the wedding photo, but in Grandmother's photo, Karin's hands were thin with long bony fingers.

With this discrepancy, Karin's facial features began to look more different as if on cue. It was now apparent that the Karin in Inna's photograph and the Karin in Grandmother's photograph were two different women.

Anna stared at Karin's wedding photograph in disbelief at the truth that was emerging. A sense of betrayal erupted from her belly while she stood motionless for several minutes, letting it swelter within her.

How could she just lie? To Grandfather? To me? To everyone? Anna paced around the room in a circular motion.

"Anna!" Inna's voice called from the kitchen.

Anna stopped in her tracks and exhaled a long deep breath. *Things can't be that simple,* she thought. *There has to be an explanation.* Calmly, Anna walked back to the kitchen.

She headed back to the Kendler Hotel, hugging the package of jars filled with stewed vegetables, braised pork, and sliced apple poppyseed cake.

Anna opened the balcony door of her small room and gazed into the night sky. She wanted guidance from the moon, but it was nowhere to be seen.

None of this makes sense. She once again stared at her photograph. Grandmother's young face was serious, lacking a smile. Her hair pulled back with a ribbon giving an even more stern expression, similar to the photograph of the child that hung on Inna's wall. Her mother's arm encircled Grandmother's shoulders, finding a resting place below her collarbone. Karin's right arm peeked from behind the arm of Grandmother's father, Kurt. The family stood in a sort of furniture shop with rows of mirrors on the wall above them.

Suddenly, the frustration she thought she had breathed out at Inna's home pulsated its way back through her body. With irritation and an unexpected surge of energy, it became her primary mission to open the ridiculous frame and free the photograph—and to break it if she had to. Anna's nails dug fruitlessly into the glued backing of the frame. She began frantically searching around the room, looking for something sharp, something pointy, but there was nothing.

With the gold key in hand, Anna sneaked down into the dimmed hotel lobby that stood empty. Sneaking through the dining-room door, she grabbed a knife from one of the preset tables and, triumphantly, ran up the three flights of stairs back to her room.

She used the knife to pick at the glue with purpose. Nothing. Annoyed, Anna drove the tip of the blade hard into the corner of the frame. This did not affect the bond, but the corner of the frame started to splinter. Anna pushed harder—thrilled, accomplished—until the right side of the frame separated itself, leaving a thin slit between the glass and glued back.

Carefully, slowly, Anna shook out the photograph, which breathed air for the first time in more than half a century. It fell into her hand delicately, a rose petal of a moment captured on film.

There it was, larger than the palm of her hand. It had always looked so much smaller underneath the wide frame that cropped the image. The right side of the photograph showed the burnt damage, which had made Grandmother bind it into a sealed frame in the first place to prevent further deterioration.

Anna turned it over. On the back, written in long elegant letters in a woman's hand: Berlin 1937.

Berlin? A family trip maybe? With delicate fingers, she studied the photograph attentively. Beautiful mirrors behind Great-Grandmother Karin and Grandmother Helga lined the wall from floor to ceiling. The mirrors were of different shapes and sizes. Engraved angels, mermaids, and maidens reached their arms towards the mirrors' crowning points.

How beautiful, thought Anna, continuing to examine the different designs. A small dark outline of a figure caught her eye at the very top of the photograph. *What is that?*

Anna moved the photograph right up to the top of her nose and narrowed her eyes. The mirror that hung above Karin was a horizontal oval that arched downward, catching the reflection of Karin's beautiful hat. Next to her... *My God...*

Next to Karin in the photo were two men, seen from behind: a taller man in some sort of military uniform and a shorter, thicker man next to him. Two men, not just one, that the photo had initially burned away.

Who the heck is that? Kurt wasn't in the military; he was a doctor. Inna herself said he had been against the war with all his might. Then who was in this photograph, and who was the second man that Grandmother had essentially edited out?

Anna could not sleep. Inna knew nothing of Grandmother's or Karin's piano abilities. The Karin on Inna's wall did not match the Karin that Grandmother claimed as her mother, and now Kurt was wearing a military uniform next to another man who Grandmother never mentioned.

Anna went over this again and again in her mind. Everything else matched up. The town, the relatives; they did know Helga, the story was the same. Even the part about the German officer who Grandmother had loved and lost in the war.

I have to be exaggerating. Maybe the piano lessons had been secret for some odd reason. Maybe that was not even a military uniform at all! Maybe doctors had to wear something similar during the war.

Yet, the problem of Karin remained. If that was not Karin, then there was a good chance that that was not Kurt, either.

She needed to take a closer look at that photograph to enlarge the two men's reflection. That would actually prove to be relatively simple. Anna decided that Grandfather would know exactly who to send it to. He had an entire crime lab at his disposal for Christ's sake!

She grabbed her phone and was about to call him until a thought made her freeze. Grandfather was old; he had already been obsessed with this whole thing for months. And now Anna would send him even more reason to be suspicious. She recalled how it had affected him—how weak he looked when he left her car the day after their lunch date. Her hand went loose, letting the phone slip. She needed to stop relying on her family. This was her business now, and she needed to count on herself.

Anna opened up her social media and started scrolling through her list of friends. *Who is tech-savvy? Real tech-savvy?* She landed on Kenny from her cinema class. He was now a student at the University of Southern California, which housed one of the wealthiest film programs worldwide. They were distant friends, but he messaged her every so often with a belief in her to "do great things in the world," whatever that meant. He had been and still was the type of guy who had spent his teen years consumed with making short movies of everything and everyone, living through his edits instead of reality itself. Anna was sure that he would soon be swimming in his own success. You couldn't buy that sort of passion.

Anna typed out a long pleading message emphasizing the need for a clear enlargement of the photograph, especially the reflection in the hovering mirror. The west coast was nine hours back; it would be around 2:00 p.m. Anna waited impatiently for a response. She used the next two hours to send messages to her father and grandfather.

When a notification pinged to announce a new message, Anna beamed. She read through Kenny's response of breaking into the school's digital photography lab if he had to. "But really, Anna, it shouldn't be too big of a problem; you should see the kind of equipment they have here! I guess George Lucas' $175 million donation went to good use! Email me a high-resolution scan...or send me the photograph overnight express—that would be best."

Anna wondered where the hell she was going to find a high-resolution scanner.

On Monday morning, armed with a language translation app, Anna made her way back to the Town Hall to see Frau Hoffmann.

"Ahh, Anna. *Guten tag*!"

Anna expressed her gratitude for being directed to Inna. "You saved the day, Frau Hoffmann. Thank you!"

"Ahh... Super, Anna. Super. Vee are family now!" Frau Hoffmann clapped her hands.

On seeing the woman's delight, Anna began her translated request to find a high-resolution scanner to send a critical photograph to her parents.

"Frau Hoffmann, *Ich muss meinen Eltern ein Foto schicken. Es ist sehr wichtig. Wo finde ich einen hochauflösenden* Scanner?"

Frau Hoffmann cast her eyes to the ceiling in thought about Anna's strange request. She then retrieved her phone and spoke to someone for several minutes. Anna watched her draw a simple map on a Post-it.

"Anna... Mmm... My brozer, Simeon, architect. You go zere." She pointed at the map.

Once again, Anna expressed her gratitude and followed the Post-it away from the Town Hall.

She stopped in front of a two-story cottage that housed an architectural office. She knocked on the door and was immediately greeted by a cheerful man in his early thirties.

"You are Anna?" he asked before she could muster a "*Guten tag.*"

"Yes!" Anna said excitedly at the sound of his English.

"Come on in, Anna. I am Simeon."

They shook hands and Anna stepped into the small office that housed two standing desks, a large-scale printer, and several architectural equipment pieces. Simeon inspected the photograph Anna had handed him with artistic precision.

"I am not sure how great the burned part of the photograph will scan through, but I will try a few different light settings."

Anna sent Kenny a text: Scanning now and about to send over!

Anna's phone beeped with a response from Kenny minutes later: Heyyy scan looks good, but I'll need some time there's a lot to clear up. Also, #its6amhere 😃.

Anna thanked Simeon, texted Kenny an apology and left to further explore Sankt Gilgen's cafés, shops, and forested paths.

Several hours later, the sun began to set as Anna walked the stairs up to her hotel room. She opened the door to her balcony to see the last remaining rays, but a beep from her phone made her jump. It was a message from Kenny: Let me know if this works!

Anna dashed to her laptop and opened Kenny's email. She examined the photograph attachments carefully. Kenny had done an amazing job. Not only had he sent the edited photograph, but also a magnified version of the mirror reflection she had specifically asked him to pay attention to.

The photograph no longer had the appearance of an aged relic. The lines contrasted sharply between the shades of gray that had at one point made the entire image blur together. Even the short feathers on her great grandmother's hat were clearly visible. Anna inspected both the mirror image on the full photograph and the cropped version. Details were lacking, but there was no doubt that the tall man on Karin's right wore some kind of military uniform. The shorter, thicker man next to him appeared to be a teenager, sporting a buzzed haircut.

Silently, Anna's finger rested on the alleged Kurt on her screen. *Is this my great-grandfather or someone else entirely? It still makes no sense. I need help, an expert...an expert in military uniforms? Maybe in World War II military, in general. Where can I find one?* Anna mulled it over for a minute. *Where did history and/or war experts work? Universities, museums, libraries, archives?*

She did an online search for "military museum in Austria." The first entry in the search results pointed to a museum whose name Anna could not even try to pronounce. The Heeresgeschichtliches Museum was in Vienna was described as the oldest and largest purpose-built military museum in the world.

This place has to have plenty of military experts to tell me where this uniform is from!

She looked up train travel to Vienna, and learned it would be a three-hour trip. But she had one more thing to do before she left Sankt Gilgen, and that was to visit Inna.

The following morning, Anna was treated to an assortment of home-made strudels, fish salads, breads, and tea at the small table in the center of Inna's kitchen. Worn, wooden cabinet doors with clear-glass inserts displayed their perfectly arranged contents. Each kitchen item stood in line with the others like little soldiers arranged by uses and sizes—strictly how Grandmother had kept her immaculate kitchen. Anna felt her grandmother's presence in the way Inna bustled around the stove, telling her more stories of relatives and who was doing what, when, and why. Yet the photograph nagged at Anna and in a moment of silence she sprang into the once again sensitive topic.

"Inna, I know Kurt was a doctor here in Austria, but did he ever serve in the military? As a doctor, I mean?"

Inna seemed annoyed at having to repeat what she had already said before. "Anna, I told you, he hated military and vould never be involved."

"That's right, I thought so. I'm going to see Vienna for a few days," Anna said abruptly changing the topic.

"Oh! That iz good," Inna replied, "Wien is magical city."

Anna embraced Inna one more time, promising to return before she flew back to Arizona. She needed to think.

Who the hell were these people? Was Grandmother even related to them? She felt like a guest at the Mad Hatter's tea party where everything was upside down. And if Grandmother wasn't related, then why would she claim to be a part of Inna's family?

Anna began to understand how Grandfather had felt all these months, filled with uncertainty, anger, and endless questions no one could answer. It was maddening.

I can't find any more answers here, Anna said to herself. *It's time to visit Vienna.*

Chapter 8

It's time to visit Vienna! Her train's boarding-ticket read in vibrant font. All around her, the First District gleamed like an opulent white cake. Anna's taxi whizzed through the quick-moving traffic that wove around the buildings and streets of Vienna's city center, forcing Anna to cling to her seat. All was too grand and too bright for her to look away—the perfect distraction for the negative emotions Anna had experienced just days before.

There has to be a logical explanation for Grandmother's lies, Anna told herself. This city would give her some answers, but until that moment came, Anna could not let her theories ruin the Vienna experience.

The taxi pulled up in front of the Hollmann Beletage hotel, a paradox of sleek ultra-modern design constructed into a nineteenth-century Viennese building.

Anna quickly checked in and burst out into the onset of a Viennese evening. A drizzle had started to fall, blurring the lines of reality. Anna breathed in the sweet smell of rain and wandered amidst the royal architecture of Vienna's past: the Hofburg and Neue Burg Palaces, massive in size while delicate in their beauty and structure.

The grand ball that was Vienna was thrown in their honor every evening. Around the royalty, God watched as a protector cascading divine light down onto Anna's face from the top of St. Stephen's

Cathedral, which rose above Vienna's skyline. The ball always started with his blessing.

To the west, the Parliament kept a watchful eye on the royals. Built in Greek Revival style, it challenged the crown's power by guarding public interests. To the Parliament's left, the Rathaus, or City Hall, stood as a chivalrous knight in Renaissance-style armor, ready to protect and uphold the law.

Anna walked south. The Natural History Museum faced its architectural twin, the Museum of Fine Arts and it seemed that they were lost in chatter over the gardens of Maria-Theresien-Platz. To the east, the Vienna State Opera house appeared—a constant culmination of drama, comedy, and love. Around the royal palaces clustered elegant buildings fussy with their balconies and porticoes; guests doing their best to please those who reigned over their very souls.

Vienna gleamed with such vigor, and its sheer beauty gave it the sense of an artificial city where people did not exist. Small in their presence, mice at the feet of the court towering above them, citizens walked down magnificent streets carrying on with ordinary lives.

The drizzle turned heavy and drummed the pavement in a rhythmic beat. Anna withdrew into the warmth of a late-night Viennese coffeehouse and mused at the city's luminous glow through the rain-washed window.

Once the rain died down and the soft waltzes she'd enjoyed in the café had switched to a jazz track, Vienna had to retire to its quarters; she needed her beauty sleep for yet another dance tomorrow.

At 9:00 a.m., Anna walked to the U-Bahn train platform. Surprisingly, it was based on the honor system. There were no turnstiles, nothing to prevent you from neglecting to buy a train ticket. *How odd... In*

New York, this would never be possible. Can the people here be that much more honest?

She emerged at Südtiroler Platz station a few blocks from the Heeresgeschichtliches Museum, a former military complex that Emperor Franz Joseph I dedicated to his army's glory. The heavy building reminded Anna of a giant red sandcastle. Its corner towers stared down like loyal soldiers, awaiting a command.

Inside the museum, multiple frescoed cupolas formed a stunning ceiling supported by gold Corinthian columns around which life-size statues of the Austrian Empire's most famous strategists stood back-to-back in marble solitude. They looked at her, annoyed that she did not know who exactly they were.

Anna bought a ticket and walked over to the information desk. Behind it, a woman sat with short-cropped brunette hair; her neon blue half-moon spectacles focused intently on a computer screen.

"Guten tag!" Anna started, "Sorry, is English okay?"

"Yes," she answered distractedly, her eyes still on the screen.

"I am an exchange student here from Arizona State University's history department; I need to speak to someone specializing in the museum's World War Two collection for my thesis." Anna smiled as innocently as possible.

The woman behind the desk did not seem to be listening. "Have you seen zi Austro Hungarian collection? It iz far more interesting than Hitler."

Her eyes flashed at Anna slyly.

"I am not interested in Hitler. I need to speak with someone who specializes in World War Two uniforms," she said firmly.

"Yes, but I do not know such a person." The woman clicked her mouse methodically as she spoke. It was odd that she had not touched her keyboard once. "I am very busy here, but enjoy our museum. *Auf Wiedersehen.*"

Anna was getting the brush-off, that much was obvious. She looked at her own reflection in the ornate mirror that hung behind the information desk and tried to think of another angle. A king of spades caught Anna's eye; the computer screen reflected a game of Solitaire in the mirror.

Busy, huh?

She looked up at Anna with a questioning look hiding irritation. "Somezing else?"

"Yes," Anna said coolly, "you may want to move the king of spades to the top deck, otherwise you will lose the game."

The neon blue spectacles flashed nervously to her screen and back to Anna in disbelief. Anna smiled sweetly and walked away with satisfaction.

Feeling smug, she proceeded into the World War II gallery; she would figure things out herself if she had to. Army trucks and even a Nazi fighter plane hung from the ceiling. To her left, something caught her eye. There were about ten mannequins in military uniforms on display. She got out the enlarged photograph from her purse. Not one of the uniforms matched it. Worst of all, the descriptions on the installation were only written in German.

Someone had to set up this display and write those descriptions... Anna felt her spirits lower, but she made her way to the remaining second-floor exhibitions anyway.

"The art of war," she said to herself. The phrase was a paradox and, as seen in many military museums, it was the glory of war that was put on display. Prisoner photographs in silver frames, mannequins modeling the uniforms once worn by human beings amidst a conflict not of their own making. The pain and horrors of war were lost amidst the glass cases displaying polished weaponry, official documents, and badges of courage given to mask a lifetime of trauma.

Through the window, Anna could see a group of children—a field trip perhaps—looking at the tank collection in the outside courtyard, fascinated by the machines of destruction feeding more of the violence that already exists within them inherently as humans. These young minds saw the glory of war, the fame of courageous leaders—but not the millions of tortured, starved, and murdered people.

A display on the aftermath of World War II cited an estimated fifty to eighty million casualties. It was a mind-boggling number that carried with it no emotional association. Just another statistic.

Anna thought back to her conversation with Grandfather in Phoenix. *So, was war really art? Or just our unconscious obsession with violence?*

An exhibition showcase held a photograph of Hitler giving the Nazi salute from his automobile. The famous portrait of Napoleon Crossing the Alps by Jacques Louis David came to Anna's mind. It showed Napoleon mounted on a horse with an outstretched hand in an almost identical salute.

Napoleon Crossing the Alps by Jacques Louis David juxtaposed with Hitler's photograph.

Did Napoleon's brilliance as a military tactician outweigh the simple truth that his egotistical thirst to dominate left millions of Europeans murdered? Hitler may have taken it to an extreme, but both men had the same intentions: to rule supreme, no matter the cost. Yet, somehow history celebrates Napoleon as a world leader instead of a murderer.

Anna stepped outside and took a seat on the main steps. She noticed a woman, slightly older than herself, in a security uniform. Her blonde hair was in a bun and did not help in hiding her eyes, which were downcast in concentration to her phone on which she was busy typing a text message.

"Excuse me," said Anna, catching her off-guard. The guard quickly shoved her phone back into her pocket, but, on seeing that Anna was just a visitor, her face instantly relaxed.

"Yes?" she answered.

"Do you speak English, by chance?"

"Yes." The young woman blushed slightly.

"Oh, great!" said Anna excitedly. "Listen, I was just inside talking to the woman behind the desk by the gift shop, with the short brown hair, but she wasn't very helpful."

The young woman rolled her eyes automatically. "Oh, yeah," her voice dropped to a whisper. "She is…odd."

"Okay, so it's not just me, then." Anna smiled. "Listen, I really need to find someone knowledgeable on the World War Two military uniforms that the museum has on display. It is part of my college thesis. Do you know of a person like that here?"

The young woman listened thoughtfully and paused after Anna finished speaking. "Mmm… Probably Doktor Bodart. He was our museum director."

"Yes, that would be perfect! Is he here now?"

"No, he just retired. But he has been coming in the later part of the day to sit in the café and make sure things are running well. I think it's been hard for him to let go of this place; it is his life. I'm sure he would help you. Just say I recommended you, he likes me. I'm Julia by the way." They shook hands. "Doktor Bodart is easy to recognize. He is tall, has a cane, and will be wearing a suit. Try an hour or two before the museum closes."

Anna thanked Julia and killed time wandering around the Schweizergarten and the Belvedere Palace a few blocks away. At 4:30 p.m., she returned to the museum and took a seat at one of the white plastic tables that sharply contrasted the ornate, golden-domed ceiling of the central room.

Soon a tall gray-haired man bearing a polished wooden cane stepped into the café. His eyes darted about assessing the crowd. Anna stood up quickly and approached him.

"Dr. Bodart?" Anna stretched out her arm. "My name is Anna, and I am Julia's friend. She told me that you might help me."

Dr. Bodart's handshake was firm, but delicate. He reminded Anna of her grandfather. The thought saddened her.

"Aaah, Julia, yes. She is a smart young woman, getting her degree in history, you know."

Anna smiled warmly, "She is lovely. Julia recommended that I speak to you because I need some expertise on military uniforms."

"I am sorry to disappoint you, Ms. Anna, but uniforms are not my specialty.... I am just here to..."

"Dr. Bodart, would it be alright if I ask you a personal question?" Anna asked to avoid any brushoff.

"Well, possibly," he answered, thrown off by her audaciousness.

"Why did you become a historian?"

"Well...to be a historian is to be a keeper of the world's memories, which turn into stories—and I have always loved stories."

Anna let out a deep sigh. It was an unexpectedly beautiful answer; one she could easily relate to.

"Dr. Bodart, you research and analyze deep into the world's memories, living and breathing their stories. Yet to us ordinary people, only a fraction of them are on static display at museums such as this. I, too, want these stories to be as real for me as they are for you. However, there is a disconnect because I do not possess this knowledge, but I need it desperately to complete my own story. I know your day is filled with things far more important than me, but, please, without the help of historians like yourself, we are left staring at unfinished chapters."

"Well..." Dr. Bodart started after a second of contemplation. "That is quite the plea. You must be a writer or poet." He chuckled. "I do not want to be the cause of unfinished business... What is this story you need to finish?"

Anna smiled with relief and said, "I saw the World War Two collection, but I could not find what I was looking for."

Dr. Bodart's eyebrows furrowed; gray and white strands poked out as if ruffled by such a possibility.

"What in particular are you looking for?"

Anna pulled out the photograph from her purse. "This uniform here," she said, pointing to the enlarged printout of the two men who stood next to her great grandmother.

Dr. Bodart removed a pair of thin reading glasses from his brown blazer's inner pocket and adjusted them carefully. He held the photograph to the light for several seconds, examining it this way and that. Anna held her breath.

"And who are these people that I am looking at? If you don't mind me asking." His eyes glanced at Anna curiously.

"It is my grandmother as a little girl, her mother and father, and a man whom I do not know..."

"I am guessing your grandmother is unable to explain?"

"She passed away before I had the opportunity to ask her."

"I am sorry to hear that." He looked at the photograph again and handed it back to Anna. "I can tell you that the uniform the man wears is not Austrian. It is a German military uniform."

"Are you positive?" Anna was perplexed. *If that is a German uniform, then the man in the photograph could not be my great-grandfather Kurt.*

"I am not sure what military division that uniform belongs to, but it is a German World War Two uniform most definitely."

Anna was stunned. *Who in the world was this man?* She began to understand why Grandmother never mentioned the presence of a Nazi in her photograph!

"Are you alright?" Dr. Bodart had been staring at Anna, who was having a frantic conversation with herself in her head and had completely forgotten she was in the midst of a real conversation with Dr. Bodart. He looked worried.

Anna smiled apologetically. "Dr. Bodart, is there any way I can find out more about this uniform? Exactly what division of the German military it is and what rank?"

Dr. Bodart thought about it for a moment. "I do have a colleague, but he lives in Berlin. He is a professor of history at Humboldt University. I can ask him about it, but, to be frank, it may take a while for him to respond, and of course, he would need to see the photograph himself. Whoever edited the photograph for you did an excellent job, but the details are still very vague. It would take someone with real expertise to recognize the uniform just from this. As you can imagine, such knowledge keeps him a very busy man."

Anna looked disappointed. "If he is a professor, he has to have time to meet with his students in between classes... Would it be possible for me to meet with him if I went to Berlin?"

"Oh... I do not know...."

"I know this is a big request," pleaded Anna, "but this is so very important to my family and me and my grandmother's peace. I would not ask otherwise."

"I do see that, Ms. Anna. You are willing to go to Germany after all." He hesitated for a second. "Let me see what I can arrange for you."

"Dr. Bodart, I would be eternally grateful!"

"I, too, cannot help but pry into the past." He winked warmly. "Here is my business card. Phone me on either number tomorrow morning. I will give Professor Rozek a call."

Chapter 9

"I will give Professor Rozek a call when I arrive in Berlin," Anna said to herself as she looked over Professor Rozek's address and the appointment time Dr. Bodart had written for her. She sipped her black tea slowly, letting the cube of sugar dissolve in her mouth and morph the bitter taste to a sweet tang. She could not sleep. Anna thought of her grandfather and typed in an email to him: "I'm on my way to Berlin. Sankt Gilgen was a dead end."

Vienna faded swiftly from view as her overnight train made its way to Germany. The soft veil of early evening descended on the stretches of fields until only the outlines of fences and scattered cottages remained. In nine hours, Anna would be arriving at the Berlin Hauptbanhoff. This thought made her nervous.

Berlin had invaded her mind much like it had invaded half of Europe in 1914 and again in 1939. Obviously, it was now a different place—a different nation altogether. However, Anna still felt it difficult not to associate it with death, with the Holocaust, and with her grandmother's near demise. Yet, here she was, going toward it at full speed.

Anna's eyes wandered around her sleeper compartment. A single yellow flower peeked from a small vase by the window. *What would Grandmother have said had she known I was headed to Berlin? Would it have even mattered?* Their entire relationship called itself into question.

The saintly qualities Anna had attributed to her grandmother no longer held substance. On some level, her grandmother was a liar. Anna popped another brown sugar cube into her mouth, hoping to sweeten that thought.

Anna heard a knock on her compartment door. It was now early morning, and Anna had not even remembered falling asleep.

"*Guten morgan.* Breakfast..." The knock came again. Anna slid the door open.

"Alloo," a pleasant woman smiled, her hair pinned into a neat updo. She handed Anna a tray with black tea, fruit, and pâté, placed neatly on small white plates on top of white paper napkins. Berlin beckoned to her with a long-curved finger. "I am just an hour away," it whispered to her. "Enjoy your jam."

Anna savored the sugared berries and stared out the window, as the outskirts of the city came into view. They looked innocent; no different than any other city. She sighed with some relief up until the train came to its final stop at the Hauptbanhoff, Berlin's central station.

Tentatively Anna pushed Calvin onto the arrival platform first as if to test for danger. Eager passengers maneuvered around her as she pretended to struggle with the suitcase. In reality, the struggle was with herself and the forbidden country she had been raised to avoid.

With both feet on German soil, she rode the escalator from the lower level upward, emerging into an ultra-sleek international train station stacked into five glass-walled floors with a gigantic steel-and-glass curved roof.

Cafés, shops, and amenities lined each level. Backpackers, tour groups, students, and businesspeople all hurried to make trains or stopped to stare down the station's center that remained open, casting a long view to the underground U-Bahn tracks. On the top level, soft morning sunshine hit Anna's eyes as it bounced off the approaching S-Bahn train. She had three days before her appointment with Professor Rozek, during which she planned to explore the city's curves.

The afternoons were hot and sticky. She wandered in and out of the streets, losing herself on purpose just to see where the city would lead her. It was on such detours that she found gems of fascination. Balconies overgrown with hanging flora, a vast park and community garden that was once the runway for Berlin's central airport, buildings laced together by a corset of street art. Everyone was outdoors going somewhere, eating something, or simply coexisting within the city's vibrant energy.

Berlin reminded her of elsewhere, but she could not quite place it. It was not until hours later of day one, returning exhausted back to her boutique hotel, that it hit her: Berlin could have been a possible love child of New York City and Portland, Oregon.

The pace, the innovation, the culture, and the drive of a big city, but with an air of freedom, and of a community still tied to the past notion of anarchy in the sixties. It was the dream to do whatever the hell you wanted and not be judged for it. That's what it was. A smile came across Anna's face. Berlin was grungy and brand-new all at the same time. Everyone belonged.

And yet, the reminders of a hell on earth persisted. The scars of World War II refused to go away, no matter how many new skyscrapers rose from the ashes of the Berlin skyline or how many artists drew upon the Berlin Wall remains, proudly renaming it the East Side Gallery.

The flags of liberation waved proudly: United States, United Kingdom, Soviet Union. Numerous museums held artifacts, documentation, and photographs of the German war machine. Anna walked among pines through Berlin's Tiergarten. She passed a memorial with two Red Army artillery pieces and two T-34 tanks. A large Soviet soldier stood atop a curved stoa. Twenty-six to twenty-seven million Soviets died; eighty thousand fell during the infamous Battle of Berlin alone.

America was so much different. The everyday memory of World War II was nonexistent. The war had been overseas, far from home. Four-hundred thousand Americans lost their lives, but America itself had never known what it would feel like to survive the destruction of itself. Here in Germany, every family had someone who had died during those miserable years. More than five million Germans perished in the madness, not including civilians.

Across from the park, the Memorial to the Murdered Jews of Europe stretched out in a contemporary maze of concrete rectangles. Six million people were not just killed but tortured to death.

The fatherland had been lying to everyone, including his own children; feeding ideas to the rest of the world, excuses masking what was really starting to rise in 1939. Nazi Germany wasn't cheating; it wasn't raping and killing: it was uniting, rebuilding, purifying. It had turned out that Germany had been a bad husband to Europe all along. Now everything has changed. Germany had been wrong, but the relationship had to continue; divorce was not an option. The question remained: Would that relationship ever be salvaged? Would the world let it be salvaged?

I have changed, Germany cried. *Look at the equality I offer. All of Europe flocks to me and I accept them all.* And it had changed, it had become better, a new nation altogether. Financially stable, artistic, intelligent, no longer judgmental, no longer superior. It realized its ego had been at fault and now it was humbled.

Yet, suspicion persisted because the world had not changed. Germany was still apologizing; it was still paying debts and compensation for Nazi crimes, walking on eggshells as the world eyed it closely, waiting to see if it ever took even one step too fast.

Anger rose in Anna. *The stupidity of humans to never learn from past mistakes, whether it concerned love or war.* The two were eerily similar. Just like a new romance, in the beginning, war is meaningful and patriotically exciting. We invest further as our romantic ideals and expectations soar. Nothing can stop this love, this passion. And then there is a fight. A battle that breaks the belief that this was the right person; the right ideology to fall for. A promise is made that next time, we will be wiser. But with each new generation, the human mind erases these notions, and so, we fall in love again, go to war again, and make the same mistakes again.

On the day of her appointment with Professor Rozek, Anna headed to Humboldt University in the brisk Berlin air. She passed the statue of Alex Humboldt, the liberal Prussian founder, into a quiet main hall. Cold-white orb lamps hung low, a line of moons leading toward big arched windows at each end of the corridor.

Room 2035 was by one of these large windows, reflecting bright light off the plastic placard displaying Professor Rozek's name. She knocked sharply and entered a small, brightly lit office with a central wooden desk cluttered with papers, behind which sat a small man in his late sixties.

"Ms. Venu, I presume? Please come in."

Anna stepped forward to shake his child-sized hand as he rose from his seat to the charming height of 5'3" directly below Anna's line of vision. He had an awkward frame that reminded Anna of a cartoon worm whose bald egg-shaped head teetered dangerously from atop a straight thin body.

The tone with which he spoke was sharp and icy. As if uncomfortable in his own body, the Professor's moves were jagged. His gaze was urgent, making it clear that this encounter was to be brief so as not to waste his valuable time.

"Dr. Bodart told me a bit about you and what you are looking for. He also told me about the conversation you both had. Poetic. I enjoyed it. Do you have the photograph he mentioned with you?" He spoke quickly, sternly, and with an air of intellectual superiority, making his compliment sting like an insult.

"Yes, it is right here…" Anna handed him the original photograph and opened her laptop to show him Kenny's edited version of the image.

"Dr. Bodart told me that your expertise is my only hope to identify the man's uniform in the photograph."

The professor skimmed over the photograph with brief intensity. "Ms. Venu, I take my work very seriously. I have a hunch, but I lack time to confirm it right now. I leave for London later today. However, Dr. Bodart is a very respected colleague of mine. I will recommend you to one of my students.

"Frederick is a promising young Ph.D. candidate specializing in World War II warfare and personnel. If he cannot help you, which I doubt will be the case, then I will look into the matter myself upon my return. Frederick is my teaching assistant; I have already called him into my office to speak with you. If you would like, wait over there." Professor Rozek motioned to one of the upholstered chairs within his office next to a browning potted fern. Anna thanked him for his help and sat down in anticipation. She was somewhat relieved she would be talking to someone closer to her age and hopefully not as intense as the professor. Maybe she would even make a new friend to show her Berlin.

The thoughts dissolved quickly as her left ear picked up the sharp knock and strong twist of a doorknob ushering in a powerful presence. Anna sat up firmly in her chair.

Frederick stood 6'3" and broad-shouldered, with a strong lean frame visible beneath a rich teal collared shirt. A narrow black textured tie neatly rested against his chest. The expression he wore telegraphed intelligence and inquisition, as if his mind never rested, but was constantly churning with new ideas and innovations. Underneath horizontal dark ash eyebrows, through sleek black rectangular frames, sharp dark eyes assessed her in mere seconds as if she was not really a woman, but just part of the armchair.

His face was flawlessly sculpted with visible cheekbones emphasizing a slightly crooked nose, giving the impression that it had at one point received quite a blow. His angular chin was the endpoint to a strong jawline and full, symmetrical lips.

Anna's stomach tightened from nerves. His looks were one thing, but, combined with the strength and confidence, his entire person radiated, his presence disarmed her. In his hand, he held a book. She made an effort to make out the title written in Italian, *Mussolini Segreto. Diari 1932–1938.*

It was a work Anna was familiar with, the diary of Mussolini's lover, Claretta Petacci, who had chosen to be with Il Duce to the very end, sharing his fate of execution by Italian partisans.

Ferdinando Petacci, Claretta's nephew, now an older man residing in Tempe, Arizona, had helped edit the diaries. He had given an autographed copy to Anna's father as a gift for help in a legal matter. *What a random coincidence,* Anna thought.

Anna refocused her eyes on the two men before her, the sight of which could not have been more amusing. Next to Frederick, Professor Rozek was elf-like in stature. Seeing them together, one wondered if a circus act would eventually follow.

The professor's hand beckoned to her. "Frederick, this is Ms. Anna Venu."

Frederick nodded at Anna just enough to acknowledge her presence out of the manner of being introduced. His expression was polite but emotionless.

Anna smiled sweetly, hoping to initiate a response; however, his eyes were vacant and had already left her.

Frederick started to speak in a deep serious voice but was interrupted by the professor.

"No Deutsch... English, please," nodding at Anna.

Momentarily, Anna could swear she caught a glimpse of annoyance flash on Frederick's face.

"Excuse me, I was not aware of your language barrier," he said coolly in almost perfect English, looking down at Anna.

Language barrier? Are you kidding me? Ohh...this was going to be good.

She smiled broadly, mustering within herself the very best of her Italian, "Oh that's quite alright, Frederick. I do hope you find Claretta Petacci's diary as fascinating a piece of history as I did."

The Italian words resonated unexpectedly, and Frederick's face showed an expression of great surprise.

"Are you Italian?"

"No, just an average American with a language barrier." She smiled curtly. Anna subdued her desire to smirk as much as possible.

She was not the only one enjoying her payback. The Professor, too, seemed to relish it and hid his chuckle behind a short cough. She wondered if the professor had his own issues with Frederick. It couldn't be easy having your best student outman you physically and be on your heels intellectually. As if reading her thoughts, the professor decided to interfere before Anna assessed their relationship deeper.

"As I was saying, Ms. Venu is an acquaintance of Dr. Bodart in Vienna... You know who I am speaking of, Frederick?"

He nodded in response.

"She is in possession of a photograph. I have taken a look at it briefly myself. In the photograph, the man, a relative I believe," he looked at Anna, who nodded in agreement, "needs to be identified. His uniform is of the German Navy, that much I am sure of. I do not have the time to study the photograph. Frederick, this is your area of expertise. Put it to good use, will you?"

Frederick had started listening intently at the mention of the German Navy. "Yes, of course," he said.

You may use my office. As for me, I am late. Hastily, he shook Anna's hand and left Anna alone with Frederick.

"Well, I suppose I should tell you the whole story," Anna started, hoping to avoid any awkward silences.

"If you feel it necessary to the task at hand," replied Frederick, who had seated himself opposite her.

"Some of the story is quite relevant," Anna answered.

Since she put Frederick in his place, she felt relaxed and confident. She pulled up all the enlargements of the photograph Kenny had made and passed her laptop to Frederick. Anna began to recount her discovery of the reflection and her family history but stopped after Frederick checked his watch for the second time.

"Is there somewhere you need to be?" Anna questioned.

"Everywhere but here," Frederick answered coolly.

"I thought this was your expertise? I am surprised it does not interest you."

"It would. If it were something of interest."

A tense moment of silence nestled itself between them.

Frederick's hard stare left the photograph and returned to Anna.

"I already have your answer. This man's uniform is of a German submariner. More precisely, a captain."

Anna found it difficult to challenge his firm tone on the impossibility of the accusation.

"Are you sure...?"

"Yes," he interrupted before she could finish.

"I need to know who this captain is."

Frederick let out a frustrated exhalation. "There were fourteen hundred and one U-boat commanders during World War II. To be frank, I do not have the time to sort through them."

"But not all of them will fit the date of this photograph nor the family history I explained!" Anna pressed further, "It is the only piece of information I need, after which I will leave you alone."

Frederick again assessed the photograph. Immediately, he began to ask a series of quick questions.

"Did your grandmother have siblings?"

"No."

"Where is the location of this photograph?

"I am not sure. All I know is that it is a mirror shop somewhere in Berlin."

"Who is the second man?"

"I do not know."

"Did your great-grandmother remarry?"

"No."

"Are you certain?"

"No.... I only know my grandmother's version, but, considering what I unearthed, it doesn't give me much assurance."

Anna's gaze traced the outline of his collared shirt that fitted around his defined shoulders and arms.

"Can you send me the digital copy of the photograph? I will look at the image using my resources."

Anna silently nodded.

"I will give you a call when I have turned your assumptions into something tangible. Leave your contact information on the desk."

Anna enjoyed his little display of coolness, but it was getting old. "You're too kind," she said flatly.

"I know."

With that, Frederick shook her hand and went to the door. Just before he opened it, he turned and asked in Italian, "Where did you learn to speak Italian?"

"My family's original name is Venucci," she answered in Italian.

"Interesting..."

"I know," Anna replied, letting their eye contact linger before breaking it.

The door shut and Anna remained seated. Frederick had left her feeling heated in both senses of the word. He was maddeningly attractive, that much was obvious, but his smugness made Anna determined to knock it down a few notches at the least. However, her priorities lay elsewhere, but it was hard to resist a good challenge.

Chapter 10

It was hard to resist a good challenge, and so, Anna again attempted to sound out the German subtitles playing on the television in her contemporary hotel room. A Georg Baselitz print stared at her from across the room. It was 10:00 p.m. Her legs burned from another self-imposed all-day tour. The ring of her cell phone surprised her out of her sprawled position across the length of the bed. She saw an unknown number.

"*Guten tag.* Am I speaking with Ms. Venu?"

"Yes... This is her," she said with hesitation.

"Miss Venu, it is Frederick. I apologize for calling so late."

Anna's heartbeat accelerated quickly. "Oh, it's no problem."

"I have important news for you." Frederick's voice resonated with excitement. He sounded different from the apathetic person she met at Humboldt University.

"Oh, really? What is it?" She tried to sound casual.

"I know for a fact who the people in your photograph are."

"Wait, are you serious? You know the names of everyone in the photograph?" Her casual tone became overpowered by sheer thrill.

"Yes, yes, I am sure. I have been working on it for the past two days. Then I realized that I had made a simple mistake in my research... Anyway, it is a long story. I would like to invite you to a café tomorrow morning. I can explain everything then."

But that is hours from now! Anna broke her normal rule of elusiveness and burst forward, "Can we meet right now? I mean, if it is possible?"

Without pause, he agreed. "Yes, let's do that. Where are you staying? I can pick you up. There is a place I go to often that remains open rather late."

Anna worked on keeping her voice level since it sounded like he, too, was hoping she would suggest meeting immediately. She started pacing around the room. "Okay, great. I'm at the Art'otel hotel in Mitte. I can be ready in fifteen."

"I will see you soon."

She hung up the phone. The thrill of finally breaking open the photograph's mystery was just moments away. She dug through the minimal contents of Calvin for an outfit decent enough for such an occasion. Several rushed minutes later, she was downstairs in dark gray fitted jeans and a loose violet silk blouse paired with zip-up suede booties.

A glistening black BMW M5 pulled up sharply to the hotel entrance, promptly on time. With hesitation, Anna approached the car, hoping this would not be one of those god-awful moments of getting into the wrong front seat.

Instantly, Frederick arose from the driver's seat and strode in Anna's direction. She was momentarily startled; in the few days since they'd met, she had somehow forgotten how good looking he really was.

A slim-fitting navy-blue blazer accented his athletic frame. Underneath, a cream patterned button-down, slightly open at the neck, showed glimpses of protruding collarbones. Dark fitted jeans ended at black leather shoes. Perfectly casual, yet carelessly chic.

"Ms. Venu, it's good to see you again. Thank you for joining me so late." He held the car door open for her and smiled.

Smiled! Anna was taken aback, *Ohh... We know how to smile...how refreshing.*

His whole demeanor changed with that smile. It was boyish, yet confident, with a mysterious coyness about it.

"Thank you for picking me up," she said, sliding herself neatly down onto the black leather seat. Even the inside of his car smelled seductive. There were so many gadgets that the thing looked like a German Batmobile.

"Nice car," she commented, knowing this would potentially open Pandora's box of car talk but, it would serve as an icebreaker, nonetheless. There's nothing boys like to talk about more than their expensive toys. Frederick only smiled politely in response.

Only two ways to interpret that, thought Anna. *Either he is not a car fanatic, which would be a nice change, or he hears "nice car" too often to care.*

"We will go to a café next to my apartment here in Mitte. There we can go over the details of your photograph."

His voice had again become detached as he submerged himself into his thoughts. The smile suddenly seemed far away. Anna tried to make small talk, which was difficult in the short responses Frederick was giving.

Not giving me much to work with here, she thought. *But at least you are nice to look at.* As they drove, Frederick started pointing out specific buildings and points of interest. Her wish for a tour guide was coming true in an odd and awkward sort of way.

They parked on the side street of a lively intersection. Most of the buildings were around ten stories high with trendy penthouse apartments on the top floors. On the street level, intimate cafés lit up the pavement, and chairs and tables still filled with Berliners enjoying their coffees or beers dotted the sidewalks. Her car door was opened so swiftly that she hadn't even noticed Frederick depart the car.

"Oh, thank you," said Anna, placing her hand in the palm he offered for support. His touch was strong and warm. To Anna this was surprising, as she had already decided he lacked a soul.

"It is straight ahead, Ms. Venu"

"Please, let's drop 'Ms. Venu.' Just call me Anna."

"As you wish."

Softly, he rested his hand on her back, gently guiding her in the general direction of the café, his other hand carried a luxurious leather briefcase. He smelled of aromatic woods and rich musk.

Frederick stepped to her side and held open the glass front door. Detached or not, he had the right manners. After a few steps forward into the chic industrial interior of the café, Anna felt somewhat alone. She turned around to see Frederick walking two steps behind her. His eyes scanned the room with grave suspicion. A shiver of nervousness made its way down her spine ending in a full-body chill. *Are we in danger or something?* Catching Anna's eyes upon him, Frederick's stern face relaxed. It almost looked kind in its own obscure way.

Frederick walked caught up with her. As they entered further into the restaurant, women and men started to shake his hand or kiss him hello on the cheek. Anna was confused.

"Frederick, I didn't know you were so famous. Should we take a picture together while I still have the chance?" Anna joked.

He looked at her firmly for a second. *Damn, maybe he doesn't get that I was kidding,* Anna thought, wondering if this was going to totally backfire. Suddenly, his stern look melted and he laughed.

He laughs? It was a night of miracles after all.

"Yes, I guess it does look quite funny." He continued to smile a charming, playful smile. "I live on the top floor of this building, so I am here quite often."

He pulled out a white cushioned leather chair for Anna. She smiled brightly and hoped that maybe they would get along after all.

"So, you are not famous? In that case, I'm slightly disappointed," she mocked.

Frederick grinned and placed her grandmother's photograph on the table. Anna's expression changed. *What an idiot.* She had almost forgotten why they were here in the first place. "Tell me everything!"

Precisely at this moment, a thick sturdy man with a trimmed red beard came over and shook hands with Frederick. After a brief introduction to the owner of the café, and an order of drinks and a few select appetizers "on zi houz," Frederick poured forth his findings.

"I will be honest, Anna, you puzzled me with your photograph and story. I have a deep interest in the German Navy of World War two, especially submarine warfare. I am actually writing my thesis on it now. Originally, I did not think it would be a problem to identify which submarine captain was in the photograph."

"Wait," interrupted Anna, "how did you even know it was a submarine captain?"

"Well, that part was easy," he said, his finger pointing to Kurt's head on the photograph facing Anna flat on the table. "Look at his hat; it is tilted—also, the cut of the uniform's jacket. Lastly, the year on the back of the photograph—Berlin nineteen thirty-seven. It left no doubt in my mind."

Anna listened intently; this guy knew his stuff.

"Then, after I magnified the image on my computer, I noticed the tips of two light-colored stripes which are barely visible on the right sleeve; it is another uniform clue. As I told you prior, there were approximately fourteen hundred and one German U-boat captains during the war. I have a file on each of them.

"I began to narrow them down by those who were already captains in thirty-seven, the year the photograph was taken. I went through each file, trying to find possible matches between the date and your family information. I was not successful. No one matched the assumed family in the photograph.

"I had almost given up, but just hours ago, I realized what a simple mistake I had made. While I was busy looking through the files, I had forgotten that I kept the files for the upper echelon of German U-boat commanders in a completely separate folder. He could have moved up in ranks later if he was successful during patrols. I had not yet looked there!"

"And, what did you find?" Anna was on the edge of her seat, leaning forward and not even acknowledging how close their faces were to each other.

"The man you see in the photograph is Lieutenant Commander Hans Ritter and his family."

Puzzled and doubtful, Anna furrowed her eyebrows and asked, "Are you sure?"

"One hundred percent."

Anna's face showed her uncertainty. Frederick's temples shifted, preparing to prove to Anna his evidence. "He had a wife," Frederick pointed to Anna's great-grandmother, "a daughter, and a younger brother." His finger was now on the mirror reflection of the young man next to the commander.

He paused for effect. "The commander's father owned several popular furniture shops here in Berlin and just before the war, he decided to open a mirror store in nineteen thirty-six. Unfortunately, this was a complete business disaster because he had decided to sell Austrian mirrors, which were out of fashion in Berlin."

Frederick opened his briefcase and pulled out a small book with a soft laminated cover. A black-and-white photograph of a German submarine decorated the front cover.

"The title of this book is *My Brother, A German Hero*, written by the commander's brother, Karl, who is in your photograph. Karl later became a physician in West Berlin," Frederick explained.

He opened the book and began showing Anna photographs of Commander Ritter when he was a young navy officer, and of his wife, Vera. There was no doubt that she had striking similarities with the Karin in her grandmother's photograph. Anna sat stunned.

She flipped through the book's pages, assessing each of the commander's photographs during various stages of his career.

There was only one photograph of Ritter without his naval officer cap. For the first time, Anna examined his face. The portrait before her had a philosophical air about it that captured Anna's attention for several seconds. Ritter had the calm inquisitive expression of a man who never rushed into anything without putting in careful thought. His dark eyes seemed kind and, in them, Anna was sure she sensed her grandmother's spirit.

Lieutenant Commander Hans Ritter, 1942

The photographs showing the commander during his long patrols stood out the most. The composition of each shot gave the image a reality that transcended time. She could almost smell the sea air as it lapped the side of a surfaced U-boat, too big to fit into the scenic shot fully.

Two glasses of wine arrived, along with small plates of smoked meats, cheeses, pickled vegetables, and neatly arranged toasts with spread. It looked delicious, but Anna did not react.

"So, you're telling me he was a German submarine commander?"

"He wasn't an ordinary U-boat commander. He was a Lieutenant Commander and Grand Admiral Doenitz's right-hand man. He was in charge of the entire U-boat operation in the south Atlantic, which was crucially important for Germany."

"Frederick, I can hardly believe this. I mean, I am shocked, but it all makes sense. It's now obvious why my grandmother hid the truth from my grandfather. He had survived a personal tragedy at the hands of a German U-boat. So she hid from him the fact that it was her own father who directed U-boat assaults on Allied merchant ships in the Atlantic. I mean, the commander must have known about the SS *Gettysburg* sinking from the U 66 captain's report generated after patrol."

Anna took a breath, ready to dive into more details, but Frederick used the opportunity to cut her off.

"Anna, you are getting ahead of yourself. I didn't say any of that. I am just telling you who is in the photograph."

"What do you mean? My grandmother told me that this was her family, which means that the commander was my great-grandfather."

"That is impossible," Frederick stated firmly. "They cannot be your relatives."

"What?" Anna subdued herself, she was becoming defensive. "Why?"

"There was only one person in this photograph who survived the war. The commander's wife, Vera, died during a Berlin air raid in nineteen forty-four. The commander was killed by Soviet troops when he tried to sneak into Berlin after the Red Army surrounded it. He tried to save and evacuate his only daughter but never made it to her. She was killed during the final days of the Battle for Berlin. Only the commander's brother survived. They are all buried in a family crypt in the city cemetery."

Anna brought the wine to her lips and took a long thirsty drink until she felt it fill her with the encouraging effect of audacity.

"Then, how are these people related to my grandmother?"

"Truthfully, I think your grandmother was Helga Eckert and your doubts in her identity are unfounded. She could have been a maid or a friend to the commander's family."

"Then, why would she tell us that this was her family?

Anna pulled out her phone and showed Frederick an uploaded photograph of her grandmother from the 1950s. "Look, there are clear similarities between the child in the photograph I gave you and my grandmother."

Frederick skimmed through the photographs and then analyzed the child's face in the mirror store photograph.

"Anna, I have never seen your grandmother, but if one compares these images, no one will be able to confirm with certainty that this is the same person at different ages. I think that you are influenced by a pre-existing mindset. For years you have been told the same story of who is in this photograph." Frederick took a pause. "The Commander's daughter is dead and that is a historical fact."

"But how do you *know*? Maybe she secretly survived?"

"I don't want to disappoint you, but I will repeat it once again. It is a historical fact."

Anna's eyes refused to give in.

Frederick continued to push forward. "Karl, the commander's brother, was a very well-known physician in West Berlin; he helped rebuild the medical care system after the war. He recovered his brother's body and re-buried his relatives in a newly built vault as the family's last resting place. He was present when his sister-in-law and his niece's shallow graves were opened, and the bodies moved to the crypt. He identified her remains."

Anna was quiet for a moment. "Frederick, you are going to have to help me find this book in English."

Frederick's eyes narrowed questioningly, but now it was Anna's intense gaze that looked through him, refusing to explain anything further.

"Please, you have to!"

"I'll see what I can do, Anna."

During the car ride back to Anna's hotel, the two remained quiet. Each submerged in their own thoughts. The BMW came to a smooth final halt in front of the Art'otel.

"Tell me one more thing, Frederick—" she turned to face him. "What exactly was up with you when we entered the café? You scouted the place as if it had hidden assassins lurking behind the curtains... Are you always that paranoid?"

Frederick smiled slightly. "You are very observant, Anna. And yes, I always assess my surroundings."

In her hotel room, Anna studied the Berlin skyline. *What really happened so many years ago?* Anna took a deep breath, filling her lungs with Berlin, wishing to inhale any possible clues. The conversation with Frederick had given her answers, but they were not the ones she was looking for. In fact, they had angered her. Despite her best efforts, her grandmother's real identity remained even more elusive.

There was no pattern that she could identify. The only thing she was now sure of was that her grandmother's photograph was of Commander Ritter's family and that Grandmother herself was not his daughter as she had claimed.

Why would Grandmother keep a photograph of a deceased family saying it was her own? It was a disturbing question. *Maybe Frederick was right.* It's possible that she had lost her own parents, just like Inna had said, and she could have identified the Ritter family as her own to ease her trauma. They could have even adopted her. Either way, there had to be an answer.

The lights in people's windows went out one by one as midnight set in. Someone out there had clues, and Anna needed Frederick's help to find that person, whoever they were.

Chapter 11

Whoever they were in relation to her grandmother, the Ritter family swam in and out of Anna's thoughts, ignoring the anxiety they brought with them. Anna stared out her hotel window in a daze. It was a mild clear day, incompatible with the fog within her mind. Frederick had called an hour earlier. Karl's book, *My Brother, A German Hero,* was not available in English.

Though the news disappointed Anna, it did not surprise her. Impatiently, Anna begged Frederick to translate the book to her himself. It was her only lead, and she was willing to fight hard for it. Frederick had taken a long pause on the phone, thinking of the best way to explain that he simply did not have the time.

"An hour a day, that is all I ask!" Anna had pleaded. "I will come to you, plus, you know the book by heart since you have cited it widely in your thesis, right?"

Frederick continued to decline politely, but Anna persisted. It was then that she started to admit that it was not only the book she was interested in but Frederick himself. His keen mind, sharp looks, and overall presence intrigued her. She wanted to see him again, and this was the only way to make that possible.

"Frederick, listen, I know you are super-busy, I get that, but this whole thing is a mystery. A real-life mystery that involves not just my family, who are, of course, no interest to you but also the family of

Commander Hans Ritter—a man you hold in high esteem. Aren't you curious enough to figure out a part of history that no one else may know? I mean, how the hell did the photograph of his family end up in Arizona? It may be nothing important, but what if it is? What if it changes everything?"

Frederick was silent again, but Anna knew she had him. She felt it.

"Alright, Anna. Alright. I cannot promise you my complete attention, but I will walk you through the book when I can."

They had hung up the phone with a set appointment for the next day. Though he had promised her hour-long increments, Anna had the feeling that once he got started, he would lose track of time. She could not have been more right.

The following day, Anna met Frederick, notepad in hand and ready to take down any relevant information that could lead to possible clues. They sat outside a small café with two cappuccinos and a plate full of memories, neither of which were their own.

"The commander was an incredible man," Frederick said with admiration. "He was intelligent, brave, and honorable. He was a man in service to his country and *not* to the Nazi regime or their atrocities. The wealthy family merchant business he was born into was of no interest to him. Instead, he enrolled into the Imperial Naval Academy in Kiel in nineteen sixteen as a sea cadet. The end of World War I coincided with his graduation from the academy in nineteen eighteen. The Versailles Treaty, which Germany was forced to sign, humiliated the entire nation and was the first stepping stone toward World War II.

"That all triggered Germany's great economic decline and eventually led to the election of the Nazi ruling party. The Versailles Treaty limited the German Army and Navy to a comical size and restricted any practical training for young officers. However, this did little to stop the Germans from secretly sending their young pilots and tank commanders to train in the Soviet Union."

"The Soviet Union?" Anna asked in disbelief. "But, weren't Germany and the Soviet Union mortal enemies?"

"Don't forget, this was during the twenties," replied Frederick. "Before both countries became enemies, they were allies. You may know about the secret Ribbentrop-Molotov Pact, which split eastern Europe into two major influence zones between Germany and the Soviet Union?"

"Yes," Anna lied.

"Well, in the nineteen twenties, the Soviets secretly provided military training to German officers who would later invade the Soviet Union with lethal precision and operational skills. History is filled with ironic twists, and this is one of them."

"What did the Soviet Union have to gain from helping Nazi Germany?" Anna asked.

"Stalin's initial idea was that Germany must be kept as a counterbalance to England and France. When Hitler came to power, Stalin hoped that Hitler would attack France and England first. Both sides would then exhaust themselves in the struggle, and then the Red Army would step in and take over all of Western Europe, spreading Communist ideas around the world. This is why Stalin helped the Germans from the very beginning. You can imagine how the quick fall of France, as well as the rest of Europe, shocked him!"

"So, how does this tie in with the commander?" Asked Anna.

Frederick smiled as if he owned a secret. "Commander Ritter had a best friend named Walter. This was in nineteen twenty-two. Back then, the commander was just a young navy officer on one of Germany's torpedo boats. Walter was a pilot in the Luftwaffe, and it so happened that he was headed to Lipetsk, a city in the Soviet Union, for secret pilot training. For this, he had to learn Russian, but that was not a problem. Berlin was filled with White Russians who had fled the country after the Bolshevik Revolution. Walter found himself learning from a kind woman called Alexandra, who he took a great liking to, but it was the woman's only daughter, Vera, who really impressed him.

"For weeks, Walter, who was happily married, told Ritter about Vera's beauty and kind disposition. He finally convinced Ritter to start Russian lessons with Alexandra for the sole reason of meeting Vera. The book quotes Ritter saying he fell in love with Vera after he first laid eyes on her. And so began his journey to conquer her heart. Vera's mother was a Russian Countess, Alexandra Chukhnina, who had been one of the lucky few to escape Russia with her husband, a White Army Colonel named Yuri Chukhnin, and with little Vera. The family settled in Berlin, one of Europe's main centers for the White Resistance. Colonel Chukhnin became a local military leader, which inevitably ended his life in an assassination by a network of Soviet spies who infested Europe at that time. Vera and her mother were left without an income source but survived by giving Russian language lessons.

"The year nineteen twenty-five gave Ritter a new sense of purpose; Vera's hand in marriage and, later, the birth of their daughter, Maria. His life unfolded beautifully, as did his military career, which caught Captain Doenitz's attention, who was building the German Navy's U-boat arm. Doenitz was the first to visualize U-boats as powerful weapons instead of just a form of support for the surface Navy."

"Umm… Sorry to interrupt you, but," Anna's tone was doubtful, "are you talking about the same Doenitz who was accused of several war crimes during the Nuremberg Trials?" She pulled out her phone and quickly validated her claim next to an image of Doenitz' portrait.

Grand Admiral Karl Doenitz

Frederick gave an exaggerated sigh and said, "Anna, your education is so one-sided."

With effort, Anna bit her lip to refrain from argument. Frederick's tone was defensive. Reminding him that the crimes were, in fact, committed and questioning his storytelling could jeopardize his help completely.

"You have to remember that the Navy was the only branch within the German military during World War Two which was *not* involved in planning or executing Nazi crimes."

Anna tried her best to keep a straight face.

"To be a submariner on either side was heroic, but for German U-boat crews, it was even more so. Watch the movie *Das Boot*, if you want to get a glimpse of what it was really like to be a U-boat man.

"Despite both of his sons perishing in the Atlantic, Doenitz remained a patriot but was never a member of the Nazi party."

Anna stared at him and asked, "If Doenitz wasn't a member of the Nazi party, then why would Hitler choose him to be his successor after his suicide?"

"It is pure irony, I know," Frederick explained, "but out of Hitler's entire entourage, Doenitz was the only one who didn't betray Germany," Frederick stated proudly.

"But from a different perspective," Anna pressed, "I am pretty sure Doenitz refused to surrender German military forces for several days after Hitler's suicide. More and more people had to die because of it."

"Ten days. He surrendered Germany in ten days. Doenitz could have refused his appointment as head of state, but he didn't. He wanted to let as many German civilians and troops get to the western part of Germany to escape the Red Army. Do you know how many Germans were saved by his decision?" Frederick shot passionately.

"I will give you the English edition of Doenitz's memoir *Ten Years and Twenty Days*. Maybe you can understand his intentions that way."

They were once again off-topic. Anna tried to steer them back to the plot that most interested her. "What was the relationship between Ritter and Doenitz like?" she asked.

"I think that Doenitz saw Ritter as his younger self. After five victorious patrols in the Atlantic and the Mediterranean Sea, Ritter became known for his bravery, cool head, and good luck. The military successes of the U-boat fleet gave Doenitz and Ritter leeway to not pledge their allegiance to the Nazi party."

"Ritter was even allowed to stay married to his Russian wife, though she was considered of an 'inferior race.' However, his marriage did raise suspicions and Ritter was always under watch. The moment finally came when Vera was arrested."

"Who arrested her?" Anna asked with genuine interest.

"According to the book, she had been hiding a Jewish boy in their summer home. There is evidence of Vera's arrest and release, but there are no official records on the reason for the arrest. Personally, I think Karl threw in the story of the Jewish boy because it made his brother look better to new generations."

"The next year brought unending disaster to Ritter. His beloved wife died during an Allied air raid on Berlin in forty-four. Ritter had to remain present in France, so the responsibility to take care of his daughter, Maria, was bestowed onto Karl, her uncle. When Karl and his family evacuated Berlin, Maria refused to leave her friends despite Karl's pleas."

"As soon as Ritter learned that his daughter was still in Berlin, he and three volunteer sea cadets from the academy tried to get into Berlin before Soviet troops encircled it, but time was not on their side. They were spotted by Soviet patrol. One of the cadets was shot to death. The commander was severely wounded but was able to guide the other cadets into a cavern where they successfully eluded Russian troops who searched the entire area."

"At night, Commander Ritter committed suicide, knowing his cadets would refuse to leave him behind, which would have ended their lives and any possibility of Maria's rescue.

"The two cadets entered Berlin, found Maria, and drew her a map with the location of where they buried her father. Unable to evacuate her, Maria was killed just weeks before Berlin's garrison surrendered."

"Wait, but how did Karl know all of this?" Anna asked, perplexed.

"That is the most interesting part of the story..." Frederick moved in even closer. Anna picked up a whiff of his cologne; its seductive notes were amplified by the story's building tension.

"According to this book," Frederick's finger tapped the cover firmly, "in August of nineteen forty-five, Karl and his family returned to the American sector of Berlin. Immediately, he started to work on restoring medical services for Berliners. Upon visiting the graves of his parents and the commander's wife, Vera, he saw the relatively fresh grave of his niece, Maria. Karl did not know anything about her death or about the fate of his brother. All of Karl's efforts to find the commander's location in POW camps were unsuccessful.

One day, a young woman appeared on his doorstep and told him about his brother's and niece's fate. She gave him a map of the commander's burial site located close to the Ritter's summer home. Karl knew the area well; however, that part of Germany was under Soviet control. Karl used all of his connections within the military administration to get permission to examine the possible gravesite. He assembled a small search party, found the shallow grave, exhumed the body, and transported it to Berlin. As I told you before, he built a vault on the family plot, finally uniting all his relatives.

"The book has many photographs, including one of the map itself. Critics suggest that Karl invented this mysterious woman to add a layer to the story. However, in several interviews, Karl insisted the woman was real and living in West Berlin. It was her wish to remain anonymous, and he said he would honor that wish. Yet skepticism still ran high. I tried to get in touch with Karl's son several times to get access to his family archives to retrieve information for my thesis, but I was unsuccessful."

"What a horrible ending," said Anna.

She sipped her now-cold cappuccino. The tragedy of an entire family turned into deep disappointment for her own family. So far the biography had given her no useful information. Anna sighed. Reaching a dead end meant she would have to once again start from the very beginning. Anna closed her eyes on what had been her best lead yet.

Chapter 12

Anna closed her eyes on what had been her best lead yet and opened them to a solution so obvious that she had missed it completely. She spent the next day mulling over the probability that she could be correct. When the percentage hit a high enough peak, the probability tipped, and Anna called Frederick.

"I have figured out my grandmother's identity and her relation to Commander Ritter! Frederick, I need to tell you ASAP."

She caught him in the middle of writing a new class lecture. He sounded rushed on the phone, busy with the task at hand, but her excitement drowned out the cues he was giving to decline. She knew he would eventually agree to meet her because, whether he liked it or not, he was now involved and would not have the manners to refuse her.

"A fifteen-minute cup of coffee—that's all I need!"

She pushed until he finally agreed to meet at Café am Neuen See, a biergarten on the banks of the Neuer See Lake in Tiergarten Park.

Anna arrived first. She had analyzed the possible ways in which the conversation could flow. Frederick was a crucial pawn for her advancing, and she desperately needed his help.

Frederick's tall frame approached the café in a ruffled manner. She felt his unpleasant eagerness as if he had been waiting all day to unleash his temper on just the right person: her.

The partial kiss that landed on her cheek as she stood to greet him was impersonal. The warmth of their last meeting together had evaporated, leaving a distance between them she found herself longing to fill.

"Frederick, I'll cut to the chase," she stated frankly, "the mysterious woman who brought the map to Karl that is the connection. She was my grandmother!"

"So, Helga was the mystery woman?"

Anna mulled this over for a minute. "No. My grandmother was the mystery woman, but I am sure she was not Helga Eckert."

"How can you keep dismissing the obvious facts that show your grandmother was Helga?"

"I don't have proof, Frederick. I just feel it. I met the entire Eckert family in Sankt Gilgen; they seemed so different from my grandmother. None of them played a musical instrument, let alone even knew my grandmother was a skilled pianist—"

"Wait, wait, wait," Frederick interrupted. "Are you basing conclusions off of their lack of musical ability?"

"It's not just that, Frederick, it's hard to explain, but things just don't fully add up. I am sure that my grandmother wasn't raised in the Eckert family. That is why I think there has to be a third alternative: Grandmother had to have been this mystery woman."

"Explain." Frederick exhaled doubt. His arms crossed like a wall between them waiting to be brought down.

"Well, I realized there is too much crossover between my grandmother and this woman for it to be purely coincidental. First and most obvious, both women had close ties to Commander Ritter's family. The mystery woman must have made a big enough impact on Karl for him to respect her wishes to remain anonymous. You said yourself that Karl received a lot of criticism and was accused of making her up. My grandmother had the personality to convince someone like him, and, just like the mystery woman, my grandmother also remained anonymous. She seldom disclosed her past to anyone—even her husband and granddaughter.

"This leads me to my second point: The mystery woman had to have been Maria's close friend. Why else would she have kept the map of the commander's burial and searched for Karl to 'make things right.' It is obvious this woman lost someone important to her.

"My grandmother told me that she lost her best friend who got shot during the final stages of the Battle of Berlin. I think it was the commander's daughter. Most importantly, my grandmother was still in Berlin in August of forty-five working as a translator for the Allies. She was transferred to Paris in the fall of forty-five. Even the dates match up. I mean, who else could this woman be?"

Frederick listened carefully, shifting in his seat when Anna paused for a response. "Yes, pieces of your theory fit, but I don't think the details are specific enough to conclude a match. First of all, Karl said this woman lived in West Berlin...and second of all, where does your theory leave Helga and the Eckert family?"

"I don't know where that leaves Helga. The possibilities are endless. As for Karl, he lied to protect Grandmother's identity. Do you think if he said that this mysterious woman now lives in Arizona, his critics would believe him more?"

"Giving you the benefit of the doubt, let's say they do match. Why then would your grandmother tell you that the commander's family is her family? If she is the mystery woman wanting to stay anonymous, she would then discourage such ties instead of perpetuating them."

Anna bit her lip slightly annoyed that he pointed out the only hole in her logic she was hoping to avoid.

"There could be many reasons. She may have been an orphan and identified herself as Maria's sister. She could have told us all of this knowing we were far too removed from Germany to make the connection."

Frederick leaned in toward her and said, "The emphasis is on two phrases you just said yourself: *could have* and *may have.* Those are both assumptions, and you cannot base facts on assumptions."

Anna stared at him tensely. Her eyes narrowed. "I can't. You're right, but what I can do is turn assumptions into facts." She paused for effect as Frederick raised his eyebrows curiously.

"I'll need your help to do so."

With that, she once again felt Frederick's loss of interest.

"Anna, I apologize, but I lack capacity for this project. Even if I was not obligated to my work, family, and thesis, I still do not see how I could help you."

Anna waited patiently with understanding eyes until Frederick finished his spiel. She had already predicted this response. It was now time to lay down her trump card. "Remember when you were telling me about Karl, and how you tried several times to gain access to his family's personal archives, but his son would not budge?"

With each word, Frederick's face became more and more engaged.

"What if I told you," Anna continued seductively, feeling as if she was playing the role of a vixen, "that I could get into those archives. Do you think that would help your thesis stand out in the world of historical academia?" To enhance her offer, she ran her fingers down Frederick's hand.

To her complete surprise, Frederick's serious expression collapsed into laughter. Collecting himself, he reached for her hand and stroked it gently. His eyes locked onto hers with longing. Anna's chest tightened. With the same seductive tone, he whispered to her, "Yes, Anna, it would, but you, of all people, have no way of achieving that."

Anna blushed. Her vixen strategy made her look foolish. Apparently, she was dealing with a different sort of man altogether.

The embarrassment swiftly faded as her gaze grew firm. "You don't have the slightest idea who you are dealing with!" Anna snapped, pulling back her hand. She paused, breathing in the shock of her own intensity. "Tell me everything you know about Karl's son and connect me with him. I will get through to him no matter what."

Her authoritative demeanor had utterly wiped the smile of superiority off of Frederick's face. The determination she exuded forced him to sit up a little straighter, eyeing her with scrutiny. "Alright Anna, if anything, I am curious to see what you come up with, but I am going to warn you now, Karl's son is the most obnoxious, pretentious, egotistical person I have ever met. A real son of a bitch."

"Well, I figured he had to be something like that if he was unresponsive to even your attempts," Anna said with sarcasm.

With no reaction, Frederick continued, "his name is Benedikt Ritter. He works as a prominent tax and civil attorney here in Berlin. The clientele he takes on is very elite. The only problems that concern him are money and the prestige of his own family.

"I exhausted all my connections to review anything at all from Karl's archives, but all my attempts were met with a stern, 'no thank you.' To me, this means one thing; some of the information in the archives does not put the Commander or Karl in the best of light, and by association, Benedikt's own name. Otherwise, there would be no reason for him not to be interested in giving himself and his family name even more credit and publicity."

Anna nodded in agreement. "That totally makes sense."

Frederick's tone was getting heated from the recollection. "To even schedule an appointment with him, you have to first go through his viciously protective secretary."

Anna thought back to the secretary back at the museum in Vienna. "Oh, I am familiar with such gatekeepers."

"There is more. Many of the photographs from Karl's book were originally taken by a young sailor named Gunter Krauss, from the U-boat's crew during one of the commander's patrols. He either sold or licensed the rights of the photographs to Karl. I think that Karl and, later, his son supported the old man. I am sure they bought him out for whatever reason. Gunter rarely gave interviews and when he did, they were to official media only. All questions had to be submitted beforehand and each interview had to be scheduled through Benedikt's law firm.

"Approximately five years ago, just before Gunter died, I asked my friend, a very respected journalist, to arrange an interview with him and take me along as an assistant. I observed the old man for an hour. He repeated pieces out of Karl's book like a parrot—and shared nothing else.

"As we had agreed, my friend left the room pretending to go to the bathroom. When we were alone, I asked Gunter one question: *Did Commander Ritter or his brother ever express direct support for the Führer or the Nazi party?*

"Surprisingly, Gunter panicked and started claiming he was having chest pain. He ended the interview."

"What do you think they are hiding?"

"The family will do whatever is necessary to preserve the commander's saintly image. What they are hiding has to be big enough to taint the family legacy, so I don't think it is something personal such as an affair or even financial fraud. I believe..."

Frederick paused and took a sharp look around before continuing, "I believe Commander Ritter had a closer association with the Nazi regime than Karl portrayed. There is no other explanation for such extreme secrecy."

They sat in silence for a minute.

"But you are correct in one thing, Anna. No one can explain how one of Ritter's original photographs came to be in Arizona. That adds a big twist to our story."

Anna nodded in agreement, excited that Frederick identified himself with her mystery. *Our* story.

"Here is Benedikt's office number and address." Frederick sent a text.

"Perfect. Always a pleasure doing business with you, Frederick." Anna held out her hand in an exaggerated manner. "I will be calling you with a game plan soon."

Frederick smiled his charming boyish smile. "May I invite you for a walk through Tiergarten Park?"

Anna leaned back in her chair, evaluating the validity of his offer. "I would, but don't you have all of your work, your family obligations, and your thesis to worry about?" she teased.

"I need to refresh my mind," he answered coyly.

This was the first instance Frederick had asked her to be with him for no particular reason.

It's about time. She smiled.

They made their way along the winding dirt path. A pleasant warm wind fragranced the air with the scent of a fast-approaching summer. Around them, Berliners lounged in the open fields of Tiergarten

Park. Some sat on the edges of the Landwehrkanal Canal reading or kissing, while others played with children or threw Frisbees. Berlin was at peace.

"It is so beautiful here."

"Yes, but it is hard to believe that at one point there were no trees left."

"Do you mean during the war?" asked Anna.

"Actually, the trees were cut down for firewood after the end of the war. Now look how nature replenishes itself."

Anna tried to imagine the green stretches of lush grass covered in ash. It was a depressing thought.

They were making their way across the Landwehrkanal Canal, and Anna spotted a llama grazing in the distance. A tall fence secured the animal.

Confused, Anna pointed, "Is that a petting zoo or something?"

"That is the Berlin Zoo, the oldest zoo in Germany and the largest in the world. It is very famous."

The words "Berlin Zoo" hit close to home. A sudden urge to run to it came over her.

"We must go there!" she blurted out. Her excitement threw off Frederick's leisurely stroll. Her hand pulled him toward what looked like the entrance. Two stone lions sat atop a big gate.

"Do you mind if we go in now!?" Her voice was eager, guiding Frederick into the ticket line. Moments later, she was studying the map of the zoo.

"I have to see the zebras!" Her hand once again pulled Frederick forward in a hurry. He tried to point out other animals, but Anna made it obvious she was set on one thing. They breezed along the winding paths until finally, creatures with black and white stripes stood out against green foliage. Her heart soothed.

"So, here are the exotic Berlin zebras!" Frederick said sarcastically.

Anna playfully pushed him, "Shut it! Do you think these zebras could be the descendants of those zebras that were here before the war?"

Frederick gave her an odd look. "That's very doubtful. All of the animals were either transferred to different zoos before the bombings started or they had to be shot. Some of them escaped during the bombings and were hunted in the streets. I even heard a story of an escaped elephant who was spotted by a Soviet general who assigned food rations to the animal and kept it protected."

Anna wondered if the zebra exhibit had always been right here and if Grandmother had admired them in this same location. Melancholy set over her, and she stepped away from the exhibit.

"Okay, we can leave now..." Her eyes fluttered away as she moved toward the exit sign.

"What about the other animals? Don't you want to see the rest of the zoo? I thought—"

"I know this sounds strange, but I kind of want to get out of here."

Anna saw the perplexed look on Frederick's face and knew she would have to explain. As if he read her thoughts, his next words were just that.

"Can you explain to me why in the world we had to run in only to see zebras?"

Anna sighed heavily. "It's kind of a long story…"

"Well, we have the time if you want to tell it, but let's go back to the main entrance. The Elephant Gate is famous; you should at least see that."

"You know, my grandmother never said much about her time in Berlin during the war except for one story. Her best friend, who I still think was the commander's daughter, Maria, had just been killed. To find some sort of inner peace, she left the shelter in the early morning before any shelling started and walked through the streets alone. Three blocks from the zoo's main gate, she met a zebra who'd escaped from the damaged zoo."

Frederick was silent, listening to Anna intently as they walked beneath the green-tiled roof of the Elephant Gate, which gleamed like the back of a curved dragon, showing its red underbelly.

"After my grandmother fed the zebra her last piece of bread, the animal turned to leave— and a round of artillery shells landed in front of the zebra. The animal was instantly killed, but by blocking her way, it saved my grandmother's life."

Anna finished the story with a heavy sigh. For a few minutes, they both walked along the street in complete silence. Frederick suddenly stopped and turned around. Anna looked at him with a silent question.

"You said your grandmother was standing three blocks from the zoo's entrance, right?"

"Yes, that's what she told me."

Frederick took Anna's hand and walked with her across the street. When they reached the middle of the intersection, he stopped, took her shoulders and gently turned Anna to face the zoo's Elephant Gate glimmering in the distance.

"Right now, we are three blocks from the Elephant Gate. This is the only street that faces the zoo's main entrance. Your grandmother had to have been standing right about here."

A cold sensation flashed through Anna's body. She shivered in the afternoon heat. Frederick was saying something, but she could no longer hear him. His voice started to blend with the street noise until it all became one big murmur. The sun was getting too bright, blurring her vision. She wanted to rub her eyes, but her arms hung heavy.

In front of her, the brightly colored gate had become dull and lifeless; a wicked and sickening feeling grew inside Anna's stomach. The hazy outlines of the buildings around her started to deteriorate. A paralyzing sense of confusion shot through her. And then she saw it, white and black stripes flashing in front of her. Suddenly, a terrible screeching noise shocked Anna's ears.

"Oh, God!" she dropped to her knees as the noise grew louder and closer, gaining on her.

"Anna! Anna!" Her name came back to her with the immediate stop of that terrible screeching sound. Someone was shaking her. Color flooded her eyesight. Frederick's face materialized in front of her, his hands firmly on both of her shoulders.

"Are you alright?!" Frederick's hand cupped her face, examining her for any signs of distress.

"What was that sound?" Anna managed to ask. "The screeching..."

Frederick nodded his head to the right, where a trail of skid marks stained the roadway nearby. "There was almost an accident, but the driver was able to stop. Are you sure you are alright?" He carefully helped her to an upright position.

"Yes, I just...I'm not even sure what happened."

"It looked like you had a panic attack. Do you have them often?"

"No... I... It felt like a flashback of sorts, but it was not my memory." Anna wondered how absurd she was sounding. "Have you ever felt like you were in two places at once?" she asked, clinging to Frederick's arm.

"When you turned me around and I looked at the gate, somehow I lost my own footing in reality..." Her voice trailed off as Frederick pulled her into his chest. She exhaled letting Frederick's strong embrace support her.

"I understand," he said. "The past, even if it is not our own at times, has a way of finding us."

He pondered this for another minute. "I think Berlin itself is in two places at once. It is odd to be standing in the past and in the present. Many people find it difficult to comprehend. Berliners have at least one place in the city where their feet stand in two frames of time.

Some people naturally avoid those places, others learn to avoid them, and still, others can't help but seek them. I, myself, am prone to the latter."

Anna nodded, letting herself be led further from the past, closer to reality, among streets filled with H&M and Bershka fashions on display.

Chapter 13

The H&M and Bershka fashions on display would not do. Anna needed something high-end if she would fit the role of an elite client to trick Benedikt into meeting with her.

After visiting multiple luxury boutiques, including Yves Saint Laurent and Dolce & Gabbana, Anna decided on an impeccable gray-toned Alexander McQueen spring pantsuit in a smart Prince of Wales check pattern. With it on, she felt chic, powerful, and sharp—the perfect combination for her con.

Anna ordered a ride-share back to her hotel and reviewed the plan in her head. After two restless days of brainstorming the best approach to get in front of the lawyer, Anna decided on the most realistic option. She had to involve her grandfather. He had the credibility to interest a man like Benedikt. With Grandfather on the phone, she explained that Benedikt had information linked to unraveling her grandmother's past.

Anna spent a long time convincing and justifying to Grandfather exactly why he had to partake in her scheme. As a prominent lawyer himself, Grandfather felt his morals were at stake. However, his desperation to uncover the truth outweighed everything else.

It was agreed that Grandfather would call Benedikt's secretary in search of a well-to-do lawyer to handle his ten-million-euro estate in Germany, now that his brother had passed, leaving him as sole heir. He was too old to travel himself and therefore, his granddaughter, Anna, would be arriving as a representative on his behalf.

As Grandfather spoke, she could feel the dry Arizona air. His voice, like the desert heat, wrapped her in warm comfort. When the phone call ended, she was left with the reminder of how far away she really was.

Two hours later, the phone rang again.

"Everything went as planned, Anna. The secretary will be giving you a call tomorrow at ten. As soon as I mentioned the estate and choosing the right lawyer to handle the job, she turned extremely pleasant. I have looked up their competitors, Grewlich & Kruger. I would throw in that you have a meeting with them, too."

Following her grandfather's advice, Anna did just that when the secretary called her promptly the next morning.

"Yes, Ms. Venu, we have you scheduled for next week on Monday. Does that work for you?"

Anna casually responded, "Oh that's fine. I have an appointment with Grewlich & Kruger the day after tomorrow anyway."

There was a slight pause and, as if on cue, the secretary's voice rose sharply with fake surprise.

"Oh, you know what? I just received a cancelation email. It looks like Mr. Ritter will have availability tomorrow at noon."

Anna pleasantly faked the same surprise, "Well, aren't I lucky! Tomorrow afternoon works just fine."

The morning of her meeting, she stood in front of the mirror of her hotel room, clad in her power suit, practicing the best way to make Benedikt understand that this whole matter concerned him just as much as it did her. If he obsessed and guarded his family secrets as much as Frederick said he did, then her own association would be of interest. Grandmother's photograph could be just one item from a collection of historical documents that she could theoretically possess.

The Ritter Law Firm took residence within Grunewald, one of Berlin's most prestigious districts. Anna was buzzed into an extravagant lobby. Walls paneled with dark wood led to a high, coffered ceiling in black walnut. Three grand chandeliers emitted golden light, which bounced off the polished cream marble floors, balancing the imposing room atmosphere.

If Anna had not been wearing a $3,500 suit, she would have felt uneasy. The décor, even the scent—cardamom, leather, and woods—gave off an air of luxury and unabashed pretentiousness. The office was designed to intimidate those who did not belong.

The secretary, or so Anna guessed, walking toward her was tall and lanky with a fake thin-lipped smile. Her big round dark eyes opened wider as if taking in Anna's persona with them.

Anna feigned the kind of boredom that frequently comes with an over-privileged lifestyle. She let her own eyes dart judgingly over the woman's black ruffled blouse that only added to her already ostrich-like appearance.

"Ms. Venu. A pleasure. Welcome to the Ritter Law Firm. You found it alright?"

"Effortlessly."

"Please, have a seat. I will let Mr. Ritter know you have arrived." The secretary's voice had an eerie sweetness to it.

She left through a set of paneled double doors, which remained open, leaving Anna to gaze at the woman's extremely neat desk. Even the paper clips were organized according to size in stackable silver containers. There were no photographs or personal touches. A series of pinned green beetles hung on the wall behind her desk under thick glass. Holding down a stack of folders was a bright orange beetle captured forever in glossy amber.

Anna could think of no better hobby that could emit such a feeling of control as catching and pinning life to permanent death inside ornate glass frames that one could always admire.

"This way, please," the secretary's voice beckoned as her sharp face reappeared in the doorway.

Anna stood up with thunder at her feet. She was here to prove to herself to Frederick—and to this exclusive lawyer, that he was nothing more than a man, a human with a big ego that could be conquered like all other egos, with sheer indifference to its existence.

Fearlessly, Anna walked into Benedikt's office. He was thick in body, balding, and with the kind of red face that ignored suggestions from his doctor to stop smearing thick globs of butter onto his morning toast. The office was themed in vivid cherry wood with green accents and artificial ferns meant to impart a sense of organic warmth.

Benedikt stood out against the red and green backdrop like a sinister Santa Claus. The environment was calmer than the opulent lobby, and Anna wondered if this was done purposely to elicit a sense of intimacy.

"Ms. Venu, it is a pleasure." Thick, sausage fingers cupped Anna's small hand until she could no longer see it. "Please, have a seat." He motioned to a plush set of green velvet armchairs facing his desk.

"May I get you something to drink? Coffee? Tea?"

Anna sat down, not wanting to push her luck with time. "I'm fine, thank you."

"Straight to business then!" Benedikt laughed wholeheartedly while rubbing his hands together in a disgusting way as if he were about to slice into a baked stuffed pig. Benedikt let his weight sink into the dark burgundy chair behind his desk.

"Okay, Ms. Venu. Your grandfather very briefly described the situation concerning your late uncle. I am sorry to hear he has passed."

Tensely, Anna removed the photograph from her purse, but kept it to herself. "I am actually here for a different reason."

Benedikt's eyebrows darted up sharply in confusion.

"You and I have a mutual connection. I believe the woman who gave your father the map to find Commander Ritter's body in August of nineteen forty-five was my grandmother, who recently passed. I need your confirmation."

"What are you talking about?" Benedikt sputtered out. "Whose estate is this?"

"There is no estate," Anna said quickly, trying to switch the topic back to the photograph.

"The woman who gave your father the map…"

Benedikt wasn't listening or looking at the photograph. Anna had made a mistake.

"Is this a setup?!" he roared, jumping from his chair. His cheeks swelled to ripe tomatoes about to burst with their own juices. A web of veins made themselves known in bright shades of red and plum.

Anna's chest tightened with the fear of a volcano of a man who was about to erupt with anger. One of the sausages pressed the intercom on his desk phone and barked something in German. Before Anna could assess the situation, the secretary burst through the door nearly running toward Anna wide-eyed and furious. Bony cold fingers closed around Anna's upper arm like jaws.

"You have to leave now!" the secretary screeched as she literally lifted Anna from her seat, pulling her toward the office door.

Anna yanked her arm back sharply, momentarily escaping the jaws. The secretary left her claw marks on Anna's skin.

Anna turned to Benedikt, attempting to show him the photograph, but the ostrich had grabbed her once again, yelling, "Gustav! *Berichterstatter*!"

A scrawny young man burst into the room with confusion on his face. The secretary yelled out orders like a sergeant to the young cadet. He finally understood and grabbed Anna's other arm.

"What the hell?!" Anna quickly realized she would be thrown out permanently; she only had one chance. Sharply, her foot stabbed its stiletto hell into the man's shoe. Squealing in pain, he released her. The secretary's grip loosened briefly, and Anna swung her arm and shoulder backward freeing herself in one motion.

She darted over to Benedikt's desk; the pig looked petrified as if she were going to attack him next. He pushed his chair away from her.

"This!" Anna yelled, shoving the photograph in his face. "This is part of the photograph of your father, your uncle, and his family. For God's sake, I need to know the identity of the woman who gave your father the map!"

Anna felt herself pulled back as the support staff grabbed her under her arms and dragged her backward. Anna flung the photograph at Benedikt seconds before being pulled from the desk. He stared at the picture dumbfounded.

"Lasst uns in Ruhe!" Benedikt yelled firmly.

Instantly, Anna was released. Her arms felt like they were bruised. The red in Benedikt's face became lighter and lighter as if someone from inside his body was turning down a dimmer switch. She heard the door shut behind her leaving her and Benedikt alone.

"This is one of my father's favorite photographs," Benedikt began tensely, "and it solely belongs to me. Where exactly did you get a copy of it, and who the hell are you?"

Anna tried to sound composed, but her nerves were on edge. "Everything I told your pleasant secretary about my family and me is true."

Benedikt scoffed. "You mean the ten-million-euro estate?"

"That part was a lie, yes, but I had good intentions. It is your own fault. Money seems to be the only way to arrange a meeting with you." She spoke with hostility straight at Benedikt's arrogance.

"Like I said before, this is my grandmother's photograph—she gave it to me before she died. She said this was her family."

Benedikt continued to inspect the photograph with scrutiny, evaluating its validity against the images he'd seen in his collection.

"That would make your grandmother my great-uncle's daughter, Maria, but that is impossible. The only person in this picture who survived the war was my father."

"I know that," said Anna. "I have read your father's book."

Benedikt raised his eyebrows with slight surprise. "If you are so well-informed, Ms. Anna," he said sarcastically, "then what exactly are you here to talk about?"

Anna took in a deep breath and once again summarized all the information she had so far collected.

"And that is how I ended up at your office," she concluded tensely.

Benedikt remained quiet, setting Anna with a hard stare. It was difficult for her to assess what he was thinking. The silence seemed to drag on uncomfortably. It broke with the sound of Benedikt's chair that squeaked under his weight as he leaned back against it. His sausage fingers connected in neat little rows on top of his suit-clad belly.

"You are right about two things. One is my father's sister-in-law, Vera, and his niece, Maria, in the photograph. The other two men missing in your version of the photo are my father and my uncle. However..." he took off his spectacles only to refit them back onto his meaty face. "The woman you are referring to, who gave my father the map, is not your grandmother. I knew her personally. She died twelve years ago here in Berlin, where she lived her entire life."

The words hit Anna so hard that she suddenly had absolutely nothing to say. She must have looked dumbfounded, but her expression was fixed beyond her control. Benedikt grunted into his fist in an attempt to wake Anna up from whatever daze she may have been in. When Anna did not react to it, Benedikt's face flashed with genuine human emotion. "Ms. Anna, I can understand your distress, especially after going through so much trouble to piece back together a past that occurred so long ago. It is impressive, and you should be proud of yourself."

"But—" Anna insisted, "I read in your father's book that he identified Maria's remains before re-burying them in the family vault. Is there a chance that someone else was buried there instead of Maria?"

"Absolutely not! My father was a physician and he identified Maria's remains based on the height, hair color, age, and even the coat her body was wrapped in."

Anna felt empty inside. Her eyes refocused and she once again saw Benedikt's face. He was still talking, but Anna only caught the end of whatever he was saying. Something about offering her soothing tea.

The string of disappointments suddenly immersed her into a state of calm focus.

"This was my last lead," Anna said sharply. "My only remaining direction is to uncover how this photograph got to Arizona and why."

Her tone rose quickly, "I will track down more historians, World War Two veterans, anyone who can give me a clue. My time and capital is unlimited as is my persistence. After all, I am here speaking with the most exclusive lawyer in Berlin."

Anna paused and watched Benedikt's frown turn upward. He licked his thick lips. Her determination must have tasted foul.

"Your family and its reputation is of no interest to me, but it is of great interest to you. Simple discoveries can ruin a carefully crafted reputation. And there is no telling what I will dig up." Benedikt's expression hardened, but Anna ignored it. "I can promise you that any information I find, I will direct to you first, but in return, I ask for your assistance in helping me now."

Benedikt snorted with amusement and said, "Is this some sort of American blackmail?"

"Mr. Ritter, I do not deal in malice. I am not a threat to you or your family. The only thing I am interested in is the true identity of my grandmother. When I have it, I will leave Germany. There is nothing for me here. However, until I do that, I will continue to dig up every single corner of Berlin, and if your family's reputation gets caught in the crossfire, consider it a civilian casualty. Yet, like all battles, this can be avoided through compromise. That is what I am asking for. It is your choice. Help me in my search, and I will present any discoveries to you first."

"Your detective game would be amusing if it were not pointless. There is nothing to find."

Between her two fingers Anna held up the photograph like a cigarette. She twirled it maliciously.

"Look, you thought you had everything sealed safely away, but I have this photograph, which is a mystery that concerns us both. Wouldn't you agree? Every new discovery always leads to another."

Benedikt pondered this for a minute.

Anna's jaw clenched. She felt like she could sit there for days in a silent cold stare if she had to. She wasn't leaving empty-handed. The minute of silence had the weight of five hours. Benedikt's voice finally broke. "I will accept your deal, Ms. Anna. I do not have much to lose from it, but we both will sign a contract."

"Fine," Anna stated firmly without hesitation.

"Please take a seat in the waiting room while I meet with my assistant."

Benedikt led Anna to the waiting area as Gustav limped back into the office giving Anna a dirty look while she politely smiled back, silently mouthing "sorry!"

Forty minutes later, Anna read a two-page non-disclosure agreement preventing her from publicly discussing or using any newly discovered information associated with Benedikt's family name without written consent from the Ritter Law Firm. She signed the paperwork, followed by Benedikt and Gustav.

Gustav left the office and Benedikt eyed Anna suspiciously. She stared back with an innocent expression as her defenses once again ignited.

"I am guessing you are a student?"

"Yes," Anna answered simply.

"Law?" Benedikt questioned.

"Pre-law. Yes."

A smirk crossed Benedikt's face. "I thought so. You have a ruthless way about you. It is surprising. Your opponents will never see it coming."

"Why is that? Because I am a woman?

Benedikt once again snorted. "I have met plenty of women lawyers, much more vicious than any man. No, it is your face and eyes. They look too angelic for law and will conveniently mislead your opponents."

Benedikt took the photograph and looked at it one more time.

"What still perplexes me most..." mused Benedikt, "is how this photograph got to America."

She too wished she knew the answer.

"I always thought that only one original print existed, the one in our family archive. It was always on my father's nightstand, but how did a copy end up in Arizona?"

Benedikt was in conversation with himself rather than with Anna.

"I think my father was right when he said that old fox Ada had hidden something. You know, my father was never able to get over not being able to protect his brother's family."

Immediately, Anna's ears pricked up.

"May I ask who Ada is?"

"Ada was a dear friend of Maria's, my uncle's daughter. She helped Maria bury her mother and, sadly, buried Maria herself. Did you know poor Maria was shot dead during a crossfire in a makeshift hospital? Maria died in Ada's arms, asking her to deliver the map to my father."

Benedikt's eyes grew distant as his thoughts recalled the sadness with which his own father had told him the tragic stories. He sat up a little straighter, pushing away the memories that had become his own.

"Regardless, my father felt he owed a lot to Ada. she had survived the horrors of the Battle of Berlin and kept her promise to Maria by finding him against many odds. At the time, Ada herself was barely getting by on city rations and she had a newborn. My father took it upon himself to aid her whenever possible.

"This proved difficult because Ada always declined the help, but eventually she became an aunt to me, and close to our family. Her daughter, Maria Arnett, is now one of our biggest clients and a close friend."

Anna listened carefully and when Benedikt seemed to end his recollections, she jumped at her chance to ask exactly why his father felt Ada had hidden something.

"That's right, I got caught up in another time and forgot the matter at hand. Yes, well, my father never had any proof that Ada was keeping secrets, but he always sensed that there was something she didn't want to share with him. As if there was always something more she wanted to say, but she could never bring herself to do it. Now that you are here with this mysterious second photograph, I think our only chance to dig deeper would be to speak with her daughter, Maria Arnett."

Anna's heart skipped a beat. Not only did she feel she had another chance, but Benedikt had said *us.* For a moment, Anna felt that she was no longer alone in wanting an answer.

"Is it a coincidence that her first name is also Maria?"

"No. Ada named her daughter in honor of my late cousin, Maria Ritter. This only added to the reasons why my father felt obligated to help them both."

"Does Maria Arnett live in Berlin?"

"Yes, she does," said Benedikt. "She is a world-renowned portrait artist. I have to speak with her myself first. Leave me your phone number and the address of where you are residing."

Anna stood up and shook Benedikt's bear-like paw. "Thank you," she said, pouring into it as much appreciation as possible.

"I should apologize for the harsh treatment earlier. I thought you were another undercover reporter. People think lawyers are vicious, but we are nothing compared to those vultures. My father's dying wish was to keep the family archive out of the spotlight, but promises are not something that reporters understand."

Benedikt walked her past the secretary, who once again smiled pleasantly and wished her a good day.

Anna walked out of the lobby and exhaled a breath that had been sitting in her chest since she stepped into that place. The chandelier glistened, a crystal galaxy hypnotizing her amidst the Mars interior as she waited for her heart rate to subside.

"*Dieses Mädchen ist unberechenbar...*" Benedikt's voice could be heard from behind the closed door.

Recognizing that "*mädchen*" meant girl, Anna quickly tried to remember the rest of the sentence. Chances were that she was the girl referenced.

Once outside, she typed out the sentence phonetically into Google, but the suggested translation made no sense. Her focus left the screen and she had to shield her eyes from the glare of the sun. It blazed wildly above, warming her muscles enough to acknowledge how tired she really was.

Chapter 14

"She really was crazy and so was that Gustav guy, but the secretary took the cake. Just like you promised!" Anna was reenacting her escape from the clutches of Benedikt's staff to Frederick with a sense of gratification. She was paying no attention to Frederick's expression as he assessed her.

She paused for a sip of beer. Her line of vision fell onto the water droplets that slid down the side of Frederick's beer stein in straight lines, commanded by the Berlin sun. Anna realized Frederick had not yet taken a drink. The beer sat there idly as if it had not even been ordered in the first place. This was odd behavior, even for the peculiar Frederick.

Anna pointed to his glass and said, "Should I say a toast for you to drink?"

Frederick's lips curled upward, but his glare did not shift from her. In his eyes, Anna saw the sort of spark one gets when they discover a new interest in something or someone that they had not noticed before. Anna blushed to herself and proceeded with her story. "When I discover a new piece of information, I first have to run it by Benedikt. I can then share it with you—as long as Benedikt approves it."

This comment seemed to bring Frederick back to his usual self. With his elbows now on the café table, he leaned closer to Anna. A snarky smile removed any lingering affection Anna had for him at the moment.

"You do understand…there is little, I would even say, no chance that Benedikt would approve of you letting me use any of the information, right?"

Anna leaned back in her chair, observing Frederick and wondering if it was the perfect symmetry and structure of his face and his entire build that gave him this irritating power to not only bring up the flaws in everything but to patronize as well.

"That may be true, but Benedikt's fear has to do with others accidentally stumbling upon something scandalous. Any information that may be important for me or you can hold no threat to him. On the contrary, it could even put his family in better light. He just wants security."

"Right," Frederick said doubtfully. "My question to you, Anna, is this: Why would Benedikt agree to help you? After all, you could stumble upon a scandal and expose him like anyone else, regardless of your promise or whatever contracts you had signed. It makes no sense."

"I have given that some thought myself. I am not sure, to be honest, but that does remind me of something else I meant to ask you."

Anna pulled out the small violet Moleskine journal where she phonetically wrote out what she heard Benedikt say in German.

"After I left his office, I heard Benedikt say something like this to his secretary." Anna slid the journal to Frederick's side of the table as if it were an offer for a covert deal. Frederick picked up the notebook and sounded out the sentence. His face cracked into a smile. Anna grabbed the journal only to reread the makeshift sentence she knew she would not understand.

"What? What is so funny?"

"He said you were unpredictable," Frederick answered after a long drink of beer. His first. He enjoyed keeping Anna on edge.

"So how is that funny?"

"It's a bit lost in translation, but it's sort of like saying he thinks you are mentally unstable.... I guess you made quite an impression on him." Frederick smiled into his glass, enjoying the small victory.

Anna thought this over. "Well, that explains everything! This is why Benedikt agreed to help me. Better comply then risk someone *unstable* messing in your affairs."

"I think it is more of a control issue. Letting you dig around gives him zero control. Agreeing to work with you gives him some ability to keep things in order and set the rules. It is a very German thing for him to do."

"To have control?" Anna arched her eyebrows. A shudder ran through her. She imagined Frederick having control of her, in any way he wanted.

"Think of it more as keeping a specific order to things." Frederick neatly aligned the silverware on the table as if to clarify with an example.

Anna snapped out of her fantasy. "I should get going, Frederick."

When Anna entered her hotel lobby, she was high on endorphins. As always, the encounter with Frederick had left her both annoyed and aroused. The lingering image of him staring at her with that curious look was interrupted by the concierge who urgently sped towards her.

"Ms. Venu!"

"Yes?" Anna turned around cautiously.

"There have been several calls to your room throughout the day. A man named Benedikt Ritter has made it clear there is an emergency. He dropped off this envelope for you."

Anna ripped the envelope open while simultaneously speed-walking to the elevator. The heavy paper contained one handwritten sentence: Ms. Venu, call me immediately, this is a pressing matter!

She reached for her cell phone, but it was not in her purse. "Shit!" Anna started to panic. *What is so urgent? And where the hell did I leave my phone?*

Bursting into her room, she breathed in relief to see the little gold phone in the middle of her bed. There were seven missed calls and three voicemails from Benedikt. Heat rose within her uncomfortably. She threw off her cream chiffon blouse to cool off as she called Benedikt's mobile number. He answered immediately. "Ms. Anna! I have been trying to reach you all day."

Anna sat at the edge of her bed, cupping the phone to make sure she heard every word of whatever was so important.

"I know. I am sorry. I left my phone in the room. Is everything alright?"

"Did the concierge give you my letter?"

"Yes."

"Good." he exhaled heavily.

"Maria Arnett, the woman I spoke to you about yesterday needs to meet with you immediately. Her schedule is very tight. I could not reach you today, so we have rescheduled for tomorrow. I will be picking you up in my car at nine o'clock tomorrow morning. Please be in front of the hotel. We are headed to Wannsee. It is a bit of a drive and we cannot be late—"

"I can meet her tonight," Anna broke in. "You don't have to drive me. I can take a car there now."

"As I mentioned, her schedule is very tight. Again, I will be picking you up at nine o'clock sharp." It was clear this was a command not an invitation.

"Alright. Nine o'clock in front of the hotel," repeated Anna.

"Yes. I will see you then. *Auf wiedersehen.*"

The call was terminated and Anna was left listening to the silence. The conversation had been so direct, so immediate, that Anna did not even get the chance to ask why it was so adamant that Maria Arnett met her right away. She tried to consider the possible reasons. Maybe Maria wanted to feel her out, see exactly who was about to dig around in the Ritter family's affairs. Nevertheless, it was the urgency with which Benedikt tried to get a hold of her that made her think there was another motive.

At 8:45 a.m., Anna stood in front of her hotel. The clouds had come in overnight, bringing with them a slight chill and an isolated calmness. Anna enjoyed such days more than beaming sunshine. It felt as though the world quieted to reflect on itself, but today, the wind blew in short unsettled bursts as if it, too, were in apprehension of what the day would bring.

A black Mercedes 600 pulled up in front of her. Benedikt's round shape bounced quickly out of the driver's seat as if it were on a spring. He walked toward her with nervous energy.

"Ms. Anna, please," he opened the passenger door and Anna slid into the vehicle. Just like Frederick's car, it was immaculate and smelled of new leather. The lingering scent of tobacco replaced the musk she had inhaled greedily each time she was in the presence of Frederick or his Batmobile. Benedikt peeled away from the hotel and onto the road in one smooth motion.

Avoiding both silence and small talk, Anna was about to jump into the unanswered questions she had been left with after the phone call from the night before. However, Benedikt's edginess intruded first.

"After you left my office, I could not focus the rest of the day. I kept thinking how the photograph had made its way to America, let alone Arizona! I considered every angle and, like you, I came up with nothing."

He paused as he turned onto the autobahn. "After careful consideration, I decided to call Maria. Maybe she would know someone connected to either her mother or my family who could have left for America." Benedikt glanced over at Anna, who was savoring each word as if it were a delicacy she had been waiting to taste for a very long time.

"I started to ask her questions, but she reacted tensely and immediately confronted me. I explained your visit to my office. Things got heated after that. I have known Maria my entire life and she has always been a calm, mild person, so her attitude surprised me. She became nervous, insisting I get a hold of you immediately.

"I obliged of course, but she kept calling and calling and calling...just to see if I have spoken with you. With each call, her voice grew exceedingly panicked!" Benedikt inhaled deeply, remembering the occurrences. "I thought I was going to have a heart attack!

"You have to understand, Maria is very important to me. Not only is she a childhood friend and connected to my family, as I explained yesterday, but she is also one of my biggest clients."

Anna bit her lip. *Why was this woman freaking out?* "Do I have something to be worried about?" she asked frankly.

Benedikt waved off her question with his free hand. "You do not need to worry."

His sentence hung in the air by its lonesome. Anna waited for a further explanation to follow, but it did not.

"What do you think her reason is for needing to meet me?"

"I don't know. As I told you, my father always suspected that Maria's mother, Ada, knew much more than she let on. Maria's desperation to meet you tells me that my father was right. This leads me to remind you to remember your promise to me, Anna. Whatever she tells you goes to me first; we have a deal."

"I will uphold my promise, but are we not going to Maria's together?"

"Not exactly. I am escorting you, but I will leave you at the front door by Maria's request. I am upholding my side of the bargain, Anna. Be sure to keep yours."

Anna nodded and said, "Of course!" Excitement began to buzz within her. Benedikt was being asked to leave and, for once, someone was chasing her to give her some sort of information.

"You said she is a portrait artist?"

"A world-celebrated portrait artist. Her last painting sold for over fifty-thousand euros, to give you an idea."

Their conversation came to a halt as the Mercedes weaved smoothly through tree-lined streets. The concrete and glass of Berlin were replaced by the awakening green inhabitants from a prior time. Amidst an early blooming park-like forest stood marvelous villas, like gigantic colorful animals trying to hide behind mature oaks and beech trees. To the right, a vast lake lapped calmly at anchored boats, yachts, and the birds that perched on them.

"That is Wannsee Lake to your right. It is Berlin's most popular swimming and beach destination."

The car maneuvered farther under cover of the trees and away from strolling families and cyclists. Small roads appeared to take travelers to more secluded estates. Benedikt turned down one such road. The trees became sparser, indicating they were driving toward Maria Arnett's home.

After about a half-mile, Benedikt made a sharp right turn and stopped in front of beautiful black wrought-iron gates that curved and twisted until their bars shot upward in a spray of black spirals and loops. The iron fence encircled a magnificent white villa in the Wilhelmine-era style. The window frames, beams, and cornices gleamed black, as if someone had outlined the entire estate in black marker, giving the house a sophisticated, elegant edge.

Benedikt was busy punching in a security code in a concentrated manner, his thick finger pressing firmly on each number for a few seconds. The gate intercom was left untouched, signifying that Benedikt may have had special access to the premises.

A screeching sound pierced Anna's ear. The gate's chains and rotors started to move slowly as if a slumbering beast was being forced to awaken.

"I have been telling Maria to change the gate operating system for years now, but she refuses. She says this is the only part of the original villa that survived the war."

Once the beast's mouth was wide enough to swallow the Mercedes, Benedikt slowly drove in. They passed a beautiful garden with ferns, flower bushes, and young fruit trees. A private lakeshore stretched behind the house where a small yacht docked in a marina bobbed on the mild waves.

Anna exited the vehicle alongside Benedikt who left the car running. Before Anna stepped toward the front door, Benedikt reached out to shake her hand.

"I wish you a pleasant visit, Ms. Anna. I will expect a call from you once you have finished…"

His mouth remained open, ready to continue the sentence, but the front door of the villa opened and Benedikt was forced to leave his thought incomplete. Anna guessed it would have been another reminder of their deal. The woman at the top of the stairs nodded a hello to Benedikt who said a few words in German before returning to his car. The woman wore a housekeeper's uniform that matched the black-and-white exterior of the house perfectly.

"*Guten tag, Fräulein Anna.* Please come in."

Anna entered into the luxurious main parlor rich in black, white, and gold Art Deco design details. The housekeeper led her down the hall until Anna stepped into a high-ceilinged room themed in royal blue tones. Suddenly, Anna lost her breath. She could have sworn she just saw her grandmother.

As reality came back to her, Anna realized she was in fact looking at an incredible life-size portrait of her grandmother in an extravagant gold frame at the far end of the room. *What the hell?* She looked to be in her early sixties, sitting in a garden in the light lilac summer dress she often wore on hot Arizona days. A closed book was on her lap.

The play between the rays of sunlight and shadow eliminated any sharp contours, giving the portrait a soft dream-like appearance. Only the three-quarter profile of Grandmother's delicate face stood out from the painting. She was looking off into an unknown distance with the sort of mysterious expression one gets after finishing a captivating book, but have yet to return from the pages of its world.

A woman's voice broke Anna's thoughts. "I consider this my best work. I had so many offers to sell it, but I just couldn't go through with it."

Startled, Anna turned and met the penetrating eyes of a radiant woman in her sixties. She walked over to Anna briskly, the cream chiffon fabrics of her ensemble flowing around her like butterfly wings. Anna soon found herself cocooned in Maria Arnett's long embrace.

"You are Maria Arnett?" Anna asked.

"I am," the woman answered.

"And you painted this portrait of my grandmother?"

"I did."

"But how…" Anna's voice trailed off as her gaze returned to her grandmother's portrait and then back to Maria. "I feel like I am losing my mind."

"Anna, you can't even imagine what our meeting means to me. I have waited for you for so long."

Maria Arnett moved closer to Anna and stroked her cheek lightly. "You look just like your grandmother, you know."

Anna felt a surge of emotion rise from within her as if her body somehow remembered this woman who she was just meeting for the first time.

Without a sound, Maria Arnett placed her hands on Anna's shoulders and led her to a large arched window that opened onto the peaceful lake. A velvet blue upholstered sofa and armchairs stood centered around a low elaborately engraved coffee table piled with beautiful trays of fruits, cheeses, and chocolates. A stack of neat white papers shared the table's surface like an unbound book.

"Before we speak further, I would like you to read this..." Maria Arnett pointed to the stack of papers.

"What is this?" Asked Anna impatiently.

"This is an English translation of my mother's memoirs. I believe her story will answer all your questions a lot better than I will. If you need anything, Clara will be outside the hall to assist. I will now leave you. Let me know when you would like to talk after you are done reading." She smiled and left the room. Anna sank down into the sofa chair and flipped over the first page. It began: My Life Story...

MY LIFE STORY

Lived, Remembered, and Written by Ada Brandt

Chapter 15
Ada

I came into this world in the year of 1918 in Berlin. Back then, being a revolutionary was a prevalent thing. My parents' allegiance to the German Communist Party and world proletariat gave them the reputation of professional revolutionaries. I would lay in bed, my eyes heavy with sleep. My mother's voice said words I did not understand at the time. She was reading from the writings of Vladimir Lenin, my nightly lullaby.

Russia's Revolution ignited the German Communists with such a force that a revolution in Germany was just a matter of time. Among the majority of Germans, this possible reality was an ever-growing fear. After all, Europe had seen the bloody consequences of the Bolshevik Revolution. The fear of massacre, bloodshed, and civil war ironically gave Hitler and the Nazis a swift rise to power.

They were the only organized force able to oppose the Communists—in essence, they were the only choice. I understood the real nature of the Nazi regime much earlier than the rest of the world did, even earlier than my Jewish neighbors did.

A fire burned the Reichstag in 1933, the Nazis blamed the German Communists, which gave them the justification to hunt and arrest them by the thousands—the original concentration camp victims. My parents, alongside other communists, their families, and sympathizers, met death within the Dachau Concentration Camp's barbed-wire fences.

At sixteen years old, I was forced to move in with my grandmother who lived in a small two-room apartment within the Tempelhof district next to the world-famous Berlin Zoo. My parents' last name forever denied me the chance of a professional career in Nazi Germany, but I was seldom bothered because I hated the Nazis with all my being. And yet, there I was enjoying the new prosperity and leisurely lifestyle of 1930s Berlin that the Nazi regime had woven out of the economic horror of the previous years.

Opportunity was now available to mostly everyone; you just had to grab it—no, you were expected to grab it. I learned to type and started working as a secretary for two lawyers. Soon after, Der Angriff, Berlin's premier newspaper, hired me. On the side, I styled women's hair and even made a local reputation for myself. With the money I was making, the money Berliners were now all making; I could thrive within the cosmopolitan capital of Europe.

The time between 1936 and 1938 were some of the best years of my life, of every German's life. The city bustled with new commerce, Parisian fashion, dance halls, countless cinemas, upscale restaurants, parks with waterfalls and swans, flowers on every balcony. It was incredible. Before our eyes, Germany rose from the ashes of the Weimar Republic like a Phoenix who was not only reborn, but who blazed with the fire of a thousand suns. And we were all part of this marvelous machine that kept spinning and spinning, producing more jobs for us all to go to more restaurants; more roads, to take us to more leisurely parks; more music for us to dance to, to fall in love to.

Hitler achieved power by bringing Germany back to life. It was once said that had he died then, he would have been remembered as one of the greatest leaders in German history instead of the devil himself. And like a devil, it was the disguise that led others to disregard the dismantling of communities the Nazis were quietly doing.

A new social fabric was woven to unite Germans based on hatred and violence. Drop by drop, Hitler created an entirely new nation. These changes occurred slowly, secretly, obstructed by the incredible economic rebirth of Germany the Nazi regime had brought.

My countrymen soaked up this newfound life of pleasure like plants after a drought. Hitler used the wave of fanatical support from ordinary Germans to push for a new war, one that would establish a Thousand-Year Reich of German superiority. This new state was busy slaughtering Europe while life in Germany, especially in Berlin, continued to blossom on Europe's grave.

Between 1939 and 1942, Berlin continued to be close to euphoric, even for me, a secret Nazi adversary. It is odd to admit that even I felt a sort of National pride when country after country fell underneath Germany's march to victory. To Nazi supporters, every conquest was a celebration that solidified their love for the Führer. This love became fanatical when the French army, the largest in the world, fell alongside British forces under the German Panzer Divisions' attack. It took less than one month!

Hitler made France's surrender a theatrical performance for the world. The stage was the Compiègne Forest, where Germany capitulated to the French Army in 1918, marking the end of WWI. In this same spot, France now signed its capitulation on June 22, 1940.

The French museum even had to deliver the same railway carriage where Marshal Foch, the head of the French Army, once received the

German delegation during Germany's surrender. Now it was Hitler who sat in this carriage in the very same chair. It was all propaganda, of course, a tactic every nation uses to brainwash its citizens.

What made the difference for Nazi Germany was the silver screen. Joseph Goebbels, the Minister of Propaganda, made sure that film studios kept producing movies to entertain the masses. And he made sure they played Nazi propaganda films before each feature.

Sitting in a theatre alongside other families and children, I watched the entire attack on France, filmed from its first advances of the Panzer Divisions to complete victory. Logically, I knew war was bloody, I knew it meant death. Yet, that was not what I saw. On the screen, German soldiers marched happily, smiling at the camera. Planes flew over France, dropping bombs that exploded like fireworks into the air. Artillery shells erupted in silence, and finally, our troops marched on the Champs-Élysées. German military music took the place of the screams and destruction, the real soundtrack of war—movie after movie depicted war as theatrical, harmless, and victorious. Now every German was an expert in Blitzkrieg Theory, a conversation topic at the grocery store as common as the weather.

The blood, tears, and death our men brought to other countries was something the average German never thought about, but then again, there was no such thing as an average German anymore. The Führer preached we were a superhuman race and, after so many victories, most of us believed it.

Poland, Norway, Denmark, Sweden, Belgium, Netherlands, then Greece fell within days or weeks. Only England hung on by a thin thread that our Luftwaffe and U-boat campaign would soon cut. The Thousand-Year Reich was materializing. Soon all of Europe was conquered.

On June 21, 1941, Hitler invaded the Soviet Union. The Wehrmacht's quick and steady daily advances promised the Red Army's rapid collapse. Again, the propaganda movies showed our soldiers as proud liberators of communist oppression, marching past hundreds of thousands of Soviet POWs.

Germans elevated Hitler to the status of supernatural. There was no other way one person could defeat so many enemies unless he was chosen by God himself. And like any God, he was worshiped fanatically.

There are a few memories from that time that I can never forget, no matter how hard I have tried. Mass hysteria is one of them. Documentaries show thousands of Germans lining the streets to see Hitler wave from a balcony or drive by in his car. But the sound! The noise of those events was never captured. It deafened me to the point of panic.

The crowd would become a single screaming, moving monster with the force of a thousand voices. Women shrieked with high-pitched cries, men roared, police officers whistled to control the crowds, and deafening military music blasted from open windows.

"Heil Hitler! Heil Hitler!" they shouted in unison.

It was the very definition of madness, and it continued to wake me years after the war ended. I prided myself on my countrymen being rational, logical people, but they had all gone insane.

One afternoon, waiting for the rain to stop, I sat by a café window. Across the street, a pregnant woman suddenly knelt to the pavement. Thinking she had fallen ill; I ran over to her. She was alright, she told me, she just saw the Führer's portrait in the store window and wanted to pray for his health. She knelt there on the pavement for twelve minutes in the cold pouring rain. I no longer knew where I was. This couldn't be my country.

Nevertheless, like every other German, willingly or not, I was helping to create this madness. My job as a typist for the newspaper was complicit in spreading the propaganda. I can deny this and say I did not create the lies, I just typed them, but even the smallest screw in a machine contributes to its overall performance.

By December 1941, I noticed a change. Our editors were struggling with information. We were forced to retype the same article as it kept being edited. I read in between the lines and understood that the Wehrmacht had halted at the outskirts of Moscow for the first time in its history and that they still couldn't break Leningrad's defenses.

I had the inkling that things would change from this point on, but my colleagues saw this as a minor setback on the road to victory. Berliners continued to enjoy their happy lives.

Even the occasional air raids had little effect on their mood. After the initial shock, the air raids were accepted as our contribution to the Great War. The Luftwaffe was able to protect Berlin, detecting British planes early enough for Berliners to hide in bomb shelters or U-Bahn stations. The raids were ineffective, and most people believed they would remain that way.

Chapter 16
Helga

In 1941 two things happened. The first was the death of my grandmother, which left me utterly alone in the world. Though misery shook me then, I am thankful that she died without having to suffer the hell that awaited Berliners.

The second was meeting Helga. Helga came into my life at a time when God seemed to be ignoring my prayers. I believe she was God's answer to them.

A neighbor recommended my hairstylist work to her, and we gravitated toward one another immediately. Maybe it was because Helga, too, was alone in Berlin, or perhaps our souls had known each other in another time. Whatever the reason, our connection was instant and strong.

Though Helga came from a small quiet town in Austria, she had the perseverance of a person who had grown into adulthood, overcoming constant tribulations. I was two years older than Helga, but I felt she was more mature, more stable than I was. With her by my side, I felt protected. A feeling worth more than gold during those years.

That first month we met, both of us were in mourning. I, for my grandmother, and Helga for her fiancé, a young German officer, who was now another corpse on the Eastern Front. Helga arrived in Berlin two weeks too late. His division was transferred to Poland and his life ended on July 14 at the hands of the Red Army during the Fight for Smolensk.

Fate intervened cruelly for him and fortunately for me. There is a fight between the ramifications of good and evil in all situations.

To her parents' disappointment, Helga did not leave Berlin. She first chose to mourn her dead love in his hometown, but eventually, the city's pace seduced her. The music, the nightlife, the lights of excitement and entertainment still lit up the night sky—Berlin's grand finale.

Enrolling in nursing school helped her cope with death by teaching her tools to preserve life. She dedicated herself to save other soldiers' lives as a way to make amends with the soldier she had not been able to rescue. In return for his life, she would in time save mine.

We spent a lot of time together and soon we were sharing my apartment. Laughter had invaded our household. We hosted dinner parties for friends, spent our evenings dancing and analyzing news of Nazi progress from the Eastern Front.

The Nazis reinforced our commitment to one another. If you were against the Nazis, doubted the Führer, or disliked the war, you could never say so. Never. There were constant disappearances. Shop owners gone missing. Neighbors arrested at night. Rumors spread that they had said something inappropriate, something that justified their need for Nazi reeducation. But Helga and I picked up on each other's signals. Little codes that over time revealed that we both felt the same way about the Nazi regime.

Helga's disdain for the Nazis swelled as the number of wounded and disfigured soldiers brought from the Eastern Front outgrew the hospital's capacity. There were not enough medical personnel, not enough space, not enough supplies, but more than enough bodies. She would return home in tears and leave again for another shift.

Helga's pain escalated when she had to return to Austria to bury her parents. A Nazi truck carrying armaments had crashed into their automobile, killing them both.

Death was coming around us more often, suffocating the happiness we grasped onto. In the summer of August 1942, the Wehrmacht offensive targeted Stalingrad, a city we didn't know in Southern Russia. Nazi propaganda told Germans it would be a quick and decisive victory. Once again, the silver screen displayed our troops marching into Stalingrad with limited resistance from the Red Army. Our men fought on the streets and finally occupied the city center—another victory.

Yet, something again went wrong. By October and November, the Wehrmacht's advances stalled. It was not until February 2, 1943, that Germans found out the painful truth. The entire elite German 6th Army under the command of Field Marshal Paulus was obliterated. Completely.

German soldiers had been killed before in France, Poland, and in great numbers during the failed attack on Moscow, but this was different. Overnight, 250,000 men in their prime vanished. Shock waves ran through Germany. You could feel it. Sorrow radiated from every person. Everyone knew someone who had been in the 6th division. Germany mourned as the Nazi flags were lowered to carry black ribbons. Just days before the 10th-anniversary celebration of the Nazis' rise to power. It was a black omen for the Nazi regime.

Helga and I cried for our ordinary soldiers. Tears for lives lost for an unnecessary war. We wanted the Nazis to be stopped, for this madness to end, but not like this. We had been naïve to think otherwise. Naïve to think Berlin would always be protected.

So far, the air raids over our heads had been uneventful. That was all war to us, alarms that never actually touched us. Until finally, on the evening of November 22, 1943, they did.

The sirens rang. We ran out for our heavy coats. Outside, a sharp radio announcement cut through the air.

Luftgefahr 15!

Meaning *air-raid danger 15*. This indicated that an extensive airplane formation was approaching Berlin. We had been through this before. Thirty to sixty planes would terrorize us like nightmares. The sun would shoo them away once again, letting us step into our beautiful city. Just like before, we crowded into the zoo bunker, hundreds of us. The Flaks drilled the air with ammunition. A deafening *clack clack clack* sound that we were sure would scare the enemy away. Instead, a different noise came into existence—endless earth-shattering explosions.

Above us, bombs fell like a meteor shower. There were no lulls like before. No time to even take a breath. We held each other quietly, but our hearts pounded with the earth. Eyes shut to the present moment and to the falling plaster above our heads. The thought of death was on everyone's mind. Would this be it? Would the walls and ceiling above us collapse? Would we be crushed under the concrete?

Almost a thousand planes rained fire on Berlin that night. The Allies called it Saturation Bombing. Two thousand five hundred tons of explosives fell on us that day at a rate of thirty-four planes per minute, but the sheer horror of those couple hours was nothing, absolutely nothing until we left the shelter at dusk.

We must have gone through some sort of portal, for we stepped outside and into some version of hell. A strong cough overcame me immediately. I gasped for air but only inhaled burning fumes thick with smoke and debris. Helga put a handkerchief to my mouth. I tried to look around me, but my eyes stung from the ash-filled air. The outline of a desolate burning city lay before me. I no longer recognized where I was. It would have been pitch-dark, but the sky above me bled. Deep red from the firestorms ignited all over my city.

Cries and screams erupted from everyone. This could not be reality. Helga had left my side; she made her way to the children in the crowd, making sure they were protecting their lungs.

An awful gust of hot wind slashed at my back. I turned quickly to face an entire block enveloped in deep flames across the street—a live furnace fed by the draft between doors and windows, ignited by the firebombs. Red demons stuck their fiery tongues from shattered windows, licking away any remaining life. Sparks flew at me like electric eels from the burning electrical wires.

Officers were shouting to keep our mouths closed; people had swallowed the molten embers thrown from the buildings that burned their throats and lungs. The angel of death was visiting Berlin, riding on the dry winds that picked up force in the city—spreading and igniting more fires. Why did the Allies bomb us? There were no troops here, just terrified civilians.

I wanted to make myself useful, but I didn't know what to do. Fear paralyzed me amidst the rubble. The air kept getting thicker and hotter. Men threw dirt onto the fires because the explosions wrecked the water pipes.

Helga appeared out of the smog covered in soot. I let her lead me toward our apartment building. She wanted to see if it was still intact. We walked past the corpses of women, men, and children who did not make it to the bunkers. Their bodies had burned completely. Inhaling the disgusting smell of charred human flesh, I swallowed vomit and grasped Helga's arm.

Wittenbergplatz, a heavy-traffic intersection, was filled with the skeletons of buses, trams, and cars. Through their windows, I saw the charcoaled bodies of passengers still upright in their metal coffins. Again, vomit rose from deep with me and this time left my body with uncontrollable tears. My city was dead. The whole world was dying. Helga guided me, turning my head away from the terror as we walked onward.

When we reached our block, we neither saw nor smelled fire and only the windows of our building were shattered. I thanked God and squeezed Helga's hand. My body was vibrating from nerves. Helga sat me in our building's main lobby, where a few of our neighbors had sought shelter from the chaos.

"I need to go help the wounded. Don't go upstairs in case a fire starts. Stay close to the exits. I will be back in a few hours. Will you be alright by yourself?"

I nodded, my teeth chattering. I did not want her to go. She knew that, but it would have been selfish of me to beg her to stay and she knew that, too.

Helga got her medical bag from our apartment. She brought me a blanket and water from the emergency buckets we had filled. She then returned to the burning city. Heavy, wrenching sobs sent me into exhausted sleep amidst the rubble-filled floor of our lobby.

Chapter 17
Maria

I did not wake until I heard the sharp pronunciation of my name. Helga was walking through the doorway of our building; she was covered in dirt and blood. My adrenaline peaked, and I was on my feet instantly, ready to do anything for her. Seeing the panic on my face, Helga told me to calm down; the blood covering her jacket was not her own. It was almost dawn.

The sun had come up, but no one could see it. The smoking nightmare of the previous night still hung in the sky. Everything rushed back to me.

"Ada, I need your help. Help me get this girl into our apartment."

In the faint light, I saw the outline of a thin young woman leaning against the wall behind Helga. She could barely hold herself up. I could not even make out her face because it was covered with crusted blood and soot. Following Helga's lead, I carefully lifted the girl's left arm and set it around my neck, and we helped her up the stairs and into our apartment.

"I need to examine her. We need to get these clothes off of her and clean her up," Helga commanded. Her face showed exhaustion, but her body moved with the swiftness of someone fueled by sheer will.

I boiled water on the stove and laid out towels. Once we removed the girl's coat, things got complicated. Her clothes were stuck onto her body, encrusted with blood. Every effort to remove them made the girl wince with pain. We decided to cut her clothes off layer by layer.

The whole time she was clutching a single piece of paper in her right hand. I was not able to remove it until we transferred her into the bathtub.

As we washed the dirt and blood from her, a gentle aristocratic face emerged from beneath the layer of ash. Her name, she'd later whisper to us, was Maria.

While we bathed her, Maria remained silent. Numb to the outside world. I figured she was in shock. When Helga instructed her to raise her arm or leg, she did so. An automatic response without any acknowledgment of the behavior.

Helga discovered a deep gaping wound on the left side of her head that was the cause of severe bleeding. Dark red streaked through her pale blonde hair in strange contrast. Maria's fingers were raw open wounds that Helga bandaged up. The rest of her body seemed fine, aside from heavy bruising and deep cuts.

"I need to get to the hospital and bring some sutures to close her head wound. I'll be back in half an hour. Watch her; she definitely has a concussion."

Helga helped me carry her to the couch and left. I helped Maria get dressed in my clothes and made her coffee while we waited for Helga.

When she returned, she closed Maria's wound with a few sutures, and we put her to bed. Finally, we sat in the kitchen, and I asked Helga what had happened.

"Bombs hit three buildings, and two partially collapsed," Helga began. "I went to the closest building still standing and helped to evacuate and care for the injured, but it was nothing compared to the building after that. You don't even want to know what I saw there. There was a fountain in their courtyard; the water was boiling from the heat of the firestorm. The entire building had collapsed, and the bricks radiated a scorching heat. People from the neighboring buildings, police, and troops worked frantically to dig through the ruins—everyone trying to help survivors trapped under the rubble.

"I tried to focus my attention on the wounded, tried not to look around and get emotional, but out of the corner of my eye; I noticed this girl. She was covered in blood, digging through the rubble with her bare hands with this fanatic determination. With an unnatural force, she moved large pieces of brick, cement, and wood. I ran over to her to try and stop her. In such a heightened state, a person could break bones and not feel them splintering. She didn't even notice me speaking to her. I got the attention of nearby rescue workers.

In an hour, they were able to pull out what this girl must have been digging for: the body of a middle-aged woman. She was dead. Upon seeing this, the girl dropped to her knees and put the woman's head in her lap. She froze. Such a deep state of grief enveloped her that it resonated like some sort of energy field that saturated my own body just by standing near her.

Her face lost its life—a beautiful, eerie statue, as white as a corpse. Without the slightest sound or sob, tears poured from her eyes, cutting two clean lines through the dirt on her face. She looked like an angel who personified the grief, the tragedies, and the misery the war brought to every human being.

The woman in her lap resembled her, so I assumed it was the girl's mother. The coroner service tried to place the woman's body into a car, but the girl started to wrestle with them for possession of her mother's body. She remained silent as her face and body mustered all its strength to protect the only thing left that was hers. They tried to reason with her without any success. So, I decided to intervene.

I promised her that we would take care of her mother's body first thing in the morning. It took me almost an hour to talk her into coming with me and leaving the body with the coroner. She didn't have a place to stay, no relatives close by, or anyone to be with. Of course, I brought her here."

"Do you know who she is?" I asked.

"I have no idea. She barely said a word the entire time I talked to her. She would just nod at me. I only know that she lost her mother under the collapsed building," Helga answered.

That night, I lay awake wondering why Maria came into our lives and how things would be different. My intuition told me she was not just someone passing through.

Restless sleep caused me to wake early in the morning. When I walked into the kitchen, Maria was already there. She was sitting upright and very still, staring at something that only she was able to see.

Softly I spoke her name, wanting to make sure she was still conscious. Her eyes were vacant for a moment before acknowledging my presence. They were ringed with dark circles from the bruising that had developed overnight. The left side of her face had also swelled.

This empty shell of a person attempted to thank me for letting her stay in the apartment and for taking care of her. I stopped Maria's words because it was evident that any movement was causing her severe pain. Turning to the stove, I started to make coffee but heard Helga's footsteps behind me. She, too, must have lacked sleep.

Helga entered the kitchen and Maria's eyes immediately lit up. Maria stood and walked over to her with regained energy, silently hugged her, and placed her head on Helga's shoulder. She remained there, motionless. Helga and I stared at each other in complete surprise until the kettle came to a boil.

Maria slowly let Helga go and looked into her eyes. With a trembling euphonic voice, she said, "Thank you."

To this day, never have I heard a more sincere and elegant "thank you" in all my life. Helga fought back tears.

Tears. They filled the city of Berlin like an ever-growing ocean. The Führer was quick to respond to the horrors of the Allied bombing. Firefighters were sent immediately from other cities to help us recover somehow. A great effort was made to keep the newspaper running.

The east side of Berlin, just a few miles away, remained mostly unharmed. We received water and other provisions. Berliners pulled together to try and continue living. It was the only thing left for us to do.

For Maria, the only thing left to do was bury her mother. Helga kept her promise and worked to help her make the necessary arrangements. The intuition I had the first night Maria stayed with us resurfaced when we arrived at the cemetery.

We came to find out that the burial site belonged to no ordinary family. Maria was the daughter of Lieutenant Commander Hans Ritter, one of Germany's most celebrated aces of the German Navy U-boat division. Her father's striking face came to my mind instantly. I had seen him multiple times in various propaganda films that featured

U-boat successes in the Atlantic. Now his daughter was staying with us in our apartment.

The irony was not lost on Helga, who then helped Maria get in touch with her father. Commander Ritter could not leave for Berlin. He was in France directing the assault of the Second U-boat Flotilla. Instead. he sent an unexpected visitor in his place to retrieve Maria.

The knock that came on our door a few evenings later had an official air about it. As if the door itself should open on command at the knocker's touch. A heavyset man in small rectangular glasses was at our entrance. He was here to see Fräulein Maria. He said this with a pompous air. I invited him in—a decision I regretted almost immediately. His eyes scanned our small apartment with obvious critique. My expression turned sour, as did Maria's when she saw him. This was her Uncle, Karl Ritter. A man she would later confess to hating.

Helga and I left for the other room to give them their privacy. We figured Karl was here to deliver Maria to her father, and we were partially right. When we saw Maria fifteen minutes later, she was close to tears. Her father arranged for her to live with Karl's family. Maria looked at us with pleading eyes, asking if there was any chance she may stay with us instead.

I felt terrible, but the thought of a third person we barely knew sharing our cramped living quarters was overwhelming.

She must have read this on my face because she smiled and apologized. "I'm sorry for being so bold; I am a stranger to you," she went on, her voice a soft bell. "It was completely inappropriate for me to ask such a thing." She left to get dressed.

Helga pulled me into the kitchen, her eyes beaming with that same determination I saw when she first brought Maria to our flat.

"Ada, maybe Maria can stay with us? I can share my room with her, and she could help pay the rent. Think of the perks we will get having the daughter of Commander Ritter live with us!"

Even though I liked Maria, I barely knew her, as it had only been three weeks. And yet, the thought of possible benefits won me over. Helga and I went into the corridor where Maria stood, ready to leave with her uncle.

"Maria, we would like to invite you to become our roommate," Helga said warmly.

The proposal had a euphoric effect on Maria. The first time a full smile adorned her lovely face. This is what she must have looked like often, before the war, I thought.

Karl's face reddened and swollen. "Impossible!" he sputtered. "I gave your father my word. We are leaving here together!"

"Maria is of legal age to make her own decision," Helga asserted. "She can choose where she lives."

Karl looked like he wanted to kick something, yet his manners stopped him. Instead, his thick foot stomped the ground like an agitated bull. Not only was this woman messing in his family's affairs, but she was doing so with an arrogance he did not like.

They both went at each other arguing until Helga opened the front door and commanded him to leave our apartment immediately.

Karl hesitated momentarily. I could understand his frustration. His niece's life was at stake, and his brother was counting on him to bring her to safety. But Helga's eyes were on fire.

I think Karl understood that if he were going to get Maria back, it would not be while Helga was at his heels like a dog.

He opened his wallet and threw down a wad of bills onto the console. "This is your monthly allowance from your father."

Karl looked at Maria one last time before putting on his coat and leaving without another word. His stare was cold, hard, and filled with remorse that would only deepen with time.

From that day onward, the three of us lived together quite amicably. Helga and Maria moved into the larger bedroom and Maria's monthly allowance cushioned our combined household income.

Maria's physical wounds healed quickly, but her emotional wounds would need more time. The only thing that seemed to help was Helga's presence. She listened to her every word and shrouded her with attention.

My curiosity started to get the best of me. During dinner one night, I asked Maria about her family. Maria spilled her past without reservation, as if people who turned you in to the Gestapo did not exist.

Surprisingly or not, it turned out that Maria was raised in a world detached from reality. It was filled with private tutors and a first-rate education without ever stepping foot into a school.

Maria explained that her mother did not want to expose her to Nazi brainwashing. Both Helga and I had looked at each other, completely puzzled. How could her mother be anti-Nazi?

"But Maria, isn't your father a Nazi hero?"

Maria was unfazed by our surprise. "My father fights for Germany, not for the Nazis, and my mother, she is Russian."

"Russian?" We sat in disbelief as Maria sipped her tea, oblivious to how bizarre the situation was.

Her mother was of Russian aristocracy, Countess Vera Chukhnina. As a White Russian, her family had escaped the Russian Revolution, settling in Berlin and eventually meeting the young Navy Officer Hans Ritter. Their love brought Maria into existence in 1925.

The commander's successes within the Navy went from bringing family fortune to family tension. After all, he was now taking orders from the Nazis.

A part of Maria's story stood out to me because I also witnessed it. The year I'm referring to is 1938. That autumn, the murder of the German diplomat Ernst vom Rath in Paris, by a young Jewish man, was used by Hitler and Himmler as an excuse to start the extermination of German Jews.

In a single day, any sense of normalcy—of morals—disappeared, and in its place, insanity materialized. Like many others, Maria's family had to choose how to behave within this new world. Involvement was inevitable either way. This involvement came by way of Mr. Rhilke, a celebrated pianist of the Berlin Philharmonic who gave piano lessons to gifted and wealthy students. A good friend of Vera's, he took Maria as his student alongside a young Jewish boy around the same age named Herman.

Young Herman was blessed with the gift of music. Yet he was cursed with existing in the wrong place, at the wrong time—Nazi Germany.

The Nazi regime stripped Jewish citizens of all their rights. This new policy also punished any German providing assistance to, or having a relationship with, a Jewish person.

Herman's lessons had become too dangerous. Mr. Rhilke asked Vera for a personal favor. Would Maria stay an hour in Mr. Rhilke's apartment following her piano lesson as a cover so that Herman could continue with his? Vera agreed.

Throughout several lessons, Vera became friends with Herman's mother, Rosa. The yellow star Rosa was forced to wear exacerbated Vera's hatred for the Nazis. Maria said she saw it on her mother's face every time they walked home from Mr. Rhilke's apartment. The situation worsened.

On November 9, 1938, S.S. troops alongside willing German citizens stormed Jewish shops and restaurants. They burned synagogues and severely beat, killed, and mass-arrested the Jewish people. Germany was covered with broken glass. That night was named *Kristallnacht* meaning Crystal Night. A beautiful name for a hideous reality.

I remember hiding in my apartment, feeling scared and helpless. My ears rang with the screams of people and the piercing sounds of shattering windows. I did not know what to do.

In the morning, I understood what had happened and helped sweep up the glass on my block. My neighbors avoided eye contact and I wondered if they were as disgusted with our country as I was. The evening was quiet for me, but Maria's home received a visitor.

Vera carefully opened the front door as Herman briskly stepped in. His thin, delicate face showed terror. Without a single word, Herman handed Vera a piece of paper. It was a short letter from Rosa, begging Vera to save her son's life. The Gestapo was there to arrest the entire family. Immediately, Herman followed the escape plan Rosa had prepared for him, out through the kitchen window. The boy hid in the attic till deep night fell before running to Vera's apartment.

What happened next was a series of unimaginable actions taken by Maria's mother to try and save a child from death. Herman could not stay at their apartment. Neighbors and Nazi party visitors eliminated that option. Vera paced the room that night as Maria pretended to sleep listening to her mother's footsteps. By morning, she had developed a plan.

Herman would stay north of Berlin in their summer home until Vera found smugglers to take him to neutral Switzerland. The risk was severe and there were endless ways in which the plan could fail. The slightest mistake would result in the arrest of both Vera and her daughter. And yet, to abandon a child knowing the horror which lay ahead of him was impossible for Vera to do. Step by step, she put her plan into motion.

Herman dressed in Maria's clothing, disguised as a female cousin, Gertrude. Vera came home with a wig, shoes, and canned and dry foods. She tied a scarf around Herman's neck. Under Vera's instructions, he coughed into it often throughout the car ride.

The three of them arrived at the summer home safely. The house was nestled at the edge of a forest near a small village. Maria recalled that they had stayed with Herman for three days before leaving him alone in the house. Under no circumstance could he go outside, turn on any lights, or make loud sounds. Maria and her mother would return every other weekend.

I couldn't imagine a child entirely alone, forbidden from doing anything for days on end following the immediate loss of his family.

Maria's father was with his flotilla. The secret was well-kept. Until, like all secrets, it started to want to make itself known. The icy winds of late fall shed the leaves off branches. Temperatures dropped severely. The house stood cold and exposed to both the roadside and the elements of the approaching winter.

Herman lay under piles of blankets, his little body freezing. His mind possibly living somewhere among memories of dinners, family, and fire. Vera and Maria came every weekend now to heat the house by running the fireplace.

As soon as they left, the warmth of the fire—and of any compassion and protection—left with them. There was a moment when things started to look up. Vera found smugglers to lead Herman into Switzerland. She thought she would be able to pull it off. And she almost did.

Nobody knew what exactly had happened. Local police arrived to inspect the summer home of Germany's hero—it was thought to have been burglarized. Or so the locals had later said. A young Jew was found. The Gestapo arrived immediately. A Jew hiding in the home of a Nazi Naval Commander was serious business. Herman was interrogated on the spot.

Vera created a backstory for him that the poor boy used. Years ago, Frau Vera had invited him and his family to this summer house. After his parents' arrest, he remembered the summer home. He walked nights until he reached the house where he had been staying since last week.

Of course, no one believed this. Vera was spotted coming to the house every weekend. Immediately, the Gestapo took Herman to the local police station in an open car to later be transported to Berlin for a real interrogation.

The Gestapo would make this boy talk. The connection between him and the commander was something they could not wait to uncover. Knowing what lay ahead of him, Herman jumped out of the car while it slowed uphill. His last chance to escape. He was shot in the back: death, a better alternative to torture.

Vera was next on the Gestapo's list. They arrived at her house within hours for questioning. Vera was allowed one phone call to arrange a caregiver for Maria. A courtesy she was entitled to as the commander's wife.

However, it was not her husband that she called but Olga Chekhova, actress and queen of the German silver screen. When Olga heard Vera ask if Maria may stay with her for several days, she understood everything.

Maria's mother had met Olga several years back. Both being Russian in an anti-Russian society had united them in friendship. Ironically, Olga had been drawn into the highest echelons of German society, all the while coming from an *inferior* Slavic race. The Führer, a devoted fan of her work, even invited her to sit next to him on several occasions.

Olga immediately used her Nazi party connections to inform the commander of his wife's arrest. She hid Maria in a remote village until Commander Ritter returned to Berlin.

This was my favorite part of Maria's story. Chekhova was my favorite actress, and I must have seen her film *Bel Ami* at least ten times.

The commander resolved this dangerous situation quickly. Vera was released. The pieces of conversation Maria overheard later suggested he made a direct appeal to his superior, Admiral Karl Doenitz. Doenitz called Himmler, personally threatening to go to the Führer if the Gestapo continued to harass a German Navy hero's family.

Herman wasn't saved, but that was not the only causality. The relationship between the commander and his wife died, too. Maria's father could not forgive Vera for putting their lives, including Maria's, at risk for a neighbor's boy whom it was impossible to save anyway. And Vera could not understand how someone who considered himself a decent human being could even think to do otherwise.

After the incident with Herman, Hans Ritter rarely visited Berlin, staying mostly with his flotilla in France. His brother, Karl, and his wife, Agnes, both Nazi fanatics, now despised Vera, too. We understood Maria's refusal to go live with Karl's family.

I found myself frequently thinking of Herman and Vera over the years. The scenario played in my head and I wondered what I would have done. Vera was brave, but she was an exception. Many Germans turned in the very children their kids played with mere months ago. I realized that even I would not have had the courage to do what Vera did in Nazi Germany. Humanity was a paradox.

Chapter 18
Life in Berlin

Maria's sheltered upbringing helped me understand her dependence on Helga. Any feelings of jealousy disappeared from within me. Life normalized itself. Helga and I continued with our jobs, and Maria swiftly picked up the skills necessary to run our household.

In the beginning, the poor girl could hardly peel a potato and yet she was quick to prove us wrong. Limited ingredients scattered around our kitchen turned themselves into delicious dinners under her command. Each time a forkful of food hit my mouth, I pondered how much longer I would have such a luxury.

Helga said that we needed to prepare for the worst. Slowly our little stock of canned foods, sugar, and wheat grew until our small apartment resembled a pantry. Mildly comforting. But we all knew, one bomb from one air raid would destroy everything.

The year 1944 spiraled downward with each month. Our relationships strengthened, but life in Berlin disintegrated. There were a few things that kept our spirits up. Frequent visits from the commander was one such thing.

He always arrived looking polished in his elegant navy uniform. Small gifts and provisions for us made his visit feel like Christmas—as if things would be alright, because he would protect us and we needed to believe this.

We entertained him in our living room with jokes and his daughter's fabulous cooking, or he would treat us all at restaurants still in business. Commander Ritter told us harrowing stories of his life at sea; we were captivated for hours.

Maria was always the epicenter of his attention. Bittersweet for Helga and I, who no longer had any parents. The commander must have known, because he went out of his way to make us feel cared for. Numerous times he thanked Helga and I for the friendship we had shown Maria. How mature she now was. How grateful he was.

It was strange to think this charming, caring man was responsible for the deaths of so many others. I justified it in my own way. We were at war and he was defending our lives by taking the lives of others. Not a fair trade, but one we hoped to win.

Winning. Something that was preached to us by the Nazis even while our country was running out of men to fight its battles. We were *winning* when the Red Army entered Poland in June of 1944 and when Allied forces landed in Normandy. We were *winning* when Paris was liberated and when the Red Army defeated the Wehrmacht in East Prussia. And we were still *winning* when Berlin became a city of women and children fighting for survival.

The three of us grew very close. We became each other's friends, mothers, fathers, and sisters. It was a struggle to go on living normally. Food rations, bombings, and constant news from the front lines made it close to impossible.

We tried to do nice things for one another. Lift each other's spirits. I would save up my salary and buy a small cake or we would take turns buying each other trinkets—simple things like that.

Though we had one another for comfort, each of us still struggled daily for various reasons. Helga's were the most obvious. Coming home each day after trying to save injured soldiers, some of them mere teenagers, was painful. Witnessing so much death could drive one mad. Maria still grieved for her mother and trembled each time an air raid siren sounded. Myself, I was panicked daily by the updates I read at work.

The rest of Berlin had access only to propaganda and the approved news content, but I had news from the USA and the BBC in London. Translations we had to type to then twist in the Nazis' favor. The situation was grim.

At home, things were changing. I did not realize what it was at first. The atmosphere became sort of electric. When Helga arrived from work, she would be in high spirits. Maria would give her a long hug. Then they would stumble together and grab me. We would all fall over laughing, our arms still interlocked.

Maria spent more time creating desserts without butter, milk, or chocolate—none of which was readily available. She would hum tunes all day, smiling to herself as if lovesick.

I asked her if she had become friendly with a fellow. She blushed horribly, but kept her lips sealed. I teased her anyway. There were hardly any young men left in the city. I couldn't imagine who it could be.

The following night, I lay awake in bed. My mind raced. When would this all end? Would we make it out alive? A woman's moaning interrupted my thoughts. I sat up in bed holding my breath. The moans came again, more frequently. They were coming from the bedroom Helga and Maria shared. I couldn't believe it.

Suddenly it made sense. The long looks they gave each other. The weekends they would spend curled on the couch together reading. The hugs that always seemed just a bit longer than my own.

I felt stunned, but not because of their relationship. I was a Berliner after all, and before the Nazi regime outlawed same-sex relationships, Berlin had been the cosmopolitan capital of Europe. During the 1920s and 1930s, freedom of art, thought, expression, and love defined Berlin's very core; these kinds of affairs were common and widely accepted by Berliners. How could anyone deny another human being the right to love?

My reaction quickly turned sour because they kept a secret from me as if I were an outsider; they didn't trust me. I felt painfully alone.

By morning, I had calmed down. Rational thinking told me they were probably embarrassed. But, aided by a lingering bitterness, I decided to confront them anyway.

"I heard the both of you last night."

Immediately the clanking of breakfast forks stopped. I felt smug as all eyes turned to me. "Is there anything you want to tell me?" I pushed onward, watching Maria's face turn crimson.

"It's alright, Maria!" Helga stood to calm her. She then turned back to me with a confident look about her and said, "Ada..." she took a pause. "Maria and I are in love."

The three of us stared at each other. I didn't expect to hear what I had just heard, and they didn't know what to expect from me either.

I wanted to say, "Where does that leave me?" What I ended up saying was, "Then, of course, I am happy for you."

Their poor worried faces erupted with so much joy and relief that a fit of laughter took over all of us.

Looking back, I understand now what I couldn't at the time. War destroyed many things in our lives, especially relationships. Neighbors turned to traitors; friends vanished; survival became the dominant driver for everyone. Suddenly, each of us found ourselves terribly alone. I was devoted to my friendship with Helga and Maria, but it was not enough for them. They needed a deeper connection, a shared vulnerability that made them stronger together, and the hope and perseverance that only love could bring. They needed to find refuge within each other to survive this war.

Afterward, the only thing that changed in our household was the openness of Maria and Helga's affection for one another. Being without a relationship of my own, Helga and Maria never excluded me and instead doted on me until I could no longer take the attention.

At work, I typed up the "promise of a secret weapon soon to be employed to win the war." By that point, only Nazi fanatics continued to swallow down such lies. The war was already lost. It was no longer a question. What continued to worry Berliners was: who would take our city?

Germans who had escaped the East Prussian capital of Konigsberg after Red Army occupation added grim detail; the Red Army's thirst for revenge against us was unquenchable.

Hitler proclaimed Berlin an impenetrable fortress and yet the Red Army had reached the East banks of the Oder River on April 16, 1945, leaving a mere forty-one miles between them and Berlin.

Allied air forces now ruled our skies and air raids continuously bombed us without rest. Berlin crumbled further.

Protection. It was taken away from me a little at a time. Our building was hit twice. The bombs inflicted deep wounds. I used to gaze at the sky for hours, lost in daydreams. Now the sky stared at me every time I entered our building lobby through the partially collapsed wall.

Still, we had a lot to be thankful for. Our apartment, two others below us and our lobby were intact.

We did not know about the war crimes on the Eastern Front or the truth about concentration camps yet, but we did understand that no one cared if we lived or died. The Nazis made that clear when they forbade anyone to leave Berlin unless they were granted special permission.

Simultaneously, thousands of refugees fleeing the approaching Red Army arrived in Berlin daily. Families, children, and the elderly; walked for days, drove horse carts, or used overcrowded trains. And nobody cared where they would sleep or what they would eat. They came anyway.

The closest and largest bomb shelter to our apartment was the zoo bunker, near the Berlin Zoo. It was a vast, intimidating concrete structure with anti-aircraft and anti-tank guns on its roof. Every night, Maria; Helga, if she was not working; and I crowded in with the 8,000 people it was built to hold.

I suppose God decided who got which end. Mothers tried to comfort their children by letting them sleep on the floor in little piles like puppies. Several of them died in their sleep that way. After such horrible accidents, we lit candles to place on the floor. We knew the oxygen level was dangerously low when the flame extinguished. Everyone lifted the children, the elderly, and the wounded upward, three to four feet off the ground. New candles were lit. We waited till the next deadly signal.

In the war's final days, up to 30,000 Berliners were crammed in there. Our neighbors, the Mazok sisters, told us afterward that many people suffocated; the air simply pressed out of them. Only after the zoo bunker surrendered to the Red Army did the bodies of the dead finally drop to the floor. Their corpses had been held upright all those days, supported by the pressure of those around them. Had we been there, I doubt I would have made it.

The only way I could survive those horrid nights was to disassociate from my body and my senses. To go somewhere else. I suppose that was how people went mad, but to me, madness was becoming something I envied.

The zoo bunker had become so unbearable that we crowded into our building's basement or the nearest U-Bahn station. That decision saved us.

Three things now governed our lives: shelter, food, and heat. We were no longer living, merely surviving. I do not recall the exact month that humanity left Berliners. Like predators, people became numb to each other's pain.

One morning, Maria and I were making our way home from a U-Bahn station. Deathly screams caused us to quicken our pace toward the dreadful sound. The screams were in English. In front of us, a sickening sight unfolded. German Air Defense had hit an American bomber and the pilot had parachuted down and crash-landed straight onto a metal-spiked fence. He was hanging upside-down, immobile, while two metal spikes pierced him through each thigh. His parachute was tangled below, while his own blood sprayed onto his face and body uncontrollably. He must have hit an artery. With each exhalation of air, bubbles of blood formed around his mouth.

We ran to him immediately. Around us, a small crowd gathered. They stared at us bluntly while Maria and I tried to untangle him from the parachute, which was pulling him downward.

I called to the crowd for help, but everyone turned away from me. They just walked off. Frantically, I looked on the ground for something sharp to cut the parachute off with. His screams deafened my ears. My eyes searched for a sharp stone or piece of glass. Anything!

"Ada! Ada!" I turned around. Maria was calling my name, soaked in his blood from trying to hold him up.

"He is dead..." she said, in tears. We dropped to the floor, holding each other for several minutes. The agony of a young human life taken in such a horrendous way. Right in front of us. In front of so many others who looked on like machines. What God-forsaken world were we now a part of?

When Helga returned from the hospital, we were still a mess. Worried, she asked what had happened. After hearing our story, Helga's response was a bitter smile.

"At the hospital, I see such things daily."

A few days later, a demanding knock beat at our door. I froze in my tracks, my heart pounding. The first thought that came to mind was the Gestapo. Had someone reported us trying to help an American soldier? My mind raced for various excuses, but Maria went to the door without hesitation. Though she stumbled back a bit once she saw who was standing there. A well-dressed buxom woman locked her callous eyes onto Maria as if she were prey. I breathed a sigh of relief. She had thin wide lips and a thick nose. It gave her a mean, masculine appearance.

"Hello, Aunt Agnes," Maria said politely.

Ignoring my presence, Agnes strictly stated a command, "Maria get your belongings. We are to leave Berlin. Immediately!"

"Where is Uncle Karl?"

"He is waiting for us in the hospital. It is difficult for him to walk for long distances and there wasn't any transportation available. I walked half of the city to get to you. The hospital finishes its evacuation this evening. Get your things; we have no time!"

Maria took a deep breath. In the same polite tone, she explained that she could only go if Helga and Ada could also be evacuated. Agnes glanced at me with annoyance.

"Your uncle has permits only for his direct family members. He cannot take anyone else," she stated firmly.

"Then I will remain in Berlin."

Without saying a word, Agnes shrugged her shoulders and walked away from the apartment. I think my mouth dropped to the floor. Immediately, I tried to convince Maria to go with her aunt. She was making a huge mistake! It could cost her, her life! But all she did was hug me, doing her best to calm my panic.

"Ada, you and Helga—you are my family now. We survive together."

At the hospital, Helga was facing a similar situation. Wounded soldiers were to be evacuated before the Red Army encircled Berlin. Helga was ordered to go with the wounded. To everyone around her, it was a blessing. Official permission to leave the capital meant survival, but like Maria, Helga could not take the offer. Instead, she proclaimed her patriotism and love for the Führer; she refused to go. Officials could not say no. Another nurse immediately took her spot. The real reason was that Helga could not take us with her.

She was transferred to work in one of the small makeshift hospitals opened in each U-Bahn station within the passenger cars. Maria decided to volunteer alongside Helga in this hospital. Being away from Helga for hours on end caused Maria severe anxiety. Her pacing ended only with Helga's return each night.

I distinctly remember April 20 of that year. A deafening silence engulfed the city that day. We dared to think a miracle occurred. The bombardments from the air had stopped. Immediately, rumors circulated. The war must have ended. There was a secret agreement between Hitler and the Allied forces—or maybe even the Soviet Union.

The following morning, I jumped awake from the severe pounding of artillery fire. The Red Army started Berlin's encirclement. I was alone and terrified. Watching from the bedroom window, I could see the smoke on the fringes of the city.

When Maria came from the hospital for a break, I said I would return to the hospital with her. With Maria and Helga around, I felt safer.

We made our way to the underground hospital in the Friedrichstrasse U-Bahn station.

Though I knew I would see injuries, I was not prepared for the extent of what I saw—soldiers and civilians with faces marred by severe burns. Blood-soaked bandages, amputees, and disfigured bodies were everywhere. After a few minutes, I blacked out. With the passing days, it somehow became more bearable. However, it is impossible to grow accustomed to the magnitude of such human suffering.

For patients wounded in the chest or abdomen, a quick death was a blessing. For others who had a wounded or injured extremity, the only available treatment was amputation. A large cup of schnapps was the only anesthetic. The gut-wrenching screams of patients made my stomach fill with bile. It was gruesome. To this day, any scream or yell brings me back to that terror.

The surgeries were performed in the passenger cars of parked trains. Maria and I carried the amputated legs, arms, and hands far into the U-Bahn tunnels. With desperation, I would concentrate on the tunnel walls or ceiling up until I ultimately faced the graveyard of amputated limbs, a feast for the rats of the city. We would add to the pile and drown them with chlorine, but that only did so much. With time, the stench of rotting flesh made living conditions unbearable. We breathed through handkerchiefs and scarves.

We lived like that for three days until the horror ended with the worst of tragedies. Helga had two rival patients, both soldiers. Dirk was a young SS officer and a Nazi fanatic. He had been shot in both legs, and they were amputated above the knees. Martin was an older Berliner who had been forcefully enlisted into the *Volkssturm*, the People's Militia, by Joseph Goebbels' henchmen. After being handed one Panzerfaust to shoot at the enemy, he had been sent to the outskirts of Berlin. There he was to fight against Russian tanks. When launching the Panzerfaust, the launch tube exploded, severely burning the right side of his face. His arm was also amputated below the elbow.

When Martin entered the hospital and heard Dirk's patriotic rants, he became outraged. No one had paid any attention to Dirk before, but now, he had a witty opponent. Whenever their confrontations started, patients would perk up. Martin had a humorous disposition and was a lot smarter than Dirk. His sarcastic and comedic rebuttals were something the patients began to look forward to as entertainment.

We should have stopped their bickering—something I will forever regret. During one episode, tensions really rose. In a loud fanatic voice,

Dirk bellowed, "We don't have any choice but to fight the Russians to the very end! Till the last soldier has fallen!"

"Said who?" countered Martin. "There is always a choice, and to surrender right now would save thousands of lives."

"You old fool!" Dirk shot back. "Don't you understand that if the Russians do even a part of what we did to them, then we as a nation will no longer exist! They will destroy everyone! Until there are no Germans left in Germany!"

Hearing this from an SS officer who fought on the Eastern Front during Operation Barbarossa, silenced everyone. The rage and revenge the Red Army would unleash on us, on Berlin, the heart of the Third Reich, suddenly became very real.

Martin broke the silence by accusing Dirk of unjustly killing Russian civilians first. Again, the argument gained momentum. Each jab is more bitter, more personal. I tried to calm Martin down. It was dangerous for patients already so weak to exert themselves in this way.

Helga tried to subdue Dirk. Suddenly, the sound of a shot rang through the U-Bahn tunnel. I turned toward the blast. Dirk had pulled a gun from under him—and aimed it at Martin.

Helga tried to wrestle the gun from his hands. Then, he accidentally pulled the trigger.

By the time I turned around, Helga had already fallen to the floor. The scream that escaped me contained the pain of the past four years. I ran to her. Maria was already there, trying to stop the blood gushing from Helga's chest. In sheer panic, I held pressed bandages to her to compress the wound. Helga grasped Maria's hand. Her body stiffened as life started to leave her eyes.

"I love you," she whispered. Her eyes glazed over. "Survive… You have to survive. Please…"

I screamed into the unforgiving air. My voice echoed off the station walls. A hundred voices screamed with me. "Those bastards!" The rage that coursed through me was so powerful that I would have murdered both Dirk and Martin if I had a gun. My heart was broken.

I cried into Helga's stomach within the silence of the station. Enraged, Martin got to his feet and began beating Dirk on the head with his improvised walking stick. Unable to move, Dirk wiggled like a worm.

He screamed apologies. "It was an accident! I didn't mean to shoot Fräulein Helga!"

Martin continued to beat Dirk with the intention to kill. The other nurses and patients finally subdued him.

Then, the two nurses were trying to remove me from Helga. I stumbled back only to see Maria, who was cradling Helga's head on her lap. While I raged in agony, she had been completely silent without the slightest sob. It was even more unsettling. An expressionless mask replaced her face. Unstoppable tears poured downward. They hit Helga's eyes and ran down her cheeks. It appeared that she, too, was crying.

I thought back to Helga's description of when she first saw Maria holding her dead mother. This was what Helga must have seen.

The absolute grief that radiated from Maria stopped everyone. It even stopped my hysteria. Maria became a statue. It shook me to my core.

After a few minutes, I went to Maria, to hold her, talk to her. She did not see me or hear me. Another twenty minutes passed, and Maria didn't move. My nervousness grew. I couldn't lose her, too. I was afraid she was having a nervous breakdown. It took the other nurses and me over an hour to get Maria out of her catatonic state. Only then did her facial expression return to this world. This horrid, horrid world.

Chapter 19
Battle of Berlin

Something needed to be done with Helga's body. I breathed in deeply. Someone had to take control of the situation. Helga was no longer here. As the oldest between Maria and I, it was now my turn to take the lead. Above us, the shelling of the past few days continued.

"Maria," I started carefully, "we need to move Helga's body deeper into the U-Bahn tunnel and dig a shallow grave. When things quiet down, we can rebury her."

Maria's wet eyes assessed my words with a frost that chilled her tears dry.

"That is absurd. Helga will be buried properly. Next to my mother, in our family gravesite."

"Are you insane?" The words flew out before I could stop them. "The whole city is under fire! We will be easy targets!"

"Calm down!" Maria's voice was smooth and unconcerned. "There is a break in artillery fire between three and five in the morning. I just asked Peter, and he agreed to drive. The car should have enough gas to get to the cemetery and back."

I looked over at Peter, the ambulance driver who was also a recovering tank operator from the banks of the Oder River defense. When his tank had burst into flames, Peter managed to crawl out while his flesh cooked, disfiguring his face. A misfortune that became a blessing when it had saved him from being sent back to the front line.

At the hospital, Helga had carefully coated his burns in honey. I could not say no to Helga when she took the small jar we had managed to save. Instead of melting on our tongues, the honey helped alleviate Peter's pain, disinfect the damaged skin, and lessen the severity of his healing scars.

Forever grateful for such kindness, Peter assisted Helga with whatever she needed. Most of the time, he was a skilled driver who could navigate the ambulance through ruined Berlin streets and find limited medical supplies. Peter helped re-bandage a wound on a newly arrived soldier, but kept glancing over at Maria as if waiting for a signal.

"Don't feel obligated to come, Ada. I can go alone."

I got defensive. Offended. "Of course I am going. Helga was everything to me!"

"Good," Maria stated, knowing all along what my answer would be.

"How are we going to bury her?" I asked.

"We will take three of the wounded soldier's shovels."

"Three?"

"Peter will help."

Around three in the morning, the artillery fire quieted. Amidst the silence Helga's death left in the station, we moved her body onto a stretcher. The medical staff and patients who were mobile rose to their feet as best they could for a final salute to Helga as we moved her body out of the U-Bahn and into the ambulance. A solemn goodbye to our beloved Helga.

The night had a damp, icy chill that nipped at every part of my body. Or maybe death himself was still with us walking alongside Helga.

Peter slammed on the gas, weaving the car around collapsed buildings and mountains of rubble. Each street leading to yet another detour. I lost my sense of place. Only the moon dimly illuminated the piles of ambiguous wreckage Berlin's streets had become: splinters of wood, chunks of concrete, damaged furniture, doors, and pieces of glass.

Several times, we dashed out of the car to move the fragments of our city out of our way. Once, it was a full leather sofa—beacons of a city no longer of this earth.

Peter's expertise got us to the cemetery in forty minutes; a ten-minute drive under normal conditions. The cemetery's iron gates looked at me like two sad eyes that reflected the world of the dead. The sky cradled a bright half-moon—a perfect semicircle of light and dark; life and death. The simultaneous smell of wet dirt and green vegetation demonstrated this continuous cycle.

Maria and I took the lead holding the stretcher's bottom end, while Peter followed behind with the top end. The shovels lay at Helga's sides. Both my arms and heart were heavy with her death. It weighed down on me.

It was getting more difficult to walk as my footsteps sank into the soft mud formed after an earlier drizzle. Scanning the path ahead of me, I swallowed any fear. The demolished crosses and weeping angels looked sinister under the half-moon. Tombstones cracked down the middle. Coffins peeked from gaping holes in the soft earth the bombs had produced. In Berlin, even the dead could not get peace. Terrified,

I stared ahead. I told myself we were there for a purpose—unspoken protection.

Finally, we lowered Helga's stretcher onto the wet earth that she would eventually become a part of. Immediately, Maria, Peter, and I started working on the grave. After twenty minutes, I was exhausted. Maria's long pale figure blurred in front of me. She looked like a corpse herself. Her hair white in the moonlight. Glowing pale skin. Dirt smeared on every part of her as if she had just risen from the dead.

I awoke to Peter gently slapping my face. I had fainted. The lack of food, water, and sleep, paired with severe stress, had taken me elsewhere. Peter apologized for having to leave us. He had to make it back to the hospital before the artillery fire began with dawn.

Maria took three steps toward him until her lips landed on his. She held the kiss for several heartfelt seconds. A silent thank you. When she withdrew, Peter hesitated, caught off-guard, wondering if he should stay—if there could be a spark of something between them.

Maria's immediate return to concentrated digging told him otherwise. Peter left.

My attempt to stand failed me. When my feet buckled, Maria told me to rest for a few more minutes. Dewdrops gathered on my face. I licked them off. Maria's consistent digging was a morbid lullaby. It eased me into a half-conscious state, but then a thought snaked through me, clear and fluid like a mountain river. I sat up extremely alert and called, "Maria!"

She looked up, alarmed. Annoyance flashed across her face when she saw I was alright. I crawled into the grave with her. She continued to toss out heaps of dirt. My voice was a whisper.

"You are the daughter of a famous Lieutenant Commander of the German Navy and a White Russian! You will never survive Red Army occupation once they find out who you are!"

Maria ignored me. She shoveled earth like a machine.

"Maria!" I wrestled the shovel from her. "Listen to me!"

Maria stumbled back, agitation in her eyes. "We need to switch your papers with Helga's. Maria Ritter needs to be buried here. You have to take Helga's identity."

"What?! Ada, that is ridiculous! Helga deserves a proper burial. With her real identity. With respect." She paused. "It doesn't matter if they find out who I am. I will probably die anyway."

A deep desire to slap sense into Maria came over me. "Don't you remember Helga's last words! What did she say?"

"Of course I remember—I will always remember them!" Maria's voice rose with anger.

I silenced her mouth, knocking the both of us down to the grave floor. We sat there staring at each other under the moon. My dirty hand pressed firmly against Maria's lips. Above us, Helga's corpse lay listening.

"The last thing she said...was to *survive.* With her last breath, she begged you to survive! You have no right to die, Maria. If you love her, you have to fulfill her last request."

Maria's hard stare formed pools of tears. They released themselves one by one. I relaxed my hand and she spit out specks of dirt.

"I look nothing like her," she said.

I sighed with heavy relief. "This war has changed everyone's faces. No one looks like themselves anymore and nobody cares."

"What about our neighbors?" she asked.

"We will worry about them later."

Artillery fire started again with the rising sun. It must have been around five in the morning—we had been digging for over an hour. Carefully, we took off Helga's coat and replaced it with Maria's. I tried to look away from Helga's face. Dawn lit death up all too clearly. Maria removed the photograph from her identification card. With matches, I burned off any evidence that the photograph had been removed. Purposely, I left Maria's full name legible. We placed the card into the pocket of Helga's newly acquired coat.

Under our feet, the ground shook from artillery fire. The Soviets were getting closer. Using the coat's sleeves, we lowered Helga into the grave. Maria kissed Helga on her forehead and covered her face with a handkerchief before blanketing her body with earth. We placed a simple cross made from two sticks we assembled. With my pocketknife, I carved: Maria Ritter 1927–1945. We took a moment of silence.

I cannot even explain how we made it back to our building. Block after block of gray debris, the pounding of the earth with artillery fire made me feel completely present and aware. The ear-splitting gunshots, the pain in my feet each time they hit the corrupted pavement.

Scattered around us, a few Berliners in dark trench coats, rags around their faces, scurried to safety with approaching daylight. Creatures of the night returning to the underground. We ran past the hollowed frames of buildings that stood like demolished funhouses. Staircases that led to missing floors. Doors in frames amidst shattered walls.

And then something completely normal would appear. A café table and chairs waited idly on the pavement for the next customer, while behind it, the rubble of whatever café it had belonged to. An old man tended a small garden in between fallen concrete slabs, unphased by the prospect of death. A lost sparrow rose upward to the heavens. Such visions were painful. A reminder of a normal life that was incongruous with the present.

My lungs burned with inhaled ash, but I kept running anyway. Our building collapsed on the left side, but our apartment was still intact. I wanted to cry from relief, but I had no tears left.

Our corridor, kitchen, bathroom, and my bedroom were almost whole underneath the thick layer of rubble, glass, and large chunks of plaster. A shell had hit our neighbors' apartment, taking with it Helga's bedroom. The sky replaced the ceiling and we could see three floors down when we opened the door to her room. It was almost appropriate that Helga's room was also no more.

The exhaustion that took us over was so severe that I no longer cared if I would be hit by a shell. All I wanted was sleep, but I had to keep moving. My body operated without me, possessed by spirits. I dashed to the Primus stove and poured in the last of our precious kerosene. Once the flame ignited and the water in the kettle boiled, I let the steam soften the glue. Carefully, I peeled Helga's photograph from her *Volkskarte* ID and replaced it with Maria's photograph. Maria ran for my scissors and immediately I chopped at her hair as if she were Medusa. Outside, the shooting drilled through my ears. We couldn't stay; our building could crumble with us inside.

"We need to find a collapsed building with an intact basement!" I yelled over the artillery fire.

Skipping the broken steps, we ran downstairs and back onto the open street. Maria's new haircut bobbed in front of me. Covering our faces, we ran into a storm of artillery fire. Immediately, I regretted our decision. Fragments of rock, stone, and glass shot through the air piercing through my jacket like bullets. I started screaming; I thought I was hit. We had heard artillery fire before; we had seen it but never had we been in it. Eruptions deafened us from the right then from the left. I tried to muffle my ears from fear of my eardrums bursting.

Maria's blonde head guided me toward the sides of a shelled building. Suddenly, an explosion blasted behind me, knocking me to the ground. Spitting out dust and blood, I crawled to Maria. Our hands groped around each other's bodies, checking for blood.

"Keep running!" I screamed.

With our coats over our heads, we ran as fast as we could, periodically tripping and falling over debris. Rocks tore into my flesh and ripped my garments. We were going to die.

"To the right!" Maria yelled to me, spitting out more blood.

I looked in the direction of her pointing arm. There appeared to be an uncovered hole amidst the rubble of a collapsed building. Two steps peeked out from this passage to the underworld.

Half-crawling and half-running we, finally fell forward and tumbled down the concrete steps. The door was blown off. A strong cough came over me as I hit the black floor. Then, followed by a frightening sensation. The whites of several eyes stared at me alongside a strong smell of coal.

"Ada!"

My eyes adjusted to see the blackened face of a woman approach me. Behind her, the eyes of the cellar's inhabitants continued to gawk silently. I reached for Maria's hand. She gave me a soft, reassuring squeeze. "It's me, Sisi!"

In silence, I continued to stare at the hollow cheeks and dim eyes. Finally, it hit me: This woman used to work with me. Upon seeing her, I wondered if I looked as horrible. She helped us up and shared a bit of her water.

"You were saved by an angel today!" she said quietly. "There is no other way anyone could survive that barrage."

I looked at Maria. We both had Helga on our minds.

Sisi made room for us against the left sidewall. "This cellar used to store coal," she explained. The fuel was all gone, but the dust and heavy smell remained. There were a dozen other women, seven children, and two old men. No one said much. It took energy to speak, energy we could not replenish. Sisi whispered prayers to herself, and I fell into an exhausted sleep.

The next couple of days passed grimly. My body was severely bruised from the debris that had propelled into me, but I was alive.

During the day, Maria and I stayed in the cellar. I played with the children to keep their spirits up while Maria mostly slept. She had fallen into a deep melancholy. At night, we sneaked back to our apartment to eat from our depleting stock of food. In the morning, we brought back canned vegetables to feed the children and the sick. Everyone received a few spoonfuls of food. Not a lot, but better than nothing. We had to pace our supply.

On April 25, we returned to the cellar relatively late. Maria had been significantly depressed. She begged to be alone for half an hour and left to gather her thoughts. I insisted on trailing behind her, but she promised to stay close. With no choice but to let her go, I proceeded to feed the children.

Twenty minutes must have passed when an explosion sounded in the near distance. Everyone in the shelter held their breaths for more, but silence followed. I ran to the entrance to look for Maria. Before I could reach the first step, a man burst into the cellar entrance, knocking me over. Apologizing, he helped me up and yelled that the shelling was getting nearer. One had hit Frau Roth's perfume store, killing her amidst all her bottles. That was the blast we had heard.

Frau Roth had been one of my devoted clients. Over the past few years, I gave her stylish haircuts in exchange for small French perfumes testers. I tried to drag her into the shelter on numerous occasions, but she was a stubborn woman. So obsessed with her material possessions, her cherished collection of expensive perfumes, that she lost her life protecting them.

Then several explosions hit our street. Desperately, I ran outside, but I couldn't see Maria anywhere. Hiding behind piled ruins of the neighboring building, I scanned the smoggy ruins for her. Approximately 100 metres from me, my gaze fell upon what looked like a fallen horse.

Underneath it peeked a blonde head. I ran over to it. The scene unfolded in front of me like a mirage in a gray savanna. There lay an unconscious woman covered in blood; half her body pressed under the upper back of a zebra! It was Maria. Was I losing my mind? It took me a minute to put things together. I stared at the surreal image, my feet frozen to the ground, my heart pounding. A zebra? An African zebra in the middle of a war, in the middle of Berlin? But how? Maria moaned and I was rushed back to reality.

"Maria!" I examined her head and upper body. It did not look like the blood was her own. A shell had split the entire right side of the zebra. It was now a carcass of entrails, blood, and muscles.

Frantically, I started trying to shove the large animal off of Maria. It was useless. Grabbing Maria's arms, I tried to pull her free, but she started moaning with pain. Shells began to explode all around, covering us with gusts of ash and debris.

"Maria, wake up! You have to get up *now*!" I yelled, slapping her face. Her eyes fluttered open a bit but she did not seem to see me. I continued yelling. "Get up! *Get up now*!"

She started muttering to herself. I didn't understand it at first, but she was whispering into the zebra's fur, "Thank you...thank you..."

"Maria! Please, please listen to me!"

She finally saw me in front of her and partially sat up. A shell landed at my left and I dove to the ground, covering her with my body. I saw urgency rush to Maria's face. She realized she was trapped and that I couldn't free her.

"Ada, find a thick piece of wood!" Maria yelled, keeping her hand on her temple, trying to get her eyes to focus. She had obtained a concussion from the explosion.

Running to the ruins, I dragged back a part of a crossbeam with a strength I did not know I possessed. I understood Maria's idea.

Having moved several bricks next to the dead animal's head, I shoved the beam with all my might underneath its spine. As I pushed down on the beam with everything I had, I prayed to Helga, "Help, please. Helga, help us please!"

Slowly the zebra's upper body shifted. Barely enough for Maria to pull herself from underneath. I grabbed Maria underneath her right arm, got her to her feet, and we ran as best we could back to the cellar.

Once inside, I got dizzy immediately. Dropping to my knees, I clutched my chest; my heart was going to beat out of it. I was trying to inhale air without the ability to breathe it in. My sight plunged into darkness, but I remained lucid. That was the first panic attack I ever had. It took ten minutes for me to regain myself.

Maria lay against the wall in a daze, softly stroking my back. Her concussion was taking its toll. We both drifted into sleep, but Maria did not awake till late into the night.

Aside from a nagging headache, she seemed to feel better, though she remained reticent.

When the shelling came to a stop, she finally spoke. "Are there any volunteers to go with me to get food?"

Thinking she was talking about our apartment, I said I would go. Two more people offered to come, and I wondered if she wanted to bring the rest of our food supply to the basement. The idea worried me, but it was too late to voice anything. Maria then secured two knives from the crowd and proceeded outside. She led us in the opposite direction from our apartment. This confused me, but then I saw the zebra.

"This animal died just this morning; we need to bring the meat back to our shelter immediately."

No one moved until Maria pierced the animal's skin with a knife. She carved out chunks of vibrant red meat and wrapped them in cloth. The rest of us followed, our hands stained with the animal's blood. We had become our prehistoric selves, ripping meat off an animal's body with our bare hands. Once back in the cellar, we stoked a small fire to roast the meat on sticks.

No one had had a filling meal, yet alone fresh meat, in what must have been an eternity. The sizzling steak tasted like a life I had lived long ago. The meat was lean and had a mild sweet flavor—finally, real nutrients. Unanimously everyone decided to get more. Maria, myself, and four more returned to the zebra.

Before us lay a sight straight out of a nightmare. In our absence, the occupants of neighboring shelters descended on the animal.

Famished vultures covered in blood and entrails, heaping chunks of meat into their arms staining their clothes red. Though some of our party went forward, Maria and I left the zebra to other families and their children.

As we walked back to the coal cellar, I looked at Maria. I mean, I really looked at her. Something had changed. Her face gained a look of inner strength and wisdom. Like that of her father whenever he talked about his battles at sea. Determination accompanied her every step. She was radiant.

The following morning, the Russians had moved into the southern and eastern parts of the city. German soldiers who had once paraded in front of us, strong and proud, were now ghosts of their former selves. The sight of our men retreating from the Southern Front through our streets was disturbing. They walked lifelessly, exhausted from a war they should not have fought in the first place. We saw them, but they did not see us—or maybe they chose not to.

Many were mere children, twelve years old, fourteen. Uniforms taken off the dead and given to the only boys left.

Grief came over me. I wanted to call out to them, "Boys, it's over! Take off that ridiculous uniform!"

I knew that was not an option. If they refused to fight, the SS who roamed our streets looking for deserters would hang them off lampposts as an example to others of what happens to traitors. They would all be dead soon.

A small Wehrmacht unit positioned itself within the remains of the building where our basement was. The lieutenant in charge placed several *Volkssturm* militiamen and Hitler Youth fighters armed with single-shot Panzerfausts.

They would shoot at approaching Russian tanks from doorways, ground-level windows, and basements from both sides of the street. It was a good strategy, but it made the civilians who took cover in these places, military targets. We were of no concern to those who had sworn to protect us.

They told us the Russians were in Hermannplatz, two kilometers south of our shelter. A shudder passed through each one of us. No one knew what to do, and we had nowhere else to go. The situation was desperate. My mind tried to evaluate possible solutions, but I was drawing a blank.

When a sharp tug yanked at my arm, I turned to see Maria pulling me aside.

"Listen, we need to return to our apartment when the shelling subsides," she whispered.

"What? Didn't you hear a shell landed on Frau Roth's store? It killed her instantly!"

"Ada, listen, the Russians will be here by tomorrow—if not sooner. All-day long I watched the soldiers position themselves in every cellar, setting up traps for the Russians. The lieutenant stationed troops on each building's first two floors to be better positioned for street-level fighting. Russians will blast anything that shoots at them, including this cellar! We will be safer in our fourth-floor apartment, and we have food there."

I paused to think this over. Maria's eyes blazed with firm confidence. It seemed her father's strategic combat genes were making themselves known finally.

"That makes sense, but what about the shelling?" I asked.

"Once the Red Army approaches, they are going to have to yield shelling. Otherwise, they will be hitting their troops who are advancing—and taking building after building."

"Okay," I whispered.

Maria was right. We waited until 4:00 a.m. before leaving the basement.

Our legs carried us to our apartment building, but Maria kept on running past it. She stopped in front of a destroyed brick building and carefully went inside the half-fallen interior.

"Maria!" I hissed. A newly wrecked building had the potential to collapse further.

"Look for perfume bottles!"

"What?" I whispered in disbelief.

"Ada, why are you whispering? Afraid the Russians will hear you?"

I grimaced at her even though she could not see me. In the darkness, my eyes hit part of a damaged sign that read PERFUMERY. We were in Frau Roth's shop. Maria's voice came from across the room. "When was the last time you had hot coffee?"

Immediately, I understood and looked for the shiny metal cases where Frau Roth kept her most expensive bottles. We secured several intact bottles from the ruins; our pockets filled to the brim. Maria jumped over rubble and back into the street. A thick book bound in purple velvet was under her arm. My eyes lit up, matching her high spirits. We now had everything needed to make a small fire.

Once in our kitchen, Maria opened bottle after bottle, and poured the exotic perfumes into our Primus stove. I was hypnotized.

Auf wiedersehen, Tabac Blond! Goodbye, Chanel No. 5! *Arrivederci,* Bandit! *Au revoir*, Cuir de Russie!

The smell of fire and ash that was a permanent fixture of my daily existence was put to rest temporarily. Notes of vanilla, lavender, sandalwood, expensive musk, and florals swept over me—a long-forgotten dream.

Maria lit up the stove and poured water into a saucepan with two spoons of coffee. The heat further released aroma of exotic lands and faraway places—of a beauty that I had forgotten existed somewhere outside Berlin's walls. My eyes closed as my mind flooded with the memories each fragrance note evoked.

Elegant ladies at parties, roses in the garden, the leather smell of my parents' sofa. There was nothing left of those moments. Absolutely nothing. Still, the inviting scent of coffee soothed me as the water came to a boil. Taking it off the stove, I glanced at Maria. She was sitting on the floor with closed eyes. She, too, was lost in memory.

I looked around at our poor surroundings, now flooded with the scents of luxury. It was absurd. I used to drool over the exclusive perfume bottles that glittered in Frau Roth's shop. Priceless in the opulence they represented. And now I possessed them, but they were reduced to mere fuel for me to drink cheap coffee substitute with. It was absurd.

Since then, I have never truly yearned for any material possessions. They were all just distractions from the only things that truly mattered: happiness, love, health, and the blessing of life.

Maria and I continued to sit in silence. The stovetop flame danced and glittered in the reflections of our precious perfume bottles. In the near distance, the sky continued to light up with the glow of destruction. But tonight, it was beautiful.

Minutes passed slowly. We awaited what we were sure was inevitable death. A Russian shell could bury us in the rubble of our own home. But for once, I had no fear. At this moment, we were together, our throats and stomachs soothed by hot coffee, surrounded by the scents of heaven. My mind remained in the peaceful past of memory, a sensation I had forgotten, but now it wafted over us in the most tranquil of ways.

I awoke to blaring artillery fire. It was dawn. We spent the entire day under the first-floor doorway. Being close to an exit was crucial if any shelling hit the buildings on our street. With the darkness of night came relative peace. Returning to our apartment, we made more coffee and ate canned vegetables—our daily meal.

The next morning, Maria shook me awake. Sitting up, I covered my eyes from the glare of the morning sun. Something was different. It took me a minute to realize the lack of noise. My ears rang unaccustomed to the silence. Explosions erupted here and there, but they were far and muffled by the distance.

"This is it," Maria spoke with a hardened voice. "Today, the Russians are going to attack our district."

Upon hearing these words, my heart began to race. There was no escape. We would confront the Red Army face-to-face.

As if on cue, a knock sounded on our apartment door. I jumped from terror. It couldn't be them already—it was too early! Scrambling to the kitchen, I grabbed a knife while Maria went to open the door. Two heavily armed military men in thick brown leather jackets faced us.

"Is this the residence of Fräulein Maria Ritter?" Maria relaxed upon seeing the badges on their jacket sleeves; they were U-boat men who likely represented no threat to the commander's daughter.

"Yes. I am Maria Ritter."

Though they looked very different from one another in height, build, and facial features, the amount of dirt and blood covering their matching jackets gave them an almost indistinguishable appearance. They introduced themselves as Lukas, a stout gunner bearing an Iron Cross, and Max, a cadet in his early twenties. Both served under Commander Ritter. I offered them food, but they refused, only taking water.

"Fräulein Maria, we tried to get to you earlier," Lukas said firmly.

I saw Maria take a deep breath, steadying herself for what she was about to hear.

"My sincerest condolences. Your father was a great leader and a true hero. This is where we have buried him." Lukas handed Maria a crudely drawn map.

Immediately I put my arms around Maria, but she did not crumble like before. "Please," she said with an even tone, "tell me what happened."

The younger seaman, Max, cleared his throat. He smiled sorrowfully with bloodied lips. In his dark eyes, I found comforting familiarity—as if I had known him before. When he began to speak, his gaze gravitated to me after each sentence, as if it was returning to its natural resting place.

"Commander Ritter intended to extract you from Berlin. Lukas and I, alongside our other crewmate, volunteered to help him. He had become a father to us. Admiral Doenitz permitted Commander Ritter to take part in Berlin's defense. We proceeded to get to you as fast as possible under this order, but the Red Army had already encircled Berlin when we arrived.

"Commander Ritter tried to dissolve our group and proceed alone, but we refused to abandon him. I am sure you are aware, your father knew the forests very well because of your summer home in that area. Carefully, we moved behind the Russian front line, but we were spotted by patrol. During the fight, as we ran for cover, the commander was wounded. Our crewmate was shot dead.

"We followed Commander Ritter to a narrow split in between two boulders escaping Russian patrol who ran past us. Commander Ritter wanted us to continue onward without him. We were now behind the Russian front line and it was safer to move forward into Berlin. Again, we refused to leave him there alone. The commander knew this. He also knew he had no chance at survival.

"During the night, when Lukas and I fell asleep, a shot rang out. Immediately, we sprang to our feet, but the shot was from the commander. He had killed himself not to be a burden. We covered his body with rocks and continued forward until we approached German defense lines. Before taking position with our new combat unit, we needed to find you so that you would know the truth." He sighed heavily. "It was a true privilege serving under your father."

"A real honor," reiterated Lukas. "Please, do your best to survive; it is all Commander Ritter wanted."

Maria thanked both men with that pure sincerity only she could evoke. Max reached into his jacket, withdrawing a half-empty pack of cigarettes.

"It is not much, but it is the only comfort we can offer." He handed them to Maria, keeping his gaze on me.

Lukas and Max left in a hurry to get to their military unit before the Red Army's assault began. The whole conversation lasted less than twenty minutes but had the impact of several hours.

Lacking any words, I only held Maria's hand. Even I felt great loss. Her father had been our provider and protector. Now, with the death of both him and Helga, we were truly alone.

Poor Maria endured so many losses in such a short time that I constantly feared a breakdown of her mental state. However, my fear never materialized. Maria took this morbid news with unexplainable strength. Maybe she had prepared for him to die in the war already. Or maybe she was in denial. Whatever the reason was, no tears came. Instead, she lit up two cigarettes and handed one to me.

A protective shield now encircled her. I didn't understand its nature or where it came from. Inhaling the smoke, I let the nicotine travel through me soothingly. I had smoked rarely before the war, but this was an entirely different experience altogether. The severe stress we were always under exhausted our brains. The flood of nicotine was the only form of relief people could give their bodies. Max had gifted us a lifeline in those tightly rolled cigarettes.

The following day sounds of heavy fighting erupted south of us. My mind would race to Lukas and Max. Were they already dead?

The gunfire and explosions got closer and closer. We remained hidden in our apartment on the fourth floor. Ignoring my warnings, Maria periodically assessed the situation on the street below from our window. Several times she would say my name, but then say nothing further.

"Maria, what is it?" I finally spat out. "You're making me even more nervous."

The look she gave me felt like an evaluation. As if she had to make sure I was stable enough before proceeding.

"Ada, listen, we have to be prepared. The Red Army consists of hundreds of thousands of angry men. You remember the rumors. I think that they will take advantage of us and other women. There is not much we can do about it. I don't want you to make a stupid mistake, which will kill you or the both of us. You need to prepare yourself mentally for the worst. I intend to survive this nightmare for Helga, my father, and my dear mother. I know you will do the same. We will be happy again; I promise you that."

There was such firm conviction in her voice that I realized Helga's plea for survival was the driving force behind Maria's transformation.

The idea of rape and beatings had always been a dark terror lurking in the back of my mind. I used to ignore it. Now it could be reality. Maria ignited my fears, but the more she talked about it, the more I built up my defenses. Whatever pain I would experience would be temporary. My body would heal. Nobody could hurt my soul. The strength Maria exuded helped me develop my own. Our roles reversed and I gladly surrendered myself to her leadership.

All day long, gunfire blasted just one street south of us. With the onset of evening, the last worn-out German soldiers retreated to our street. They positioned themselves in our building and within the neighboring ones that still provided shelter. Across the street, only ruins remained with no places to hide.

Large groups of the notorious Waffen SS soldiers occupied the first and second floors of our building. We saw them come in and heard them take their positions downstairs. This made me extremely nervous. Though the night remained quiet, I barely slept. Maria did not wake up once. It felt as though I had taken on her worries as well as my own.

Finally, sleep had come to me when the roar of a tank engine scared it away.

Scrambling to the window, I saw a Russian tank creeping its way down the middle of our street. Behind it, the infantry secured buildings on each side of the street. There were no Germans in sight. This only meant one thing: Our soldiers were in position, ready to attack from their hidden locations as soon as the time was right. I left the window and let Maria look down at the formation below.

"The tank is almost under our window," Maria said. "This is where the SS fighters are hiding."

As if reading her thoughts, the SS released their first Panzerfaust warhead. It missed its target, but a second blast instantly followed. It hit the tank directly on its right side, immobilizing it in its tracks. Now, aggressive gunfire erupted between the German soldiers and the Russians.

"Another Panzerfaust hit the tank! There's black smoke coming from its engine! Take cover!"

Before I could ask what was happening, Maria dove away from the window and covered me with her thin body. A thunderous explosion erupted through my very core. Chunks of plaster hailed down on us from the ceiling. Plates, pots, furniture, and books smashed to the floor in one loud crash. Maria continued shielding me from debris.

The remaining skeleton of our building was violently shaking. *This is it*, I thought. *It's collapsing!*

My eyes squeezed tight as my arms clenched onto Maria's sides like a scared child. Gunfire pounded my ears, but it was coming from the other side of the street. Maria slowly peeled off me, her back drenched in a thick layer of dust. Our hair matted in white plaster.

"We just survived the tank attack!" Maria laughed hysterically through chattering teeth. "This house…this house survived the tank blast!"

Heavy pounding tried to push its way into our front door.

"Stay here," Maria whispered and took several deep, calming breaths. She unlocked the door and was instantly pushed against the sidewall. Two Waffen SS stormed into our apartment and locked the door behind them. Their guns were aimed at us both.

Frozen in terror, I remained fixed to the floor as they went from room to room, lowering their guns only after it was secured. Their faces were not visible behind the layers of dust, dirt, and blood.

"Only two of us survived the blast from those pigs," one of them, a lieutenant, told us as he looked down from our window. "They are hunting down every German, floor by floor." The severe edge in his voice sprang me to my feet.

"We need to prepare," he continued. "We have one chance and that is to trap the Soviet scum here." He pointed at our apartment floor as the second SS inspected our bathroom.

"The bathroom is the closest to the front door," he said.

"What is the plan? We are ready," Maria said firmly. They stared at her as if to confirm that such confidence was indeed coming from a woman.

The lieutenant pointed to the bathroom and said, "The Russians will enter the apartment and probably ask if there are any Germans here. Both of you need to point to the doors at the far end of the corridor. As soon as they head that way, we will jump out of the bathroom and gun them down from behind. It is easy; they will be trapped in your narrow corridor."

My heart beat so loudly I thought everyone could hear it. I knew we would be caught in the crossfire; we would be in the corridor, too. Maria walked over and squeezed my hand reassuringly. She must have read my thoughts.

"Alright, that will work, but I will open the door by myself," Maria stated. "The both of us will crowd the corridor and reduce their mobility in this small space."

Once again, the two men eyed her suspiciously.

"Alright." said the lieutenant. He stepped into the bathroom, but turned around swiftly. "I will be listening and watching you..." His finger pointed to the small decorative window that faced out of our bathroom and into the hallway. "Any foul play and I will shoot you first."

I remained utterly silent, numbed by fear, but Maria was quick to retort. "We are Germans, just like you, and we have chosen to stay in Berlin, just like you. Just worry about your job!"

The lieutenant smirked in approval and closed the door. Maria led me into the living room. Buzzing with nerves, I took in several long breaths, trying to calm myself. Maria leaned against the window, analyzing the street battle, unafraid.

"Make sure to stay in this room," she murmured.

Each minute dragged endlessly. I would get a hold of myself, but then a creak or footstep would throw me into panic all over again. The inevitable came approximately twenty-five minutes later—heavy pounding against our door. Maria walked to answer the door, as planned; I stayed in the living room. Male voices with strong Russian accents were sharply repeating, "Where are soldiers? Where are soldiers!"

Then the awful gunfire started. I covered my ears, wanting to scream. Silence followed. I waited two minutes, scared even to breathe; slowly, I then peeked into the corridor.

To my utter shock, Maria was calmly speaking with a Russian officer with perfectly round eyeglasses. Two Russian soldiers leaned against the wall listening to the conversation. I saw the tips of more rifles outside our front door. The remaining soldiers must have come up to assess the situation.

Accidentally, I made eye contact with one of them, who immediately pointed his rifle in my direction. I threw up my hands in surrender. Maria said something, and the gun was lowered. The two soldiers then proceeded to check our kitchen and remaining bedroom.

As they walked past me, a fourth man entered our apartment from the hall. He had a scarred face and eyes like a cold-blooded killer. With slow, heavy footsteps, he made his way down the corridor of our apartment and locked eyes with me. Immediately, I stood to the side. He looked me over and said something in Russian with a sinister tone. He turned on his heel and spoke in Russian to the two other soldiers who had by now checked our whole apartment. All three men went back up our corridor and into the bathroom.

To my horror, they dragged out the two bodies of the SS leaving a heavy trail of blood out the front door. Soon I heard two dull thumps. They must have thrown the bodies over the railing to the ground floor.

The Russian officer saluted Maria and said, "Thank you," to us both in broken German. The remaining two soldiers followed him, but the last one to enter lingered behind. He gave me another sneering look and then focused his attention on Maria. With a dirty, thick hand, he reached toward her face, but she stepped back instantly. Enjoying her reaction, he laughed to himself. After whispering something to her, he finally left.

I ran to our bathroom. It looked like a slaughterhouse, drenched in blood and bullets. Clasping my hand over my mouth, I briskly walked back into our living room. Maria followed suit, but said nothing. She took a white pillowcase and secured it to the outside of our window. Uncomfortable energy had built inside of me and I was pacing around in a circle.

"What just happened?" I spat out. Maria took in a long breath and rubbed her temples. She, too, was on edge, though she showed nothing.

"When I opened the door, I pointed to the rooms at the end of the hall as agreed. Under my breath, I whispered, "in the bathroom," in Russian and pointed to the bathroom with my eyes. The officer and his soldiers understood. They came in as if headed down the corridor, but then opened immediate fire on the bathroom. The SS were shot through the door."

I couldn't believe my ears. Anger swelled in me.

"How could you do that?" I yelled at her. "How could you betray your countrymen?" Her eyes stared at me blankly, which only enraged me further. "These men risked their lives protecting you, protecting Berlin!"

Maria shrieked, "oh, Ada. *Heil Hitler!* Do you think those SS cared if we lived or died?! They were just using us. They weren't like Max and Lukas—they were SS!" She practically spit out her words. "The most inhumane and insane division of Nazi Germany. The ones who killed your parents!"

I shut up momentarily, but continued to fume. "You still conspired with the enemy, the Russians are here to kill us, to exterminate Germans, and you helped them!"

Rage lit up Maria's face, I knew I went too far, but I didn't care.

"I just saved your life, Ada! Instead of thanking me, you sound off the propaganda Goebbels has been feeding all of Germany. The Russians are here because your precious Führer started killing them village by village. Don't forget that I am half-Russian—those are my people, too. And even so, what do you think would have happened if we had followed the SS's plan? Once the Russians realized their officer and two soldiers were killed in our apartment, we would be shot on the spot. At least this way they will remember us as helping them, which can give us an advantage. The war is lost! We are in a conquered city now and we have to play by their rules if we want to survive. If you want to die for Nazi Germany, then do it on your own time, not under my watch."

Maria slammed the bedroom door shut and left me to myself. I knew she was right. We would have been killed. After several minutes of silence, I got up the nerve to apologize. It did not take much to smooth things over. The stress of every day was so high that arguments did not hold authority for long.

Outside, we saw most of the windows on our block were now covered in white cut-up sheets and pillows: signs of surrender. It was shocking. So many Berliners were hiding when I thought there were so few.

"What did you and the Russian officer talk about?" I asked.

"After they killed the SS soldiers, he asked me if I was Russian and if I had seen other German soldiers on our floor. I explained I was from Austria and had a Russian speaking nanny and there were no other Germans on our floor. They started to leave, but then I asked the officer what to do with the bodies. Thankfully he ordered his men to drag them out."

"Did he tell you his name?" I asked.

"Yes, George Razumov. He was different from the other two. Intelligent, well-spoken, and polite. Wars take away courtesy, but it had not left him. It was a refreshing change." Maria sighed.

My mind drifted to the man with the disfigured face. "The last man, the one who looked like he just escaped prison, what did he say to you?"

"He was disgusting." Maria nodded in agreement. "He said he would pay us a visit real soon, and that we will like it."

I swallowed hard. "Are you serious?"

Maria stared out the window. "The soldiers seemed to have a lot of respect for Razumov. I think he will be sure to tell them to leave us alone."

I prayed for this to be true. Suddenly, intense gunfire blasted through the air further along our street. The earlier blast to the tank had left it immobile. Continuing forward without its cover, the Russian infantry now made it to the front of our former hiding place, the coal cellar.

It dawned on me that inspecting our building was only the beginning of the Nazi plan. Now that the tank was out of the way, the Russians were exposed and the Nazis unleashed a firestorm.

Bullets rained down on the Russians from doorways and second- and third-story windows. Our soldiers had the advantage, and they used it while the Russians fled from the open streets leaping for cover behind the jagged remains of buildings and rubble.

The German trap had succeeded. Several Russian soldiers lay dead or wounded in the street. My eyes spotted a young Russian nurse. She ran to Razumov and said something. He began shouting and giving a vertical hand signal to his men.

The soldiers around him began shooting at the windows across the street and soon, the rest of the Russians followed in suit. Not wasting a moment, the young nurse and two helpers ran into the middle of the street, checking the fallen men's bodies for signs of life.

She dragged every wounded soldier to safety. In front of our eyes, the drama of life and death unfolded. One of her helpers fell to the ground, shot in the leg; another appeared to be shot in the abdomen.

The young nurse swiftly pounced like a small agile fox. Only after she made it to safety did I feel the pain of my nails digging into my palms as I squeezed my fists in fear. She started treating her helper and the soldiers. The man shot in the leg assisted after treating his bloody wound. They were like machines running on pure adrenaline.

German resistance was extreme as the Russians fought their way to the top floors. Later I learned that those fighters were Berlin's defenders from the French SS battalion known for their fanaticism and fighting abilities. Even they did not stand a chance because new Russian troops arrived by the end of the day. They brought something we had yet to see: a small cannon that looked like a toy.

Night fell and the both of us retired from the window, exhausted. How the soldiers felt, I could not imagine. My empathy started to move between both sides, to Germans and Russians. They were all just human beings. Sleep came to me quickly that night; my body shut down without the permission of my mind, which attempted to continue to race.

Gunfire shattered through the night; grenades and the deafening Panzerfaust blasted with the rising sun. Would this ever stop? We saw the Russians employ their small canon from our window, pulling it up surviving stairway steps to the second floors of collapsed buildings. From there, they blasted the buildings across the street, silencing any resistance. I thanked God that the small canon came after our building was secured. Four surviving SS soldiers were shoved down the stairs and taken as POWs.

By evening, the Russians had secured our neighboring block and proceeded out of our line of sight. We decided to try and make our apartment somewhat habitable. This was our refuge and we needed to stay busy so as not to lose our minds. Maria found a gun in the bloodied bathroom belonging to one SS, which had slid far underneath our bathtub.

"It is a Walther," Maria explained, a gun she had sometimes used when target shooting with her father at their summer home. I told her to toss it, but she refused, instead hiding it by the front door.

Severe gunfire blasted through the neighborhood the following day. Sequestered in our apartment, we had run out of drinking water, though we still had some canned goods left. When night fell, Maria grabbed an empty bucket and left for the street fountain to get water. I begged her not to go, but she insisted. I stayed near the window, trying to look for her figure, but it was pitch-dark. I was a nervous wreck. After a few minutes, a knock came at our door. I breathed in relief, thinking, thank God, Maria has returned. I opened the door to a dark heavy figure. Panic shot through me, but it was too late.

Cold steel rammed itself under my chin. It was a rifle and it belonged to the disgusting brute that was in our apartment looking for German soldiers days prior. Maria was wrong; he had come back as promised. The rifle pushed against my throat until I walked backward. He was saying something to me in Russian in a nasty hoarse whisper. My entire body tensed in complete terror. His rifle pushed hard under my rib cage. It directed me back toward the bedroom.

I tried not to look at his thick, jagged face, but he grabbed my chin to stare into my eyes before shoving me downward. His forearm pushed against my throat, pinning me down. The smell of tobacco, sweat, dirt, and onions overpowered me. I wanted to vomit.

His dirty, sweaty face was breathing on me. Closing my eyes, I tried to detach myself and thought of what Maria would do. He pushed into me painfully. The inability to have control, to be at the mercy of this disgusting, foul ogre, made me start to cry. This aroused him further and he began to laugh, releasing his chokehold. I realized he wanted a show out of me. To make me suffer. If I remained quiet, he would further assault me until he got what he needed to get off. And so I completely gave into my emotions. Releasing months of built-up pain.

His body tensed; he was about to ejaculate. Suddenly a shot rang out and I screamed. I thought he shot me, but instead, he fell on top of me, dead. Still screaming, I scrambled out from under him. Maria was there. Gun in hand.

"My God! What did you do Maria? The Russians will kill us! You said to not do anything stupid, remember?!"

Maria lowered the gun. "I know what I said, but I couldn't stand by and watch this monster rape you."

As the reality of the events hit me, a complete panic came over me. It had happened. An animal had raped me and now his pathetic death would cost us our lives.

I paced the room, constantly checking the window. Maria remained in deep thought and I prayed to God for her to think of a solution. Maria watched me.

"Ada, are you alright?"

I looked at her through my tears and cried, "I am not alright! I am not alright! We are going to die…"

Maria embraced me fiercely. "Don't worry, Ada. Everything will be fine. That pig is dead, and you are here with me. She looked at the soldier's back carefully, then scanned around the room. Afterward, she went to the front door and peeked outside. I wanted to yell, "Don't even open it!" But I kept my mouth shut.

"Okay, Ada. Here is what we are going to do as quickly as possible."

Earnestly I listened to whatever instructions she was about to give me. With fast robotic movements, Maria dashed to the closet and retrieved a thick quilt.

"Help me roll him onto this," she commanded, laying it on the floor. He fell with a heavy thud.

"Now, Ada, clean up every drop of blood off the floor and make the bed. Quickly!"

I mirrored her swiftness while Maria opened up his uniform. The bullet had gone through his back into his heart. The thick padding in his uniform had been soaking up and retaining the blood. Maria sped out of the room and returned with Helga's medical kit. With precision, she began to bandage the wound. I asked what she was doing, but Maria ignored me.

"Alright, Ada, grab the end of this blanket, we are going to drag him out of the apartment. The blanket slid easily on our wooden floor. I was almost out the front door when Maria yelled, "Stop!" She had noticed the thick layer of debris outside our front door.

"The body will leave a wide trail and the Russians will see this instantly! We can't drag him downstairs."

"Well, we can't carry him!" I shot back.

Maria eyed me, madness in her stare.

"We need to carry him down to the first floor," she responded. "He is heavy, but we can do it, Ada. We have to do it. It is all about positioning, and he can't be more than eighty kilograms. Don't let the uniform padding fool you."

I ate her lies up. Maria left to the bedroom and returned carrying a sheet and scissors.

"Hold this!" she barked.

I watched her cut the sheet into two long strips of fabric. "Quick—bend his knee and tie his left ankle very securely to his left thigh, wrap it multiple times. I will do the same to the right. His feet can't drag on the floor.

"Okay, Ada. Now, listen carefully! We need to squat on both sides; you will grab his left arm and I will grab his right. We will pull him up to his knees. Then put your right shoulder under his left armpit and I will do the same on the right side. Get as close to his body as possible. On the count of three, we will lift him. It will be easy for us if we bend forward and squeeze his body from both sides while going downstairs. Be sure to control its position by holding his left arm while pulling it forward—and don't let his body slide backward!"

With our shoulders underneath his arms, we counted to three and carefully lifted the body. Immediately, my shoulder started to kill me under his weight.

"We need to move together completely synchronized," Maria squealed, "on the count of three, take a step with your right foot forward. Watch for debris where you step and don't lose balance in the dark. Pull his left arm down as far as you can to control the body."

Together we stepped forward. Maria watched my steps and adjusted her pace to mine. We squeezed his body from both sides and moved as one, carefully exiting our apartment and going down, step by step, trying to maintain balance. If we dropped the body, we'd need to start all over, and we were running out of time.

By the time we got the body downstairs, my right shoulder was completely numb to the level of screaming pain. When we reached the last step, Maria told me to turn my back to the building entrance and face the first flight of steps.

"On the count of three," she said, "we will drop the body backward."

It hit the floor with a dull sound. Maria pulled out scissors from her pocket and cut the ties holding the man's knees.

When I looked down on the body's position, I understood Maria's idea. It now looked like the soldier was shot from behind as he was about to walk upstairs.

Maria pulled the empty Walther cartridge from her pocket and placed it to the right of the body. What she did puzzled me, which Maria noticed.

"They are professional soldiers. An empty cartridge must be to the right of the shooter."

I looked at her with admiration. The pain in my shoulder was beyond intense, but some relief came to me nonetheless.

"Should we go back upstairs?"

"No, we will wait." Maria's voice remained strained.

I felt she was worried about possible outcomes that I could not comprehend. "If no Russians come in the next fifteen minutes, I will go and find that Russian officer.

"I'm going to explain how I was carrying water from the fountain and I saw a Russian soldier entering our building, then I heard a shot and a Hitler Youth ran from our building into the darkness. I ran into the building and I saw the soldier lying on his back bleeding. I recognized his soldier and quickly ran upstairs, grabbed bandages, and asked you to help me care for the wound. He died in our arms."

She went silent for a moment. "Grab his rifle from the apartment and bring a bucket of water back here and don't spill one drop on your way downstairs!"

After I returned with the water and rifle, Maria and I took our positions next to the body. I sat with his head in my lap while Maria bent near the wound, ready to pretend to put pressure on the bandages. About ten minutes passed until we heard the sound of several boots approaching at a run. We sprang into action. Officer Razumov and three soldiers appeared in our lobby.

"What is going on here?" shouted the Russian officer. Maria told him what happened in Russian. His eyes darted around with high suspicion. Carefully he examined the dead body and inspected the entire area. Squatting, he picked up the empty Walther cartridge, scrutinized it, and put it into his pocket.

With one soldier guarding the body, the officer took the remaining two soldiers and us upstairs to inspect our apartment. Again they looked it over with careful detail. I swallowed my heartbeat from stress. As they inspected our bedroom, Maria watched from the window. Her arms crossed over her chest with a look of discontent openly on her face. Razumov began to pay extra attention to the bed when suddenly Maria said something to him in Russian. Her tone was heavily unpleasant.

Razumov reacted with slight embarrassment. Without a word, he turned and left with his soldiers. From the window, we saw them carry their comrade to the main camp north from our building.

Maria was breathless when she came back upstairs. Exasperated, we both collapsed onto the bed.

"What the hell did you say to the officer?" I asked.

Maria smiled, her first in ages. "I asked him if he thinks that we killed his soldier and that if I were him, I would appreciate our efforts to save his soldier's life."

"You said that?" I asked, stunned. "You could have easily set him off! We could be dead right now!"

"But we're not!" She turned to me, still smirking. "He is a smart man. When I verbalized his thoughts and suspicions, I put him in a defensive position. Plus, in front of his less-intelligent soldiers, he would look arrogant considering that the same two young women had saved his and his soldiers' lives just the other day. And now here we are, trying to save their comrade. Smart men have their weaknesses, especially around women," she said mischievously.

"Since when did you become such an expert on men? You've never even been in a relationship with one," I said sardonically.

"True. But, Ada, I've read a lot in my life. Everything that you need to know was already lived through and written about by someone else. You just have to learn from the experience of others instead of making your own mistakes. And as you just saw, it worked," she explained casually.

I stared at her. "It's like I don't even know you anymore!" I said in jest, although that was precisely how I felt.

She looked at me warmly, but then her smile faded. "I know," she said quietly, staring into our crumbled ceiling. "I feel like I no longer know myself."

Over the next day, the Russians slowly advanced along our street in the direction of the Reichstag. Intense gunfire and explosions to the north kept us on edge. When our door was pounded on the following night, our hearts dropped. The Russians had found out we had lied, or the remaining SS saw us assisting the enemy.

"Let's not open it," I begged Maria. Naïvely.

Once again, Maria opened the door. A decision we thanked our lucky stars for. A Russian soldier handed us two loaves of bread, butter, and salt, compliments of Officer Razumov.

Overjoyed, I licked the butter off the bread, letting it melt into little moments of happiness on my tongue. I then licked the salt off the back of my hand like a cat lapping milk. It was incredible. Little did we know that this was just the beginning of our good fortune.

Chapter 20
The Russians

On May 1, a Russian patrol car equipped with speakers blasted a message to the German people: The Führer was dead. We heard rumors that Grand Admiral Doenitz was now Germany's leader. Doenitz was someone Maria had met several times when she was a child.

On May 2, General Weidling, commander of the Berlin garrison, surrendered the city to Soviet troops. We waltzed around the living room. The war was over. Whatever struggle was ahead of us could not be worse than what we had somehow lived through. That fact alone was cause for celebration.

Maria and I peered from our window down at the celebration happening on the streets. Russian soldiers drank, danced with each other, and sang at the top of their lungs as they fired shots into the air. The war was really over, but I found it hard to stay in good spirits. So many were dead. In just a few years, life had turned 180 degrees.

"Isn't it funny how different they all look?" Maria said, observing the dancing soldiers. "Remember the Nazi parades? All our soldiers looked identical, as if they'd been made in a factory."

Following her gaze, I examined the crowd on the street. There were Slavic, North European, Southern, and Asian faces. Even mere boys were among them, orphaned by the war and adopted by military units. Maria was right; it felt like the whole world had descended on our street to celebrate the end of the war.

I knew Russia was a big country, but seeing all the diversity in one place felt odd. Curiosity struck me. Propaganda had told me that Russians were Mongols and barbarians looking to destroy Western civilization. I did not fully believe this, of course, mostly due to my parents' involvement with the German Communist Party, but nevertheless, propaganda—sticks with you.

When the Russians began beating our troops on the Eastern Front, my perception of them changed. They had to be an efficient war machine but the men I saw on the streets were something else. They were all just so very random—everything from their ages to their backgrounds to their military equipment. Next to highly mechanized artillery units stood a wooden cart and an entire Cossacks unit on horses equipped with sabers and rifles. However, it was the number of women in the Red Army that I really noticed. They weren't just nurses or cooks. There were female officers; some even had medals they had earned from battle glittering on their uniforms.

Nazi philosophy categorized women's role in society using three simple words: *Küche*, *Kinder*, *Kirche*: kitchen, children, church. These Russian women would have spit on our confines.

I watched as a few soldiers entered the first floor of our building. Holding my breath, I listened for their footsteps on the stairs, but none came. This happened a few more times and Maria reminded me of our still-standing spacious lobby.

"They are probably using it for shelter." The idea worried me at first, but it turned out to work in our favor. Headquarters for the Red Army division that had secured our block before Berlin capitulated had set up in our building. This was good news, mainly because of the relationship we had somewhat developed with Officer Razumov.

On May 3, we met him again when he and three of his men came to our door to inform us that the lobby and first floor will be officially closed off to Germans who will now need to use the back entrance.

In this more relaxed second meeting, I was able to get a better sense of him. Razumov stood 180 cm tall with a fit, strong build. When he spoke, he exuded the calm confidence of a man who always knew exactly what to do and how to do it. His facial features and dark hair hinted at the influence of mixed Slavic and Southern European blood.

I guessed his age to be mid-thirties, though he could have been younger; war stole youth away. He gazed at us assertively but with perception. I noticed his stare linger on Maria.

"I want to make it clear that all weapons must be surrendered to the Red Army immediately. Anyone possessing a weapon will be shot without trial, according to martial law," he said this in broken German and stared directly at Maria.

I waited for her to surrender our gun, but she remained completely silent and looked at him with a blank sarcastic stare as if it were ridiculous that he even tell us such information.

Razumov explained the new rules Berlin citizens must follow, including a curfew hour, but Maria leaned against the windowsill unfazed. Behind her, sunlight from the window backlit her frame into a curvy silhouette. With her left hip popped outward, she rested her left elbow on her right forearm, which was wrapped, underneath her breasts, pushing them upward. A smoldering cigarette—from the U boatmen's pack—dangled between long, elegant fingers.

The U boatmen had gifted us those cigarettes! I swallowed my outrage when Maria chose to casually light up our last prized possession as soon as Razumov entered. Sheer smoke released itself slowly from her pouty lips. From behind this veil, she focused her mystic gray eyes on Razumov.

He was getting distracted. His concentration faltered and he started to take pauses in between words. If it hadn't been for the other soldiers in the room, I would have left, uncomfortable with the building tension in the air.

Maria responded to him in German with a calm unattached voice. "We appreciate your kindness, Officer. Thank you for taking the time to update us on all of the changes."

She blew out smoke in between sentences, taking her time with each exhalation. Razumov nodded to us both and left the apartment.

I turned to Maria and said, "What was that? Were you flirting with him?"

Maria gave me the remainder of the cigarette and led me into the bedroom away from the front door.

"We already had a glimpse of what might be ahead of us when that piece of shit raped you. We need a protector. Razumov is the perfect candidate for that job," she said with a faint smile.

"You think seducing Razumov will keep us safe?" I asked in disbelief. "He can just use you and let others have a turn!"

Maria shook her head. "He is not like that. He is an intelligent, well-bred man. Believe me; he won't want to share. Men are possessive creatures, and, Razumov? He has a good heart Ada, I can feel it. When he falls for me, he will protect us both."

"You are talking like this is some sort of a business plan. Your body for his protection." Maria rolled her eyes. "Don't be so naïve, Ada. You already experienced the other alternative once. If you would like, you may undergo it regularly, but I am determined to do everything in my power to avoid it, even for the price of Razumov's seduction. At least this way, I will have some control."

I had to think about this. Even if Maria was right, I wondered how I would fit into this equation. Razumov may take care of Maria, but that did not guarantee any protection for me. Suddenly I felt very sorry for myself.

"Ada, I won't let anything happen to you." Maria noticed my downcast eyes. I tried to smile.

The following day, the Russians set up field kitchens and started to feed us lucky Berliners who had survived the war. Many were barely alive. Hunger and malnutrition had removed life from people's eyes. Hope came in a bowl of soup and a piece of bread. It saved countless people. We stood in line waiting our turn surrounded by gawking soldiers.

The women tried to keep themselves ugly with each passing day. Dirty faces, mangled hair, and fake hunched backs, to appear as unattractive as possible; the complete opposite of our goals before the war.

Abortion clinics seemed to spring up overnight. The local commander threatened to arrest perpetrators and the rapes diminished temporarily.

In a few days, we received a carefully timed knock on our door after sunset. My eyes looked to Maria for strength. As usual, I prepared for the worst.

When Maria opened the door, Officer Razumov was standing before her holding food, sugar, vodka, and cigarettes. Politely, he asked for permission to enter, which Maria immediately gave. He removed his military cap revealing a thick scar on his left temple that ran jaggedly into his hairline. Asking to refer to him as George, he proceeded to take a chair and pour us each a glass of vodka.

Upon seeing him again, I felt an odd sense of joy—as if I was seeing an old friend. Razumov looked dapper and had a more informal air about him. He was freshly shaven; an attempt to clean up from a war that still hung heavy in his calm, intelligent eyes.

"I still cannot believe this horrific war is over," he said in broken German. "I want to celebrate, but after the death I have seen...the inhumanity..." He paused and took a shot of vodka. "I find it hard to be merry."

Maria and I nodded. "It is strange how we have not gone insane," I said.

Razumov half-smiled. "I am not so sure I have not."

Maria proposed a toast: "To a future better than our past!"

The vodka relaxed us a bit and so we did what all strangers do. We shared stories and talked about ourselves. Razumov was not married and he had no children. A mother and sister awaited his return in Odesa, a port on the black sea. He had been in the war since the very beginning and found it hard to remember anything else.

Maria went next. She told Helga's story, adding a few details of her own, such as her love for the piano. I finished off the discussion with my own story and the fourth shot of vodka.

The evening had fallen into the night. My eyes closed happily from the alcohol. With Razumov there, I felt safe and comforted. A similar sensation to what had commander's visits had given me, but then a thought struck me out of my fantasy: He was not Maria's father. He was a Russian officer who had gotten the both of us drunk. He was probably here for sex. Most likely with the both of us! I sat up extremely alert.

Both Razumov and Maria turned to me.

"Ada, are you alright?" Maria asked.

I looked at Maria, panic-stricken.

Suddenly, heavy pounding sounded on our door. I nearly jumped out of my chair. Razumov turned and walked toward our front door, his hand on his gun holster. He swung the door open, revealing four drunken laughing soldiers. Their faces glowed red from alcohol. All eight glazed-over eyes stopped at the sight of Razumov. After a brief exchange of drunken banter, the soldiers had stopped laughing.

Razumov had pulled out his gun and aimed it directly at the forehead of their leader. They slowly retreated from our door. Under her breath, Maria translated to me. "Those pigs came to *'show us what real love is.'* George told them to forget this apartment because his women live here. The pigs tried to enter anyway, telling him not to be so greedy and to share the wealth. That's when he pulled the gun."

Razumov waited till their footsteps faded before leaving the front door. Maria mischievously threw in an "I told you so" at me with her eyebrows.

I cracked a smile, but the phrase "my women live here," stuck with me uncomfortably. So he was here for sex. Razumov came back and poured himself another shot. We sat in silence for a minute before Maria decided to petrify me further.

"George, you do know your soldiers rape women nightly, correct? So why is it that you do nothing to stop them?"

My eyes nearly popped out of my head.

"My battalion is well-disciplined, and sex is the last thing on my men's minds because they are so exhausted beating death every minute of the day. The best rewards for us are food and sleep. When I tell my men to behave, they do so out of the respect they have for me, but I cannot control the others. The street battles just ended. Military police are not fully operational yet and the court-martial system is not in place, either. We, as commanding officers, cannot detect and prosecute perpetrators. Priorities come first and setting up food kitchens to feed your starving city has been the main one. Those four idiots are not my soldiers," Razumov said sharply. "They weren't even supposed to be out on the street."

He fell silent. Maria's mouth opened, ready to push the conversation further, but his deep hardened look stopped her. Razumov was working through something painful in his mind.

"I have a soldier in my battalion," he began again more to himself than to either of us. "After we liberated Belorussia, we were given a few days rest before continuing onward. We were close to his village, and so he asked for permission to leave for the day and visit his family. His joyous visit became hell on earth. There was nothing left of the village. Only stray dogs and a locked and burnt community building. Inside were the charcoaled remains of his wife, his two children, and every single friend and relative he knew. The Germans had forced the entire village into this building, barricading it before burning it to the ground.

"Some windows were shattered by those who tried to escape, but the Nazis had encircled the building and gunned them down. Every single man, woman, and child was burnt alive.

"Among them, he found his poor wife still clutching to his two small children even in death. He recognized her by a missing finger on her left hand that she had lost in a work accident before the war. He dug the grave to bury his family himself.

"Afterward, he lost his mind and became a cold-blooded killer. Always first to run from the trenches to attack the Germans. No bullet could stop him; he has the devil on his side now.

"He keeps a personal tally of each German soldier he kills; he carved notches on the stock of his rifle until it ran out of room. He killed even those who surrendered to him. I didn't have the guts to report him to superiors. We just kept quiet.

"Another one of my men came from a big Jewish family in Kyiv. The Nazis simply wiped out twenty members of his family. They did not evacuate from Kyiv, because his sister, who was in her final weeks of pregnancy, was very sick and might not have survived the journey.

"A week after Nazis occupied Kyiv, all Jews were told to take their belongings and line up to be escorted to a ghetto. Those who would not show would be executed.

"Thousands of Jewish women, children, and the elderly gathered on the street. The Ukrainian Auxiliary Police who collaborated with the Nazis led the Jews to Babi Yar's entrance, a deep ravine, and ordered them to strip naked. Soldiers formed a corridor through which the Jews were forced to march in groups of ten. They were then told to lay face-down in the ravine on top of their neighbors' and friends' corpses while Nazis gunned them down. In this disgusting way, a neat layer of bodies piled on top of each other until the ravine was filled.

"It's impossible to imagine that close to thirty-four thousand people were murdered in two days. Think about that: almost thirty-four thousand people waiting in line naked for their own death—for the death of their children.

"Not everyone died immediately, and the ravine stirred with the mortally wounded for another full day. The Ukrainian nationalist police guarded the area so that no one could assist the half-dead. They only left after the earth stopped moving. His whole family died in this way."

A heartbreaking silence followed. My eyes welled with tears and I looked at my feet.

"Every soldier in my battalion has horrible, tragic stories like these. They entered Berlin knowing that your soldiers raped their mothers, sisters, and daughters. People never learn that violence only breeds more violence."

Maria again opened her mouth to speak, but closed it. I knew what she wanted to say—that that did not justify the continuation of pain; that there was no need to prolong the cycle.

Razumov threw back another shot of vodka and cleared his throat. "My division participated in the liberation of Auschwitz. I lived through an entire war seeing terrible things. I killed people, many people, some with my bare hands. But never..." His voice cracked. "Never in my worst nightmares could I imagine what Auschwitz had brought to life. It haunts me at night, and I wish I could erase all of it."

He told us his eyewitness accounts until I asked him to stop. I was swallowing bile that rose from my stomach.

"After Auschwitz, I lost the decency I tried to keep toward Nazi soldiers. I asked my men to restrict themselves as best they could, but I could not be responsible for those outside my battalion."

He poured more vodka. My mind raced in circles. "How could this be? How could those same handsome German soldiers do such horrible things?"

"I don't believe you!" I said suddenly, loudly, unable to control my outrage. "Our men wouldn't do that!"

Razumov only smiled at me sadly. "I wish I were lying to you, Ada, but I am not..."

With that, he took his last shot, thanked us for the company, and stood to leave. He turned at the front door momentarily and locked his eyes on me. "There are no winners in any war."

He shut the door behind him. I turned to Maria and the both of us cried. It was impossible to get the visuals of his stories out of my head. We talked for another hour, attempting to regain our composure.

"You know he stayed here to protect us," Maria said. "He must have known soldiers from other divisions were going to be on our street tonight."

I nodded in agreement, refraining from sharing the reason I had originally thought he had come to see us.

"He is second in command," Maria continued. "I think rumors from those four bums will circulate. We should be left alone...at least for a little while."

Razumov's visits became more frequent. Maria had started to get giddy. The nervousness a knock on the door usually elicited turned into excitement. In response, Razumov's face lit up whenever Maria answered it.

Maria's affections were markedly different from her past relationship with Helga. Back then, she had been so reliant and even submissive, but now Maria had blossomed from a dependent girl to a strong woman.

Razumov seemed to bring out her inner femininity and strength. We enjoyed each other's company often, but I began giving the two of them more space. They spoke Russian when alone and sat very close to one another, hand in hand.

One time, I left for my turn to wait in the field kitchen line. "Could you take your time today?" Maria asked me. "George is coming over..." her voice trailed off suggestively and I snickered and chased her around the room teasingly.

Admiral Doenitz unconditionally surrendered all German forces to the Allies on May 7. Russian troops continued their celebration. World War II was officially over. Downstairs, the Russian soldiers laughed and cried and held onto one another; they were the only family some of them had left.

Some German women joined in on the celebration, too. They were tired of the constant fear, struggle, and pain. Most just wanted to experience happiness again, that long-forgotten emotion.

Berlin was going to be divided. The Allies, we heard, were splitting it amongst themselves like a badly burned pie. Soviet, British, American, and French; four occupational sectors that would dictate our futures' progression.

Razumov explained that Stalin's orders were to withdraw Russian troops from Berlin. The motherland was waiting for her broken boys. I noticed Maria's eyes when Razumov said this. They shouted, "No! Don't go, George," but her lips remained closed.

"The Soviet Military Administration of Berlin has assigned me," Razumov stated, "I will remain in Berlin for now."

Relief flooded Maria's face, which triggered a warm discreet smile on Razumov. They attempted to keep their actions subtle, but it remained clear they were falling for one another.

This didn't surprise or faze me. Maria was not the only woman who had developed an attraction to a Russian soldier. Two buildings down from us, our neighbor Emma was in loving relations with a

Soviet soldier. She bragged how he had managed to find a toy for her eight-year-old among the ruins.

Even our friend Sisi was presumably seeing a Russian, although she kept it quiet. This idea was debated among our women hotly. It seemed as though all of our German men were gone overnight. Killed, placed in POW camps for the so-called de-Nazification, or shipped off to rebuild the countries they had destroyed.

The entire male population of our once-great European metropolis consisted of mere boys and very old men. Aside from the physical loss, I think we lost respect for our men for failing to protect us. During the siege, they no longer cared what would happen to us. We simply became collateral in the war, and that was difficult to digest.

Some women sought Russian and later Allied officers, solely for benefactor reasons. Before the war, men may have gifted furs and rings, but now they gifted extra food and cigarettes. Others sought affairs for protection from other brutal men or because they needed extra ration cards to feed their children. And finally, there were those women who were lonely, tired, and just wanted companionship.

Not everyone in Berlin had been pro-Nazi, though we had to pretend we were. These women especially saw Allied soldiers as liberators. Others still claimed them to be pigs. I had no judgment for anyone. We had all suffered. I was too tired to have opinions. I just wanted peace.

The promise of it came in a way, and someone had to step up and begin to normalize life again. That was us—60,000 German women. Every female between the ages of fifteen and sixty-five was part of the first force to rebuild our city. Food ration cards were issued depending on the person's contribution to Berlin's recovery efforts.

To the young and able, this was an advantage. It was a step closer to death to the old and weak, though it beat the alternative, which was nothing. Maria and I were assigned to be *Trümmerfrauen*, or Rubble Women, earning us second-tier ration cards.

Each night, I fell onto our bed exhausted after clearing the streets from heavy rubble. My hands calloused and worn to the bone, an ache in my back and debris in the nooks and crannies of my face that the water I splashed with could never reach. My eyes closed while Maria found the energy to meet Razumov. Proof that love truly is a lifeline. Maria had begun calling him by first name.

"George is so caring," she would say. "George is so intelligent... I have never felt so comfortable being with a man aside from my father... We talk about literature, art, and life's complex journey..."

I would eye Maria coyly and say, "Admit to me right now that you are head-over-heels in love with him!"

Maria's serious expression broke into a blushing smile. "I suppose I can't contain my secret anymore!"

She gushed and we twirled around the room like children. Time passed quickly in this way. A calmness came over our household. Under Razumov's protection, our fears subsided, and we fell into a routine that was in itself comforting. I prayed for this normalcy to continue, but as all things, even this came to an end.

Razumov's courteous knock never sounded on our door that night. Instead, he stormed inside and yelled, "Who is Maria Ritter?"

I had buried the name deep within myself, never accidentally to call Maria by it; she had become Helga.

Now the name brought back with it the fear, the sorrow, and the tragedy that we both thought was behind us.

Maria looked at me, stunned. "Will you give us a moment, Ada?"

She led Razumov into the bedroom and closed the door.

I paced the kitchen frantically, prepared to go along with whatever story Maria would craft. To my surprise, she told him the truth. When they returned from the bedroom, Maria was ghostly white.

"George knows everything," she paused. "There is bad news."

Earlier in the day, Razumov had been reviewing the requests for assistance with arrests that the NKVD—the Soviet Secret Police—were supposed to carry out the next day with the help of Razumov's men. The address of our apartment immediately caught his eye and with it, was an order to arrest Maria Ritter.

"One of your neighbors must have informed the NKVD about your false identity," Razumov said solemnly.

"In two weeks, Soviet troops will leave the Tiergarten district and it will be turned over to the British to be a part of their sector. The both of you need to go into hiding until the British come. If they don't find Maria Ritter here, then they will arrest you both. You must leave tonight."

"But we have nowhere to go!" I shrieked.

Razumov paced the floor. "Think of anyone you know. Maybe a distant cousin or friend, anyone! I can send you off with some supplies you can use as a bribe to stay."

Maria and I fell silent. In our heads, we went over each person within our circle of existence. All my relatives had abandoned me after my parents were arrested for being communists. The only person I could contact was my grandmother's friend Lara, but I did not know if she had stayed or survived Berlin.

Maria broke the silence. "We can go to my mother's friend's home in Potsdam, they are..."

Razumov cut in, "Going to a friend of Maria's will completely reveal you. As you said, Maria is dead and buried. You are Helga, and you should not contact any of your relatives or friends. Ever."

"My only solution is Lara, my grandmother's friend," I chimed in. "I know she lived in Berlin, but I have not seen her since last year. She may have left or died."

"What borough of Berlin does she live in?" Asked Razumov.

"Neukölln."

Razumov sighed and said, "That is good. That should fall into the American sector. Whether she lives there or not, we need to get the both of you there tonight."

"We can leave early morning when the streets quiet down." I proposed.

"Ada, right now, the streets are filled with our troops and military patrol. Walking is too dangerous; I guarantee that you will be stopped for violating curfew. I cannot escort you myself because that will raise suspicions, but I have someone who can..." His voice drifted off as he formulated the details of his plan. "Give me a few minutes. I need to think of how this will play out. In the meantime, gather your things, and bring all of your provisions."

Maria and I began racing around the apartment. Razumov sat deep in thought, watching as we layered on our few remaining items of clothing.

"Wait!" he commanded.

I shoved my head through my last sweater, only to see Razumov walking briskly toward our closet.

He pulled out a thin garment bag holding an evening dress that remained as shiny as the first day I had bought it. I had never worn it, always saving it for an occasion special enough. Ironically this would be it.

"Do you have another evening dress or skirt?"

Maria and I both looked at each other and nodded.

"Perfect. Put them on and any makeup if you have it. Try to look as seductive as possible." He blushed a bit when he said this.

Maria said, "We understand, George."

Razumov smiled knowingly. "Right. Just do your best to look like you're headed to a party."

"A party?" I asked. "What kind of party would we possibly get away with going to now?"

"To be frank," Razumov began, "and I do hope I do not offend you, but a party that requires prostitutes."

We stared at him blankly.

"I will send Arak with a Jeep to pick you up around midnight. Watch for him from your window. As soon as the Jeep pulls up, run downstairs and get in. Most likely, the car will be stopped by our patrol. When this happens, the both of you need to giggle, flirt, and... well...act like willing prostitutes. Arak is our general's personal chauffeur. He will explain that he is driving the both of you to our general for some late-night company. Arak is well-known, so it should not be a problem."

Razumov then paused. "If either of you acts nervous, it may set off the patrol's suspicions and they will ask more questions. Take some shots of vodka before you go."

Maria and I let the plan sink in. It sounded easy enough, but the possibility of being shot down by the NKVD if things didn't go as planned made the whole ordeal extremely intimidating. I bit my lip.

"Who is Arak?" Maria asked, "and are you sure we can trust him?"

"I would not risk your lives if I had any doubt in him," Razumov answered sharply. "Two years ago, my unit was sent on a reconnaissance mission behind the German front line. We were ambushed." Razumov pointed to the deep scar on his left temple. "Arak was next to me, unconscious, but I managed to drag him back to safety. We were the only two survivors."

He is a Chechen from the Caucasus Mountains. In that part of the country, personal sacrifice is a badge of honor. He declared me his blood brother and swore an oath that he would do anything for me, even give his own life. That is one of the reasons he stayed in Berlin with me, securing a job as the general's driver."

He paused to let this sink in. "Do you feel more confident in Arak now?" The question was directed at Maria.

"Yes, thank you George."

Razumov looked out the window, deep in thought, until his gaze came back to us sternly. "So, which one of you killed my soldier and why?" I nearly swallowed my tongue, but kept my lips sealed, waiting to see if Maria would tell him the truth on this, too.

"I shot him," Maria answered firmly. "I walked in on him raping Ada. I stand by my decision."

"I thought so," Razumov responded.

Maria looked at him puzzled, "You thought so, what?"

I caught a hint of a mischievous smile on Razumov's face. "I consider myself an expert in two things: survival and combat. After three years in the army intelligence service and eleven successful crossings of the German front line, I would be a fool not to know one of you shot him."

He paused for effect. "I admire your creativity, Maria, but you placed the empty cartridge too close to the body. The blood on the soldier's *telogreika* was much drier compared to when you claimed he died, and there were two small droplets of dried blood near the bed."

The both of us felt ridiculous, thinking we could outsmart a professional officer.

"If you knew we were lying," Maria began in her testing tone, "then why did you not inform your superiors?"

"Because you did me a favor. That soldier was an NKVD informer assigned to my battalion to report any suspicious behavior among my men to the secret police. That jackass was directly responsible for the arrests of several brave soldiers who cracked unwise jokes about Stalin and the Communist Party. We all hated that coward, but could do nothing about it."

"Did he ever get you in trouble?" I asked.

"Unfortunately. I am on the NKVD's watch list because of him. I received four official thank you letters from the Communist Party for my actions during the war. The night I received the fourth letter, my soldiers and I drank to celebrate. Thinking I was among friends, I foolishly joked that I already had three official letters, so I am ready to exchange the fourth letter for some warm blankets for my men. You know, something useful. That bastard somehow heard me and immediately notified the NKVD. The next day, I was arrested. Luckily for me, our major's intervention saved me from being sent away to a work camp. I only wish I could have killed that piece of shit myself."

He leaned over and lightly kissed Maria. "Alright, both of you understand the plan, yes?"

We nodded in agreement.

"I will try to visit you in two to three days." Razumov stood to leave. I hugged him goodbye and went to prepare while he and Maria shared their farewells.

We spent the next hour applying old remains of blush, eyeliner, and shadow. The mascara had dried, and our lipsticks had turned to a sticky wax consistency, but we smudged them on anyway. I trimmed some playful wispy bangs into my hair and refreshed Maria's haircut.

We stood before each other in our evening dresses in our half-collapsed apartment—ghosts of our former carefree selves. It was a surreal experience, but we looked beautiful. Razumov's bottle of vodka met our lips.

Our eyes earnestly searched the night for the lights of a Jeep. When it finally approached, my heart flipped. This was it. We ran downstairs and threw ourselves into the car without even looking at the driver.

Arak turned to us with dark, penetrating eyes. "Remember what to do," He said harshly in Russian. Maria whispered the translation to me as Arak pressed on the gas and moved the vehicle forward rigidly.

The drive through the broken streets was quiet and tense. Soon the vodka seeped into my blood and relaxed my nerves. Ten minutes or so must have passed when we saw the bright lights of another vehicle. It was Russian military patrol. I grabbed Maria's arm and squeezed it until my nails felt her bone.

"Ada!" Maria hissed in my ear as she kicked me and let out a flirtatious laugh.

"I know you love him!" she continued, "just admit it already!"

Her thin fingers began tickling my protruding rib cage as the Jeep slowed to a halt. We continued to play-fight with each other exchanging devious giggles while Arak spoke to the patrol in Russian.

The patrol officer recognized Arak immediately and, after shining a bright light on both of us, he joked around with Arak for another two minutes. The Jeep finally began to move forward. I took three deep breaths and thanked God. The next stop was Lara's apartment building.

"That is where her apartment was," I whispered, pointing to the completely collapsed left side of the building." Maria followed my gaze.

"That does not mean she is dead. Let's search the rest of the building. Either way, we have to get out of sight; otherwise, Arak will get into trouble. If we don't find Lara, we will try and blend in with the other rubble women here where no one knows us."

We grabbed our food and clothes and thanked Arak. Carefully we climbed our way up the partially collapsed staircase past the blown-off apartment doors. Inside, giant gaping holes in the floors made the rooms uninhabitable. My hope was sinking. The remaining part of the building was abandoned.

The door to Lara's apartment on the third floor was closed. I knocked on it softly, twisted the doorknob, and let myself in when a gust of wind hit my face. Confusion hit me. Instead of the inviting air of someone's home, the chill of the street welcomed me. I was in a corridor that ended with a complete drop to the first floor. Maria was behind me on the other side of the door.

"Lara!" I called. "Lara!" A soft whimper came from behind a door to the left of the collapsed corridor. Softly, we slid our feet toward the door, feeling each floorboard for stability. I turned the knob and rounded the door frame into what was the kitchen.

I gasped. On the floor, a skeleton of a woman with loose skin was moving her fingers.

"Oh, my God!" I cried, "Lara!"

She was emaciated—practically dead from starvation. Maria and I quickly got to work. Emptying our supplies onto the floor, we began to make a small fire using pages from the perfumery book we had brought with us.

The kitchen was empty, aside from cookware. In a small pot, we mixed one of our cans of vegetables with little water to make a broth. Lara was half-conscious and did not know who I was. Cradling her fragile head, we fed her spoonfuls of soup like a helpless child. Eventually, Maria fell asleep beside her. I stayed awake stroking Lara's thin white hair, wondering if the arrest warrant for Maria Ritter had occurred so that we would find and save a dying Lara.

In the morning, she remained in bad shape, but at least she recognized me.

"Everything will be okay now," I told her. "We are going to take care of you."

She smiled weakly before drifting back to sleep. Little by little, we fed her soup, making enough for the three of us.

We quietly stayed on the kitchen floor during the day, hiding from the rubble women working on clearing the streets just below.

Late into the night, Maria or I would wake up to sneak down and get clean water. Four days passed and Lara regained some strength. I asked her why she was not getting food from the Russian field kitchens.

"I was," she spoke slowly, "but I am too old to work. I was issued the lowest ration card, the *Friedhofskarte.* It is called the 'cemetery ticket' for a reason." Lara exhaled mournfully.

"I became so weak that I decided to die in my apartment, or what is left of it...." Her voice drifted off as tears welled in her sunken eyes. "But then you angels came... You brought life back to me."

The tears escaped her pale lids and I squeezed her hand.

"Don't cry, Lara," I whispered.

As Lara's senses returned to her, she noticed our nervousness. She understood our need to hide from the Soviet secret police until the Americans and British could establish control of our sector.

A complication arose: we were running out of food. Razumov had not shown up as promised. Maria began to worry that something had happened to him, but I started to develop a different theory. I was not proud of it, but it was where my mind naturally drifted.

I assumed that Razumov had created this whole ruse with the NKVD to get rid of Maria. Being in love with a German woman who was also a White Russian would not play well with Soviet authorities. This way, there would be no painful goodbye that would be inevitable when the time came for Russian troops to leave Berlin.

Two more days dragged through our empty kitchen. We both feared Razumov would not return, but my worry centered around food and supplies instead of love.

Maria began considering returning to our former apartment to look for Razumov.

"That is pure suicide!" I hissed at her. "They will arrest you and then torture you until you tell them where I am hiding. Three lives are at stake here!"

Maria was a woman in love and reason no longer played a role in her decision-making. I had to knock logic back into her, and so I told her why I really thought Razumov was not returning. Maria was furious. For the entire day, she wouldn't even look at me, but I knew I had planted the seed of doubt in her mind and slowly, she began talking about it.

"He wouldn't do that, Ada. He loves me."

"I know, Maria. I am not saying that he doesn't love you, but put yourself in his situation— what is he supposed to do? If he stays in

Berlin with you, the NKVD will go after him or his family!" Maria gave a solemn nod and said, "You are probably right...."

I wasn't. At dawn on July 2, a knock sounded on our door. Lara had been the first to hear it, and she woke us up to usher us into the broom closet. Pressed against one another, we held our breaths in the darkness of the small space.

We heard a man's accented German, and Maria burst outward. "It's George!" She squealed. "Oh, my God, George!"

The initial happiness in her voice had dropped to heavy shock. Following her, my eyes landed on a man I no longer recognized.

George's head was shaved; his oval face was swollen round with dark bruises covering his cheeks and eyes. His nose looked broken. Only his voice was familiar. Maria was already in his arms, crying from joy and sadness.

"What did they do to you, George?"

Next to his feet were two sacks filled with packages of food. I felt awful for doubting him, and even more so after his severely beaten face smiled at me warmly.

"It is good to see you, Ada." He hugged me and I began crying, too.

Lara and I left Maria and George to speak in the kitchen. We sat in the corridor by the front door. Maria was crying, kissing him, pleading, and crying again. I understood nothing, but even in Russian, it was obvious the conversation was doleful.

After about forty minutes, Razumov proceeded to leave. Lara and I thanked him for the food. The color in his face had drained and even his bruises seemed paler. He nodded to us and left without a goodbye. In the kitchen, Maria sat on the floor lifeless. Those silent tears poured from her eyes once more, staring into that abyss that only she could see. I knew she was gone.

When night fell on us and Lara began a light snore, I started talking to Maria. She remained seated in the same position with her back against a cabinet. Her mind had seemed to return to her. I could tell by the way her eyes flickered to different parts of the kitchen. Boiling some of the tea and sugar Razumov had brought, I handed her a cup.

The amazing taste of strong sweet black tea flooded my mouth for the second time that day. I savored it, quietly watching Maria gulp it down without emotion.

"Is George leaving to go to Russia?" I asked delicately.

She nodded in response.

"Will he return?"

"No," she whispered.

A long silence ensued. I waited till Maria was ready to speak again.

"When the NKVD did not find us in our apartment, they set up a trap waiting for our return. After two days, they began an investigation and easily connected us to George. Everyone knew he was visiting our apartment often.

"They arrested him with the charge of informing us of our arrests and of covering up the murder of the NKVD informant. He was tortured and beaten. And it was all because of me!" Maria burst into tears.

"I can't believe he didn't give up our location... He really loves you, Maria."

"I know..." She sobbed. "He said that the thought of me was the only thing that got him through all the beatings during his days of imprisonment."

"How did he escape?"

Maria took a few breaths to settle down. "The charges were dropped only after a detailed interrogation of all his soldiers who were with him when they found the informant's body in our lobby. George's major, who had saved him before from the NKVD, got the secret police to free George on account of his loyalty to the Soviet Union and the Communist Party during the war. The major and the NKVD colonel were drinking buddies. Now George is under constant watch. I don't even know how he got out here to us."

I squeezed Maria's hand.

"We are supposed to be together, Ada, I just know it. Even our pasts are intertwined."

"Your pasts? What do you mean?"

"Razumov isn't his real name; it's Razumovsky. He is the direct descendant of Kirill Razumovsky, the Hetman of the Ukrainian Cossacks."

"What? How did he keep that a secret from the Communists?"

"His father was executed after the Russian revolution for being a part of the Russian aristocracy when George was just two years old. His mother escaped with forged papers under the name Razumov. She remarried quickly and was able to go on living."

"Why did he fight in the war on the side of the communists?" I asked, bewildered.

"I asked him the same thing, but he told me he was fighting for his motherland, for Russia, not for the communists. He hates the communist regime, especially Stalin."

"Can't he return to Berlin in the future when things settle down?"

"No," Maria answered bluntly. "In Berlin, the Americans would turn him over to the Soviets because they are Allies. Even if we ran away together to a neutral country, the communists would execute his mother and sister for being a family of traitors.

"I am so sorry, Maria..."

"I feel that God is against me, Ada. First my mother, then Helga, and my father, and now George. I am given love and then it is brutally taken from me."

I said nothing because she was right. I could not understand why Maria was dealt such tragic fate. "What did Razumov say before he left?"

Maria smiled at me tearfully. "He said, chances are, our ancestors knew one another, danced together at the same royal balls within the walls of the Czar's palace and maybe were even in love. He then kissed me deeply and said he would never forget me—that we would always belong to one another before we belonged to anyone else."

"What happens now?" I asked cautiously.

"We wait for the Americans. George said they would be here in two days."

Chapter 21
The Americans and the British

Razumov had been right. In exactly two days, soldiers we had never seen before appeared on our streets. They came in with round olive-green helmets and matching uniforms. Relief washed over me: no more hiding, no more fear of the NKVD. The future seemed brighter than it had in a long time.

Maria remained unaffected by the changes and mostly stared out the window, though she no longer cried. For some reason, I had the idea that our lives would drastically change under American occupation, but each day continued to begin and end quite the same.

Starvation haunted Berliners as it had before. Food rations were so small that seeing someone collapse on the street from malnutrition was not uncommon. I suppose things shifted more than they actually changed. Rape diminished, but it was replaced by soldiers using extra food as a trade-off for sex, knowing that some women, especially those with children, would have no choice but to give in.

At least we were not in the French sector, where rape continued until September. Word got around that only the British left the German women in peace for the most part—and that is where we got lucky.

With the Russians gone, Maria and I made our way back to our old apartment, which was now a part of the British sector.

Our attempt to convince Lara to come with us failed as she insisted on staying with friends in her building. We agreed to visit her often to make sure she had enough food and supplies.

When we entered our old apartment, I felt as though I were seeing an old friend. Familiarity in itself is enough to soothe distress. Though Maria may have felt otherwise; our walls held the memories of both Helga and Razumov. She did not mention either.

With the passing hours, my recollections of this apartment began to nag at me, too. I lay awake exhausted after work; Maria lay on the bed beside me, no longer hurrying off to see Razumov, but it wasn't Maria's presence I felt; it was that brute who violated me. The image replayed itself over and over—his boorish face, jagged and angular, stared at me through my mind's eye. The stench of sweat and onions overpowered my senses.

I sat up with beads of sweat on my forehead, my abdomen cramped. I tried to swallow the nausea the memory conjured up but only tasted onion and cheap tobacco.

Quietly fleeing for the bathroom, I vomited his presence out of me. Weak, I slid to the bathroom floor. The grout between the tiles remained stained with the blood of the murdered SS soldiers. Anger pulsated through me. Anger at myself. Why did I open the front door? Why was this still affecting me? It had happened once, briefly, and the bastard was now dead.

Disgust refused to leave me no matter how much I had scrubbed my hands and face with water.

In the morning, I threw up again. It came naturally—the need to purge myself of the contamination. Afterward, fatigue would come, but I dragged myself to work anyway. Anything for more ration cards.

Sadness consumed me. I began to believe he was haunting me from another world, sucking my life force from me in return for taking his. "Damn him!" I repeated to myself.

Maria noticed my odd behavior, but I denied its existence and blamed it on the demands of physical labor. I continued to suffer in silence. It was the seventh day in a row that my morning was plagued with vomit.

Panic hit me, as did a horrible realization.

"Ada…" Maria spoke to me softly, "is everything alright? Are you sick?"

My eyes avoided Maria's with the inability to uphold the lie. "No. No, it's not alright. I think I'm pregnant…that bastard." I spat violently at the thought of his face. "Even dead, he ruins me."

Maria stared at me, concerned with the anger that exuded from me.

We sat facing each other on our bedroom floor.

"Are you sure?" she asked.

I nodded. "I can feel it within me. A part of him he left behind to grow and drain my vitality. I have been so exhausted, I feel disgusting. I want it out of me!"

At this point, I was shaking and thoroughly enraged. "I want to be clean again!"

"Alright," Maria said calmly and took my hand. "Tomorrow, we will go and find a clinic."

When I awoke in the morning, I was fearless, ready to undergo the procedure that would return me to myself.

Hand-in-hand, we stood in a long line outside a makeshift medical tent just to try and make an appointment.

"There are no openings," we were told. "Try next month."

We went to the next clinic, and then the next. By sunset, the only thing aborted was my ambition. Every clinic had turned me away.

Back in our apartment, I lay exhausted.

"We just need to get food or money, something to barter with at the abortion clinic," Maria stated.

"How?" I asked bluntly. The question lingered in the air for several seconds of quiet.

"I will figure it out," Maria answered with conviction. "We have always figured it out," she added, squeezing my hand.

I believed her. With all my faith, I needed to believe her.

There was talk among the other rubble women of back-alley abortions. "I am awaiting an opening at a clinic," I told them.

Several of them scoffed. "By the time they get to you, you will be delivering," they told me. "You need to find someone else to do the procedure before it is too late."

Following this advice, I began asking around. The stories of others poured forth from neighbors about women who had died from complications surrounding the unsafe abortions done by amateurs. Yet some survived.

As for our German doctors, most were dead and the nurses left lacked the required training. Abortions had been illegal in Nazi Germany.

"We have to get you into the Red Cross clinic," Maria said when I told her my options. "They know what they are doing," she insisted.

A week passed and, through word of mouth, I managed to find a more reliable option—the daughter of a nurse who had learned the procedure from her mother. The downside was that that was the only thing she knew. If there were any complications, the girl had no further medical knowledge.

"She accepts payment in ration cards," I told Maria, who became livid upon hearing my plan.

"Ada, are you insane! You survived the whole war only to risk your life at the hands of a teenager?"

Maria was shaking her head in disbelief.

"I can't take this anymore!" I yelled. "I need this thing out of me! It is killing me!"

Maria paced the room anxiously. "Give me two days..."

"For what? What can you possibly do?" I could hardly control my skeptic tone.

Maria's eyes narrowed onto me. "Damn it, Ada! I need two days!" she barked, firmly cutting off the conversation.

When I awoke, Maria was already gone. I went to work, but she was not there, either. Evening fell and worry plagued me. I tried to remain calm. It's finally happened, I thought to myself. I have pushed her to do something crazy. Another twenty minutes passed as my legs carried me in circles around the kitchen. I should not have told her. I should have solved the problem myself.

The door finally opened, and Maria leaped through it. She was glowing with excitement, completely distracting me from my worried state.

I hurried over to her and said, "Maria, what is it! What happened?"

"Darling, Ada— Before you stands the new employee of the American occupying forces of Berlin!" She announced with an animated American salute.

"What do you mean? Are you working for the Americans?" I asked, stunned. "But—that's impossible!"

"It almost was. First thing in the morning, I went straight to British headquarters to secure a position as a translator. I was there for hours waiting to speak to someone. Finally, when I did, they didn't want me! 'We already have translators,' they said. I insisted anyway. 'Not only am I fluent in German, but Russian, English, and some French!' They didn't bat an eye but just politely escorted me out like I was some mad woman.

"Ada, I was livid! Then I realized I had gone into action without a backup plan, but I still had a shot with the Americans."

"So, I proceeded directly to the headquarters of General Floyd Lavinius Parks!" she reported in an exaggerated military manner.

"And, who is that?" I asked.

"Really?" Maria's shoulders slumped in defeat. "You are so detached from reality that it's almost shameful. General Parks is the American Military Governor of Berlin's sector three, where we lived with Lara."

"So you saw the general and he hired you? Doing what?" I asked in disbelief.

"Well, I didn't see the general just yet, but I would be happy to do so in the near future." Maria piqued my curiosity.

"You see, after several long hours of trying, begging, and insisting, I finally got the chance to speak to a major who was the general's Chief of Staff. He runs the American Headquarters' bureaucracy machine, so to speak. That was phase one. Next, I offered myself as a translator again. He wasn't interested in me...at first," she added mischievously. "But then we got to chatting... And I began phase three. 'I am an excellent addition to your office,' I explained. 'I speak Russian, German, English, and even a little French. Being separated from my family in Austria and working as a nurse in Berlin's hospitals has left me feeling so disconnected, so isolated.' I looked longingly at him when I said this.

'You must understand how it feels to be so far away from everything you know. To wake up each morning alone, not remembering how the touch of another human being feels like because you are so lost in surviving this horrible, horrible war… Please, I just need a distraction…to stay sane.'

"Mind you; we had already been talking for an hour before I ended with that bit of seductive dramatics."

"You mean to tell me he fell for that?" I asked doubtfully.

"Ada, every man wants a woman to rescue. I made him feel like he was that person. And in a way, he could be. So, starting tomorrow, I report to the American headquarters for work!"

"In exchange for what?" I questioned gravely.

"Don't you dare make a face. We need money and connections to get you in at an abortion clinic. It was partly my fault that I left you alone in the apartment that night. You just

worry about regaining some strength and I will worry about everything else." She left to make tea.

That was when I finally realized that what was keeping Maria running were two things: Helga's dying plea for her to survive and my safety. A steady job in the American administration was like winning a lottery ticket. It meant survival.

Maria left for her first day of work early. With her nightly returns, she brought with her bizarre stories that made me gasp.

"I can eat whatever I want there!" Maria said excitedly with big eyes. "And not just me—any German employee. The military kitchen has real meat and even fruits! But imagine this: We are not allowed to take any of our leftovers home to feed our families!"

"What do they do with it?" I asked wide-eyed.

"Toss it in the trash!"

"No!" I gasped. The thought of food going to waste because of some stupid rule while people starved drove me up the wall. Why do people let suffering continue when it is so easy to stop?

"We need to figure out how I can sneak out some food," said Maria.

That night, I sewed strips of fabric into the lining of Maria's long skirts.

And when Maria returned from work the next day, she lifted her skirt and twirled around comically. Half a loaf of bread dangled from the thin fabric she had laced through the crust. In her stockings were wrapped pieces of salami.

"If there were any dogs left in this city, they would have nipped at my heels!" She laughed.

In that way, Maria managed to bring home hard cheese, sachets of sugar, breads, dry sausages, and even some caramels.

"The Americans are very segregated from us," Maria explained. "Razumov…" She paused after saying his name, remembering that he was no longer part of her present. "He used to tell me that the Soviets eventually adopted a policy to engage with locals."

"Not that that is always a good thing," I chimed in dryly.

"Yes, well, it's strange because the American administration forbids any fraternization." Maria continued, "Interactions are subject to court-martial. I don't see why they do it. It is only widening the gap between Berliners and the Americans."

"Maybe they want the distance from us," I offered.

We sipped the rest of our weak coffee in silence, wondering how Hitler's ruined dream would affect our futures. The thought of the rest of the world hating us became a genuine concern.

I became noticeably pregnant while Maria did her best to secure relationships with the Americans, especially those who had connections to medical staff in clinics. We were getting closer and closer to our goal, but then, the life inside me kicked.

My mind cleared in an instant. There was an innocent being within me. Like me, all it wanted and needed was love. Right then and there, I knew I would not be able to go through with it.

I began avoiding serious talks with Maria and changing the subject when she spoke of clinics or who she had managed to befriend. I felt terrible. My secret, of course, did not last long. Maria was becoming clearly annoyed with my behavior. She cornered me one night after work.

"Ada, listen. I finally secured a spot for you with a lot of help from a few Americans I befriended. I know you are scared, but I will go with you to the appointment—we have to go tomorrow."

I looked down at my feet miserably. I made Maria go through so much effort and now I was backing out.

"I can't," I whispered.

"Yes. You can..." Maria said reassuringly.

"No, the baby moved and I…I just can't." I looked up at her cautiously. Her eyes were ablaze.

"Why the hell didn't you say anything! I have been working tirelessly to get you what you wanted!"

"I know…I'm sorry, it just happened!"

Maria had already walked out, slamming the door behind her. I stood staring at our front door, immobilized by guilt. Ten minutes passed and then ten more. The stairwell remained quiet. Gathering my inner strength, I proceeded downstairs to find Maria and make things right. The thought of giving birth and raising a child without Maria's love and support was inconceivable.

I did not have to look far. Maria was sitting outside the lobby door on a wrecked cement slab. She looked small and fragile in the moonlight, though this clashed with the surreal inner strength that I knew pulsed within her.

I took her hand in mine. "Maria, this was all so unexpected, I…"

"It's alright. There is no need to apologize. This is your decision."

The night wrapped around us quietly, echoing our words off the stone graveyard that was Berlin. An image, no matter how many times I saw, I still could not get accustomed to.

"It is not just my decision," I said. "It must be *our* decision. You are my only family." Maria's eyes met mine. They were pale, reflecting the full moon above. She said nothing. Instead, she stood and embraced me. Relief swept over me. In the darkness, we felt our way back up the stairs into our apartment. Maria entered our hallway, and suddenly turned to me, animated with whatever thought had crossed her mind.

"We can make this work, Ada, but only on one condition."

"What is it?" Concern returned to me.

"I will be our baby's Godmother!"

The urge to laugh suddenly came over me. "Who else would be?" I shouted excitedly, knowing I had made the right choice.

With that decision, a joy was lit within me, and, over the next few months, a love like I had never known before grew alongside my belly. My appetite grew as well. I was ready to eat anything and everything in sight. With Maria's job, we had a steady supply of stolen provisions, but a problem soon developed.

"Two of the girls got caught taking food home from headquarters." Maria walked through the front door after work. "They were shoving leftovers into their stockings and, wouldn't you know, one of them tried smuggling a can of tuna. Of course, the damn thing slid down her stocking and hit her ankle as soon as she started walking. Right away, one of the officers began checking everyone else. Then another poor girl got caught. They were fired immediately."

"What are we going to do?" I asked anxiously. "Soon, I won't be able to work heaping rubble! What ration card will I get then?!"

"Ada, don't worry about anything! Stress is not good for our baby!" Maria knelt to speak to my stomach. "We love you so much, little one," she whispered. "I will figure something out."

Maria began working long, late hours. Some nights, she did not even return home. Those nights, I did not sleep either. When she did return, bags of canned goods and bread were under her arms. I did not ask where they came from, although I had a good idea.

My presumption was soon justified when the major's driver began arriving to deliver the groceries once a week. The major was risking his military career doing so. I wanted to thank him, but I knew it came at a price: Maria. So, I thanked her instead.

Before Christmas of 1945, I gave birth to a healthy baby girl bearing the woman's name solely responsible for my survival: Maria. I had been calling Maria by the name Helga for so long that this seemed to give my friend a second chance at a new life. It was beautiful to hear the name in the house again.

December turned into January, and a bitter frost set on Berlin, the coldest winter in history. As if the war had not killed enough people.

Maria's job and relationship with the major was our savior. On our block, women and children crowded into our lobby sleeping in heaps like dogs in the arctic for warmth. We would share some of our food with the children and elderly—small portions to not raise suspicions.

The frost died down in March, taking with it the lives of sick and weak Berliners. By the spring of 1946, we all prayed that from now on, death would only visit those whose time had come naturally.

In April, we celebrated little Maria's five-month birthday. It is a memory I cherish for two reasons. The first being the feeling of a fresh start, of a hopeful future. The Berlin streets had been cleared by rubble women who now shifted their attention to ruined buildings. The sky above us was a clear bright blue as if it had never seen the war. People smiled in the warm spring weather around us, riding tarnished bicycles and going about their days. Friends took their breakfasts in the dining rooms of their upper-floor apartments that still lacked walls or ceilings. Nobody cared; we were just happy to be alive.

We took little Maria to what was left of Tiergarten Park. As we walked, we read the messages people had written on walls to find each other.

"Emma, are you alive? I am residing at Otto's."

"Walter, I am looking for you endlessly, my love. Frieda."

Sometimes there would be responses, "Yes! I am alive! I am coming to you!"

Those rare moments made me hug little Maria close. Spring flowers opened to new life, perfuming the air with the soft smell of approaching summer. Maria and I wondered what the new Berlin would be like. The old Berlin had been the center of cosmopolitan Europe, but its soul had been killed years back. What would it be now—and how would we fit into it?

The second reason this memory is crucial is because of what followed it a few days later. It was a Wednesday. I held my breath the entire time Maria explained to me that she had been offered a job in Paris. The US Military Intelligence was transferring the major to Paris and he insisted she go with him. I felt myself exhale only after Maria assured me that she had, of course, turned down the offer. Yet, I had relaxed too soon.

The next evening Maria returned home anguished. "I saw Karl today."

"Who?" I had forgotten the name altogether.

"My uncle," she answered with slight irritation. "Karl."

"Karl, of course! Where in the world did you see him?"

"The worst place I could see him: American headquarters."

My eyes lit up. A hundred thoughts flew past me. "Did he see you? He can expose you instantly!"

"I know!" Maria was blatantly worried. "He did not see me, but he still has the chance."

"What do you mean?"

"That Nazi rat got hired by the Americans to restore Berlin's medical services."

Her answer paralyzed me. "My God…what are you going to do?"

Maria's apologetic eyes told me what I feared before her lips phrased it. "Ada, I no longer have a choice. I told the major I am accepting his offer to go to Paris."

I instantly broke into panicked tears. "You can't leave me! You can't! What will I do? What will we do?"

Prepared for such a reaction, Maria was armed with a bevy of solutions to calm me. "This is temporary. I have already arranged it so that you will receive my pay every two weeks. All you need to do is pick it up at American headquarters. You have to be strong. Both of us do. Karl can find me and he will expose me. The Americans think I'm Austrian, and if they find out I lied about my identity, I will be fired or worse. If that happens, then little Maria will have no support. We can't be selfish. It is her life we are both worried about now."

I knew Maria was right, but I was devastated. The thought of being on my own was terrifying. Maria promised me that the major had given her permission to visit Berlin in three to six months. Ultimately, that was one promise that Maria would be unable to keep.

In just a few days, we said our tearful goodbyes filled with the comforting phrase of "just a few months." We had no way to know that those few months would turn into fifteen long years. The next time we would see each other would be in 1961.

After her departure, I was left with a task to accomplish. I was to find Maria's uncle Karl and tell him the location of his brother's grave within the woods in hopes that Karl could locate and properly rebury Commander Ritter's body. Secondly, I was to tell him the unfortunate end to his brother's life and his niece's, Maria Ritter.

Karl was not difficult to find. He was a prominent man around Berlin and, as a physician hired by the Americans, he stood out even more. Getting a meeting with him was also simple. After all, I was carrying news of his brother and niece.

To say the least, Karl was gravely upset. He remembered me when I walked into his makeshift office. I thought he would be cross. Maria did choose to stay with us, supposedly costing her life. Still, on the contrary, Karl was extremely thankful for the map of his brother's grave, the U-boatmen's story of the commander's final moments, and the circumstances leading to Maria's death.

In a few weeks, Karl showed up at my door, unexpected, much like the first time I met him, but now under much different circumstances.

He said, "I secured papers to investigate into the outskirts of Berlin. We found my brother's body."

We held each other for a moment. I too, loved the commander. Karl was disturbed by Maria's death, and I shared his emotions completely. In a way, she felt dead to me, too.

"We buried my brother next to his wife and poor Maria. Ada, I cannot thank you enough. How are you living? Please, let me help you."

From that day, Karl was extraordinarily kind to me, taking care of everything, from renovating my apartment to finding proper food for little Maria. He was honored by her name, and, in an ironic turn of events, we became friends. The man who had at one point almost taken Maria away from me, a decision that would have cost me my life, was now providing little Maria with a better life.

Chapter 22
Aftermath

Maria and I kept in touch through letters as best we could. It helped us move onward with life, knowing we were not alone in this crazy world. In a few months, the major she had been working for returned to America, leaving Maria a secured position in Paris.

"He was a good man," she wrote at the end of their affair. "But as you know, I had no emotions toward him. We helped one another cope, I suppose."

The next letter I received held exciting news: In a strange twist of fate, Maria fell in love with a young American officer from New York, whom she eventually married.

I was astonished at first, but it led me to evaluate my own life and Maria's. The both of us suffered severe loss and heartbreak, but Maria kept moving forward, refusing to give in to her inner demons. And so, life rewarded her with its greatest gift: love.

Unlike Maria, I kept my heart closed. The following years haunted me with a past I could not put to rest. Any male relationships that developed would break with one thought: If we were at war, you would act just like the rest of them. It was irrational.

The only man I could have loved was Max, the young U-boater who gave us those cigarettes. Maybe it was because I had met him before I lost my faith or because there was genuine honesty and tenderness about him. I relived the moment our eyes met over and over. Without success, I looked for him after the war. At that point, I left it up to fate to join us, but fate never did. I assumed him dead.

My love concentrated on raising my daughter. It was odd. Odd to think that I could love someone so much who came from someone I hated so deeply. Just like many instances during the war, it served as a reminder that terrible situations can bring forth blessings.

Maria helped me raise little Maria both financially and emotionally. Even after she married John and moved to the United States with him, she kept sending financial support.

Each year was better, but still extremely difficult. Germany had to rebuild itself from the desecrated ground up.

I read about Maria's new life. She traveled across America filling her letters with vivid descriptions, but even then, there was an underlying sadness to them; It was as if the pen with which she wrote could not ignore her deepest thoughts. Of course, I knew why without her having to tell me. Maria continued living under Helga's identity, and this heavily burdened her life.

"Why don't you just tell John the truth?" I asked her once. He loved her so much; I knew he would not care, but Maria was too terrified. She blamed herself for not being honest before their marriage and now, the thought of losing him was enough to keep her mouth shut forever. Although, we had some close calls.

In 1951, a stranger came to my door. His name was Kent Sullivan. He was from the United States and he was here to find Helga. Immediately my guard went up. What sort of trap was this?

I invited him in and put on some coffee. Though I was suspicious, my intuition told me that this man had more problems of his own; that he had come on a personal matter. In a few minutes, I found out my intuition had been right.

Kent Sullivan was the major Maria had worked for in Berlin, with whom she moved to Paris and who helped us through that winter. I was bewildered. Here he was in my apartment, years later, looking for the woman he said was the love of his life.

My first impulse was to embrace him. We had survived because he had let his affections toward Maria overpower his concerns for himself.

"I want to thank you…" I started to say, but immediately stopped when confusion lit up his face. He did not know who I was or what he had done for little Maria and I. Quickly, I switched my words, "for loving her." I finished. "She was an incredible woman."

"Was?" The word left his lips in one shaky breath.

Understanding the danger Maria was in, I attempted to explain that we had lost contact with each other. The man's expression fell.

"You must know something?" he pleaded.

"Have you searched for her in Paris?" I asked, hoping to switch the man's direction.

"Of course!" he answered. "After I returned to the States, Helga never left my mind. It ruined my marriage..." He paused. "I just could not stop thinking about her. I searched for her everywhere. She either stayed in Paris or returned to Austria or Germany. Paris had nothing for me. Here I am again, ready to turn West Berlin upside down for her! Even your apartment—I had no idea where it was. I found my old driver, flew him here, and he found your building from memory!"

He was on the verge of tears now. "Please tell me you have a clue for me!"

I swallowed my nerves. The only thing I wanted was to give this man hope. Some sort of relief—an unspoken thank you for what he had done for us. But, how could I? Maria was happily married.

Taking his hand in mine, I did my best to convince him again that we had lost contact after her move to Paris. "I am so sorry, Mr. Sullivan, but I think she died there, because one day her letters stopped coming from France."

He left my apartment and I watched him walk down the street from my window, an emotionally broken man with nothing left to live for. I prayed for him.

Over the phone, I retold the story to Maria. She sat silently on the other line for a minute.

"How many years will it take for the war to stop crippling us?"

"Endless years," I answered.

"Neither of us have that sort of time."

One day in the winter of 1961, Maria said, "Ada, I will be in Paris in three months. John is going for business. Will you meet me there?"

My heart raced. "Of course I will be there!"

This meeting remains forever vivid in my mind. I waited for her under the Arc de Triomphe. Cars ran circles around me, and my head was a daze filled with the faces of strangers as I searched for Maria.

"I will be in a pale-yellow rain jacket," she said.

Every spot of yellow made my heart race: a child's sweater, an umbrella, the damn advertisement poster on a passing truck. And then, I saw her. Clear as day. The same beautiful girl that comforted me, protected me, and breathed life into me during the darkest times of my life was walking toward me, now a beautiful vibrant woman.

Once her gray eyes locked with my own, we ran to each other like mad-women; colliding in strong embrace in the middle of the road. Cars swerved around us, honking for us to move out of the way. People gawked at the commotion. I saw their curious stares through tear-filled eyes.

They could never understand the meaning of this moment. It felt as though we were embracing not only each other, but our former selves. We cried heavily. Those memories, all of them came rushing back one by one and we wondered how we went on living; how we were still living. Happily, nonetheless. We promised each other that once a year, we would meet again. We had to. We kept this promise.

The story of mine, of Maria's and Helga's life, is rare. Not because of our experience in wartime, but because of the true love and friendship we found within it. We discovered the ultimate life force, surviving because of it, continuing onward because of it.

I look back at my life now and I am confronted with regret. The war had ended so long ago. It had been years, but within me, the conflict continued. I let it continue. I see now how it has crippled my choices and their inevitable outcomes. I should have left the war, Berlin, all of it behind.

I did not understand this then because, during the war, I ignored as many emotions as I could. I had to keep my sanity, but those experiences, never left me. Instead, they appeared when I was most relaxed, unexpected guests I had hoped never to see again.

The most frequent, was rape. Countless years I spent obsessing over the same pointless question. Why? What had I done to deserve it? What right did this soldier have to do what he did to me? To countless others? It was not our faults that the SS and Nazi fanatics had murdered their families.

Deciding to face my trauma head-on, I began seeking it to understand it. The Balkan civil war that had started in 1991 led me closer to an answer. Before it started, the Serbians, Bosnians, and Albanians lived together in relative peace within the same country. The onset of war brought up pure evil, pinning one group against the other. Bosnian Serbs took rape to another level, establishing genocide rape camps. There, hundreds of Bosnian Muslim women and girls were raped repeatedly by Serbian paramilitary until they were impregnated. An estimated 12,000 to 50,000 women suffered in this way. Bosnian Muslim men were killed.

The goal was to change Bosnia's genetic makeup, by ethnically cleansing out Bosnian genes and replacing them with Serbian genes.

Less than five years later, the same atrocities plagued Serbian women by the Kosovo militiamen. These rapes were a preplanned military strategy. Systematic. Effective. Inhumane. I continued to follow these repeated atrocities with horror.

During the year 1995, the exhibition War of Annihilation: Crimes of the Wehrmacht 1941 to 1944 opened to the Berlin public. Many Germans protested in the streets, outraged at the photographs and documents which showed the atrocities committed not by the SS but by our regular Wehrmacht soldiers in the Eastern Front and the Balkans.

At least 100,000 children were born due to the estimated 800,000 to 1 million rapes German soldiers inflicted across the Soviet Union alone. Our men, our common good, well-mannered army boys, had been as brutal as hardcore Nazis. I left disgusted and devastated with a heightened hatred toward all men.

Yet the more I dissected the pain within me and around me, the more I realized that it was not just about the act of rape: Rape was just a strategy. It was about war. I remained struck by the notion of how we continue to let it happen.

I have heard the theory that humans are violent by nature. I do not believe this, and I will say this much: Ordinary people do not start wars. Power-hungry leaders use nationalistic pride to feed their own thirst for greed and power.

Their fellow citizens, you and I, are disposable. To them, the value of human life is nonexistent. We are the ones who pay the price of our leaders' decisions, as they escape responsibility and go on to get rich, and give documentary interviews after losing power. The families of the dead are left to forever grieve.

Who will end this madness if not each of us? We hold a responsibility to ensure the lives of one another, and that is the only way to ensure our own.

—Ada Brandt

Chapter 23

Anna turned the last page, stunned. Around her, the light had dimmed, but she failed to notice. The room itself sensed the setting sun, and automatically turned on soft accent lighting. Anna snapped out of her trance. Her vision refocused on the garden outside the window bathed in dusk.

She shifted her gaze around the room right until it landed on her grandmother's portrait. The painting blended into the room's shadows; a carefully positioned light illuminated Grandmother's figure giving it the impression as if it were floating.

They stared at one another. A deep understanding carved its way into Anna. Grandmother had lied to her family, to a lot of people, to Anna. She had broken laws, moral codes, and societal taboos. She lived under a false identity her entire life and yet, she had done it all to ensure the survival of Ada, herself, and little Maria. Anna continued to admire the painting, fully realizing how extraordinary a woman her grandmother truly was.

The door opened and Anna laid eyes on little Maria, now an older woman and the only other person who knew the truth. A sudden desire to hug Maria Arnett consumed Anna. It must have been evident on her face, because Maria Arnett swiftly came over to her. As if on cue, the met each other in a long embrace. Tears wet the sheer sleeves of Maria Arnett's blouse, but Anna could not stop them. They held one another, the granddaughter and goddaughter of the same woman who silently gazed at them from the portrait.

"She is with us, you know," Maria Arnett said. "In this very room. At this very moment."

Anna nodded; she, too, could feel her grandmother's tranquil presence. Anna wiped her eyes and regained her seat on the sofa. There was a lot that needed to be said.

"I did not know this story myself," Maria Arnett began. "Not until I came into my later years. I flew my mother to see Maria in France in 2003. You were there, too." She winked at Anna. "But you were only a toddler; do you remember anything from that trip?"

Anna did remember, but she was never sure where the memory had come from. There were no photographs to match that specific recollection.

"Yes. There was a garden," Anna said. "I mostly recall sensations—the sun hitting my face through flowers and tall grass. A feeling of carefree happiness, laughing female voices, but that is about it."

Maria Arnett smiled in response. "That is a lovely memory, and you are right; there was a garden. The four of us stayed in a villa with a marvelous lush garden that grew unrestricted by any sort of design. It was so very freeing sitting there, and you especially enjoyed exploring it. Some of the flowers and ferns were taller than you!"

Anna beamed, savoring each detail of an existence she barely remembered.

"My mother was very ill then, dying of cancer. She knew that this was probably the last time she would see her friend. That is why she brought her finished memoir with her. In the villa, she gave it to Maria to read. I did not know what it was at the time. Back then, I had thought it was just a captivating story because your grandmother sat reading it in the garden from breakfast until early evening.

I, too, came into the garden hoping to snap some photographs of the flowers but instead caught sight of Maria. The book lay closed on her lap. I remember the expression she wore vividly. It conjured so many emotions. Fear, love, strength, hatred. As if they had all combined to create an entirely new expression. Her presence was elsewhere. She was in another space and time foreign to the rest of us. The artist in me had to capture it. Quickly, I snapped a few photographs, hoping to seize the moment in secret. And I think I did."

Maria Arnett then nodded at her grandmother's portrait. Anna stared back at the portrait in disbelief.

"Do you mean this painting is from the photograph you took after Grandmother finished reading Ada's memoir?"

"Yes, exactly!" Maria Arnett answered. "After we returned to Berlin, I showed the photographs to my mother. Curiosity led me to question what was behind Maria's surreal expression. Silently, my mother left the room and returned with the same purple book Maria had been reading in the garden.

"Maria agreed with me," my mother told me. "Our truth is yours. After all, you are a part of it."

Immediately I began reading it. Like you, Anna, I was shaken to my core. My mother had always told me that my father had been a German U boatman who had heroically fought his way into Berlin past the Russian front line to help evacuate my mother and Maria. She had even described him to me in detail. He had kind and sincere dark eyes. She said his name was Max, that he died protecting us.

"Then I found out that Max was someone my mother had only met once. My birth father was a rapist. Such a horrible excuse for a human being that even his comrades did not want to associate with him.

"A fortune teller once told me that the creation of a child out of anything but love would inflict hardship on the child's spirit. I finally understood what she had meant. My spirit had always known its own struggle. Since that realization, my art has shifted to express freedom and peace."

Maria Arnett stared with adoration at Anna's grandmother's portrait on the wall.

"This piece was my first in this new style. It became my salvation. After finishing the memoir, I locked myself in my studio and purged every bit of chaotic emotion out of myself to create it in one exhausting week. My mother's pain, Maria's sacrifices, tragic losses, and their strength; everything went onto the canvas. I was a mad-woman armed with a paintbrush crying, yelling, laughing. The war was running its course through me as I layered the paint thick and angular.

"The painting was a mess, but then a calm fell over me. With each brushstroke, I smoothed out the oils until Maria came to life. She glowed with perseverance. I was finished. Afterward, I collapsed into sleep for two days."

Maria Arnett laughed at herself and continued. "It sounds ridiculous now... Poor mother was so worried, but since then, I have found such peace. I can only hope you find your own path to it."

Anna sat in a silence heavy with sentiment. Thoughts raced through her, but there were too numerous to verbalize correctly. Maria Arnett patiently stroked her hand.

An antique writing desk stood in the corner of the room. Maria Arnett walked over to it and unlocked the top drawer with a small key kept in a cast-iron zebra-shaped jewelry box. Anna watched her remove a book and walk back to the couch. The book was purple velvet. Anna's eyes widened.

"Is that the original?" she asked softly.

Maria Arnett handed it to her. The once-thick book felt heavy in her hand despite missing over a third of its ripped-out pages. A faint smell of dust, fire, and perfumed oil drifted into her nostrils.

"It is," Maria Arnett answered as she watched Anna flip through the tiny cursive German words.

Every delicate page was covered in writing from top to bottom with no blank margins. Some of the sentences were even written upside down with arrows pointing to where the reader ought to go next.

"It is a bit more than that." She paused, waiting for Anna to meet her gaze. "The only paper my mother felt appropriate to write the memoir on was within this book—the same book Maria had found in the bombed-out perfume store so long ago. My mother had kept it all these years as a symbol of hope and survival. Eventually, I typed up the memoir and translated it into English myself—knowing I would meet her family one day."

"What do you plan to do with your mother's writing?" Anna asked.

"As you now know, my mother came up with the idea that your grandmother take on Helga's identity. Even though it saved her life, it was something your grandmother could never free herself from—a blessing and a curse. My mother knew this and set out to put the issue to rest as best as she could. The result was this memoir. Written for me, for Maria, and for her children and grandchildren.

"My mother did not want the truth to die with her and Maria. The truth was not just important; it was extraordinary and extremely human. After my mother passed, I asked Maria if I could publish it anonymously in Germany using altered names. The world needed to read it, I argued. To understand what Berliners had gone through and what the war really did to people. Maria agreed to the idea, but only after her death. This past year, I stopped hearing from Maria, and I began to expect the worst. When you showed up at my doorstep today, my suspicions were sadly confirmed."

Anna nodded solemnly and said, "It has been more than a year now. Grandmother died peacefully. Reading." She tried to smile.

"Anna, I am truly sorry, but I am also grateful that her passing has brought you here to me. This is now our story and we have to decide what to do with it—together. Let me show you something."

Maria Arnett took the book from Anna and flipped it to the last page where an envelope only a few centimeters wide was taped. From it, Maria withdrew a passport-size photograph of a young woman with short hair. The woman's full face looked familiar.

"This is Helga's passport photo, which my mother had peeled off of her *Volkskarte* to replace with Maria's photograph. My mother kept this picture on her nightstand, and carried it with her on each trip to see Maria. She believed that, in this way, Helga was always a part of their reunions in spirit."

Anna studied the photograph carefully. "This should be with Helga's family. I think we should return it."

"Whatever you wish, Anna, but we need to find them first."

"I have already found them. Helga's relatives are still living in Sankt Gilgen—in Austria. They desperately looked for her after the war. If you don't mind, I will give this photograph to them. They only have one photograph of her as a child."

Maria Arnett nodded in approval. "Of course."

The two women sat in prolonged silence. They soon returned to the portrait of Maria, who continued to listen to their conversation.

"You know I was offered hundreds of thousands of euros for this portrait," Maria Arnett began, "by art dealers who saw it while visiting my studio. But I never wanted to sell it. How could this woman who had meant so much to my mother and to me be truly appreciated while in some random person's home or as part of a museum display next to the paintings of flowers and seascapes? The art dealers would tell me that the painting evoked a certain mystery for them but of course, they will never know it nor the circumstances under which I painted this piece."

"I can understand that," Anna agreed.

"She is my best work, but she no longer belongs to me. It is time for her to go home." Maria Arnett squeezed Anna's hand. "To you and your family."

Choked with emotion, Anna tried to reason a fair exchange. "Maria, I can't take this—"

Maria Arnett cut her off each time with curtness in her voice. "Anna, this is a gift. You cannot refuse gifts."

Anna once again embraced Maria Arnett, who could not even imagine the impact this painting would have on Anna's grandfather and the rest of the family.

With the thought of her grandfather, Anna's mind returned to the present, which she had temporarily forgotten about.

"Maria, you said that this memoir is my story, too..." She paused, evaluating Maria Arnett's reaction. "I hope this is not too forward of me, but I have a close friend, Frederick. He is a historian working on his Ph.D. focusing on the German Navy during World War II. I think this memoir would be a breakthrough for him and, if it weren't for his involvement, I would not have found you. May I let him read it?"

A twinkle shown in Maria Arnett's eye. "A close friend?" She teased, "As in, a boyfriend?"

Anna blushed, giving herself away. "Not exactly, but I'll admit I am more than infatuated."

"Anna, if this man has helped you find me, then I am grateful to him. You can even bring him here to examine the original. I know how historians can get with copies of documents," she added playfully.

Anna sat on the outside steps of Maria Arnett's villa, waiting for Benedikt's arrival. Her thoughts wandered. In Arizona, the word memories had held a general meaning, such as Anna's memories from childhood and so forth. It lacked the significance it held now, which was synonymous with the definition of a key.

One by one, Anna had connected the memories of people, of cities, of books, and of silent photographs. Each memory had been meaningless when alone but became weighed down with significance once it was linked to its counterpart.

Anna thought back to her friends and the people around her. How many memories were idly waiting to be connected so that they too could become magnificent stories that would possibly change absolutely everything?

BOOK II

THE WEB OF TRUTH

Chapter 24

Memories from Ada's journal flooded Anna's mind uncontrollably. Maria Arnett had offered for Anna to stay till morning, but the only thing she wanted was to be alone with her thoughts among the few familiar things that had nostalgically traveled with her from a now distant life.

Benedikt's luxurious Mercedes pulled slowly into the driveway like a creeping panther against the night, but Anna's thoughts were still in 1945. Helga's last words to her grandmother, "I love you...please survive..." were the force behind her grandmother Maria's courage and determination to defy all odds. In a sense, her grandmother lived her life happily for herself and for Helga.

"Thank you, Helga," Anna silently said to the heavens. "You saved my grandmother and, in turn, my father and me."

In front of her, Benedikt opened the passenger side door and Anna got in, she would return, and she would be bringing Frederick.

"Ms. Anna," Benedikt impatiently began, "I assume things went well?"

Benedikt was unsuccessfully attempting to contain his desperate need for information. The thick flesh that made up his lips pushed together tightly; two balloons ready to pop.

The panther turned onto a curvy road illuminating the way to Berlin with its bright headlights. Anna calculated how long she could remain quiet before Benedikt erupted. She estimated a taut four minutes. After a long drink of water from the Pellegrino bottle she'd taken from the blue room's table, Anna decided to get right to it.

"Ada gave your father the map," she began, "and she told him about Maria's death in the makeshift hospital."

Benedikt nodded once, keeping his eyes on the road.

"What she didn't tell you was that it was Helga—their friend—who had died there. Maria survived. She was my grandmother."

Benedikt jerked the car and pulled over on the side of the winding neighborhood road. His small glistening eyes beamed at her. The lip line of his mouth now hung slightly open. "Maria survived?" He asked in disbelief that tinged with anger. "Why did she let all these years pass without saying anything to us!"

Anna left the last question unanswered. Benedikt spoke more to himself now, or possibly to the moon that hung low and full in the sky. "My father had reburied her himself! How could he have made such a mistake? How could Maria deny us the right to know the truth!"

A sort of camaraderie began to form between Benedikt and Anna. She understood the confusion he was feeling far better than he understood it himself. She had been in his shoes before. After all, she had been coping with it since Austria.

"Grandmother took on Helga's identity to save herself from the Soviet secret police. After the war, she married my grandfather, a U.S. Military Intelligence officer who had lost his best friend to a German U-boat attack. She could not bring herself to admit who her father had been. Fear stopped her from ever reclaiming her true identity or contacting anyone."

Benedikt was deep in thought. A few minutes passed and Anna closed her eyes. The day had truly drained her. She wished Benedikt's questions would fade away into silence. This, of course, was unlikely.

His voice sounded as if to spite her hope for peace. "You are, then, my second cousin—a blood relation. All the way from Arizona!"

His words caught Anna off-guard and popped her eyes back open. Somehow the idea of being related to a man such as Benedikt did not fully register until now, but he was absolutely right. It was an uncomfortable feeling.

Benedikt's bulky body then shifted awkwardly in its seat toward her. "How funny is it that you, too, are pulled toward the practice of law. It must be genetics, indeed. Generations pass, but certain traits remain."

Benedikt's initial aggravation toward Maria was replaced with a sort of pride for Anna's similarity to him.

"Even the ridiculous way in which you tricked me the first time we met! That is something I would have done myself." Benedikt continued, bemused, "I should have recognized my blood in you, but back then, it was an impossibility."

Benedikt's amiable disposition only made Anna more annoyed. *Would Grandmother have approved of keeping a relationship with the family she had detested?*

The thought of Ada calmed Anna's concerns. Karl's and later Benedikt's immense support of Ada and her daughter had to counter whatever negativity was left.

"I suppose we are family then!" Anna answered in artificial delight.

"This, I never expected." Benedikt shifted himself back to face the wheel of his car making the entire automobile bounce under his weight. He pulled back onto the road and continued to ask follow-up questions, many of which surrounded possible negative details about Commander Ritter.

Anna disclosed that Ada had known about Karl's allegiance to the Nazi party during the war. She watched Benedikt's jaw muscles clench. They pulsated until she affirmed her promise of eternal silence.

"I wonder," Anna began in a soft voice, "the portrait of the older woman, which Maria Arnett painted—I assume you have seen it?"

"The woman in the garden? Yes. Art is not my expertise, but I consider it Maria's best work."

"It is stunning," Anna answered, "*She* is stunning…"

Benedikt eyed her suspiciously from behind the wheel. "The woman in the portrait, you mean?"

"Yes, she is Maria Ritter..."

The car jerked to a stop again and Anna felt her body slam into the car's seat belt.

"Don't play these games with me, Anna!"

Benedikt turned to her, heated. An unexpected reaction. Anna found herself entertained by the ability to unnerve Benedikt. She smiled innocently. "I don't play games, Benedikt."

"That portrait is of Maria Ritter?"

"Yes," Anna confirmed, "your first cousin."

Benedikt shook his head in what Anna assumed to be disbelief and once again pulled onto the road. She watched Berlin through the window as her hotel came into view several silent minutes later.

Anna parted ways with Benedikt and eagerly made her way to her hotel room, where calming solitude awaited her.

Falling backward onto the bed, Anna inhaled the smell of the Berlin night wafting in from her open window. It somehow reminded her of Frederick. The idea of telling him this grand revelation recharged her and she sat up in bed searching for his name in her phone. The usual nervous energy with which she called him was gone. She just wanted to speak to him—to someone who would understand the importance of this discovery without being too emotionally involved.

Frederick answered on the fifth ring.

"Frederick...." Anna paused, calming her eagerness, "I have figured it out. Are you busy tomorrow?" she asked without waiting for a reply.

She could hear Frederick switch the phone to his other ear.

"Anna, hello."

For once, his voice was soft, but in the sort of way, a voice gets after a long day of speaking. Not for her specifically.

"I have a full day of lectures tomorrow. What exactly did you figure out?"

"You should cancel your lectures," Anna spoke firmly now. "It turns out that Commander Ritter is my great-grandfather, just like I told you."

Frederick was silent. Anna prepared to counter his doubt. Smugness filled her, but she said nothing.

He finally spoke into the phone, "Anna, whatever you discovered can't be right. You can't be the great-granddaughter of Commander Ritter. We covered this several times."

Anna was amused, "Frederick, your thinking is too linear. It is possible. More so, it is a fact proven by documents."

More silence followed.

"What kind of documents?"

"The kind that could turn a thesis into gold. You can see it all for yourself tomorrow, but only tomorrow. Maria Arnett possess something you must see, and she is leaving for Spain afterward."

"Maria Arnett? The painter?" Frederick asked with surprise.

"Obviously."

"So we are going to meet with Maria Arnett tomorrow, who has some documents that prove that the family of Commander Ritter did not all die, even though they are currently all buried together?"

"Exactly. Turns out, my grandmother was her Godmother."

This time his hesitation was brief. "May I pick you up at ten in the morning?"

"I will see you then."

The blue room at Maria Arnett's was drenched in afternoon sunlight. Anna joined Frederick on the royal blue upholstered sofa after he read the memoirs in solitude. Anna observed him curiously. His slate-gray patterned blazer was tossed carelessly to the side. He had a ruffled way about him, as if he had just lived through the journal's events. His fingers ran across the faded purple binding and the ripped book seams. Frederick's actions were indeed meticulous. He reminded Anna of a paleontologist who, after a long exhausting dig, finally found the bones of a creature that could change the story of evolution. The original journal sat on his lap, but he had only skimmed through it.

Under Anna's instruction, Maria Arnett only gave Frederick access to an edited version of the memoirs, blaming the journal's delicate state. In this way, she was also able to hide sentences highlighting Karl's pro-Nazi sympathies. Anna's promise to Benedikt had to be kept. If Frederick was suspicious, which Anna knew he was, he said nothing. After all, Maria Arnett was doing him a favor.

For the next hour, they discussed the memoirs in detail. Frederick was charged with electricity.

"The story is captivating. You should definitely publish it," said Frederick. "Although I'm not sure if Herr Ritter would want real names used. On the one hand, the commander lives up to his heroic image, but, on the other hand, his daughter was bisexual and cooperated with the Soviets. Contemporary Berlin will accept this, but Ritter's conservative circle may not."

Frederick quieted and looked at Anna. His eyes did not flinch, and Anna found herself feeling uncomfortable. Eventually, she averted her own gaze to the outside garden.

"I owe you an apology." He broke the tension with this unexpected sentence. Anna turned back to face him. His thoughtful expression made it clear that he was serious. "I doubted you."

"That much was obvious," Anna remarked lightly.

"Yes..." He took a drink of wine, giving Anna a moment to breathe. "You were right all along, Anna." Frederick resumed his intense stare.

Her ears picked up the loud drumming of her heart. She prayed that he could not hear it.

"I would like to show you Berlin tonight, the way you should see it, as an apology, if you will let me, of course."

This is it, Anna thought. *A date.* Something she had been hoping for in the confines of herself. However, now that the moment arrived, she found herself wanting to say no—to throw him off, to show him that he didn't have her like he thought he did, that she wouldn't just give in after his standoffish attitude.

Frederick must have sensed her hesitation.

"I understand I have not been on my best behavior with you..."

With you. The last two words made the statement personal. Intimate.

"But you owe it to Berlin to see it how Berliners do. After all, your grandmother was a Berliner."

"Using my poor grandmother to get your way, are you?" she asked coyly.

"I have resorted to this, yes," Frederick grinned. "But also, you have been running around nonstop completing mission impossible. You simply haven't had the chance to really explore our magnificent city."

Anna broke into a deep smile at his reference, a smile that had wanted to free itself since she saw him this morning.

"Let's enjoy Berlin and have fun tonight, Anna."

Chapter 25

Let's enjoy Berlin and have fun tonight, Anna... She repeated Frederick's words to herself curiously.

"Alright, Frederick, but I want a time I will always remember," she had answered with a sly smile.

That night, Anna looked up at the sky, but there was no moon. Or rather, a new moon had risen but was not visible to the naked eye. The city lights blazed brighter than usual against the darkness. They merged with the stars and reflected in the glass walls of the posh high-rise lounge by the hundreds. Anna floated amidst this cosmos, lost to the world that went on spinning down below her.

"Berlin lights up for you tonight, Anna," Frederick said with a smile as he handed her a martini.

Unbeknownst to Anna, the moon watched undetected as she sipped the drink lustily, wholly engulfed by Frederick's charisma.

The night stretched itself forward and onward through morning coffees, afternoon city wanderings, and evening dinners until a full moon now appeared heavy in the sky, filled to the brim with Frederick's extravagance and Anna's newly obtained hedonism.

Had Frederick been an average man, then the past two weeks would have secured physical intimacy between them. Had Anna been an average woman, she would have been confounded as to why nothing had yet to occur. Not even a kiss had been exchanged between them.

Still, Frederick always found ways to touch her: the small of her back, her shoulders, running his fingers up and down her spine until Anna winced with shivers. He caressed her, respectfully or teasingly, never going too far. Amidst this sort of atmosphere, even their innocent lunches became intimate affairs.

Their relations formed a sort of routine, which uncomfortably played on Anna's emotions. In front of the Art'otel, a car door would open. Frederick's outstretched hand would smoothly pull her from the vehicle into his embrace. A kiss would land on her cheek instead of her lips, close enough to where she could almost feel what it would taste like, yet too far to satisfy the building desire for more.

Sent on her way, with the clean smell of his aftershave under her nose, Anna walked toward the hotel lobby casually, refusing to be bothered by his lack of increasing affection.

At the glass lobby doors, she would meet herself, a reflection that showed a different truth. She bit her lip to deny it. *Damn him!*

Frederick looked at her with a gaze that prompted Anna to inquire what he was thinking, although she never did. Often, she would catch his mind elsewhere, in deep thought, far away from her. She wanted to know what his inner world was made of.

He was not keen on talking about himself or his family. All she could muster out of him was that his father owned some sort of construction company. A quick online search revealed that the business was a multi-million European construction behemoth.

"So that *is where his family money came from."*

A search on Frederick, however, produced a rather bare social media presence. He had configured himself into another mystery that she was adamant on deciphering but felt no rush to do so. With each passing day, what had been a tightly closed bud of a city was now being unraveled by Frederick's presence, petal by petal, until the entire metropolis was in bloom. The sensation was incredible.

Frederick opened a beer and handed it to Anna. The heat of that particular Saturday afternoon caused the outside of the bottle to drip with condensation, melting icy streams down her forearm ending at the angle of her elbow. He guided her towards the Berlin Badeschiff—the bathing ship—a big rectangular swimming pool, which floated comically on the River Spree. The perfect solution to the otherwise contaminated river water.

Berliners covered the man-made beach in swarms like the seals on San Diego's shoreline. The locals sprawled on top of one another, fighting for their piece of sun, something Anna, or anyone else from Arizona, was not used to lacking.

Similar to her past experiences by Frederick's side, he seemed to know everyone or, rather, everyone knew him. In a private cabana, a group of his friends laughed while sharing a jovial toast that had spilled beer on everyone.

"Frederick!" exclaimed a tall, curvy blonde planting an exaggerated kiss on his cheek. The top of her black micro bikini left two wet triangular imprints on Frederick's linen shirt. Anna's confidence remained fully intact.

An intense desire to understand the German squeals of something apparently hilarious came over her. Frederick's hand landed on Anna's shoulder.

"Introduce yourselves!" Frederick shouted to the cabana crew over the music. "This is Anna; she is visiting from the USA, from Arizona."

With that, the handshakes and smiling faces turned to confusion as everyone tried to pinpoint where exactly Arizona was.

"It's next to California, below Las Vegas."

"Ohhhh California! California knows how to party..." one of the guys burst into a Notorious B.I.G song.

The blonde cleared her things off a lounge chair, inviting Anna to join her next to an equally attractive brunette casually exhaling vanilla-scented smoke that wrapped around her long-tanned legs.

"Those e-cigarettes are shit, Bernadette; if you're going to quit smoking, then do it correctly," Frederick said with masked seriousness.

Bernadette stuck her tongue out at Frederick. "You never understood me. I don't know what I ever saw in you," she continued mischievously.

"It remains a mystery to all of us," Frederick said with a grin, but he held his gaze on Anna, who was making herself comfortable on the plush lounge chair.

"I'm not about to witness a battle of exes, am I?" Ann asked casually.

"Hardly!" the blonde chimed in. "Frederick may be a heartbreaker, but a classy one." She held her hand over her heart in an exaggerated manner. "Frederick, it still stings..." she cooed.

Frederick sighed and extended his hand to Anna. "Anna, please join me before these two lure you into their devious circle."

The brunette beat off his hand and said, "We are just teasing! Leave Anna to us!"

Anna laughed alongside the crowd, hoping to eradicate the uncomfortable sensation she felt internally. She thought herself to be a good-looking woman, but to be sitting in between two Maxim-model look-a-likes who were also exes was disheartening. No wonder he had been so casual toward her. It seemed that none of them took anything too seriously when it came to past relations.

Anna shook off the feeling immediately. *It doesn't matter!* she told herself. She was here in Europe, immersed in a new world altogether.

Taking a big sip of beer, she focused her attention on Bernadette, who had begun telling her about her graduate studies surrounding Berlin's green efforts.

"Berlin is green, both literally and figuratively. The entire idea of the Green movement blossomed here during the nineteen eighties in West Germany. It gave the green name to the world's political eco-movement as we know it today."

"I did notice that myself," replied Anna. "Everything in Berlin seems to be sporting the label of bio or local."

"It is not only that, green politics is an ideology rooted in social justice, sustainability, and nonviolence."

Anna nodded in agreement. "There is a similar wave on the rise in the U.S. too."

Bernadette arched an eyebrow. "Some places, yes, but you have a lot of catching up to do."

The onset of dusk fell, and the music grew louder and the crowd livelier. The masses of sunbathers thinned out as families packed up and young Berliners kicked up sand dancing with whoever happened to land next to them.

Anna tried to keep her attention off Frederick's shirtless physique by making it her mission to talk with as many people as possible. His friends from Spain, Australia, the UK, and Brazil explained how they were unable to leave after visiting Berlin.

Two strong hands landed on each of her shoulders, interrupting her conversation. "Having fun?" Frederick's voice asked from behind her.

Relaxed by the strong Bavarian brews, Anna let her head fall back and hit his firm chest. She looked up to find his eyes. "Yes."

Taking her left hand, Frederick guided her away from the cabana and down the zigzagging boardwalk ablaze with lit torches reflecting their glow in the sparkling water. Effortlessly, he picked her up and propped her onto the top of the wooden railing. Frederick stood facing her, aligning his gaze with hers.

"So…what do you think of Berlin now?" he asked.

Anna let her mind wander before answering the question. What did she think of Berlin, or what did she think of Berlin with Frederick? She had the same answer to both.

"Captivating, but full of secrets."

"Secrets?"

"Yes. Guarded secrets."

Frederick leaned his arms against the railing, inches away from her face. "That should not bother you then, since you are such an expert at uncovering secrets."

Frederick's body pushed further toward her while his hands met the curves of her waist.

"I always welcome a challenge," Anna responded with a breath that was unexpectedly captured by Frederick's lips. Endorphins shot through her, tingling her body with sensation. Wrapping her arms around his neck, Anna greedily pulled him closer to prolong the moment.

Frederick's right hand ran up her spine and held the back of her neck, leaning her further over the edge of the railing until Anna's laugh broke their kiss. She let the upper half of her body fall further downward until she could see the lights of the city blaze upside down. Softly, Frederick pulled her back up and, once again, she met his lips. He kissed her softly, pulling on her lower lip. Her body tensed against him with the weight of every moment in which she had craved him.

"Are you ready to leave?"

Anna arched her neck, letting Frederick's lips explore its surface. His breath against her skin further charging the electric current within her.

"Let's go," she responded.

The building elevator stopped at twelve— the top floor of Frederick's building. Exhaustion from the Berlin sun partially killed the nerves Anna would have felt as she stepped into his moonlight- drenched apartment.

Modern black couches and sleek furniture adorned the spacious room cast in the night's shadows. Under the vaulted ceiling, large curtain-less windows opened to the Berlin sky, the lights of other buildings twinkled like clustered stars. In the dark, amidst the scent of musk, leather, and cool night air, Frederick kissed her again. Her arms wrapped around his shoulders as she pulled him closer to her.

Their kissing became deeper and heavy; her body was restless against his. He lifted her mid-kiss and carried her until she felt her head gently fall onto plush pillows. His grip loosened, but his eyes remained fixed. Locked under him, her gaze had nowhere else to go. He kissed her teasingly, running his thumb along her lips, smearing what was left of her lip gloss.

His gaze hypnotized her into losing herself—into closing her eyes when she could no longer match his stare and into letting his hands undress her, trusting that he knew what to do. Against her, she felt the weight of his chest. Lips brushed the nape of her neck, sending continuous chills down her body. Frederick's hands made their way along her back, untying her cream bikini top and tossing it onto the hardwood floor alongside her sundress. Anna felt herself melting in his hands. His toned arms maneuvered her frame easily as if she were just a puzzle piece being placed into the position that fit best.

Her whole body was abuzz with sensation. Frederick observed her curiously. Noting when her breathing accelerated and when her lips parted in anticipation. She ran her hands through his hair and down his back until Frederick pinned them above her head with one arm. Never leaving her body, his other hand continued to caress, explore and possess the various parts of her. He breathed in her exhalations until the air between them became one breath.

At the peak of sensation, unable to stand the tease, Anna pushed herself upward and onto Frederick to take the lead, but in an instant, her back once again hit the pillows. Knowing what she wanted, Frederick pulled her hips into him and pressed into her until a moan escaped her lips.

Words sounded hot against her ear, but she didn't understand them. Lost amidst the sensation of pure pleasure, her mind completely blank, she tried to regain clarity. The words came again, soft, but with a firm edge to them. Frederick was speaking to her in German.

The sounds wrapped around her, an erotic spell. Heat spread through her every muscle until she no longer felt the physical presence of herself. Consumed by Frederick, waves of dopamine rolled through her rhythmically matching his movements. His tongue collected the light perspiration gathered on Anna's lips. The added sensation further heightened her arousal.

Frederick went deeper and kissed her harder. Anna's fingers clawed against his back from the building pressure within her. Her sweat-drenched body tensed against his chest. Sounding his name with the tip of her tongue plunged her into complete release.

The sensation vibrated through her. With inhibitions suspended, the previous months' worries, stresses, and emotions rushed out of her with intensity. Anna's eyes moistened from the shock of emotion. She buried her face in Frederick's collarbone and let her body pulsate with an aftermath of chills. He continued to kiss her slowly and lightly.

Anna was lost. She had entered a frame of existence where only herself, Frederick, and Berlin maintained an unspoken dialogue with each other. Yesterday felt like another lifetime. This love triangle was the new reality.

The morning air that blew in from the open balcony was crisp, perfumed with flowers and dew. The sounds of Berliners bustling, starting car engines or setting down espresso cups, which chimed in rhythm against glass saucers, floated up from the street below.

Anna opened her eyes to the view from Frederick's apartment. She had never seen it before, but already it felt familiar. Arizona was a past dream from another life; one that was lost in the wheel of time. Momentarily, this scared her, but Anna let it pass. The only thing she remembered clearly was the sensation of the night before.

The sound of a starting shower distracted her. She smiled. The rays of the Berlin sun beat against her eyes blindingly. She let the sensation linger until her corneas produced colorful shapes. Anna felt different. The cool wooden floor grounded her feet as she shimmied into her sundress and left the bedroom.

She recalled the apartment as a blur of mischievous sensuality. With the morning, it lit up into a spacious modern penthouse, immaculate in its design and sophistication but lacking the personal touches needed to create the feeling of a home. There was no way to tell the apartment belonged to Frederick specifically. Then again, maybe that was exactly what made the apartment his.

Anna followed the halls of the L-shaped layout from the bedroom toward the corner and the longer part of the L, which held the living room and kitchen. A protruding wall stopped her. From the corner of the L, an angled room stuck out as if someone had taken a cube and fitted it perfectly into the middle of the living room. The cube had one door which faced the bedroom; it had no windows.

"What a strange way to design an extra room," Anna voiced.

"It is my study," Frederick answered her from the bedroom.

She turned just in time to see him pull on a black T-shirt. A wave of heat rushed through her. Frederick had just showered and dripped droplets of water as he kissed her good morning. Anna swallowed her building lust.

"Sooo…may I see where the master theorizing happens?" she asked with a cool smooth voice.

"No," Frederick answered curtly.

Anna raised an eyebrow. "This isn't some sort of Bluebeard room, is it? I really do not want to discover the bodies of your ex-girlfriends."

"Hardly. Though similar to Bluebeard, I allow no one to enter," Frederick said mischievously. Anna's look of doubt prompted a further explanation.

"We all need a space for ourselves," Frederick continued. "The moment I treat this room like any other is the moment the room loses its ability to be a place of insight."

"Hmm," Anna mused, "I believe Bluebeard had a similar explanation if I remember the folktale correctly."

"As always, you have caught onto me Anna, though I will correct you and say Bluebeard was not just a French folktale."

"Are you kidding?" Anna made a face and followed Frederick into the kitchen.

"His real name was Gilles de Rais. He was the Marshal of France and comrade-in-arms to Joan of Arc. Simultaneously, he was one of the most prolific serial killers in human history who tortured and killed up to six hundred people—mostly children and not his wives, as folklore suggests. Eventually, he was caught and executed only because he kidnapped the local priest."

Anna swallowed the disgust that had built in her throat. "Frederick, that is sick."

He nodded in agreement. "I will spare you the rest of the details."

Anna looked around the sleek kitchen to distract her from her imagination. The kitchen contained only one piece of life: a hanging cluster of ripe bananas. They looked out of place among the steel appliances.

"May I offer you some coffee?"

Anna nodded and stepped to the window to admire the view of Berlin.

"Did you sleep well?"

Anna blushed at her reflection in the glass.

"I did…" She let her answer linger in the air. "Last night…was very intense."

She turned around to meet Frederick's knowing stare.

"I am curious…" she continued. Frederick arched his eyebrows in question.

"We had not been physical before, yet it felt like you knew me intimately," Anna said. "Tell me your secret."

Frederick responded with a playful smirk. “My secret? I pay attention to details.”

“Explain?”

“It is simple,” Frederick said casually. “When we would see each other, I observed your reactions to my touch. The human body has always fascinated me. It cannot lie. There are always signs when something doesn’t feel good or when it does. Most people do not pay attention, or they go off of what they have learned is supposed to feel good or erotic to their partner. I looked for your body to tell me. Then I learned and adapted.”

Anna thought back to her past sexual experiences. They now seemed amateur, even misguided. Frederick was right—as usual.

He eyed Anna for a prolonged moment while her thoughts lingered obviously on her past encounters. Frederick handed her a cup of coffee to coax her to the present moment.

“I would like to invite you on a trip with me.”

Anna took a long sip of the perfectly brewed dark roast and set down her cup, coyly resting her chin on the back of her hand.

“Where are we going?”

“Germany’s heart and soul.”

Chapter 26

Germany's heart and soul had led them to Regensburg, a picturesque Bavarian city in southeast Germany. Colorful historical houses up to six stories tall surrounded the building whose sign read: HISTORISCHE WURSTKÜCHE.

"So the same family has been serving sausages here for over eight hundred years?"

"That's what I'm telling you, Anna, and it's the oldest open public restaurant still in operation since the twelfth century. From generation to generation, the family continues to cook three thousand bratwurst sausages daily."

Anna could not help but laugh at the thought. "That's commitment."

"You are *literally* eating German history right now!"

She bit into the slightly charred meat topped with house-made sauerkraut.

"I didn't expect German history to be so delicious!" Anna leaned across the wooden table and planted a kiss on Frederick's lips.

She finished her beer and followed Frederick across an arched stone bridge; the Danube River flowed gently beneath them.

Anna glided her hands along the thick blocks of stone that had felt the fingertips of countless others. "How old is it?" she asked.

"Twelfth century. It is the father of all future European stone bridges."

She gazed at Frederick's profile against the setting sun, the backdrop of Regensburg behind him. He symbolized the new Germany: beautiful, intelligent, powerful, chivalrous, nothing like what her grandmother had taught her to fear. Anna felt her way up his chest and kissed him deeply.

Anna awoke the following morning from the sounds of Frederick's determined packing.

"What is happening? Why are we rushing?"

Frederick knelt in front of her, moving a cup of fresh coffee back and forth underneath her nose.

"No time to explain," his face was animated. "Today we start the journey to the place where it all began."

"Where what began?" Anna gulped down the hot liquid and cringed. It was bitter and black.

"Germania."

Frederick swooped Anna onto his shoulder and carried her squealing into the shower.

"I'm going to go and get us breakfast for the road. Any requests?"

"Something with jam!"

Driving north on highway E 37 led them to the small town of Bramsche. A light mist had grayed the once-sunny skies. Anna breathed in the scent of wet leaves greedily. It was one of her favorite smells. She scanned the horizon of green fields, grazing animals, and lonely single cars for something out of the ordinary. Compared to their travels through Dresden, Frankfurt, and Regensburg, Bramsche seemed to be the mousy kid sister.

Noticing her boredom, Frederick broke the silence. "We are headed to Varusschlacht, a museum, and park on Kalkriese Hill." Anna waited for him to continue.

"Look around you. These fields may look innocent, but they are the remains of the deep Teutoburg Forest."

Anna's ears perked up. *So there* was *something unique here after all.*

"Where does the forest begin?"

"We are in it now."

Anna could count the sparse trees on her fingers.

"The forest was cleared long ago to make room for farming fields in between protected remains of the forest. At the time of Roman conquest, it looked much different."

Anna frowned in slight disappointment. "How misleading. The weather is perfect for a trek through a dark fairy-tale."

Frederick authoritatively cleared his throat. His tone lost the lightheartedness of the past week.

"The Romans received anything, but a fairy-tale."

"Romans?"

"Yes. That's where we are going—to the place where Germany's history as a nation began."

"Where do the Romans come in?"

"Imagine yourself living during the Roman Empire, under the rule of Octavian Augustus when Rome was at its prime militarily and economically. You were at the center of the world, part of the most advanced and inguinal nation, and an unstoppable war machine.

"To your North was Germania, a barbaric land inhabited by tribes who lived in small villages deep within the forest. A people without a political system, without any order, who attacked each other, and sometimes the neighboring Romans. As a Roman, you want these wild people to be controlled and you want your northern borders to be secured."

Anna thought this through. "Okay. As a Roman, that makes sense to me. So, how do we secure our borders?"

"Does the idea of bribing and promising military support to various fractions to split opponents into smaller, more manageable parts sound familiar to you?"

"Possibly. Should it?"

"Definitely. Julius Caesar's divide-and-conquer rule or *divide ut regnes* concept is still relevant in politics today. Think of how the Western countries have dealt with African or Asian countries."

Immediately, Anna thought of the Middle East. "Alright, so the Romans became allies with one tribe of Germans, and then pin them against each other?"

"Yes and no. They were much more devious. Over the years, Rome developed a very successful political strategy. They would take the sons of local chieftains as noble hostages to assure the tribe's loyalty to Rome."

"Wouldn't that cause more tension between the tribes and Rome?"

"You would think, but imagine yourself taken by the Romans from your village deep in the forest around the age of twelve. Suddenly, you get thrust into the center of the world surrounded by great architecture, people of importance, exotic foods, wines, and beautiful women from every corner of the Empire. You get a top education, military training, and access to everything Rome has to offer. You even get that time's most prized possession: Roman citizenship. As an adult, you are sent back home as a friend of Rome. Now, would you ever rebel or attack Rome? It's part of your identity now."

"I suppose I wouldn't," Anna answered, but in a second, she added, "Unless I somehow remained connected to my roots."

"This is *exactly* what happened to Arminius, the son of Segimerus, chieftain of the powerful Cherusci Tribe. After growing up in Rome, he became a military commander of the German auxiliary forces and became a Roman Knight. In short, he had it all."

"Let me guess: Having it all wasn't enough?"

"Basically, but to give Arminius credit, it was on a personal level. He never forgot his people, his village, and his family. Rome failed to buy him out."

"Do you think he saw through the Roman plan of seduction?"

"Definitely. Arminius was brilliant. He took advantage of what Rome gave him, but he knew it came at a price."

Frederick had turned off the single road that ran through the forest and into a parking lot. In front of them was an artistic modern burnt-orange building. It stood out from its natural green environment. Attached to its main floor was a rectangular tower that led to what looked like several observation points.

Frederick took Anna's hand and together, they walked through wet grass toward the building. The air was fresh, and Anna could taste the mist that hung heavy in the air.

"Emperor Augustus wanted to expand Roman rule over the rest of the Germanic tribes west of the Rhine and to protect the Empire's northern borders." Frederick continued, "So, he sent Publius Quinctilius Varus, his friend and distant relative by marriage, to make this a reality. Varus chose twenty-five-year-old Arminius to be his right-hand military commander and personal adviser. This was in seven A.D. Immediately, Arminius saw this as his chance to free Germania from Roman rule and he sprang into action."

Frederick nodded to the museum guard, who knowingly shook his hand upon entry. They proceeded upstairs. Exhibitions of Roman armor decorated the walls, as did several maps and digital images. Frederick stopped before a large depiction of the Roman army in small figurines marching in stilled silence alongside fake trees and painted marshes.

"These are Varus's legions," Frederick pointed to the model. "As soon as they got to the first fort, Arminius started to sneak away under the cover of night. He rode to different Germanic tribes and persuaded their chieftains to unite in an uprising against Rome. Racing against the rising sun, Arminius returned to his Roman camp undetected.

He then arranged a second meeting with all the chieftains to convince them to mobilize. Again, he rode against the night, probably meeting men clad in animal furs in the depths of this forest."

"How did he convince them?" Anna interrupted.

"I would die to know what he said to them, and how he created peace among the tribes and persuaded them to rise against their common, powerful enemy Rome."

"Did they actually understand what they were up against? Wasn't the Roman army the most powerful in the world?" Her eyes returned to the hundreds of figurines.

"Completely! The chieftains were risking the total and cruel destruction of their people if they lost. The Romans had a zero-mercy policy to anyone who raised their weapons against the Empire."

Anna thought back to the scene in *The Gladiator* when the Romans crucified their own General Felix's wife and son. The scene still haunted her. It was puzzling how Romans could be simultaneously advanced and cruel even to their own people.

"I don't know how he did it," Frederick broke her thoughts. "Arminius must have had not only tact, but a hypnotizing charisma, because all the chieftains followed."

"What was his plan?"

"One morning, Arminius rushed to Varus's headquarters with grim, urgent news. He told Varus that the Germanic tribes in the north were planning to rebel. This uprising needed to be crushed before it spread like wildfire through the rest of Germania and even to the precious Gaul Province—now modern France.

"Obviously, Varus panicked. He was supposed to be responsible for keeping peace in these provinces. If he failed, Augustus would be furious, but this reaction was exactly what Arminius was hoping for."

"So, Varus believed Arminius without a doubt?"

"Yes. The arrogant belief that Arminius would never give up the glory of Roman citizenship for his barbaric Germanic roots, blinded him into Arminius's trap.

"Immediately, he ordered three of his legions to get ready for battle. Two days later, this massive column of troops began the long trek north along the Teutoburg Forest's edge. And who was providing the army with protection as they marched?"

"Arminius?"

"Exactly. Remember, Arminius headed the Germanic auxiliary cavalry in charge of scouting for danger up ahead. Just picture this; each legion consisted of around fifty-five hundred trained battle veterans along with another five thousand supporting troops.

Merchants, doctors, weapon masters, prostitutes, healers, fortunetellers always followed. Herds of cattle trailed along to feed all these people. There were around twelve to thirteen thousand people per legion, and now multiply that by three, and you have an idea of the size of the Roman military force Arminius and his under-trained and under-equipped Germanic men faced. It was like a large town on the move."

"Arminius obviously knew this, right?"

"Of course! He was trained as a Roman commander," Frederick's voice boomed, getting the attention of several museum visitors.

"The Roman legions formed a vulnerable twelve-kilometer snake as they slowly progressed north. The Roman Army was only unbeatable in solid battle formation, but that in itself would be their problem. Germans hid within the thick forest, watching the vulnerable Roman snake slither along its edge, trapped by swamplands on its other side. Suddenly, Germanic tribesmen pounced out of the trees armed with swords and spears. Arminius and his cavalry switched sides and began attacking their own legions."

"Why would the cavalry follow Arminius?"

"Remember, they were also originally Germanic."

"For three days, the Germans ambushed the legions from the safety of the forest. Imagine yourself a Roman soldier. You don't know what the hell is going on. Your protection has turned against you. You're hungry and exhausted from saving your own life, and you are in the middle of nowhere—swamplands, dense forest, a rainstorm, and the threat of a spear or arrow gutting you at any moment. That thought alone is enough to drive a man insane. You can't even make camp because as soon as you close your eyes, you will be murdered. You only have one hope: to get to the nearest Roman fort."

"Frederick, how do you know all of these details?"

"Captured Roman soldiers were made into slaves but were eventually freed by the Romans and left personal accounts."

"Well, why couldn't the Romans just turn back?"

"It was too late! The road back was longer. Varus was devastated. His only choice was to push onward to the nearest Roman base at Haltern, ninety-six kilometers away.

His immediate plan was to assemble the legions into battle formation as soon as they reached a large enough clearing at Kalkriese Hill, but it was too late.

The Romans' famous discipline had been broken. The soldiers were exhausted. They had no sleep, not enough food, the constant stress of battle, physical exhaustion, and their brothers' death to deal with. Varus knew it was the end. He had led the legions to their doom and fell on his sword in suicide, abandoning his army."

Anna looked out in front of her; they had reached the top of the observatory. An innocent field stretched out before them. It was hard to imagine that a deep layer of this very earth was once heavily soaked with blood.

Frederick marveled at the model reconstruction of the battle within the observatory museum, while Anna couldn't help but focus on the vast loss of life for whatever good it accomplished. She stared at the thousands of miniature soldier figurines, representing real people who were all murdered.

"What was Augustus's reaction? Did he retaliate?"

"He almost went mad. The Roman historian Suetonius wrote that Emperor Augustus, a reticent man, was devastated. He tore his clothes, refused to shave or cut his hair for months as a sign of grief, and banged his head against the walls of his palace like a madman repeating *Quintili Vare, legiones redde!* meaning *Quinctilius Varus, give me back my Legions!* The defeat hit the Roman psyche so hard that these legions were never restored as military units—not even after their deaths were avenged."

"Avenged?"

"As you would imagine, Arminius became a legend among Germans and other tribes, but pro-Roman chieftains were jealous of his status. After Tiberius became the next emperor, he refused an offer to poison Arminius, saying that, 'it was not by secret treachery, but by arms that the people of Rome avenged themselves!' Seven years later, Tiberius sends his nephew Germanicus to defeat Arminius's forces and return the three defeated legions' sacred eagles. Guess who helped Germanicus?"

"Germanian chiefs?"

"Exactly, and Arminius's father-in-law even gave up his pregnant daughter Princess Thusnelda to Germanicus, who paraded her and Arminius' only son Thymelicus through the streets of Rome at his triumph."

"Did the Romans kill his wife and son?"

"They were the family of Roman citizens, so no, but his son later decided to become a gladiator and died in the arena. I can only imagine how much spectators enjoyed his death. The son of Arminius killed, final revenge for the humiliation his father had caused the entire Roman Empire."

"What happened to Arminius?"

"Conspirators in his tribe who wanted to be aligned with Rome killed him."

"So, all this blood for nothing? Arminius didn't really achieve anything."

"No, he did. He halted Rome's expansion into Germania and gave our ancestors freedom. He showed not only to Germans, but to the entire world that when united, ordinary people can defeat an ultimate power."

"Ironic, isn't it? Germany defeated a world power and relentlessly tries to take that same title destroying half the world in its conquest."

"You generalize, Anna," Frederick fired back quickly. "Germany hasn't been the only aggressor. A quick look at the rest of European history can easily prove that."

"So, Arminius remains a German hero then?" Anna asked.

"Sadly no. On the two-thousand-year anniversary of Arminius' victory, Chancellor Schröder refused to celebrate this day as an event of national pride in two thousand and four. Instead, the German government labeled it as propaganda of Germany's militaristic past."

"Maybe he had a point?"

"Tell me how winning Germany's independence from Rome and World War II have anything in common."

"I just mean maybe the government felt it was too soon to celebrate German nationalism."

"They are cowards and Schröder in particular. Even one of your senators called him a political prostitute." Frederick spat out the words with a strong sense of passion.

Chapter 27

A strong sense of passion and their travels together through Germany had synced Anna and Frederick closer to one another. On their return to Berlin, Anna now connected to a new life that she shared with Frederick in the district of Mitte.

Anna spent her days studying German or touring the Berlin streets while Frederick went about his routine. The nights were spent together, and the weekends filled with day trips, lazy afternoons, or nights out amidst the glitter of the city. Anna had even connected with Benedikt, who, unexpectedly, adopted her into his family. Benedikt solidified their common lineage through a copy of two photographs he gifted to Anna. The photographs were of her grandmother's grandparents Yuri and Alexandra Chukhnin, dated 1902—before the Bolshevik Revolution destroyed the Russian Empire.

Alexandra and Yuri Chukhnin, 1902

It felt bizarre for Anna to obtain a sort of new identity that encompassed people she never knew existed. It gave her the urge to connect her family back home to what and who she had discovered in Germany.

She considered flying to Arizona, but immediately crossed out the option. Leaving Frederick when they were just falling into a romance with each other was risky. What if something changed? What if, under the notion of *out of sight out of mind*, he forgot about her? And yet Grandfather, the man responsible for her even coming to Germany, remained in Arizona awaiting news from Anna.

I have been so selfish! Anna thought. She needed to tell him everything, but explaining that his wife was a completely different person over a Skype call felt insane. *How would he handle that?*

The foam of her cappuccino further melted into the espresso as if it, too, was giving up from lack of options. Around her, the modern café walls contradicted the costumed soldiers posing with American and Soviet Flags at Checkpoint Charlie just down the street. She liked being in the present with such a close reminder of the past. Most mornings, Anna watched Berliners walk past the tall glass windows, but today she opened up her laptop and began to type *Dearest Grandfather*. She took her time with every thought she wanted to express. The detailed letter soon became an outlet for herself, which she returned to composing each morning at the same café while Frederick went to work.

A week passed. It was 12:30 p.m. and the afternoon sun was hitting her eyes and making the letters on the screen illegible. The final sip of cappuccino hit her tongue in a disappointingly cold splash. A few drops trickled onto the sleeve of her blouse.

"Damn..."

Anna left her table and made her way to the bathroom situated at the end of a narrow corridor. After soaking her sleeve, she proceeded back to her table, but quickly turned around. A man's voice had called her name.

"Fräulein Anna Venu?"

The voice was clear, but had a hint of a strange sort of humor in it, as if the sound of her name was a sinister joke. She turned. In front of her stood a balding man in his mid-forties. There was nothing special about his features. In a way, he looked like anyone on the train or walking down the street or reading a newspaper at a café. Yet the man's face held a strange smile that eerily contradicted a cold, dead stare from curious eyes.

"Fräulein Anna Venu, I presume? May I have a couple of words with you in private?" He asked while sliding open a side panel door to the café's back office.

So that's *where he materialized from*, Anna realized. "I am sorry, but I do not know you to talk to you in private," said Anna while backing out of the hallway.

A government ID card flashed in front of her face.

"What is going on?" Asked Anna defensively. "I am an American citizen who is legally in the EU and Germany."

"Ms. Venu, *please*, do not worry. My presence here concerns only your safety." His response caught Anna off-guard.

"My safety?"

"Correct. *Please* step into the office. This won't take long."

Anna hesitated, but did as he said. Her right hand gripped her cellphone as if she would have time to call for help.

"I sense your worry, but again, please relax. My name is Agent Vogt. I am who I say I am. I'm not here to trick you or murder you or whatever scenario you have crafted within your head."

Did he just mock me? Anna quickly accessed the situation; it felt off. Just because the man had identification did not make him trustworthy. He could be anyone, and her foreign identity put her at a disadvantage. *I need to observe how this unfolds.* A Leonard Cohen lyric entered her head: *"If you're squeezed for information, that's when you've got to play it dumb."*

She gazed up at the man's face innocently. "Thank you very much, Agent Vogt. Please tell me what I can help you with?"

The agent studied her carefully, reacting to Anna's change of attitude. *Had it been too sudden?* Anna timidly moved a strand of hair from her face.

"I left my things on the coffee table," Anna said. "I should go grab them."

Agent Vogt locked his hands in front of him and, with mild amusement, said, I already took care of that."

"What do you mean?" Anna asked abruptly.

"Feel free to check on your table, but it is essential that you don't fully extend your head out of this corridor.

Was this some sort of joke? Anna turned her frustration of not having control of the situation into feigned naïve concern. Slowly, she pushed herself out of her chair and made her way to the door. Anna peered out into the café and, at first glance, missed her empty chair.

Upon the second scan of the room, her eyes found her laptop, but someone was using it. Anna's breath stopped.

What the hell? She was using it! In front of her laptop sat a girl that looked just like her! The same teal blouse on a slender body. The same hair hitting the same heart-shaped face. Even the girl's black flats slightly beat against the floor of the café in the same way that Anna's would.

Anna's eyes flashed back to the agent, "What the hell is going on?!"

"Ms. Venu, please, do not worry. That is one of our agents. She is your decoy."

"Ha, my decoy! My decoy for what?"

"I have a question to ask you that may clear everything up." The agent proceeded casually, his fingers spinning an unsharpened pencil. "Ms. Venu, did you or your family members back in the United States hire private bodyguard protection for you?"

"Yeah, because I'm so important, I have bodyguards. Who do you think I am?" Anna answered, bewildered.

"What about friends or relatives that may have taken it upon themselves to look out for your well-being without your knowledge?"

"I wish I had friends like that. My family wouldn't waste money on personal bodyguards anyway."

"Ex-boyfriends? Ex-girlfriends?" The agent seemed to be enjoying himself. "Anyone who would be concerned with your safety?"

"Agent Vogt, I think you have made a mistake."

"I hardly ever make mistakes, Ms. Venu, but *please*, let me prove it to you. Would you mind going for a short ride?"

"Yes, I'd mind. What's going on and why would I trust you?" She asked, looking directly into his eyes.

The Agent let out a mild laugh. "Ms. Venu, although I find it amusing that you think so highly of yourself to imagine, I would set up this elaborate ordeal to kidnap you, or whatnot, please understand that you are of no interest to me. Your existence crossed my path by mere accident. It's the people who are watching you who I'm curious about, not you."

Whenever this man said "please," something inside Anna squirmed. It was a "please" that both asked and commanded; just like the man's smile, it had a peculiar tinge to it.

"I understand your confusion and I can explain further, but for that, you will have to follow my lead."

Anna paused while her brain quickly analyzed possible scenarios. *I cannot walk away now. The presence of my twin outside the office is much too strange. For me to find out anything, the game has to continue.* She let out a mock sigh of defeat. "Alright. Fine, I will go with you. I mean, what choice do I have? It's not every day you get to be part of a Jason Bourne novel."

The agent smiled after receiving the answer he wanted.

"Before we step outside, please put on this jacket and hat; we don't want to give away your decoy's operation."

"Of course we don't."

Anna reached for the short-brimmed navy-blue hat and gray spring trench coat. "How very espionage of you," she mocked.

"Yes, we try to keep in line with spy stereotypes as much as possible. We don't want to disappoint the public," he answered flatly.

The door slid open. She followed the agent out the back door. Anna glanced back at her decoy, who continued to type away on her laptop. *What was she even writing? Was she reading my letter to Grandfather?*

The agent opened the door to his parked black car, and Anna moved into the front seat. The car started almost silently and made no noise as it drove. *Was it electric?* He wheeled around the block and back onto the main road in front of the café. She could see her decoy get up and order a coffee.

"Looks like your agent is getting nice and comfortable," Anna remarked. "Hope she knows what I order...."

The Agent smiled that same strange smile. "Of course she does, a cappuccino. She needs the extra caffeine to keep up with your active lifestyle."

He looked at her from the corner of his eye. Anna could tell the man was probing her reactions. Anna smoothed her blouse nervously but remained silent. *I'll be just as anxious as you want me to be,* she said to herself.

The agent pulled up behind a line of parked cars. He said something in German into his mobile. Immediately a gray car began to reverse out of a parking spot.

"Oh, look, we have luck on our side today," he said sweetly while pulling into the empty spot.

"Ms. Venu, do you see that white car second from the corner on the opposite side of the street? Its driver is facing us."

"Yes, I do."

"Let us do a small experiment. I will call your decoy on her earpiece. She will get up, gather your things, and leave the café. Upon exiting, she will continue in the direction of your hotel, where you usually go after you finish your daily writing. Two or three minutes later, she will change her mind and return to the café. Maybe for one more cappuccino. While this is occurring, I would like you to concentrate on the driver of the white car. Are you ready?"

"Sure, let's do it."

The agent spoke into his mobile again. Anna's decoy began to gather her belongings and walk towards the front door. The man in the white car immediately started the engine.

The decoy had crossed the street and was about to turn the corner. As if on cue, the white car quickly left its parking space and drove past them. Anna saw the driver, a good-looking man in his late twenties. The white car turned the same corner toward her hotel.

Anna waited. Two minutes went by and then three. The seconds passed slowly as Anna strained her vision in the direction her decoy should be returning from. The agent beside her was silent and motionless. Four minutes. Anna was about to speak up when the decoy's teal blouse appeared from around the corner.

She lightly walked back to the coffee shop, looking small and vulnerable against the city streets. *Is that what I look like?* Anna wondered. *I thought I was taller than that.* Her attention snapped back at the sound of the agent's airy voice.

"Don't turn your head, but try to look to your left."

Using her peripheral vision, Anna saw the white car drive back in the direction of the café. It slowed down as the decoy entered the shop and halted behind their car.

"Parking here is a real hassle," the agent said with artificial sympathy. "Let's make his life a little easier."

He proceeded to leave their parking spot. Anna observed as the white car immediately took their space and turned off its engine. The driver remained seated in perfect view of the coffee shop.

"What the hell…? Anna half-whispered to herself.

The agent drove two streets down and re-parked the car. He turned off the engine and looked at her. "Now, I will ask you again. Ms. Venu, can you think of anyone who would, for any reason, be interested in watching you?"

Anna stared back blankly. "I really can't."

"Ms. Venu, *please*, take your time with the question."

She watched him strike up a cigarette.

"Do you mind..." he asked without a question mark.

"No."

"Care to partake?" His pack of Marlboros drew closer to her.

"A German consumer of American cigarettes?" she asked.

"Yes. I suppose even I fell for the marketed rugged cowboy spirit of the Marlboro man." He blew out his first inhale with satisfaction.

The scent of tobacco made her think back to Benedikt. *Would he have me followed? He certainly has the means and the contacts... But why?* She then thought of her father and grandfather. Both men were protective and knew such business. Anna refused the cigarettes and reached for her phone to dial her father, but she paused to make the call and asked with genuine curiosity, "Agent Vogt, even if these people are following me, why does that even matter to you?"

He blew smoke out through the half-cracked window, but the summer breeze only pushed it back into the car. It sat under Anna's nose heavily.

The agent's hand reached to the backseat and grabbed a dark brown leather briefcase. Its corners were old, frayed, and full of cigarette burns. From it, he withdrew a folder and held it open. A man's mug shot was clipped to the corner. Anna recognized him immediately.

"That is the driver of the white car."

"Good eye."

"Who is he?"

"Rudolf Lanz, an active member of the German neo-Nazi movement. He has been detained several times due to Nazi propaganda and violent acts against Muslim immigrants, liberal organizations, and charities."

Anna's eyes widened.

"He is not the only one who follows you."

The next folder held a mug shot of a heavyset man possibly in his fifties. His wide-set eyes gave him the impression of a farm animal. Anna swallowed her nerves as fear casually began to enter her.

"He is another member of the same neo-Nazi group. You may see him tomorrow. His name is Martin Schulz. The two usually switch off. This..." The agent waved the folder and continued, "is why I am interested in who is following you."

"You are not assuming I have anything to do with a German neo-Nazi group, are you?"

The agent smiled his sardonic smile. "In my line of work, I cannot exclude any options just because you look like an innocent tourist who is legally in Germany."

His sarcastic tone was getting annoying.

"Agent Vogt, you don't understand," Anna began with inflated defensiveness, "my family, my grandparents, and parents, hated the Nazis, it's how—"

Vogt cut her off, "Ms. Venu, please. I simply mean it is a possibility. Just like me being a secret millionaire is a possibility, but, unfortunately for me, that is unlikely. Now, if your family hired someone to protect you, they could have easily stumbled upon these thugs by accident. Security is a common type of work for them."

Anna looked down at her phone. He was right. If Anna's father or grandfather did arrange something, it was possible for these men to somehow get the job.

She called her father and put the call on speaker. He answered the phone almost immediately. "Anna, is everything alright? Have you bought your flight back yet?"

"Dad, no not yet. I will call to catch up later. I just have a quick question. Did you or Grandfather hire anyone to watch over me while I'm abroad? Like, a bodyguard?"

Silence.

"What? What do you mean, hire someone? What is going on over there? Anna!"

"Dad, don't worry! Everything is fine. I will call you later today." Anna hung up the phone.

"That's too bad." There was genuine disappointment in Agent Vogt's voice.

"What's too bad?

"This dead-end. You don't have an answer for me, and I have no answers for you. Since you are the mysterious focus of two active members of the neo-Nazi underground, you will remain my focus as well."

He took a final long drag and put out the butt in an empty soda can. "We need to keep Germany green."

"What should I do?" Anna asked impatiently. She was irritated by this man's casual attitude.

He looked at her firmly. "Ms. Venu, tell me, what do you know about neo-Nazis—generally speaking."

"That they are crazy skinheads."

"Mm… And tell me, what do you know about the BFV?"

"Nothing."

Agent Vogt rubbed his eyes as if tired from explaining things to a child. "Ms. Venu, the Federal Office for the Protection of the Constitution or the BFV is a special federal police department, which deals with both ultra-left and the ultra-right terrorist organizations."

A pause sat between them. Vogt proceeded. "You see, Ms. Venu, in Germany, any Nazi propaganda is a federal crime, even the simple display of a swastika. Nazi sympathizers are both a national and personal threat; therefore, I take my work at the BFV very seriously. For me, Ms. Venu, the rise of the neo-Nazi movement or any party that harms innocent lives is something I will work my entire life to destroy. I hope that you understand me."

Momentarily, vengeance flashed through the man's eyes in such a way that it sparked slight chills through Anna. Their relationship had shifted, if ever slightly. *We have a common enemy,* Anna thought.

"I understand," she answered with newfound respect. "In what way can I assist you?"

"Ms. Venu, earlier you called the neo-Nazis crazy skinheads. You were only partially right. Crazy, yes. Skinheads, no. At least not for the last ten years. Until the late nineties, our job to monitor neo-Nazi groups and prevent acts of violence was much easier. Their skinhead looks and special tattoos made surveillance a relatively simple task, but they evolved dramatically in the last two decades. Skinheads grew hair, got more or less stable jobs, started mingling with regular Germans, and their political agenda changed significantly."

"How can an organization based on Aryan supremacy significantly change its agenda?"

"Simply. They began riding the wave of economic difficulties and dissatisfaction felt by many ordinary Germans. Neo-Nazis started to target immigrant populations: Turks, Arabs, and Africans. Clever propaganda helped them emerge from society's fringes reinvented as a legitimate ultra-conservative political force, but their goal to change Germany's established political order has remained the same. And they continue to support militia-type groups secretly.

"Prior, when skinheads organized to plan a violent act, we were able to interfere, but now, planned violence is made to look like an ordinary event that just *happened* to get out of control."

"I don't understand..." Anna said. "What do you mean by an 'ordinary event'?"

"Let's say a liberal party conducts a regular gathering. Neo-Nazis wearing the liberal party's colors join the crowd. Suddenly, several small violent disturbances in the crowd coincide, and they escalate so fast that in ten to fifteen, minutes there is complete chaos.

"It is a brilliant tactic. The media immediately picks up the story and delivers it to viewers in the form of ordinary German citizens disapproving of the liberal party's platform or agenda. This tactic is so simple and effective that it took us some time to figure out what was going on. This shift to modernize and redirect the entire neo-Nazi movement was done by someone with a high intellectual capacity."

"Did you figure out who was behind all of this?" asked Anna.

"I believe so."

"Well, what did you find?" she pushed excitedly.

"The BFV secretly tapes all neo-Nazi events and gatherings. It has allowed us to have an image gallery of active members, sympathizers, and even bystanders who stopped to listen to their propaganda. It was always an uphill battle to identify who is who on the images until we got our hands on new facial-recognition technology.

"Recently, we put all of our old videos and photographic images from the past ten-fifteen years through this software, and we've had several breakthroughs, but one, in particular, was very interesting.

"Our computers picked up one unusual bystander from demonstrations and gatherings around eleven years ago. There were five different neo-Nazi events in Germany where this same individual was present. The man would be sitting in a nearby café, watching from inside a car, or even standing at the window of a hotel facing the neo-Nazi gathering. Suddenly, he disappeared from the rallies for almost three years—until two thousand and eight when our computers again identified him. We have not seen him since."

Anna felt sucked into the story until common sense hit her. "Why are you telling me this?" she asked. "Isn't this all classified information? You said earlier, you cannot rule out the fact that I, too, might be a neo-Nazi sympathizer."

Vogt ignored the question. "Do you know what really got my attention?" he asked. "The man was continuously making notes as the events he observed unfolded."

Anna watched the agent's face. Again, his gaze had wandered off to a time and place where she was not present. "This man could have been a journalist or a writer," she suggested.

"That was my first thought, as well." Agent Vogt spoke swiftly now. "But the man was neither. He was in the German Army and seemed not to have anything to do with the neo-Nazis aside from observing their events. There was no published material, analysis of the ideology, no blog, no social media. Nothing."

"So you know the man's identity then?"

"I asked our technicians to put together all of the videos where this man was visible into one short movie. The more I watched the video, the more I got the feeling that this individual had something to do with each event itself."

"You didn't answer my questions: Who is this man and how does this involve me?"

The agent's stare turned Anna to stone. Slowly his mouth opened and his lips formed two clearly articulated words: "Frederick Häuser."

Anna's stomach dropped.

"What did you say?" The question escaped her lips in a thin whisper.

"Frederick Häuser, the man I believe you are dating."

Slowly and silently, Anna pulled in a deep breath of air to stabilize her nerves. "Show me the video."

"I knew you would ask."

Agent Vogt pulled out an iPad from the same run-down briefcase. The video expanded onto the screen and images of a much younger Frederick moved across it. He was thinner then, boyish, with an almost innocent look to him. Harmlessly writing notes into a small notebook, looking up every few seconds with concentration. A smugness fell over Anna. *This cop is an idiot.*

"Is this it?" The cockiness in her voice refused to simmer. "Based on these short videos, you assume that Frederick is involved in the neo-

Nazi movement?" Her tone rose. "He is a historian, as I am sure you know, specializing in World War Two. His job is to do research and taking notes on an ideology that began the very war he studies seem rather relevant."

"Yes. Yes it does, doesn't it?" A wicked smile flashed across his face. He reached for a water bottle.

"Is this amusing to you?"

"Yes. It is," Vogt replied. "I am always amused by the reactions of humans when they hear something they refuse to believe. Seeing the eventual destruction of their denial is rather priceless." He took a sip of water.

Inwardly Anna fumed. *The accusation was weak. What was really going on?*

"You see, Ms. Venu, I am sitting here listening to you defend your significant other as you should. I even applaud you for it. I am sure Frederick would be flattered. However, I possess information that you do not. And as I told you before, I rarely make mistakes."

"I think we are done here." Her hand moved to push open the passenger door. It easily unlocked.

"We believe that Frederick is one of the players behind the transformation of the German neo-Nazi movement," said Agent Vogt with an emotionless voice.

Her right foot stopped short of hitting the pavement. Chills ran down her neck and her stomach tightened. *That just can't be.* She turned her head and stared at Vogt coolly.

"Listen. I have had enough of this cat-and-mouse game. Either you give me all your so-called evidence, or I tell Frederick everything."

The agent smiled again with the fixated look of a prosecutor about to win. "Ms. Venu, *please*. Frederick already knows we are looking into him. In fact, it was *he* who prevented us from continuing our investigation. Well, he stopped the agency. He did not stop me." He took another sip from the water bottle. "I agree with you, and you have the right to know. Otherwise, how would you ever believe me?"

In a split-second turnaround, Anna decided to hear him out further. She shut the car door. Subconsciously, she tried to distance herself from the agent. Indifferent to her deadpan gaze, Vogt lit up another cigarette and re-opened the window. The fresh scent of Berlin hit her face. All Anna wanted was to leave the smoke-saturated car and forget the entire conversation.

"You know, I began looking into Frederick out of curiosity. He came from an affluent and powerful family, and his father publicly expressed anti-immigrant views. Or maybe it wasn't curiosity, but intuition. After years of this sort of work, sometimes you just know."

"Please get to the point," Anna responded.

"I assigned basic surveillance of his daily activities, but, to my complete surprise, Frederick spotted our agent the very next day. Immediately, we were pressed to stop any investigation on the Häuser family. Frederick's father's government connections serve them well."

"Again, you just made another assumption," said Anna.

"Frederick made a simple mistake. He showed his power too early. To detect highly professional surveillance in a day means that one was already on the lookout. Secondly, his father isolated our agency, the BFV, and my department. How was it so swiftly decided that we were the culprits, not another agency?"

"You said his father has connections; I am sure you were easy to identify."

"Ms. Venu, *please*."

Inwardly, Anna fumed from the demeaning sound of his saying "please."

"Our investigation further revealed that the written materials published by the neo-Nazis started to change exactly at the time when our cameras began detecting Frederick at their events. Compared to their previous garbage, these new texts were excellently written with a lot of historical and pseudo-historical data to illustrate Aryan supremacy, using everything from Arminius to Holocaust denial, Savitri Devi, and the widespread Muslim conspiracy to overtake Europe."

"Arminius?" The shock in Anna's voice was evident.

"It seems that someone has already educated you." Agent Vogt snickered.

Anna felt heat once again flash through her. "Frederick has never denied the Holocaust or talked of Savitri Devi. I don't even know who that is."

"Ah, well, then you are in for a treat, because Savitri Devi, the mother of the modern neo-Nazi movement, was quite the character."

"Her name sounds Indian. You are saying that a woman of color founded the Aryan-supremacy movement?"

"Not exactly. Savitri's birth name was Maximiani Portas. She was born in France into a mixed Greco-English family and took the name Savitri Devi after moving to India in nineteen twenty-nine, the literal birthplace of the Aryan nations."

"Frederick has never mentioned an interest in any of this..."

"Ms. Venu, the ideas of Savitri are extreme. Don't you think Frederick would want to further integrate you into his world before shifting your paradigm? Believe me, Savitri's writings greatly impacted Frederick's beliefs."

"I don't have to believe anything. You keep talking in abstractions. What beliefs are you referring to? Aryan supremacy? All I am hearing is your attempt to convince me that Frederick believes some lunatic."

"Ms. Venu, you are mistaken. Savitri was far from a lunatic, in the cognitive sense, I mean. She was highly intellectual, holding degrees in philosophy, psychology, mathematics, and biochemistry. From an early age, she was skeptical of Christianity, defining it as a product of Judean thinking that destroyed the original complex and beautiful religion of the Aryan race. She insisted that it was pure luck that Jehovah, a simple tribal Jewish God, wrongly obtained worldwide status and recognition. Throughout the war, she stayed in India, married an Indian nationalist, and secretly spied against the British Empire for the Germans."

"So she supported Hitler?"

"Oh, yes. In her writings, she considered Hitler the tenth avatar of the great Indian God Vishnu, who had finally come down to earth as a mighty warrior to fight the evil dark-skinned races and pave the way for the golden age of humanity. She saw the Führer as the savior of the Aryan nations from the evils of Christianity.

"After the Third Reich's defeat, she traveled to Europe on a pilgrimage to all the major sites of Nazism, starting with Hitler's birthplace in Austria. Germany was under martial law, so any Nazi propaganda was subject to capital punishment. This did not stop Savitri from starting her own campaign against the Allies. Even hardcore Nazi fanatics were in hiding, yet here was this woman, distributing more than fifteen thousand copies of her writings by hand, telling Germans to resist the Allied forces. For days, she secretly passed out her leaflets on trains, her martyrdom mission for her beloved Führer."

"Did she get caught?"

"Oh, yes. She was arrested and served two years in a camp alongside the most notorious female guards of the major concentration camps. Not surprisingly, they became very close friends. Once released, she became an international hero for the Nazi movement. Savitri Devi actively helped Hitler's favorite commando SS-Obersturmbannführer Otto Skorzeny run the *Die Spinne*—The Spider network. With the Vatican's assistance, this network helped hundreds of Nazis escape to Latin America and avoid justice.

"She was the first person who actively denied the Holocaust in writing. Every modern lunatic around the world, from German neo-Nazis to the former Iranian President Ahmadinejad, have referenced her words."

"I don't understand how she continued to hold this prestige..."

"Devi authored a unique book called *A Son of God.* There is no Nazi ideology in it; it is simply a great example of idealism philosophy in its purest form. This book propelled her name into New Age philosophy, and neo-Nazis are still using her talented writings to penetrate New Age groups and even green political parties, since she was one of the pioneers of the green movement in Europe. Believe it or not, her work has been introduced in conversations about animal rights protection and even vegetarianism.

"Within Nazism, she is famous for transforming the ugly and guilty face of Fascism into something completely new. Something sacred."

"What do you mean?"

"Hitler's predictions and promises had failed. As with any belief system, when something that is promised does not occur, it needs to be justified for its followers to continue to have faith. Think about the many times the end of the world was supposed to come, but didn't.

"Savitri turned Nazism into a mysterious cult of visionaries and martyrs who held supreme spiritual powers and were ahead of their time when they predicted the deep divide and struggle between the Aryan nations and the dark-skinned inferior nations. In a sense, they failed because the world was simply not ready."

"So you don't believe the Nazis had any mystical ties?" Anna asked curiously.

"I do not believe in mysticism, period. But, I will tell you that Nazi ideological leaders had a dogma of underlying primitive mysticism that was mostly based on superstition. It all stemmed from Hitler's initial interest in comic books."

"Comic books?" Anna found herself genuinely intrigued.

"Yes. It sounds ludicrous, but the entire Nazi philosophy that brought the world to its knees and exterminated millions of people originated from the cheap comic-like magazine *Ostara*."

"That can't be true..."

"Oh, but it is. Don't act too surprised, Ms. Venu; I believe Americans can relate since a failed fiction writer created Scientology, and now millions of people take his writings as spiritual guidance."

"Well, he is not a failed writer now, is he?"

"Exactly my point. The Ostara series was published throughout the early nineteen hundreds in Vienna by the pseudo-philosopher Lanz von Liebenfels. It is difficult to comprehend, but the main ideas of *Mein Kampf* and the entire Nazi philosophy were taken from the *Ostara* magazines Hitler collected as a teenager."

"And how are you linking Frederick to this?"

"I think Savitri has had a significant influence on his thinking and actions. I'm confident he met her just before her death when she visited Germany in June of 1982. As a prominent figure of the neo-Nazi party, she was under our twenty-four-hour surveillance. We watched her every step and filmed every contact she had, even if it was in the grocery store. Now imagine that despite all of BFV's efforts, she suddenly vanishes for more than two weeks."

"How can an old woman elude professional surveillance? Did she have supernatural abilities?" Anna asked facetiously.

The agent gave her a look of disappointment. "Not in the slightest. What she did have was sophisticated help. Our agents followed her when she went to the railway station in Bonn to buy a ticket to Frankfurt. After passing through a relatively narrow corridor inside of the station, a fight of ten to fifteen young men broke out and completely blocked the corridor. When our agents tried to pass, they were pulled into the fight and were unable to call for backup.

"When the police arrived at the scene, the fight immediately stopped and all participants melted into the crowd. Savitri had already disappeared. For two weeks, we searched everywhere, but the woman simply vanished. After eighteen days, she reemerged in her hotel room, which continued to hold all her belongings. Only after she left for England, we received a weak lead that she had been staying with a wealthy family in their estate on the outskirts of Bonn. Conveniently, Frederick's family estate is north of Bonn."

"But that's just more speculation," Anna observed.

"That may be so, but there are too many bizarre coincidences to dismiss the possibility. Think about it: After the neo-Nazis began publishing more appealing promotional materials, their physical appearance also changed. Even the structuring of their events became more efficient and friendlier to non-party members and bystanders. All of that coincided with a significant influx of money from an unknown source."

With great confidence, Vogt said, "As I am sure you have already noticed, Frederick is a secluded person. Popular with a lot of acquaintances but no close friends. He rarely stays with one woman for more than three to four weeks."

Anna hid her satisfaction; Frederick was indeed treating her differently.

"That is how we noticed your presence and later, to our complete surprise, we detected that you were being followed. Interestingly enough, this surveillance starts as soon as you are alone. If you are with Frederick, no one watches you."

Vogt paused to let this sink in before continuing. "There were two possible reasons. Your family hired protection, but if this is so, then why would you only be monitored when Frederick was not around—unless they already knew and trusted him? The second possibility is that Frederick arranged the protection for you. Since you have disqualified option one, we are left with option two."

Anna opened her mouth to challenge the agent's theory, but he quickly silenced her.

"Something about the second option is very puzzling. If Frederick arranged for your protection, then it must start as soon as he leaves you, but this is never the case. Your surveillance always starts thirty to forty minutes after he leaves you."

Anna silently mulled over the agent's explanations. She could not see what the time delay had to do with anything.

"So tell me," Agent Vogt began, "why is a tourist girl from Arizona, who is legally in the European Union, of such high interest to neo-Nazis? There has to be something about you that is so important to them that they would spend time, money and a lot of effort to make this whole ordeal look like foolish activity."

Anna felt his stare dissect her.

"I have no idea," Anna said genuinely. "All of this is a pure shock to me, but I still don't know why you would give this tourist girl from Arizona a detailed layout of your whole investigation. I am sure you considered I would tell Frederick everything..."

"It was a risky decision, but I have a tendency to gamble and thought my odds of winning were high."

"What makes you think that?"

"It's doubtful to me that the granddaughter of a man who bravely fought fascism in World War Two would make such a careless decision. I would imagine that you would like to know the truth yourself."

"You placed a good bet."

The agent's face showed satisfaction. He said, "It is in both of our interests to find the truth. Would you not agree?"

"*Our* interests?" Anna scoffed. "You just think I will work with you against the man I deeply care for? I don't even know who you are."

Agent Vogt shifted in his seat, annoyed at having to convince her further. "Ms. Venu, after we are finished, you will leave here with three options. The simplest choice is to do nothing and see what happens next; the harder choice, I would imagine, is to leave Germany behind and return to Arizona; the final choice is to stay in Germany, work with us, and get your own answers."

Anna observed the man's gaze. He already knew what choice she would make, and it aggravated her. She hated being predictable.

"I will need to think about this first, as they are all just such excellent choices," she said sarcastically.

The agent's face relaxed into a mild grin. "Of course. Here is my card. My cell is on me at all times; you may call it twenty-four hours a day."

"Do you not sleep?"

"What do you think?"

Anna noticed the fatigue underneath his solemn stare, but then it vanished. It seemed as though he flashed his true self for a moment before hiding again behind his armor.

"I will drive you back to the coffee shop and let you reclaim your life from our agent."

Anna nodded, though she was no longer sure she wanted to reclaim it. She wondered why there were always complications. *Why can't my blissful German life continue unmarred for just a little longer?*

Two minutes later, he parked the car outside the café and said, "I will expect to hear from you soon, Ms. Venu."

Anna proceeded to step out of the car.

"And, Ms. Venu …"

Anna turned and heard him say, "I am sorry."

"Don't be sorry yet," she said. "Things are not always as they seem."

"No. No, they are definitely not."

Anna shut the door and entered the café through the back door, as she'd been instructed. She returned to her table, gathered her things, and left the café. *There is an explanation for everything*, she said to herself. The only thing Vogt had been right about was her being followed, but everything else seemed like a long, intricate story held together by threaded assumptions.

When she entered her hotel room, she called the concierge. "I'd like to order a bottle of Bordeaux."

Chapter 28

The bottle of Bordeaux was the first thing Anna's eyes opened to the next morning. It stood empty on the bedside table, filled with the rays of the morning sun. Anna's head was splitting. It took her a minute to remember what she had been so worried about the day before. She popped two Advil and turned over. Her cell phone began ringing. It was Frederick. She reached for the phone but stopped herself.

Frederick... Damn. Yesterday's conversation with Agent Vogt rushed back to her. The phone beeped twice. A text message came through: "Good morning, beautiful, give me a call when you are up. I have time to go for lunch and I would like to see you."

I would like to see you too.

She sighed and sat up. She stared at the phone, unable to respond. The urge to tell Frederick everything consumed her.

What if I just asked him?

Anna covered her face with her hands. She was not naïve enough to think that the truth would be something she would get just by asking.

She thought about the white car.

"I am being followed, that I know for sure," Anna stated out loud, "and it may be Frederick's doing, but it also may not. Either way, I need an answer!"

She needed to think. Most importantly, she needed to think away from Frederick for a day or two. Seeing him, kissing him, touching him, would mask any of her doubt.

I need some viable excuse to get away...

Anna thought of her close friend Brienna who periodically had migraine attacks. Brienna had explained to her that forty minutes before an episode, she would smell the strange aroma of violets. Immediately, Brienna would take her medication and go home to lie down in a dark, quiet room, waiting for the migraine to hit.

Anna began texting: Good morning, love, you do not know this about me yet, but I am prone to periodic migraines. I just smelled violets; it is a sign that I will have an intense migraine in about forty minutes. Please do not worry! I have already taken my medication and I just need to stay in a dark room and lie down. I will call you in the morning.

Frederick responded immediately. He offered to get her to the emergency room, to the best clinic—to transport her to his apartment or to come over with anything she needed whenever she needed it.

Anna melted further. She wrote: It is nothing to worry about, I promise. I have gone through every major test at the Mayo Clinic in Scottsdale, and I know what to do. I just need to sleep, be alone, away from light, and stay away from electronics. Please understand.

Again, Frederick expressed his sympathies, but promised to let her be: Anna, I will be waiting for your call!

It was time to get to work. Anna showered and ordered coffee from the concierge. She carefully re-played the entire meeting with Vogt in her head. She tried to remember his body language, voice fluctuations, and facial expressions.

Grandfather had always told her that everything people say or do is a result of some agenda. It could be hidden or obvious, good or bad, intentional or on an unknown subconscious level. Either way, no one acted or even made a simple comment for no reason at all. Therefore, behind the agent's proposed friendly partnership was his own motive.

The BFV needed her to get to Frederick; that much was obvious. Like Vogt had told her, this case was personal to him—so personal that he risked his career at the BFV by continuing to investigate on his own time. He even contacted Anna directly, something she was sure his superiors wouldn't have permitted. Taking all of this into consideration, she decided that he could not be trusted.

Anna took a big gulp of coffee and stared out of her window. On the street below was what looked like the same white car from yesterday, but Anna could not be sure. If what Vogt had theorized about Frederick was even partly true, it would change everything. There was no way she could have any relations with a person involved with neo-Nazis.

"You gave me three options," Anna said out loud to an invisible Vogt. "To leave Germany, impossible; to let things unravel on their own, but I refuse to leave my life up to chance; or to cooperate with you, which would most likely leave me with the short end of the stick. The thing is, Vogt, you never thought of option four: I find the truth out myself. And believe me, I will."

There were similarities between the neo-Nazi beliefs Vogt had expanded on and the deeper meanings of the historical events Frederick had referenced. Still, the agent could have made it all up. He could have spun everything to work in his favor.

Maybe he is after Frederick for a different reason altogether... After all, his family has money, power, and influence. He could have been using a conspiracy theory to scare me into becoming his pawn....

Anna again glanced down at the parked white car. *Shit! He could have even set up the entire spying scheme by himself!*

Anna began pacing the room in an attempt to get into the mind of Vogt.

What did Vogt think of me? How did he perceive me? She saw her reflection in the mirror. An innocent face stared back at her.

From his perspective, I look incredibly harmless and vulnerable. Here I am, a young American girl with strong anti-Nazi roots in Germany dating a very nationalistic German man.

More coffee flowed down her throat.

Vogt has done everything to more or less freak me out. The important question is: How did he expect me to respond? Vogt insisted on me not telling Frederick about our conversation, using my family's anti-Nazi past as justification, but that is obviously a stretch. If Vogt really didn't want me to tell Frederick, then he would not have risked telling me so much information. I could have bad relations with my family. I could value Frederick over everyone else. He is too smart to assume otherwise.

Anna drew a decision tree of possible outcomes. *And I thought I would never use statistics in real life.* She smiled.

"Alright, here we go," she said out loud. "If I tell Frederick about the surveillance, and the surveillance stops, then Vogt would have some proof that Frederick is somehow connected to the neo-Nazis. It can be enough circumstantial evidence to reopen the investigation.

"If Frederick has nothing to do with the surveillance, Frederick would probably go to the police or to his own contacts to get to the bottom of this situation. Vogt could deny knowing anything and I have no proof of our conversation. It would be my word against his and I would probably lose. Finally, Vogt may have set this all up to somehow get to Frederick."

Anna tapped her pen repeatedly on the notepad. She stared at the pattern of dots it created until it hit her. *Vogt won't lose anything if I tell Frederick about meeting him. He has to want me to tell Frederick everything. If this whole neo-Nazi ordeal was made up to get to Frederick for another reason, I have no way of knowing what Vogt really wants. As usual, I can only trust myself.*

Anna confirmed into the mirror, "Okay, let's play detective. I need to figure this out without sabotaging my relationship with Frederick."

There was just one problem that began to surface within Anna's thoughts. *Vogt said that Frederick had detected he was being watched almost immediately, and that was professional surveillance. I am nowhere near that level, and I won't stand a chance.*

She kept thinking. The common-sense thing to do was hack his computer, but that was impossible. Anna was no Lisbeth Salander from Stieg Larsson's trilogy.

Where was his computer anyway? Anna began thinking back to his apartment. Frederick had a laptop, she had seen it before, but she never saw it just lying around.

"Of course— Frederick's office!"

Chapter 29

Frederick's office (a.k.a. the Bluebeard Room) was always closed and Anna had spent so many nights walking past it that she had almost forgotten it existed. Excitement bubbled within her. That would be her first step, to access his office. Would the door be locked? And if so, would the key be on Frederick's keychain?

Anna began Googling. There had to be a way to mold a key using the lock itself. There was the possibility of imprinting his entire set of keys onto a soft mold. She had only seen it in movies.

I need to look at that lock immediately!

The clock read 3:00 p.m. It was still too early to call Frederick. Anna knew she was behaving strangely, and Frederick would have questions, maybe even ask to see her medication.

I need to secure my alibi before I see him.

Anna quickly headed downstairs and out the back door of the hotel. She hailed a taxi.

"Nearest emergency room, please!"

Anna staggered into the emergency clinic, shielding her eyes from light and holding her temples. An emergency clinic would be obligated to give her a prescription for migraine medication immediately, and that was what she triumphantly left with.

At 8:00 p.m., she decided to give Frederick a call. He answered on the first ring.

"I am feeling much better. I think I want to come over…" Anna said weakly.

Frederick insisted on coming up to her floor to pick her up. Just to be safe, Anna made sure to close the front door behind her as soon as she heard footsteps in the hallway. A bouquet of pink roses turned the corner: his smile, his scent, his concerned eyes. Everything about him made her lose her senses, just like she had predicted.

"Anna, I was so worried about you… I missed you!" Frederick kissed her and lifted her into his arms. The way he said "I missed you" was so soft, almost shy. It was honest. Anna closed her eyes.

What had she been thinking? She held onto him tightly with the hope that around them, the remaining world and all its worries would simply evaporate. She kissed him longingly.

"The roses are beautiful, thank you."

Frederick's affections directed her for the remainder of the night. She even walked past the Bluebeard Room twice, refusing to give the room attention, but her conscious persisted.

During her third trip past the door, she glanced at the lock—a moment of clarity cut through to her. There was no keyhole at all. The lock was automated. Underneath the handle, four small buttons looked back at her.

How did I not notice this before? She wanted to ask Frederick about it. Maybe casually make a joke about him having such high security, but that may raise his suspicions. Anna said nothing. She could think of no way to open the door now.

Frederick called her name from the living room. Her concern for the door and the investigation faded as swiftly as it had when she saw Frederick in her hallway. He continued to kiss her suspicion away. At

3:00 a.m., her eyes fluttered open. The moon stared at her through the window.

Anna turned to face him, but he wasn't there. Anna sat up. No light or sound came from the bathroom. *What the hell?* Gliding off the bed, her toes silently met the wooden floor and she proceeded into the hallway.

The Bluebeard Room's door was closed, but light was visible from the crack beneath. Anna smiled. A new plan formulated itself. She slithered back into bed to await the morning.

As usual, Frederick woke up first. Anna felt his kiss on her cheek, but kept her eyes closed. When the shower started, Anna quietly reached for her cosmetics bag and withdrew an eyebrow pencil. Seconds later, she was on her knees in front of Frederick's closed office door. Using her eyebrow pencil, she measured the small distance between the floor and the office door's lower edge. Using her fingernail, she made an indent into the pencil to mark the distance. Anna tiptoed back to bed, her heart racing.

Frederick's footsteps left the bathroom. They stopped at the foot of the bed and remained there. Anna held her breath. He knew something was off. He sensed it. He sensed her. The pounding in her chest quickened. Frederick leaned onto the bed; her body slid toward the part of the mattress that sunk underneath his weight. This was it. She opened her eyes only to meet Frederick's gaze.

"Good morning, beautiful," he whispered.

Relief swept over Anna, "Good morning."

Frederick dropped her off at her hotel at 10:00 a.m. Immediately, she walked to the nearest pharmacy and bought a disposable cell phone, along with toiletries and snacks to lower suspicions.

Back in her room, she placed a call to Arizona.

"AZ Spy Shop, how may I help you?"

"Hello, is Steve available? This is Anna Venu."

"One moment, please."

Anna readied a pen and paper. A man's voice soon took the call. "Anna! How are you doing, kid? How's dad?"

A smile came over her. She had not talked to Steve in ages. When Anna was a child, she became obsessed with the idea of being a spy. Anna read through all the Nancy Drew and Hardy Boys books and replayed *Harriet the Spy* and *Spy Kids* dozens of times. After begging her father for real gadgets, he finally caved in. The result was a series of fun trips to the AZ Spy Shop. Her father and the store's owner Steve, a former army officer, even developed a friendship. Now Anna was calling Steve for help.

"I need to order an endoscope camera with the lens no larger than two centimeters. It needs to have high resolution, a wide-angle lens, and a light source."

"Anna, that is a really high-tech piece of equipment. I don't even carry it. I can order something for you, but it will cost a lot."

"I understand," Anna replied.

"What is this for? Should I be worried?"

Anna let out a light-hearted laugh. "Oh, no, it's nothing major. I think my boyfriend may be cheating on me and I want to know for myself. I need it shipped to Berlin ASAP."

"Berlin—"

"I'm studying abroad." Anna quickly prevented any further questions.

"Alright, Anna. I will take a look, give me a few minutes."

Anna hung up the phone and paced the room. She called Steve back twenty minutes later.

"The camera will arrive in five days," he said.

"Thank you, Steve."

Waiting for the package put Anna in high spirits. Excitement pulsated through her as it had when she was a child holding her first pair of real binoculars. The most important thing now was to chill.

I need to relax and not act any different.

For the next few days, Anna took herself for long walks, meditated, and did breathing exercises before seeing Frederick at night.

On the fifth day, she received a call from her hotel's front desk: a package had arrived for her. After inspecting the camera, she realized that assembling and learning to operate it would take her a fair amount of time. Anna began immediately. First thing in the morning, after Frederick dropped her off, she would assemble and dismantle the camera over and over.

Her fingers fidgeted clumsily until frustration forced her to take her usual walk to the coffee shop. Over a cappuccino, Anna watched for the white car, worked away on her laptop, and walked back to the hotel. Again, she worked the camera until Frederick called to pick her up after work.

The next day, Anna added another component by testing the camera underneath her bathroom door. During one of their city strolls, Anna asked Frederick to gift her a chic backpack. Immediately it began accompanying her to Frederick's house. When she was ready, the backpack would eventually conceal the camera. After a week, the process became automatic.

"I think I am ready!" she said after another quick and successful assembly. She reached for her backpack, but suddenly stopped.

"I have never been alone in his apartment. Shit, how did this not dawn on me before?"

Anna never paid attention to that realization until now, but it was so obvious. Even when Frederick had half-days, he would still wake her up, drop her off, and pick her up later in the day. *He doesn't trust me in his apartment.* Anna sat on the edge of her bed. *How do I get him to leave me alone?*

By Thursday, Anna found a solution and decided it was time to spring into action. Frederick was on the couch reading while Anna was working on her laptop. The whole day, anxiety blossomed within her. She let it fester and grow. Anna would need it for this exact moment. The camera waited at the bottom of her backpack.

"Oh, God..." Anna grabbed her temples and squeezed her eyes tight, repeating, "Violets… violets…"

Frederick looked up. "Anna?"

She began taking long deep breaths. "Frederick…violets!"

Tears formed at the corners of her eyes.

"What is the matter?" Frederick was by her side now, trying to console her.

"My medication! In my hotel! Frederick, I didn't bring it!" Her voice was escalating, rising with each syllable.

"Anna, don't panic; I am calling an ambulance right now!"

"No!" Anna shouted, they won't have it; I need my specific medication now! Frederick!"

"Alright, let's go!"

But Anna was already running to the bathroom. She locked the door behind her and began dry-heaving into the sink."

"Anna!"

Frederick was pounding on the door. Anna shoved her finger further down her throat; she was sobbing now, letting the built-up anxiety leave her body in emotional convulsions.

"Frederick, please go get my prescription—it's in my bathroom, the key is on the counter." She gasped in between sobs.

"Go now! Please!" she begged from behind the door.

Anna heard Frederick pacing behind the door.

OK, one more push. She thought and started another convulsion.

She heard him curse and run into the living room. The front door slammed. She had approximately twenty minutes. Anna grabbed her backpack and ran into the living room.

Outside the Bluebeard Room, she took one big steadying breath. With her heart racing, she assembled the camera. The endoscope slithered through the bottom crack like a snake. Carefully, she held the screen and pivoted the endoscope around the room.

Frederick's office was smaller than she expected. Anna controlled the movement of the camera from one side of the room to the other. Suddenly a loud mechanical noise cut the silence. Anna jumped and almost dropped the camera from panic. The inkjet printer in the office was printing a fax.

Anna returned the lens to the wall opposite the door and concentrated one more time on Frederick's desk. She was done in ten minutes and shut off the camera.

Suddenly, she heard the elevator doors open outside the front door.

Shit! How did he get back so fast!?

Anna ran back to the bedroom and shoved the camera into the corner underneath the bed frame. The front door opened as she locked herself back in the bathroom and shut off the lights.

Frederick came pounding down the hall. "Anna, open the door!" he commanded.

The faucet was running, and Anna splashed water all over her face. Her mascara ran down her cheeks. Slowly, she opened the bathroom door, hiding her face behind a wet towel. She looked pathetic sitting in the dark bathroom on the floor.

Frederick's face flushed red. "Are you alright?"

He handed her the bottle of medication. Anna brought her finger to her lips to signify silence.

"Thank you," she whispered and reached for the medication with a trembling hand.

She closed the door on Frederick and laid down on the cold floor, taking deep breaths until she heard Frederick walk away from the door. She flushed the pill down the toilet.

Anna could not stay in the bathroom; the camera was underneath the bed. She washed her face and slowly stepped into the hallway to thank Frederick. His back was to her, and his hands were looking through her backpack.

What the hell? Anna backed into the bedroom and panicked. Did she leave something behind? Did she make a mistake? Did he know?

She stepped back into the bathroom and made a fair amount of noise to draw Frederick's attention. He immediately came to her and walked her into the bedroom. Anna hid half her face into the pillows. She was terrified.

Frederick sat at the edge of her bed and felt her head. "Are you alright now?"

Anna nodded, "I'm sorry..."

He kissed her on the forehead and sweetly said, "Go to sleep..."

Anna could not sleep. Her eyes remained closed, but the camera underneath the bed burned through her. She felt its presence with the same discomfort had it been physically underneath her back. She drifted off only after Frederick's breathing deepened into slumber several hours later.

In the morning, Anna retrieved the camera and shoved it back into her bag while Frederick showered.

He held her hand in the car and kissed her goodbye in front of the hotel.

"I will check on you later today," he said.

"Thank you," Anna repeated over and over. "You saved me."

She left his car and walked towards the hotel entrance. Once the door of her hotel room closed, Anna took a long, loud breath and fell onto her bed. True exhaustion came over her, but she could not lay still. Anna got up and turned on her laptop. She plugged in the camera and began to upload the video.

Frederick's office was neat and organized. A laptop lay closed on his desk. Above the desk hung a framed print of three interconnected triangles. *The symbol looks Roman*, she thought. A portrait of Admiral Doenitz hung just below the triangles alongside a portrait of her great-grandfather Commander Ritter standing atop his U-boat's conning tower. It was the same picture that was featured in Karl's book.

On the right wall were more portraits; they looked like family photographs. Below them was the printer. An antique-looking leather couch stood against the left wall. Above it hung a rather large portrait of an Indian woman. Or rather, a European woman with crossed arms wearing a traditional Indian saree.

Had the BFV agent been right? Was that the mother of the neo-Nazi movement?

Anna concentrated on the portrait. Something was written in the upper left-hand corner, but she could not make it out. She would need parts of the video enlarged.

Anna resumed the video and scanned the remaining portraits. There were no swastikas or pictures of Hitler. Doenitz and her great-grandfather were there, but Frederick never hid his admiration for either man.

Anna sighed a breath of relief. A mechanical noise interrupted her calm, and again she jumped. It was the same which started working, this time in the video.

Anna rubbed her face. *Keep it together, Anna!* The camera slowly moved right, giving the printer enough time to print one sheet whose top margin hung down from the machine tray. Anna squinted her eyes. The top of the printed sheet displayed three interlocked triangles, the same symbol, which hung above Frederick's desk. Below it was one line of text, but Anna was unable to read it.

She opened her browser and typed in: *meaning of three interlocked triangles.*

It was not Roman as she had thought, but a Nordic occult symbol. One theory was that the triangles, called a valknut, symbolized the power of Odin—the Norse God of war, death, wisdom, magic, and prophecy.

Odin could bind and unbind the minds of warriors in battle. If bound, men would become helpless, and if loosened, men could ease their fear with Odin's three gifts of battle: madness, intoxication, and inspiration. These gifts were treasured by Germans in antiquity and later by Vikings. In modern times, the image was used by German and Swedish companies as a symbol of national identity, and even the German soccer team used it.

There was no mention of neo-Nazism. Anna scrolled to the bottom of the page and her heart sank. For once, she detested Google's "searches related to." One of the suggestions read: "valknut white supremacy."

With hesitation, Anna made the click.

White supremacists and neo-Nazis used the same symbol, as a racist symbol of a pure Aryan nation. In the United States, Odinism started to spread among white prisoners as a counter-ideology to the Jihadist movement. Anna closed the webpage.

"Don't jump to conclusions!" She repeated the phrase to herself three times, once for each interconnected triangle. Linked together, they formed a symbol of hate or one of Germanic historical value. It made a lot of sense for Frederick to be associated with the latter, but Anna had to know for sure.

Chapter 30

Anna had to know for sure what was written on the corner of the portrait and what was on the printout. Immediately, Anna contacted Kenny, her friend from USC, who agreed to come to her rescue once again. In two days, Anna received the email she had been waiting for: "You are giving me more work for my portfolio than my internship does." Anna smiled. She exclaimed to Kenny in a text message: "I owe you, Kenny!"

Kenny shot back a text: I cleaned up the letters on the still as best I could. Up to you to translate. As for the printout, there is only one letter in the line of text; the rest are numbers.

Numbers? Anna opened the enlarged and edited attachments. Kenny was right. The printout contained one line of numbers underneath the valknut symbol. It read: 1109220034k.

Anna opened the second file and typed the German words into Google Translate. The translation read: Frederick, my little angel. Be smart and make a difference, with love, Savitri Devi.

Damn it...

Vogt had been right. Frederick had known her personally. What in the world did Savitri's writings instill in Frederick exactly? Was the focus on animal rights or Aryan supremacy? Anna let out a forced laugh; the situation was bleak.

She drank some cabernet, but it only tasted of dry guilt. *I'm such an idiot!*

Some of what Vogt had said about Frederick's interests had been true, but Frederick had not hidden any of it. If he knew what she had been up to, he would never trust her again. Their relationship would be over, and she wouldn't even be able to blame him.

Anna finished her wine and stared into the faint outline of the rising moon outside her window. The numbers on the printout were the last piece of the puzzle. There had been nothing else on the sheet of paper. Why was only one line of numbers sent over? The fax could have been sent from anywhere by anyone. The message was so cryptic that it looked like a code.

I will make a pact with you, she said to the moon mentally. *If the numbers on the fax lead to nothing, I will drop this whole conspiracy theory. I will stop suspecting Frederick.*

The next day, Anna stared at the sequence on her laptop. *Were the numbers a code or a password?* The only clue was the letter *k. It could mean thousands of dollars,* Anna thought, *but the* k *is lowercase, not capital, and even if it was capitalized, that would signify a tremendous amount of money, even for Frederick.*

She thought it could also stand for karat, but again the number was too high to make sense.

On a notepad, Anna separated the numbers, but she failed to find a pattern. They refused to give her any clue.

Maybe, the problem is not the numbers. Perhaps the problem is me. Perhaps if I was German, I could figure out what it meant.

Anna rushed downstairs to the hotel lounge, where she saw her favorite bartender, and that was exactly who she wanted to see.

"Hey, Arlo," Anna said, having practically jogged over. "If you have a minute, I need your opinion on something."

In his late twenties, Arlo was an Australian bartender with a knack for traveling off the grid in-between jobs. They had become friendly talking about Arlo's next adventure and one of Anna's favorite routes, the California Pacific Coast Highway.

Anna ordered a gin and tonic and continued to stare at the numbers. Arlo came over several minutes later.

"What's up?"

"Alright, this is random, but I am going to give you a sequence of numbers. Do they mean anything to you—or is there, like, a pattern you can recognize in them?"

Arlo's dark features became animated. "A puzzle? A mysterious code? Let me look at it!"

He took the sheet of paper from her. "Hmmm..."

"Well, the last two digits are probably distance or speed, but I'm sure you have already figured out that much."

Anna stared at him, dumbfounded. "What do you mean distance or speed?"

The look on Arlo's face showed surprise. He pointed at the digits and explained, "Well, actually, it is distance. Look, there are two zeros before the number thirty-four, followed by a little *k* at the end. The *k* stands for kilometers and if there is no *h* behind the *k*, then the number is referring to distance, not speed. So, most likely, the last two digits of the number sequence mean thirty-four kilometers."

"Arlo, you are a genius. I can't believe I completely missed something so obvious! I still see the world in miles!"

"Don't blame yourself, Anna. Blame England for giving the United States an inferior system of measurement."

"A small price to pay for independence," she remarked. "Do you see anything else in these numbers?"

Arlo took several more moments, but returned the paper with a look of defeat. "I got nothing."

Anna returned to her room with a slight buzz. On her bed, she opened up Google Maps and looked at various points: 34 kilometers away from Berlin, 34 kilometers away from Frederick's apartment, and 34 kilometers away from his university. The location could be anywhere, but nothing jumped out in particular. She had hit another dead end.

The next three days passed, but in her mind, Anna was constantly coming back to the number sequence without any results. Feeling stressed and desperate, Anna decided to concentrate on studying German and finally making it onto social media. Her friends in Arizona had been bothering her for photos of her travels. The thought of updating Facebook or Instagram with all her adventures seemed overwhelming, but she had time to kill.

Saturday morning, she awoke to the welcoming aroma of espresso. Frederick was already in the kitchen. Anna grabbed her laptop and joined him. Their entire relationship showcased itself in pairs of frames across her computer screen.

The Munich market, the Dresden museum, the bridge in Regensburg, and, finally, the Teutoburg Forest. Anna took her time looking through the last addition of their photographs from Kalkriese Hill. She had neglected to browse them before. There were several shots of her against the backdrop of the forest. Frederick's voice repeated itself from her memory: "Keep smiling! I need to find the right light."

Being a perfectionist, Frederick paid extra attention to his shots. Anna's hair gleamed gold in the few rays that escaped that day's overcast clouds.

Only a person in love could take photographs like that, she thought as she smiled to herself.

Her index finger tapped through the remaining photos. Trees, wet earth, her grinning, Frederick at the museum's observation deck. She chose several images and added them to a new Facebook album and closed her laptop.

There, painless enough.

In the darkness of night, Anna awoke in a cold sweat, the nightmare still fresh in her mind. She looked at the time. It was 3:00 a.m.: witching hour. She sat up in bed shakily and reran the dream from beginning to end. She and Frederick were back on their trip through Germany, but they were on the run, constantly hiding to escape an unknown hunter. A sense of paralyzing fear accompanied her. Then, somehow, Frederick vanished. Anna was alone, walking naked along a forest road in cold pouring rain. Shivering and exhausted, she sat down on the dirt, hugging her knees, and leaned against a road marker. The fear had left her and was replaced by a sense of complete emptiness. She looked up and saw the number 34 written on the top of the road marker.

The trip through Germany... Maybe that is a clue to the location. I have already been there. An eerie chill played its way down her spine.

Anna removed the covers and quietly left Frederick's bed. She fought the overpowering urge to run to her laptop and instead tiptoed into the kitchen and poured herself a glass of water. She waited a few minutes for Frederick to wake up, but he didn't. Anna opened her laptop and scrolled through the photos from their trip. Her heart pounded with each click on the trackpad.

All this time, it was right there. Right in front of her. The partial solution to the riddle. Anna zoomed in on herself, leaning against or standing next to the 34-kilometer post in every single shot.

What if 34k is the location itself? The Teutoburg forest, an iconic destination for Frederick. A place saturated with historical significance; a sanctuary for him.

"Anna, what are you doing?"

Anna jumped from the sofa and slammed her laptop shut. "Frederick!"

His eyes scanned through her like an X-ray.

"You scared me to death!"

With slow precision, Frederick walked over to her and lifted the screen of her laptop.

The photographs from the trip immediately appeared. Anna held her breath.

He knows! He knows what I have been up to. He senses something. She found herself trying to mentally block his invasive stare. Anna closed her eyes, ready for an assault of accusations that she would be unable to deny.

"You can do this tomorrow. It's three in the morning. Let's get back to bed."

Anna looked up with innocent relief. "You're right, babe. I just couldn't sleep..."

Frederick's light snoring soon broke the silence of the bedroom. Unable to sleep, Anna stared out the window into the empty night sky.

Why did he take so many photos of me next to the kilometer post from different angles? Were the photos really of me or of something else that he was trying to capture?

In the morning, Anna kissed Frederick goodbye, playfully nibbled his earlobe, and ran to the front door of the Art'otel as his BMW sped away. Back in her room, the sequence stared back at her waiting for her to make the first move. 1109220034k

If 34k was a kilometer post on a small road in the Teutoburg Forest, then the remaining numbers were more likely associated with the concept of location.

What about zip codes? How would someone know where the 34k post would be without knowing the city it is in? Alright, Google, here we go again.

Anna searched for the postal code of Bramsche, the town that Kalkriese was located in, and saw it was 49565. No match. Anna expanded her search outward to include codes in the district of Osnabrück; they spanned 49074–49090. Again, no matches. Searching the number 110922 landed her in Muldrow, Oklahoma, while 92200 got her to the Neuilly Sur Seine region in France.

What else could the numbers represent? she asked herself.

Anna rewrote the numbers separating out the sequence in various ways:

110922 0034k; 110 922 0034k; 1109 2200 34k; 11 09 22 00 34k.

Anna could not help but focus on the two zeros.

There are not that many instances when two zeros make sense. It has to be time, 22:00 on the 24-hour clock, which Europe uses, or 10:00 p.m. American.

*Or...*Anna rewrote the sequence, *it could also be 2:00 on the 24-hour clock, which is 2:00 a.m. In that case, the code would read: 11092 200 34k.*

Anna first considered 2:00; in this scenario, the remaining numbers broke the two-digit pattern: 11 092 2:00 34k or 110 92 2:00 34k. She then thought about the 10:00 pm option and read the numbers as: 11 09 22 00 34k. *That feels more natural.*

Continuing to use the two-digit pattern, she was left looking at 11 09. Aligning that with a location, 34k, and a supposed time, 22:00 or 10:00 p.m., she landed on a new take: *Logically, 11 09 would have to be a date!* November 9, four months away.

Anna checked the calendar but stopped herself.

Wait a minute... I am thinking like an American again. In Europe, the date goes first, then the month, which makes it September 11!

She thought about this day, which signified so much for Americans: the terrorist attacks on the twin towers in New York City, the Pentagon, and Shanksville, Pennsylvania. There was something else about the date, which she'd recently learned from Frederick. It was an important date for Germans, as well.

What was it?

Anna opened a new Google search: German history September 11.

Immediately, several results for the Battle of the Teutoburg Forest appeared.

"Of course!" Anna scrolled through the entries. September 9–September 11 were the supposed dates of Roman defeat by Arminius.

Anna looked back at the calendar: The 11th fell on a Saturday, and it was only six weeks away. She shot out of her chair and paced the room.

September 11, 10:00 p.m. at the 34k milepost in Kalkriese. *It just has to be a meeting; too many things are adding up, but…*

Anna turned to her reflection in the mirror. "I can be completely wrong."

She needed some sort of evidence that verified her hunch. *That will be easy. If Frederick is busy the night of September 11, then I'm likely right.*

That night, Anna began fishing.

"Frederick, I am thinking of returning to Sankt Gilgen to visit Inna. I have been feeling guilty ever since I found out Helga's real identity and how she died. I want to give her Helga's photograph."

Frederick nodded in approval. "Can't you do it over the phone and then send the photograph by mail?"

"It is such a delicate matter, especially to Inna. The woman has been obsessed with finding the truth about Helga. I need to tell her everything in person. I'm thinking of going for a week. Taking some time and visiting Vienna."

"A week?" Frederick grimaced. "Why don't we go for a weekend? We can make a short vacation out of it."

Anna smiled sorrowfully, "Honestly, Frederick, I don't think it will be that sort of trip. I want to spend some time with Inna. I am thinking of going in September."

"She's not even your family..."

Anna felt agitated. "She is my family now! Can I not just go if I want to go?"

"You can do what you want," Frederick responded curtly. "I need to leave Berlin in September myself."

Anna's throat tightened. "When and where are you going?"

"It's just for three or four days, a business trip to Hamburg. From September ninth to the twelfth."

Anna drank some of her wine.

"Can I come with you?" she pressed further.

"Not this time, Anna. It's really a business retreat for my father's company and I am supporting him during the event. We will be expanding into new markets. The leadership team is expected to come alone to be fully engaged in the planning process."

"Why didn't you say something earlier?"

"The details just got finalized."

"I see. Then, I will go to Austria the same weekend."

Frederick squeezed her hand and said, "Okay."

The turmoil began to race within her like a cyclone. She looked into the eyes of the man she loved. He could be someone completely different, or he could not. There was a meeting he was going to. It could have nothing to do with anything she suspected. The secrecy could be to hide something illegal, like bribery or some sort of mafia association. After all, it was Vogt who had planted the seed of neo-Nazism into Anna's head. Either way, she needed to figure it out.

It was late evening when they returned to Frederick's apartment; Anna had been quiet the entire car ride home. This game was emotionally draining; she just wanted the truth as soon as possible.

I think it is time to tell him about me being followed, she said to herself. *Something has to change after he finds out.*

Anna climbed into bed, situating herself away from Frederick. When he leaned in to kiss her, Anna moved away.

"Are you still upset about my business trip? I told you it was just scheduled."

Anna didn't answer.

"Anna! What is the matter with you? You've been distant since dinner."

"It's not that," Anna began. Her eyes began to flood. To her surprise, real tears ran down her face, "Did you send people to follow me?" Anna sobbed into her hands.

"Did I do what?" Frederick asked with such genuine surprise and disbelief in his voice that Anna immediately felt better.

"Give me your word that you didn't hire any personal bodyguards for me while I am alone."

"I don't even know what you're talking about."

"I am really scared," Anna said with genuine emotion.

Frederick sat up and held Anna's shoulders. "Tell me what's wrong."

To enhance the drama, Anna dabbed the corners of her eyes and looked up at Frederick. "Several days ago, I realized that there are two cars with the same drivers who follow me around when I'm not with you. At first, I thought it was my imagination, so I continued not to pay them any attention, but then they became sloppy. The cars don't even try to be discreet anymore. I then thought it was my father or grandfather who secretly hired personal protection, but I spoke with them and they are not involved. The only person left who would want to protect me is you. And if it is you, then you obviously don't trust me or you are crazy overprotective, and frankly, I hate both scenarios!" Anna sobbed into her hands.

"Anna, I didn't hire anyone to follow you!"

"Then I'm being followed by some maniacs and will end up dead!"

"Please don't exaggerate!"

"Are you kidding?" she shot back. "I'm not exaggerating; they have been following me for the last two weeks!"

Frederick's voice fell an octave. "Alright, I need you to describe what the drivers and cars look like."

"There are two cars and two drivers, and they seem to alternate days. There is a white car with a young driver in his late twenties, and he was around today. The other car is tan and has a bulky older driver with a military-style haircut. He will probably show up tomorrow."

"Alright. Tomorrow when I drop you off, go back to the cafe. I will be close by."

"But how will you…"

"Anna, don't worry about it—it won't be a problem." Frederick's voice was full of confidence. As if he knew exactly what to do. "Now, try to get some rest."

The next morning, Anna walked to the café. As expected, the tan car made its appearance every time she turned a corner. Anna looked around as hard as she could, but was unable to spot Frederick or anyone else following the car that was following her.

Later that day, Anna returned to her hotel in high anticipation of Frederick's call. At 5:00 p.m., he picked her up. Anna sat on pins and needles.

"Did you see him?" Anna asked quickly.

Frederick pulled away from the hotel and onto the main road.

"You were right. There was a tan car following you today. I observed it for some time and confronted the driver a couple of hours later."

"You did what?"

"I opened the passenger door and got into the car. We had a chat."

"A chat?" Anna repeated.

Frederick pulled the car over and momentarily parked it. He looked directly at Anna.

"Anna, I am glad you told me. The man is a creep. His name is Klaus Müller, he's unemployed and has a police record for exhibitionism. You caught his eye. I have already filed a police report. He won't be bothering you anymore. I made him understand the consequences."

Anna sat stunned. "How did you get his police record?"

"This is my city; I am well connected here."

"What was his name again?" asked Anna.

"Klaus Müller, but it does not come up online. I have already checked."

Anna stared at Frederick. He was lying—right to her face. The man's name was Martin Schultz; Agent Vogt had shown her the man's mug shot.

Anna stopped herself. B*ut who says Vogt was the one being honest?* The mug shot could have been fake. Anna brought her fingers to her temples, her head pulsed from confusion.

"What about the white car tomorrow?" she asked.

"I will do the same thing tomorrow. Go about your day as usual."

When Anna walked to the café the next morning, there was no white or tan car. It seemed no car was following her at all. Again, she could not find Frederick anywhere.

"Anna, I think you made a mistake with thinking a white car is following you," he said to her later that evening. "I observed you the entire day and saw no one."

"I didn't see anyone today, either," Anna remarked. "Maybe they will be there tomorrow."

Anna had a feeling the white car would no longer make an appearance, and she was right. Over the next several days, she couldn't see any signs of being followed.

There are only two possible explanations, Anna said to herself while thumping her pen. *Frederick either canceled the surveillance, or he controlled the people who followed me.*

Either way, he was lying to her and going as far as to make up a story about some pervert. It was insulting. *Does he really think I'm that stupid?* Frustrated, Anna threw the notepad across the room.

Chapter 31

Across the room, the notepad sat patiently, waiting as Anna scrambled to retrieve it from in between the dresser and floor lamp. Her ear burned hot pressed against her burner phone.

"Basically, I need a wireless night-vision digital camera with long-lasting batteries, a wide-angle lens, and the highest possible resolution. Oh, and it needs to be as small as possible."

Silence answered her request. Steve, the AZ Spy Shop owner, was on the receiving line.

"Anna…are you in the business now or something?"

The question, which started jokingly, ended on a nervous note.

"Steve, you run a respected business based on confidentiality. I understand you are a family friend, but I need that same confidentiality from you that you give your top clients."

"I need the camera within two weeks, max. I know that is a tough deadline."

"Alright... Are you thinking of a live-feed camera or a classic model with internal storage?'

Anna considered the question. She couldn't risk being dependent on a wireless network connection.

"Internal storage," she said.

The conversation ended with Steve promising to fulfill the request to the best of his abilities. Anna had a month and a half to prepare for

Frederick's business meeting on September 11 to prove to herself that it was exactly what he had described it to be.

Following Frederick to the meeting was out of the question—that plan would fail immediately, but that wasn't her only option. Anna had the advantage of knowing the date, time, and location of the meeting—or rather, the supposed meeting's presumed date, time, and location.

After careful evaluation of all possibilities, Anna concluded that filming the event was her only chance at success. The catch was that she could not physically be there without giving herself away. Even given her fancy new gadgets and meticulous planning, Anna was an amateur and she knew this was a weakness she couldn't help.

Her first task was to buy a train ticket to Salzburg. At the Berlin Hauptbahnhof, Anna spoke as loudly as possible in broken German in case she was still being followed, which she was sure she was.

After boarding the train bound for Salzburg, Anna would leave the train at the first transfer station and proceed directly to a rental car agency. Paying cash, she would rent and drive a car to Bramsche, the town closest to Kalkriese Hill, a few days before the actual meeting, behaving as an American tourist exploring Germany.

Online, Anna found a small privately-owned bed-and-breakfast in Bramsche. With her friend Brienna on the phone, Anna reserved a room using Brienna's credit card. As usual, of late, Anna finished the call with, "I'll explain everything later!"

Next, she spent time looking for a beauty supply store in Berlin close to the hotel that carried wigs. She picked out an unassuming dark brown shoulder-length wig with bangs, and a cap for her hair. Anna wrote down the item numbers and returned to the hotel bar. Arlo was smelling bottles of open wine.

"If I give you fifty euros, will you do me an easy favor?"

Arlo arched his brows questioningly. "Sounds like it's not so easy."

Anna laughed. "It is, I swear. It's personal, so I won't go into details, but I need you to buy these items for me at the beauty store a few blocks away and drop them off for me at the concierge. That's it."

"Uh-huh… And by *items,* do you mean *party favors*?"

"Cocaine, heroin, whatever you got," Anna answered flatly.

Arlo looked around suspiciously and leaned in closer. "Are you serious?"

Anna's laugh broke her straight expression. "No, crazy! I need a wig, but I can't pick it up myself. It's a long story that I'm not willing to share." She smiled brightly.

Arlo threw a bar towel over his shoulder and raised a brow. "Ahh so it is a party favor then, sounds kinky. Platinum blonde?"

"Deep brunette."

"Sultry."

"Obviously," she said playfully and finished her drink.

Two days later, Anna received both the wig and a call from Steve notifying her that the 7000 Series Outdoor Camera with built-in intelligent video analytics had been shipped express.

The camera was a fascinating piece of equipment. It picked up nighttime images easily and itself did not generate any noise or emit any light. Anna spent her free time alone learning how to perfect its operations. However, how she would actually record the supposed meeting was a different problem altogether.

On September 6, Frederick drove Anna to the Berlin Hauptbahnhof where Anna had first arrived in Berlin, intimidated by its essence. In a way, Anna felt as though she was going backward to the beginning. After several passionate goodbye kisses, she left Frederick's embrace and descended the train platforms' stairs.

Anna boarded the intercity express train headed for Hannover, her first transfer station perfectly located between Berlin and Bramsche. She bought a disposable phone there. She then called Frederick and told him that she left her phone in the hotel and for the duration of the trip she'll have to use a disposable phone to get in touch with him.

Of course, Anna didn't actually transfer to the train headed south for Munich and then onward to Salzburg. Instead, she made her way into the Hannover Hauptbahnhof bathroom, changed her clothing, and became her brunette alter ego. Anna left the bathroom and headed out to pick up her reserved car.

With her newly rented GPS navigator turned on, Anna maneuvered the car onto the autobahn. She felt good. The plan to plant the camera somewhere by the 34k post seemed too easy to actually work, but, then again, did it have to be complicated? The mission had taken on a life of its own. The personal ties she had to Frederick somehow fell into the background, replaced by a sense of adventure and independence.

After two hours of driving, the smug look on Anna's face relaxed into a smile. She was on Bramscher Strasse weaving by modest houses and fading green fields. The cracked window let in cool, crisp early fall air. Anna pulled into the bed-and-breakfast. A young girl around nineteen introduced herself as Lilli and checked Anna into the small, simple room.

"Are you from America?" Lilli asked carefully.

"California," Anna answered.

"Oh, I love California! I watched all of the *OC*!" Lilli rambled on, but Anna's head was swimming. She wanted to get to Kalkriese as soon as possible.

Anna cut Lilli off, "Listen, Lilli, we should get lunch or dinner before I leave, and I can tell you all about California. I spent a lot of time there."

She smiled sweetly.

"Also, I have some questions for you about getting to Kalkriese. Will you be downstairs in fifteen minutes?"

Lilli nodded with enthusiasm and headed to the front desk. An exhale left Anna's lungs as she walked into the bathroom. Her reflection made her jump back. A dark-haired older version of herself stared back in surprise.

"Who am I?" Anna asked out loud while posing James Bond–style. "Alright, Anna. Be serious. It's time for a test run."

It was early evening with enough sunlight to take a quick drive east toward Kalkriese. Downstairs, Anna spent a few minutes asking Lilli about routes to Kalkriese; fortunately, there was only one main road.

Back in Berlin, Anna had spent countless hours on Google Earth, going up and down the main road that ran to Kalkriese, Venner Strasse. The 34-kilometer mark stood at a T intersection between Venner Strasse and a narrow side road that led deeper into the forest. If Anna was right, Frederick's meeting would either take place at the crossroad or down the side road. That was going to be the problem, figuring out where to situate the camera.

The main road started to curve, and Anna slowed down to prepare to turn into the side road, but the sight of a seated man who looked up at her sharply as her car approached stopped her. Anna kept her wheel straight and angled the brim of her hat downward. From the corner of her eyes, she assessed the side road.

The man appeared to be a woodsman. He sat dressed in worker's clothing. Next to him was a high stack of long logs piled high. A gas-powered saw lay at his feet. The man took a drink from a thermos but kept his gaze on her car while Anna drove further away.

Something didn't feel right. The man had eyed her car with suspicion.

Anna, you're being paranoid.

Still, Anna didn't turn around just yet. She drove onward and killed two hours. On the return drive, Anna again glimpsed into the side street. The woodsman was still there, almost in the same position.

Damn! I need a better look at the area.

The following afternoon, Anna found Lilli at the front desk and asked her to call a taxi.

"Lilli, can you tell the driver that I'd like to take a slow drive through the Teutoburg Forest toward Kalkriese?"

In the taxi, Anna prepared her camera to film the road and snap photographs. The taxi driver eyed her from the rearview mirror and asked with slight confusion, "You like fields?"

"My grandmother grew up here, but she died recently. My mother never got to see her place of birth—this is for her."

The driver nodded, satisfied with the answer, and left Anna in peace. The camera steadied itself as the taxi approached the 34k marker.

"Dammit!" Anna whispered under her breath.

The woodsman turned to watch the approaching taxi. The pile of logs looked the same as they had looked the day before. The woodsman remained at his seated post with the saw at his feet. Anna ducked lower into the car.

What is this guy's deal?

After a few minutes, Anna asked the taxi driver to turn around and slowly head back to the bed-and-breakfast. She repositioned the camera into her jacket and pressed it against the window next to the backseat. Again they drove past the 34k mark with the camera filming the crossroad and the woodsman, who did not make any unusual movements.

Back in her room, Anna viewed her recording in slow motion. The side road was narrow and unpaved. It had the capacity to hold one-way traffic. The pile of timber was stacked against the forest wall on the right. The logs were not freshly cut. They were weathered and even mossy in some places. The woodsman's clothing was clean, and his hands wore no working gloves. The woodsman looked like he had been doing absolutely nothing except reading and lifting his head at passing cars.

He can't be there every day, can he?

Anna let a few hours pass by and then took the bus to Kalkriese. It was 5:00 p.m. and another woodsman in almost identical clothing remained seated at the same place with the same saw at his feet. At the next stop, Anna left the bus and wasted time at the Kalkriese Museum café until the last bus picked up tourists in the evening.

The woodsman continued to sit. She noticed he gave no attention to busses. Anna began to panic.

It looks like twenty-four-hour surveillance! Of course, *they have surveillance if this meeting is so secretive!*

Anna wanted to hit herself. *Ugh... I'm such an idiot! How will I plant the camera if I can't even get out of the car and walk around?* Her plan was already falling apart.

Anna woke up the next morning and stared at the ceiling. She was being pulled in opposing directions. She missed Frederick already; he had become a part of her life, her new life. Anna was left in a lonely place, further amplified by texts and short evening phone calls. During each one, Anna would stare out the window into the empty streets of Bramsche and tell Frederick of the beautiful mountains of Sankt Gilgen. It pained her to lie, but Anna saw no other way. *I need to find the truth.*

Once again, she took the last bus to Kalkriese, hoping that the woodsman would finally go home. Her heart sank as she looked out the window and again saw the same seated man sitting next to the 34k signpost. Anna hit her head back on the bus seat.

What am I going to do? It was September 9—two days to go. She looked over her notes at the times she had driven past the woodsmen. They were all during daylight hours.

I'll need to go late at night, she thought. *No, I need to go during dead hours.*

At 4:00 a.m., Anna got into her rental car. With her brights on, she sped past the side road with the intent to see as much as possible and blind anyone looking in her direction. The pile of logs appeared to have no supervisor! Immediate relief and excitement swept over Anna. She had a chance after all.

Anna drove a few more miles out and parked her car on the side of the road next to a few local shops. Setting her alarm for 6:00 a.m., she let her eyes close till dawn, yet her excitement fended off any chance of sleep. When the alarm went off, Anna snapped back to reality. During the drive back, she saw the woodsman on patrol.

Anna realized that if she were lucky, she would have a short window of opportunity between 4:00 a.m. and 4:30 a.m. Back at the B&B, Anna sprang to action.

She knew she needed an alibi if she would be out snooping around and mounting a camera. *What would I say if I get caught by surveillance?* Then it dawned on her. She would say that she's a film student, doing an art project that requires filming the changing leaves at different times of day. *That's ridiculous. Think, Anna, think!*

In the town center, Anna strolled through the farmers market to clear her thoughts. Tables were filled with wild mushrooms, onions, and root vegetables. She studied the crowd. That was what she should do; pose as a local out picking mushrooms in the early morning.

A local who couldn't speak German? Anna thought to herself, biting a freshly baked strudel stuffed with meat, onions, and mushrooms. The bottom of her jeans collected dew off the wooden bench she'd situated herself on, but she paid no attention.

I could be mute... Too ridiculous. She thought back to middle school, where she took two years of American Sign Language. Aside from the alphabet and signing the song "White Christmas," she remembered nothing, but that was going to have to be her best bet.

How would I even get there? Taking her car was out of the question.

She stood and proceeded to wander around town, imagining what her life would be like if she actually lived there: how she would get around, how she would dress... She needed to blend in. *Alright, I need to get real local.*

Anna observed the town's inhabitants around her. Men in jeans and light jackets, women in boots, shawls, and sweaters. Practical, durable clothing, perfect for withstanding the afternoon-to-evening temperature change of an early fall day.

She found a second-hand shop and bought a long brown wool sweater, semi-worn leather boots, and a headscarf. Her jeans would suffice.

The only transportation solution was a bicycle, but peddling several miles to Kalkriese before dawn was unrealistic and dangerous. Anna headed to a bicycle shop and picked out a used foldable bike she could fit into her rental's trunk and a woven basket to attach to the handlebars.

Lastly, she returned to the market and bought enough untrimmed mushrooms to fill her basket, picking out the dirtiest ones.

Anna made a plan, but doubts and worries began to overtake her. She looked at the array of items on her hotel room floor: used clothing; the camera smeared with dirt for better camouflage; pieces of twine, in case she needed to secure anything; the basket of mushrooms and dirt; and the brunette wig. The bicycle waited in her trunk.

"Am I completely insane?" she asked out loud. She thought how Frederick told her about a business meeting, and then the great—let alone expensive—lengths she'd gone to, to prove to that it was just that, a business meeting and not a neo-Nazi gathering.

She rubbed her face. There was no turning back now. It was 8:00 p.m. Anna preset the camera's timer to start recording at 9:30 p.m. on September 11 and tried to sleep.

At 3:30 a.m., Anna walked to her car and drove into Kalkriese. She parked at a forest turnoff. Before dawn, the air smelled of another world, of the upside-down, where anything could occur.

At 4:00 a.m. in Bramsche, Germany, Anna was a local brunette mute girl on a bicycle, her basket filled with a camera covered by mushrooms and her ears unable to hear the sounds of the world. As she peddled hard for what seemed like an eternity, sweating somehow in the cool morning breeze, she spotted through the forest fog that familiar signpost. Closer and closer. Anna's heart beat loudly as she inhaled deep breaths of air to try to stay calm. At the side road entrance, Anna pretended to lose control of her bike and awkwardly wheeled into the side street, hitting the stack of logs with her front tire. Not a sound. No one was there.

She pretended to fall to the ground and after a few moments of clearing silence, Anna got to work. She removed the basket and set it onto one of the higher stacked logs angled to face the 34k marker. She then quickly removed and secured the camera deep in the pile of rotting wood and smeared it with more moist dirt, moss, and decomposing foliage that covered the logs. The wet earth stuck underneath her fingernails. Anna stepped back and looked at the logs; for a minute, she couldn't even find the camera.

Time to get out of here. Anna picked up her bicycle, but her ears picked up fast footsteps. Panic shot through her.

Keep calm, keep calm, she repeated to herself. *You don't hear anything.*

Anna scrambled to start carefully picking up the mushrooms she had purposely dropped from her basket when her bicycle had toppled over. The footsteps approached closer. *You cannot hear anything*, Anna continued to remind herself.

An angry male voice yelled at her in German.

"*Was machst du hier? Dies ist geschloss ene Immobilien*!"

Her adrenaline peaked, but her body made no outward flinch. Casually, she put the last of the mushrooms into her basket and got on the bike. The footsteps were behind her. She turned her bicycle as a giant hand landed on her shoulder.

Anna screamed and shoved the hand off of her with all her might while simultaneously pushing the bike forward. Caught off-guard, the woodsman stumbled backward. Radiating with rage, Anna furiously signed the first lines of "*White Christmas.*"

The gestures confused the woodsman who had stopped yelling, but Anna wasted no time. High on adrenaline, she peddled as fast as she could onto Venner Strasse.

From far away, rays of approaching dawn began to color the leaves in greens and yellows. She fought the desire to look back until she felt she had gone far enough from view. Pedaling across to the other side of the road, Anna used it as an excuse to turn around.

The road remained clear of people and cars.

Everything's fine, everything's fine, Anna repeated to herself.

Driving back to Bramsche was too risky. She would have to continue onward until the roads became busy with other cars. Anna folded her bike as quickly as possible, tossed it into the trunk, and pulled the muddied car onto Venner Strasse. She drove a few miles east and stopped in a restaurant parking lot. With her eyes closed, she took a few deep breaths.

I did it. It could not have gone better than this. Her adrenaline refused to cease, making her stomach churn violently.

Too many things could still go wrong. The camera could be discovered, it could fail to record, or the location could be wrong. The list continued.

"*Que sera, sera*; whatever will be will be." Anna sighed.

She awoke mid-afternoon on September 11, wide-eyed. A burning desire to drive by the location at the time of the presumed meeting took over Anna's focus.

What a horrible idea! She thought. *If there really is a meeting, I could be recognized immediately!* But her curiosity would not subside.

She knew that if she did go, and if she did risk it, she'd need another alibi.

Lilli.

Anna went downstairs and found Lilli at her usual post at the front desk.

"Hey, Lilli! Listen, I may have to leave earlier than planned, but I would love to invite you to get dinner tonight if you're free."

"Tonight?" Lilli flipped through a schedule book; it would have to be a bit later; I work until nineteen."

"No worries! And it's completely my treat!"

Purposely Anna picked a restaurant in Bohmte, a town thirty minutes east of Bramsche along the main road Venner Strasse.

"I figured it would be fun to see another town," Anna explained to Lilli on their drive. "I hope you don't mind."

Lilli shrugged her shoulders. "You are the one visiting. I am fine as long as it is interesting for you."

At the restaurant, Anna tried to talk about life in America and California but was on complete edge. She ordered another glass of wine to try and compose herself.

"I'm sorry if I seem uneasy," Anna began. "I just need to drive back to Berlin tomorrow and I always feel nervous the day before traveling alone when I don't have a good sense of where I am."

Lilli tried to comfort Anna, who could only think of what might happen at the 34-kilometer mark at 10:00 pm.

At 9:30 p.m., Anna drove onto Osnabrücker Strasse, the most direct way back to Bramsche. After fifteen minutes of driving, she began to pay close attention to the road markers. She maneuvered her car around a turn, but immediately slowed down. Flashing blue and white lights lit up the pitch-black road ahead.

Shit! Anna saw that the road was blocked.

She came to a halt in front of another passenger car that was beginning to make a slow U-turn. In front of them were road barricades and a car with flashing lights parked in the middle of the road.

"What is this?" Anna asked.

Lilli read the traffic sign. "It looks like the road is closed."

Anna's heart raced. *It's happening.* The police had caught on to Frederick's secret meeting and had crashed the party. They had to be at least a mile away from the 34k post.

"Lilli, can you ask the police officer what's going on? I might need to take this road in the morning, and I need to see how long it will be closed for."

Lilli got out of the car and walked toward a policeman who immediately began approaching her, as he had done with the other confused driver who had just driven away. His right hand was on his gun holster. Anna leaned across her steering wheel. The man took a few more steps before stopping to speak to Lilli in the glare of the other car's headlights.

"Oh, my God!" Anna exclaimed.

The policeman was Martin Schultz, the older driver who had followed her back in Berlin. Panic overcame her. *What if he comes over and sees me? He will recognize me immediately!*

Her hands gripped the wheel tightly, ready to speed away at any second. She sank deeper into her seat, but the officer paid her no attention and walked back to his post as Lilli returned to the car.

"There was a car accident up ahead, but the road will be open in a couple of hours. The bad news is," Lilli continued, "we have to turn around and cross over on Berlinger Strasse."

Anna nodded and changed the conversation back to Lilli and her life in Bramsche as she drove Lilli to her apartment.

Analyzing the evening's events, it suddenly dawned on her that the car at the traffic stop wasn't even a police car. It was just a regular car with flashing lights on its roof. The policeman was the same creeper from Berlin. She imagined that there was probably another fake police officer with barricades on the other side of the road. *What a simple and effective way to block traffic on the road for a secret meeting. Clever.*

Anna awoke at 11:00 a.m. to the pounding of her heart. *The camera!* She had only fallen asleep sometime around 4:00 a.m. from exhaustion and stress.

Anna scrambled out of bed and threw on a sweater and jeans. Quickly she checked the bus schedule for Kalkriese and ran down the stairs to catch the 11:30 bus with her folded bike in hand.

She pressed her face against the window once the bus passed the 34k mark. The road was clear and there was no woodsman, no barricade, and no police.

From the Kalkriese Museum, Anna casually rode to the logs and turned into the side street where she parked her bike.

She felt around for the camera and quickly found it. She shoved it into her backpack and began biking to the main road, but momentarily stopped. Below her feet, several tire tracks were imprinted into the dirt. She counted them: one, two, three. Three pairs of deep tracks weaved around each other making snakes in the wet earth until they disappeared into the forest vegetation. *What the hell?* Anna continued to the main road, where the tracks disappeared on the pavement.

The ride back to the B&B felt like an eternity. The camera inside her backpack burned into her body. She took several deep breaths when the B&B appeared in view. Anna dashed up the stairs to her room and, with trembling hands, connected the camera to her laptop and rewound the recording.

An empty road appeared on the screen with periodically passing cars. She exhaled. *Calm down, you may see nothing.* At 9:40 p.m., a covered cargo truck drove by. At 9:55 p.m., the lights of an approaching car slowed down and came to a complete stop in front of the 34k mark, blocking the post entirely.

This is it!

The driver turned off the headlights. Anna held her breath. The inside of the car remained pitch-black. They have to be waiting for a second car. Anna sat and waited alongside the driver on the screen unable to fast-forward the video for fear of missing anything important. The dancing reflection of several small lights appeared to the side of the parked black sedan.

What is that?

The lights were beaming and shaking, and they were coming from the side road where her camera had been situated.

Are those people with flashlights? But they're approaching so fast.

Anna leaned in closer and squinted her eyes. Suddenly three ATVs burst from behind the camera's view. Anna jumped from the quick movement on-screen.

Those were the tire tracks! They came from the forest!

All the drivers were wearing helmets and carried semi-automatic rifles strapped to their backs. Two of the drivers turned west and east of the car, dismounted their ATVs, and took up guarding positions facing both ends of the road. Their ATVs continued to run, sending high beams from their headlights into the night.

The other driver parked its ATV in front of the sedan, and kept the engine running, but switched to low-beam lights. A man jumped off the vehicle and Anna slightly exhaled. His helmet remained on, but even then, Anna could tell from the stocky build that it was not Frederick.

The sedan's driver's-side door opened, and a tall, broad-shouldered man began to walk toward the ATV driver. Anna bit the tips of her fingers. As he got close enough to shake the ATV driver's hand, Frederick's profile came into view in the dimmed headlights of the ATV.

It can't be.... Anna whispered, crestfallen.

Frederick guided the second ATV driver toward the sedan and opened the backseat passenger-side door. The driver removed his helmet and disappeared within the dark body of the vehicle. Frederick closed the door and returned to the driver's seat.

She deduced that Frederick wasn't the one meeting this ATV driver—there was someone else in the backseat.

Anna watched the scene for ten long minutes, but nothing changed. In another five minutes, the backseat passenger door opened. The ATV driver exited the car, holding his helmet. In the dimmed headlights of the ATV, Anna could see his blurred rectangular face. She snapped several stills of the man.

Frederick left the car carrying a sports bag, which he handed to the ATV driver. He put the sports bag on the car's trunk, unzipped the bag, and rummaged through what appeared to be stacks of cash.

"Oh, my God," Anna gasped.

Satisfied, the ATV driver zipped up the sports bag, shook Frederick's hand, and put his helmet back on. While the two men were speaking, the backseat window rolled down. Whoever was inside the car must have addressed the ATV driver because he leaned in toward the rolled-down window. When he did this, the light from his parked ATV reflected off of his helmet and momentarily illuminated the inside of the car and the passenger's face. Anna zoomed in, but, like the ATV driver, it was both blurred and unfamiliar.

The grainy outline of a man quickly disappeared back into darkness as the ATV driver lifted his head. Anna noticed the tightness of the ATV driver's body language when speaking with the man inside the car. He seemed fidgety and tense.

Whoever is in the car must be someone important and intimidating.

The ATV driver returned to his vehicle, followed by the two remaining drivers. All three ATVs sped toward the camera, blinding the lens with white lights until they disappeared behind the camera's view, back into the forest. Once the camera refocused, the sedan had already driven away.

Anna stared at the screen, lost in thought.

What was Frederick doing there and who was he meeting?

Movement on the screen caught her attention. A covered truck passed the 34k mark in the opposite direction.

Anna wondered if that had been the same truck she had seen before the meeting. She pressed rewind. It was.

That truck must have been setting up the police barricades on the opposite side of the road for the meeting to have complete privacy.

Anna replayed the entire recording and paused on the ATV driver's blurred face and that of the sedan's backseat passenger. She snapped several still-shots and emailed them to Kenny with the subject line: Emergency! and the message: Kenny, I'll Venmo you three hundred dollars if you can clear the images up and send them back to me tomorrow!

She focused her attention on Frederick's face in the recording. *Let's not assume the worst,* she told herself. *Did a shady business deal just happen? Yes, but for what reason?* There was a large sum of money involved, but there were countless explanations. She thought back to her Grandfather's childhood; maybe Frederick was paying off a crime boss, or perhaps, he was being blackmailed.

Anna woke up in the morning with her face next to her open laptop. Immediately, she opened her email. Kenny had responded with several question marks and "I'm working on the image now.... what would be even more fascinating than $300 is an explanation of what I've been helping you with for the past months."

She Gchatted him:

"So, you don't need the money?"

"You can't buy me, Anna!"

Anna cracked a weak smile. "$300 Kenny!"

"Fine—take advantage of my broke student life. I'll send it soon."

Soon came in an hour and a half, when Anna's inbox received the attachments from Kenny. Two clicks later, Anna found herself staring at the cleaned-up image of the man from the backseat: It was Frederick's father.

"So your dad is running this show?

A sense of great relief smoothed Anna's nerves. Frederick was not the man in charge like the agent had thought; it was his father, but the ATV driver's identity remained a mystery.

Anna closed the laptop and looked at her white Michele watch, a recent gift from Frederick. It was about time to drive back to the Hannover Hauptbahnhof to catch the train back to Berlin.

Chapter 32

The train back to Berlin sped Anna uncomfortably toward Frederick. She uploaded the video to her iCloud, alongside her guilt for spying.

What is going to happen to us, Frederick, and what are you involved with? I'm desperate for the truth.

These thoughts tormented her until Frederick greeted her at arrivals, kissed her senseless, and smothered her nose with the scent of lush roses.

Anna awoke restless early the next morning. Throughout the night, her subconscious had never stopped working, quietly sending signals warning her that questions remained unanswered. Her eyes met Frederick's awakened gaze.

"Good morning, beautiful. How did you sleep?"

"Better than all the nights in Austria," she lied. "I was glad to hear your business getaway was successful."

"Yes, it went better than expected. Everyone got what they wanted."

Frederick pulled her into him and kissed down her neck and chest. Anna gave into the sensation greedily. "Oh, I bet they did…"

In the shower, hot water hit her face. She scrubbed away the rising tension. The urge to demand the truth was overpowering. Anna turned up the shower to scorching heat.

Get ahold of yourself. He did tell you he was going away for business; he just didn't say that it would be shady!

Anna picked up her backpack and walked to her usual café. Since her return to Berlin, there had been no reappearing cars or stalkers. From what she could assess, no one was following her. She eagerly sipped the buttery brew, yearning for her neurons to fire a little faster.

In her mind's eye, she pictured the face of the ATV driver she had filmed on her camera. *Who are you? A criminal? The mafia? A businessman partaking in a one-time risky transaction? If I find out your identity, I can find out what Frederick and his father are up to.*

Anna had replayed the video so often that she felt she could act out the entire ordeal. The solo ATV driver's body language suggested subtle submissiveness when speaking to Frederick, but even more so to Frederick's father.

From what she saw, Anna gleaned that it wasn't a typical business meeting between mutually powerful partners, and the ATV driver was no kingpin. If anything, it looked like Frederick's father would hold that title.

Anna had already shown a still from the video she snapped on her phone of the ATV driver to Rich, the concierge in her hotel, and two of the café baristas to determine if the man was a well-known public figure, but so far, no one recognized him.

"Pardon..."

Anna looked up in complete surprise. One of the baristas hovered over her table.

"There is a man here, with the police. He would like to speak with you. He is waiting for you in our back office."

The barista ended on a note of uncertainty, trying to piece together how a police officer had taken ownership of their office.

Speak of the devil and he will appear before you, Anna thought. *The only man I desperately need to see!*

Anna thanked the barista with the composure one can only develop from having had the same experience before. As instructed, she let ten minutes pass before walking into the corridor, which led to the back office. As she pulled open the office door, her decoy stepped outward as Anna stepped inward. Again, she wore Anna's exact outfit.

That, I will never get used to.

Inside the office, Agent Vogt stood from his seated position to greet her. "Ms. Venu, thank you for agreeing to meet with me again." Anna shook his hand.

"*Please* take a seat. I would like to have a word with you. It won't take long."

She widened her eyes with fake uncertainty. It was time to play the game of ignorance once again.

"Yes, of course, Agent Vogt. Can I help you with something?" she asked with feigned innocence. She couldn't place it, but something about him felt different. The man in front of her studied her carefully; his fingers beat an unusual rhythm on the desk behind him: *tap tap ta-tap tat-a-tap*. She tried to place the melody. It sounded like something from a parade or a carnival. Anna scooted to the edge of her seat and leaned in as if to catch the agent's every word.

"After our conversation, you told Frederick about your surveillance, and someone stopped it. Imagine my surprise when the next day you were no longer being followed!" *Ta-tap tap tap...*

"Agent Vogt, I didn't tell Frederick someone was following me."

Immediately, the drumming stopped. Vogt observed her as if she were a peculiar lab mouse. "You did not tell Frederick?" he asked.

"No," Anna answered coolly.

Vogt slowly leaned back into the office chair. Anna thought she heard his teeth grinding.

"*So ein Misthaufen*," he whispered under his breath.

She continued, "I didn't tell Frederick because I didn't want to worry him. I know it's not him who had me followed. He loves me and would never do anything to hurt or scare me."

He has to know I'm lying.

Anna continued to fix him with the same wide-eyed glare, aware of the minutes ticking away. She had to break this game.

Vogt's eyes narrowed, his tightly bound lips parted, and, with an artificially sweet voice, he said, "Ms. Venu, did you notice Frederick exhibiting any unusual behavior? Or receiving guests you have not seen before?"

Anna saw her opportunity to probe. "Well..." she began with uncomfortable hesitation. "Frederick is a private person, as you know, and I've met only his closest friends, but recently there was an older man whom I had never seen before, or since."

The agent nodded, encouraging Anna along.

"Frederick and I were at dinner, and a man entered the restaurant, approached Frederick directly, and whispered something into his ear. Then Frederick got up and left with the man to a corner booth. I sat there by myself for, like, twenty minutes. I mean, can you imagine? In the middle of a date!"

Anna felt herself getting heated as if this scenario had indeed happened. "So, naturally, I ordered an expensive bottle of Merlot and—"

"Ms. Venu," the agent interrupted with a shrill voice, but quickly checked his tone, "Ms. Venu, *please*, stay focused. What were they talking about? Did you get a sense of their interaction?"

"Oh, no. They were sitting much too far. Even if I could hear them, my German is still very bad."

"Ms. Venu, if you saw a photograph of this man, would you be able to recognize him?"

Vogt, you make this too easy. That is exactly *what I wanted to hear from you.*

"Yes, definitely," Anna answered.

Without hesitation, Vogt opened his laptop and clicked around. He turned the computer to face Anna, who then began to scan through each photograph that appeared on the screen. So far, none of the men matched the ATV driver, but she asked about each one anyway. Anna needed to keep this man's mind occupied enough to keep him from probing her with further questions.

To make it easier for herself and harder for Vogt, she made sure to have visible reactions to each photograph. Suddenly her eyes landed on the man she was looking for. The ATV driver! With all her might, Anna kept her reaction similar to prior responses.

"This one looks like a typical politician, doesn't he?" she asked plainly.

"Yes. This is Walter Balke; he is an interesting fellow. He doesn't associate directly with the neo-Nazi movement. Right now, his affiliation is with a local conservative party. They refrain from using pro-fascist rhetoric and instead use German nationalistic ideas with heavy anti-immigrant sentiment. He has become more popular in Germany's eastern parts, especially following Germany's participation in the Greek bailout and the recent immigrant crisis. His group is very well-organized and disciplined. They have a paramilitary branch which, of course, they deny exists."

Anna clicked forward to the next photograph. The rest of the faces didn't look familiar.

"I'm sorry, Agent Vogt, but I don't see that man here."

Vogt returned to his hard stare.

"I will pay closer attention to Frederick's associations and friends," Anna promised.

Vogt stared at her with obvious disinterest. To him, she had become useless and that was exactly what Anna needed him to think.

Back at her table in the café, Anna made herself wait an extra twenty minutes before speed-walking home. All she wanted to do was type "Walter Balke" into a search engine.

Once she finally had the opportunity to do so, his biography and political website came up quickly. Vogt had been right. The man was interesting to say the least.

Balke was born in Dresden in Eastern Germany in 1948. Witnessing his defeated nation's struggle, he developed extreme right-wing views and was imprisoned several times by East German authorities on charges of spreading neo-Nazi ideology. The fall of the Berlin Wall and the unification of Germany had freed him from prison.

Because of his courage and lonely struggle against the communist regime in East Germany, he managed to become a local hero for many Germans, especially for those who had extreme-right views. Anna watched a few of his speeches on YouTube.

Though she didn't understand everything he said, his charisma was impossible to miss. She scanned for English sources, and gathered that his primary political platform has been anti-immigrant, especially anti-Muslim rhetoric. She clicked on his party's political website.

"No way!" Anna voiced out loud. She was looking at a smiling portrait of Balke in front of a sign—the three intersected triangles, like the icon which hung above Frederick's desk.

Frederick is conservative, and he doesn't hide it. Still, Anna couldn't fight the doubt in her reasoning. The triangular symbol on Balke's website had cut through the excuses she had been making for Frederick like a diamond-tipped blade.

She conceded that Vogt had been right about Balke, but she couldn't lean into his theory all the way.

Outside, the sun shone brightly. She wished it would rain. Anna dialed room service and ordered coffee and fruit. *Let's not get emotional and out of control.* She reached for her notebook and began writing everything she knew about the situation.

1. I love Frederick and I'm sure that he loves me. He was genuinely surprised when I told him I was being followed.
2. My surveillance stopped directly after I told him about it. I think he interfered and has power over whoever was following me.
3. Frederick's father seems to support a neo-Nazi candidate financially—either because of the party's anti-immigrant policies or because he is an actual neo-Nazi supporter.
4. I don't know why anyone, especially the neo-Nazis, would follow me to begin with. I'm no figure of significant interest to anyone in Germany.
5. Am I?

Anna carefully looked back and analyzed her relationship with Frederick. His affections had conveniently picked up after she shared her newly found identity with him. In fact, he had asked her out right after he had personally examined Ada's memoir in Maria Arnett's house.

It's my lineage.

Anna could see the Germany Liberation Party's next headline: "Recently Discovered Great-Granddaughter of Lieutenant Commander Hans Ritter Supports Fight to Restore German National Identity!

Anna grasped her chest; she could feel her heart in her throat. *I'm paranoid. This is just one scenario, just one scenario.* She repeated like a mantra. *You do not yet know the truth. It's just one possible scenario.*

Chapter 33

One possible scenario could ruin our entire relationship. Even if Frederick has no choice on whether to be involved with his father's business, I could never be with a man who associates with a neo-Nazi group....

Anna opened up her laptop, thinking about Frederick's father. *He has him so caught up in money and business that he's forgotten what supporting a group with these extremist beliefs actually means.* She scanned the web until she found what she was looking for: The Sachsenhausen Concentration Camp Memorial Museum, forty minutes from Berlin.

Being at the concentration camp will have to stir something within him. I can then appeal to his sense of morality.

Although planning a trip to Sachsenhausen was her own idea, going forth with it left her with an uncomfortable sensation. Memories from the Holocaust Museum in Washington DC resurfaced uneasily. She could still feel the dark energy of the cattle car used to transport victims. Anna recalled it feeling as though the wood had been soaked with fear, pain, and death that had seeped into its very fibers, unable to free itself. She shuddered.

Convincing Frederick to take her to the Sachsenhausen proved to be more laborious than expected.

"It will be too much for you, Anna. You and I both have read and seen enough of the terror that had happened there. Why go to a place of such human suffering? There is bad energy in that place. It will not sit well with you, and it could trigger a migraine."

Anna turned Frederick's words over in her mind. She wanted to agree with him, but found herself unable to do so. "I just want to pay my respects. It's easy to learn about a tragedy like a historical fact and then move onward with your life, but that's how more tragedies continue to happen. If people took the time to truly understand the absolute horror and pain of the Holocaust or any other atrocity, then maybe they wouldn't repeat the same mistakes in the future."

For a moment, there was silence. Anna and Frederick looked at each other with the mutual understanding that Anna's last comment was too altruistic for humans ever to undertake.

"Alright, Anna. Let's go this Friday. The Memorial is closed on the weekends."

In her hotel room, Anna stared back at her reflection in the bathroom mirror. She had one more full day before confronting him. She turned her head to the left and right. Nothing seemed to look different when singled out, but when assessed together, she thought she looked older. In Arizona, Anna had a seriousness about her that came from discipline, but now it came from her life experiences. The latter carried an extra heaviness with it.

Friday morning, Frederick's BMW pulled up in front of her hotel. Anna slid into the front seat, replacing a box of savory pastries. Frederick handed her a cappuccino.

"Are you ready for our soon-to-be-disturbing adventure?" Frederick asked with a grain of dark humor.

Anna sipped through the foam, unable to appreciate it.

"Thank you for getting breakfast." she kissed him lightly. "Let's go."

Anna was nervous. It was obvious, and she knew this. With all her effort, she brought up random conversation topics: the recent podcast episode of *Invisibilia*, the TED Talk on outer space technology, but Frederick saw through all of it. He pulled the car over in the middle of Anna's repeated recitation of new German phrases she had learned.

"Why did you stop?"

Frederick put the car in park and turned to face Anna, taking her hands into his own. "Anna, are you alright?"

She nodded with too much enthusiasm. "Of course."

Frederick sighed. "Anna, listen: I think this trip is a bad idea. You are already nervous, and we have not even arrived there. You need to pay attention to the signs your body is giving you. Why don't we head home and maybe we can go another day?"

Anna freed her right hand and gulped down the remainder of her cappuccino, pretending to consider the merits of his tempting proposal. They were a few minutes away from the camp.

"Frederick, I know it's going to be horrific and you're right; I'm nervous, but out of respect to those who suffered, I need to see it."

Frederick opened his mouth, ready to reason her back to Berlin, but she chimed in with a point he could not argue. "If it's too much, we can leave."

Frederick squeezed her hand and turned back to the wheel. "Alright, Anna...."

The Sachsenhausen concentration camp was not the first of its kind, but it was, in Himmler's words, the "ideal camp." It was at this camp where all other camp commanders were trained on how to run the finely tuned machine of death.

Since 1938, the entire Nazi concentration camp system was managed from these grounds. Here, nothing went to waste from gold fillings removed from victims' mouths to human ashes spread on fields to fertilize the land around the 1,000-acre compound.

Anna shuddered with every step her boots made onto the wretched soil. Welded into the entrance gates was ARBEIT MACHT FREI, or Work Makes You Free. That freedom was obtained through death for the 30,000 to 50,000 Jews, Germans, Russian POWs, Poles, Romani, and Serbs who lost their lives at Sachsenhausen.

They walked through the grim barracks, to Station Z, a nickname given by the Nazis to the execution trenches and gas chamber as an ongoing joke, since prisoners first entered the camp at Tower A. The remains of the extermination buildings housed iron parts of the cremation ovens arising from the ground like demons.

Frederick led her to the infirmary, an insult to the practice of medicine; physicians are supposed to take the Hippocratic Oath to do no harm. The white-tiled surgery table stood eerily gleaming. A drain in the middle to rid of the blood that gushed from the poor souls chosen for medical experiments. Anna fought back a need to vomit. She could see the procedures that once took place in the now-haunted room.

At Tower E, an exhibit explained the camp's relationship with Oranienburg, the surrounding town whose inhabitants saw the camp's inner workings every day. Some ignored it, some profited from it, and others defied it and were brave enough to help.

The plaque described one bold townswoman who threw bread to prisoners over the camp walls. *If we were all like her, if we were all brave like her, atrocities like this wouldn't happen.*

Anna stood in the middle of the *appellplatz*—the roll-call area where prisoners stood for a daily count. That was when it all really hit her, the unexpected size of the roll-call area. The sheer magnitude of the crimes committed against humanity engulfed her. She could have been here—she could have been one of the victims if she had been born into a different family at another time.

Anna quietly walked past Tower A where prisoners awaited the degree of suffering, they would endure until the camp's liberation in 1945. Immediately, her lungs felt lighter as she exited the camp. Frederick had been right; there was disturbing energy there.

"Visiting a memorial like that should be mandatory for everyone," Anna said. "If all children were thrown into learning about such wretched history, maybe they would grow up to be compassionate adults who would never think of invoking such pain and violence on others."

Frederick silently nodded and gently pulled Anna into him as they walked toward the parking lot.

The car ride back was heavy with silence as Anna tried to regain some composure. Through a sideways glance, she saw that the experience also moved Frederick.

I'm sure that he can't actually believe or justify the horrendous ideas of the Third Reich....

Anna rubbed her eyes. Seeing the camp, the reality of it all, was a sharp reminder that she could no longer live in doubt; she could not keep postponing getting the truth from Frederick. She had to convince him to dissociate himself from his father's activities.

"Frederick, can we stop? I really need a drink. There's a biergarten I found nearby."

Frederick nodded in approval and pulled off the main road after a few exits. The restaurant was busy and noisy, a review she had looked for specifically while searching TripAdvisor. A place full of people allowed her to ask Frederick questions while forcing him to keep his cool in public.

They ordered two dark beers and scanned the menu. Anna was starving but was unable to concentrate on the menu before her.

For the past three days, she had played out various scenarios as to how to start this conversation with Frederick best. Finally, she narrowed down two approaches: logically build up her case or directly ask. After careful analysis and many mirror conversations, Anna settled on the latter. She reached for Frederick's hand across the table and squeezed his fingers until his eyes left the menu.

"Everything okay?"

Here we go, she said to herself and took a long sip of beer.

"You know, Frederick, after one of our conversations, I read more about Chancellor Schröder. The more I read about him, the more I realized how different he is. Out of all the Western leaders, he was the only one who had enough courage to stand up against our former president and refuse to send German troops to an unjustified war in Iraq. Do you know how many German and Iraqi lives he saved by this decision? I wish more politicians around the world had such courage and determination."

"You could be right here..." Frederick answered after a second of silence.

Good, so far, our values are in agreement, Anna thought.

"I'm glad that we see things similarly," Anna said, inhaling courage. She pressed onward. "I need to ask you a question."

"Yes...?

"Why does your father support the neo-Nazi party?"

Frederick choked on a large gulp of beer. The intense eyes she had loved when they had first met her own, bulged out at her.

"What?" Frederick yelled in such disbelief that Anna immediately regretted her approach.

People at a few nearby tables turned to gaze in their direction. In response, Frederick lowered his voice. "Anna, what the hell did you just ask me?"

Her face remained blank. "Why does your father give money to the neo-Nazis?"

"Who the hell told you this garbage?" he asked with genuine disbelief in his voice.

"No one," Anna replied coolly. "I learned of it myself."

Without another word, she reached into her bag and withdrew her iPad. The video of Frederick's father's secret meeting began to play. Briefly, his eyes widened, but soon his facial expression returned to its usual composed demeanor.

Anna felt caught off-guard; she had prepared herself for rage and anger, but not for this. Frederick watched the screen and, after several minutes, fast-forwarded the meeting until its end. He brought the stein of beer to his lips and only then did Anna notice the extreme whiteness of his knuckles. Pressure had built within him to the extent of finding its only release in clenching the nearest object, the stein. The bottom of the glass hit the table with a firm thud.

"Who gave you this video?"

"I recorded it myself."

"Don't toy with me. That meeting was private. I need to know immediately who recorded this. Someone is trying to mess with both of—"

Anna cut him off, "I told you, I recorded the video myself."

Frederick's jaw clenched underneath his faked composure.

"Listen, I'll tell you everything, but try not to get angry with me. My reasons for doing so came out of the best intentions. I needed the truth, and it was obvious that you were never going to give it to me."

Frederick narrowed his eyes to slits sharp as razor blades. Anna knew he was assessing her, just like Vogt had, he was trying to catch Anna in a lie, but this time, Anna was telling the truth.

She started at the beginning, and, with some pride that she attempted to hide, she told him the details of her scheme. As her story progressed, Frederick seemed to be regaining his cool. "And that's how I was able to record the video," Anna said. "Of course, no one else knows any of this."

Frederick looked into Anna's eyes cryptically. A smile began to show on his lips that quickly erupted into a loud, drawn-out laugh.

Confused, Anna stared at the spectacle in front of her. *Was he going mad?* Tears formed at the corners of his eyes and he wiped them off through continued chuckles.

There was something unnatural in the way his voice sounded as if it was masking a hysterical undertone. A discomfort spread through Anna. *What am I missing here?* She thought.

"The thing is..." Frederick finally resumed. "The thing is that there actually is a hard-of-hearing young woman living in Bramsche. As soon as our watchman reported the incident, we looked into it right away." The laughter continued. "Her name's Katrina!"

Anna took a sip of water. Her mouth was parched. *Is this laughter genuine or was it masking a much darker reaction?* Frederick ignored her silence and continued his train of thought.

"You know, my mentor from army intelligence once told us that only an amateur could bring down an entire operation that has been carefully planned. I never believed him. I mean, how could that be so?

But here I am, in front of an amateur, who is my girlfriend no less, telling me she infiltrated a secret meeting that took months to plan by pretending to be a girl collecting mushrooms in a forest!"

"I'm glad you find it so amusing," Anna offered.

Frederick's smile quickly faded. "Oh, yes, it is amusing, but don't feel too proud of yourself Anna. I arranged twenty-four-hour surveillance of that meeting spot, but it got fucked up and you had sheer dumb luck on your side."

"I opened my home to you, my life, and you spy on me? In my own house? Who do you think you are? Snowden?"

Anna's eyes widened with the onset of Frederick's aggression.

"Is it in the very blood of your nation to spy on everyone, including people who love you!" Frederick spat the words out. Anna's face flushed.

"Frederick, stop it! You think this is a game for me? You think I liked finding out that the man I love is helping finance the German neo-Nazi movement?"

"I tried getting you to tell me what the hell was going on, but instead, you make up some bullshit about a pervert following me in a car. Did you really think I was going to eat that up? I knew you wouldn't be honest with me. I realized that I had to take matters into my own hands."

"I didn't know they were following you," Frederick fired back. "That's why I ended it immediately."

"Frederick, don't you see the kind of people you're dealing with? Why? Why in the world, after everything that Germany has been through, would you think in your right mind that supporting a neo-Nazi party is a good idea?"

"Anna, keep your damn voice down!"

More people were looking in their direction. Anna shot back at them with a firm look.

"Alright, Anna, fine, you want to know the truth so bad? Here it goes."

Frederick's elbows spanned the table. His body leaned closer to her until it was halfway across the table. They were almost nose to nose.

"Have you ever visited the Kreuzberg district in Berlin?"

"No."

"Really? Well, you should. Because as soon as you get there, you will feel that by some magic carpet ride, you're transported from one of the world's greatest European cities to the middle of a Turkish bazaar. Suddenly, our country's way of life is gone; our language is gone; our customs are also gone. Our chancellor suggested assimilating immigrants, and we tried it, but she was quick to admit that her dream of a multicultural Germany failed. Turks and Arabs did not want to integrate into German society. Instead, they formed their country within our country complete with honor killings of their women all in the name of Allah. Anna, you are a smart and educated woman; how does that satisfy your Western view of gender equality?

"And now, we have an enormous influx of immigrants from the Middle East and Africa who live and act according to tribal law, not German law. We are in the midst of a cultural crisis and my country is dying. France is in even worse shit than we are and I don't want my country to follow suit."

"Wow, Frederick, to hear you repeat the same fear-mongering racist speech yelled by every radical nationalist group across countries and throughout history, is for lack of a better word, boring.

"You want to throw gender equality in my face like it's a Muslim problem when really, it's a patriarchy problem. If you're so concerned with protecting women, how are you okay with the thousands of women trafficked to Germany from Eastern Europe to be sold for sex? How does that sit with your German values?"

"Prostitution is legal in Germany because it's a person's right as a profession."

"Right, but I'm not talking about sex work; I'm talking about your courts doing the bare minimum to sentence known traffickers who then repeat the same crime. I don't see you too concerned with the value of women there. But I think my favorite part of your rant is the audacity you have against the same group of people your family exploited as cheap labor and then profited from."

"What the hell are you talking about now?"

"Your father's corporation was a major sponsor responsible for bringing Turks to Germany as guest workers during the sixties and wasn't it your father's idea to build cheap cluster housing for Turkish laborers on the outskirts of major cities, purposely isolating them from German society? And here you are, accusing the Turks of creating a sense of home for themselves and not assimilating into Germany. How could they? You outcast them, got rich off their hard work, and now want them out? How very convenient for you both."

Anna inhaled deep, slow breaths through her nose. She could feel her nostrils flaring. The love she had had for Frederick faded each time he opened his mouth.

"My father made a mistake back then. He admitted this himself and has accepted partial responsibility for it publicly. Since then, he has worked to correct his errors. He is only human."

"What an interesting way of correcting his errors," Anna said sarcastically. "Throwing his money in support of a terrorist group."

"Don't talk about my father like that. The party we support does not terrorize anyone. Even if they have said racist remarks in the past, that can easily be changed. The party's leader is not the brightest man, but he has charisma and speaks in a way ordinary people can understand and relate to. We know we need to do better at steering the party in a proper direction."

Anna couldn't believe what she was hearing. With a smile, she said, "Frederick, are you kidding me? When Hitler was brought to power, Krupp and other German magnates said the same thing. They were sure they could keep controlling him but failed to do so. You know that! Now, here you are literally repeating history even though you yourself are a historian. I mean, the irony is insane! How in the world can you not see it?"

Anna threw her hands into the air, completely overtaken by the ridiculousness of the situation. "You know Karl Marx's quote, 'History repeats itself first as tragedy, second as farce?' Well, Hitler was the tragedy, and what you're currently doing is pure farce."

In contrast to Anna's energy, Frederick looked drained and suddenly much older.

He said, "Don't you see what is happening here? Germany is being ruined by immigration and the disastrous European Union. Your great-grandfather would have been devastated—and I guarantee you he would understand my point of view."

Anna exhaled and said, "I was waiting for you to bring up my great-grandfather," she began with a sharp tone. "I know how much you admire him and Admiral Doenitz."

"I do; they were brilliant men and true German patriots."

"You know, I read Doenitz's memoir, *Ten Years and Twenty Days.*"

Frederick's mood instantly perked up. "That's great. I hope you appreciated his role in German history."

"Not exactly. It was bizarre, full of technicalities, achievements, and failures of the German U-boat fleet, but the humanity was missing. Doenitz took no responsibility for anything he participated in."

"That's because he didn't participate in any Nazi crimes," Frederick stated.

"So, he conveniently never saw exhausted malnourished prisoners from concentration camps working endlessly to build his precious naval bases? How about the anti-Semitic speeches he gave, which additionally stirred up the Holocaust? Or the Laconia Order, which clearly stated that U-boat captains are responsible for only their U-boats and can do whatever they think appropriate to all others! It gave the green light to neglect and even kill enemy sailors after their ship was sunk. Killing for the sake of killing!"

"That is complete nonsense! This exact accusation was dismissed during the Nuremberg Trials. No U-boat captain interpreted the Laconia Order in this way!"

"Are you kidding me? My grandfather's best friend died at the hands of a U-boat captain after surrendering! And what about U 852 and its Captain, Eck, who killed the crew of a sunken ship with machine guns and grenades while they were in the water on life rafts?"

Seeing Frederick's loss for words only pushed her further. "I saw Doenitz's and Speer's interview after they were released from Spandau Prison. Speer at least had the guts to accept and acknowledge personal responsibility for his role in the Third Reich. He never killed anyone or ordered to have it done. Regardless, he expressed genuine remorse—unlike Doenitz, who got pissed when a journalist asked him about his anti-Semitic rhetoric. It was evident on his face that Doenitz had zero guilt. It was disgusting!"

Frederick's expression remained stoic, but Anna knew it was a mask. She wanted to shake him into a raw expression of truth. His poker face was bullshit.

"Tell me this, Frederick: Do you really love me, or do you just want to use my family's name as propaganda for your cause? Who are you really in love with? Me or my bloodline?"

Frederick's scrutinizing eyes lost their sharpness. They stared into Anna's with what she saw as humility. A silence sat between them, drowning out the typical conversations of diners around them.

"At the beginning, I was attracted to you physically; you are a beautiful woman, but, in Berlin, beautiful women are everywhere."

"Thanks, that's just charming to hear, really..." Anna said flatly.

"I'm not saying that to be rude; I am just trying to explain what captivated me. I have never met a woman as intelligent as you that has challenged me and entertained me. I'm disgusted that you spied on me, but I admire how you pulled it off. I think I'm more shocked at this point. When I found out who your great-grandfather was, I was fascinated by the bizarre situation life put us in."

Anna let Frederick take her hand across the table.

"I believe that everything that happens to us serves some purpose. If not in our own lives, then in the lives of others. Anna, think about it: What are the chances of us finding each other? I'm in Berlin working on my dissertation when the great-granddaughter of my main figure of research walks through the door from the other side of the world and my professor assigns me to help her!"

Frederick's voice rose with a passion that Anna tried hard not to cave into. He was right; their story was something out of a fairy-tale. It was too perfect to be random, but this was not a storybook. Anna bit her lip to remind her of the pain of reality.

"I can't say I didn't fantasize about how perfect it would be for us to work out and be involved together politically, especially with your background, but that was such a small part of it. I would never pressure you into a public life like that unless you wanted it. I have fallen in love with who you are.... We have our differences, yes, but we challenge one another, we love one another, and I can't imagine my life without you."

Don't cry, she repeated to herself with moistening eyes. *Don't you dare cry.*

Anna withdrew her hand. "Frederick. I love you, too. I want to be with you. Before this mess, I couldn't imagine returning to my former life without you. It's all just like you said. But this mess. This mess did happen, and I can't unknow it... I tried to reason with it. I've heard Balke's speeches online. I read the news articles and analyses and it all goes against mine and my family's values. I think if you look within yourself, you'll see it goes against your values, as well. So, I offer you this: my love for the rest of our adventure-filled lives for your disassociation with any neo-Nazi party or movement."

Frederick breathed out, retrieved Anna's hand, and pulled her across the table inches from his face. "Anna. Marry me."

"What?" she whispered.

"Anna, I know this isn't romantic, but I can't think of a more critical time. Marry me—we can work it all out. You can understand my work better; it is not as black and white as you make it out to be. There are no neo-Nazi associations. We can have everything; I will give you everything."

"Frederick...." Anna leaned back in her chair, determined not to topple it completely.

"There is no way I could support your views and your work, I'm sorry."

"Please... You talk like you know what we are doing, but you don't. You just need to understand."

A flash of heat shot through Anna. "Frederick, if I marry you and support your extremist views, I will lose my family, myself, and betray the memory of my grandmother. How could you ask me to do that?"

"The same way you asked me to give up my family and my beliefs for you," Frederick answered coldly.

The passion of just a minute ago seemed to evaporate with his sentence.

"I see..." Anna said softly. "I suppose that's our answer then." She began gathering her things to leave.

"Anna, don't make a rash decision. I want you to think about this. You're just upset right now."

Anna shook her head with increasing confidence. "No, I'm not. Frederick, I know my answer. I can't. I can't unless you stop supporting these awful ideals."

"It is unfortunate..." Frederick's words sounded defeated but firm. "I think you will regret this decision in the future."

"I just don't see how we can reconcile our differences," Anna answered.

Silence overtook their table. A desire to touch him—to be in his arms one last time—overcame her. Anna looked upward and met his eyes, but they had returned to ice.

"What are you going to do with that video?"

Chills crept up Anna's spine. Frederick—her Frederick was gone. Even with his confession of love, she still couldn't say if he had ever truly been hers. Regardless, she was now facing a wolf.

"Nothing. This isn't my country, and this isn't any of my business," Anna lied, hoping to coax Frederick out of his position of attack. He seemed to relax a bit.

"At the same time, I'm very uncomfortable with your friends who followed me for over a month. I plan to leave Germany in a couple of weeks, but I will keep the video. You have my word no one will see it if I return unharmed."

"It looks like you have thought everything through," Frederick said, slowly getting up from the table.

"Yes," Anna said. "I'll call myself a car home."

Frederick threw down cash for the beers.

"You are making a mistake. Let me know if you change your mind."

His words sounded empty as if they were said to be said. She met his eyes, but their gaze was almost feral. As he walked away from the table, a sudden sense of danger shot through her.

"Frederick!" he turned on his heel. "There are multiple copies of the file." Anna impulsively lied.

A cold dead stare radiated from the man she could no longer love. Anna turned away, unable to handle the pain. Then he was gone.

Anna began to panic. She needed to get out. Out of this restaurant, out of her hotel, out of Berlin, and out of Germany; she needed to do this with immediate urgency.

Chapter 34

With immediate urgency, Anna jumped into the approaching ride-share.

What did I just do?

Dread pulled at her until she felt like she would split into two separate people just to handle the situation better.

She inhaled long, steady breaths as Berlin's center grew into view.

Anna burst through the doors of the Art'otel and ran up the winding staircase to her room.

She felt that staying there another day, another hour was impossible. No longer was it the base of a new life—a future that she herself had so carefully crafted—with Frederick, with Berlin, with Germany. Those plans were gone; she had destroyed them herself a mere hour ago.

Scattered around the hotel room were reminders of everything that had led to this exact moment. Anna got out her phone and called Maria Arnett's number; the only person Anna could confide in. Maria's voice was a comfort Anna didn't even realize she needed.

"Maria, I need to come stay with you for a few days, before I leave Germany. I hope that's okay."

"My dear, Anna, of course! But what is the matter? You sound very upset."

"I'm alright." Anna breathed in her own lie. "I am going to pack up and head your way."

"Do you need me to get you? How will you get here?"

"No, I'm fine. I have a car. I'll see you soon."

Anna hung up the phone and looked around her room. *I don't have a car, I don't have Frederick, I don't have a plan. I don't have my life anymore...*

She dropped to her knees in front of Calvin and burst into tears.

You're fine, Anna, she said to herself. *Take each moment after the next, and then it'll be tomorrow, and then it is a flight home, and then all of this will be so very far away.*

She stuffed her clothing and necessities into Calvin until he overflowed with her newly acquired things. Quickly she called down to the front desk.

"Yes, hello, can you connect me to the nearest rental car agency—and also call me a taxi to that location. It's urgent."

The dial tone switched as it transferred to a car rental in Mitte.

"What do you have available for immediate pick-up? Only luxury models? That price is fine; I'll be there in a few minutes."

Anna took one last look around the room. The brightly lit up modern space she had loved no longer fit with the turmoil within her. She pulled Calvin down the winding golden-railed staircase and approached the front desk with hesitation. Her departure suddenly became real.

"Ms. Anna, off on another adventure?" The concierge asked innocently, as he was used to seeing Calvin wheeled back and forth in front of him.

"I would like to check out." She heard her voice crack.

The concierge's face reacted in surprise as if it were the first time a hotel guest had requested to leave. Then he switched to pleasantries, "We hope you enjoyed your stay....and.... If you could give us a positive review on..."

Anna's eyes burned through the man at the counter. She slid over the key while nodding in repeated succession.

"Thank you," she said sharply, cutting through the dialogue, "but my car is already outside."

Anna turned toward the glass door holding her breath until she exited her sanctuary of the past few months. *You chose this, Anna. Now get into the car.*

In the front seat of a new BMW 325 coupe, Anna regained a small sense of control. It felt good to be in command of a powerful car that could take her far away from this place. In front of her stretched a forty-minute drive to Maria Arnett's home. Anna's hands gripped the wheel and focused on the road ahead. Memories of Frederick passed through her mind one after the other.

Did I make a mistake?

A red light forced her to brake. Anna reached for her water bottle and brushed against a wet spot below her chest. She looked down. Drops of inky water soaked into her blouse.

What the hell? Did I spill something? Anna flipped the visor mirror. *What the...*

Her reflection showed lines of tears that had flowed from her eyes, carrying mascara with them. She hadn't even noticed.

Grandmother. A sense of focus and calm came over Anna. Grandmother's presence was with her in the car.

No! I did not make a mistake!

It wasn't about Frederick or even herself; it was much bigger than that. Memories from the past several months flashed through her, stories of the past that she had uncovered. Her grandmother's raw hands covered in blood attempting to free her dead mother from the rubble, Helga's death in the U-Bahn tunnel, her grandfather's delusional attempt to rescue his best friend at sea, the consuming feeling of pain at the Sachsenhausen Memorial, the millions of people who had experienced unspeakable tragedy in the one life they were given. *And for what?*

Staying with Frederick, with his ideals, was a betrayal of humanity, a betrayal of her grandmother, and of the millions of souls who perished in an unnecessary war.

Anna's peripheral vision caught sight of a dark object on her left and she quickly turned to see a black Mercedes pulling up relatively close to her side window.

Her gaze narrowed. *What the hell is this car doing?*

Anna looked into the darkness of the Mercedes' tinted windows. Cars passing in front of her turned on their headlights with the onset of evening briefly illuminating through the Mercedes' tint. That's when she saw it, the outline of a gun, its barrel elongated by an attached silencer. Her eyes locked on the cylinder shape. Whoever held it began to roll down the window.

Anna slammed on the gas and veered right into the flow of traffic. The loud, persistent honking of outraged drivers shook Anna to her core.

What the hell did I just do?

She tried to think of what she had seen. *Was that really a gun?* Anna's teeth clenched together.

I'm losing it. I'm becoming so paranoid that I'm a danger to myself.

She glanced into the rearview mirror. The black Mercedes was one car behind her in the neighboring right lane. *Don't panic!* Anna told herself as she switched lanes to the left. *It's just a car.*

The Mercedes remained in its lane, but Anna's hands continued to grip the wheel tightly. She stepped onto the gas pedal and began making headway. This time, the Mercedes also picked up speed, keeping to the lane next to her. Anna's breathing quickened. She maneuvered right to get one car in front of the Mercedes, but the Mercedes responded by moving left to catch up to Anna's driver's-side window. *One more time to be sure.* Again, Anna changed lanes to the far left. Now, without any subtlety, the Mercedes followed her and kept to her right side.

It's tailing me. Whoever that is, they're trying to get next to me...to shoot me! The thought was surreal. Sweat formed on her chest as her heart pulsed with panic.

"Calm down, calm down," Anna said out loud to herself, pulling in sips of air.

Every nerve, every muscle in her body united to achieve one goal: escape. A complete sense of serene control enveloped her body. She was outside herself.

Think strategically! I can't out-speed their car, the engine is too powerful, but my BMW can outmaneuver it until I find the nearest police car or police station. I need to get onto a narrow street so they can't pull up next to me.

The upcoming light glared yellow. "Fuck!"

Anna shifted into Sport Mode, stepped on the gas, and flew into the intersection. She yanked the wheel to the left, pulled the emergency brake, and immediately turned the steering wheel to the right using all her upper body strength. The tires wheezed and burned rubber making the BMW's rear skid further into the intersection before completing a sharp right turn. The car blazed forward into a two-lane side street.

In her rearview mirror, she could see the empty intersection and frozen cars. The Mercedes had passed the intersection and was now backing up despite the traffic jam she created.

Not a professional driver, are you? Probably not a professional killer either!

Anna scanned the road for police, hoping a good samaritan would report the two dangerous cars, but so far, there was no sign of blue lights. She sped past cars leaving behind her a trail of engine horns.

A few seconds later, her ears picked up another round of honking behind her. "Damn! They're gaining on me!"

Anna pulled a sharp left turn. Tires screeched behind her. The Mercedes hit the side of a curb, unable to replicate the BMW's neat maneuvers. She turned right and immediately swerved left to avoid a panicked cyclist. Something crashed into the left side rear of her car and she hit the hood of a neighboring Volkswagen. Loud honking blared at her, but she lost no time.

Behind her, she saw the Mercedes accelerate forward.

"Goddamn it!" Anna turned the wheel right and crossed two lanes while blasting her own horn.

She took the next right, bypassing cars on the left. The road in front of her began to clear.

"Move out of the fucking way!" She banged her horn and cut around other cars.

The Mercedes was two cars back, unable to fit through the smaller spaces in between lanes. Berlin froze around her. Pedestrians ran off the pavement as she weaved toward a central street.

I need to get back on the main road!

Anna looked at her GPS and made another sharp right.

"Oh, my God!" The street in front of her ended at barricades, safety cones, and construction tape. A trench about three feet wide was dug across the road. The Mercedes' headlights behind her kept her from seeing anything in the rearview mirror. She flipped it upward. Within the darkness of the car, the darkness of Berlin, she made the only decision available to her. Anna slammed on the gas and steered the BMW toward the two-foot-tall mounds of dirt covered by heavy plastic boards. This was the only way she could catch air.

I die or I die trying not to die.

The car roared forward at full speed, smashing the barricade and shattering it into pieces. In seconds, Anna felt the impact. Her body flew into the steering wheel; the seatbelt cut into her chest. Momentary weightlessness held her in mid-air as the BMW flew over the trench.

Within seconds, her body slammed harshly into the physical presence of her leather seat. The car's tires reunited with the road in a crash of metal, rubber, and concrete on the other side of the trench and immediately picked up speed, disarming the airbag's sensor. Terrible screeching noises clawed the bottom of the car as her rear bumper fully detached. She now knew why this car was called "the ultimate driving machine."

Behind her, the black Mercedes ran its engine in front of the trench. A maddening laugh overcame her.

"Go to hell!" she yelled, speeding away, flipping off the Mercedes.

The rush of adrenaline erased rational thought. *Where the hell am I going?!* Anna asked herself. Inhaling deep breaths, her mind came back to her. *Maria Arnett... I have to get to Maria's!*

The GPS directed her to the highway, but she ignored it.

It would be too easy for them to spot me. I need to stick to the streets.

Paranoid, Anna's eyes repeatedly flashed to her rearview mirror, her side mirrors, and to every single car she passed. They could be anywhere, they could have switched cars, they could be waiting for her to think that she got away.

Frederick, you piece of shit, you gave that order, didn't you? Anna smirked to herself in amusement. *Oh, Frederick, you made such a big fucking mistake. I will ruin you, and you just gave me the biggest reason to do so.*

Anna's mind raced. She considering options for the most effective way to make the information she had public.

Maria Arnett! She would know how!

Anna would give Vogt the video file in exchange for 24-hour protection until she stepped onto U.S. soil. Once the information was made public, there would be no need to silence her.

And then I will just be another girl. I will go to graduate school, I will live a normal life, I will forget all of this, and all of this will forget me.

A bit calmer, Anna turned onto the narrow road which led to Maria Arnett's villa and dialed her number. "Maria, it's me. I'm on your road..."

Anna's own scream interrupted the conversation. The phone dropped to her lap as her tires skid off the road. Something had rammed into the back of the BMW. She looked into the rearview mirror as her hands worked to regain control of the car.

The black Mercedes was pounding against her trunk and trying to push her off the road.

"Fuck!" Anna yelled and tugged the wheel left to reunite with the paved road. Suddenly, an explosion of shattered glass sliced her face and arms. Still screaming, she ducked her head.

"They fucking shot at me!"

"Who did!?" Maria Arnett's voice desperately yelled from Anna's lap.

Anna slammed on the gas, "Maria, listen to me!" her voice commanded.

"Open the gate to your house *now*! Stay near it and close it when I say."

Anna veered the car left and then right across the road, blocking the Mercedes from accelerating next to her. She had a mile and a half in front of her before the road would curve to the right and bring her to the iron gate.

Again, the Mercedes crashed into her from behind, but Anna took the hit without giving up room on either side. The right turn was a hundred feet away.

"Close the gate, Maria! Close the fucking gate!"

Anna pulled the wheel right with all her strength. The BMW's rear swerved to the left. Anna hung on to the wheel. It vibrated underneath her fingers as the tires squealed and burned the pavement. The car's left side lifted but met the ground quickly. Her chest pounded until she felt it in her throat.

She made a final right turn and saw the old iron gates in front of her squeak their way toward one another. She wasn't going to make it. They were closing faster than she had anticipated. She closed her eyes for impact and screamed as loud as she could as the sound of metal ripped into the BMW on both sides. Sparks flew everywhere.

Anna slammed on the brakes as the car began to skid out of the gates and into Maria Arnett's fern-covered property. Bushes, flower beds, and young trees scraped at the BMW, clawing at it to slow it down.

A loud crash behind her rattled her ears, eliciting another scream from Anna just as her car came to a rough final stop. Anna opened her eyes and tasted blood in her mouth.

Maria Arnett was running toward her.

"No!" Anna screamed, "Go back inside!"

Anna unbuckled her seatbelt and smashed against the car door until it finally gave way. Maria Arnett was already at her side, pulling Anna out of the car, but Anna forcefully shoved Maria Arnett down behind the BMW.

The powerful Mercedes didn't have time to stop after the final turn and had crashed into the heavy iron security poles, bending them to the ground. It didn't even look like a car anymore, with smoke and steam coming from the engine. No one seemed to be moving inside the vehicle.

Was Frederick in the car?

Anna shook her head, grabbed her backpack and pulled a frazzled Maria Arnett toward the front door locking it behind them. "Fuck him!" she said under her breath.

"My God, Anna! Are you alright? What is going on?!"

Anna ignored Maria Arnett's frantic questions and instead stared at her car from the window. How was she even alive? The BMW was stripped. The gates had taken both side mirrors and scraped off much metal on each side. Both the front and back bumpers were gone.

Anna spit out blood.

"Maria, call an ambulance immediately. I'll explain everything later." Anna pulled out a business card and dialed Vogt's cell phone.

Chapter 35

Vogt's cell phone answered on the first ring. "This is Anna…" she tried to keep her voice steady. "They tried to kill me—the ambulance is on its way."

"Who tried to kill you?"

"Whoever the hell you have been chasing... I ended it with Frederick—I'm sure he gave an order…" Anna's voice cracked.

"Where are you?"

"In Wannsee. I'll text you the address. You need to come now."

"I am on my way. Don't talk to anyone until I get there."

The agent hung up and Anna felt partial relief. Blood had created thin layers of crust that formed on the skin of her lips. Anna touched the chapped bloody craters and peered out from behind the curtains. The black Mercedes continued to smoke in the distance. No one had exited the car.

Maria Arnett hovered by her side with anxious composure. Millions of questions had to be going through her head, but she asked none of them.

"Anna, are you sure you are alright? Sit for a bit, rest." she pleaded.

Anna kept her gaze fixed on the window. She needed to speak to Vogt. She needed to figure out what to do next.

Sirens blared in the distance. Anna watched the white and blue lights of police cars and an ambulance speed toward the broken gate.

"When the police get here," Anna began, "tell them I'm recovering from shock. I will only speak to Agent Vogt once he arrives."

The German *polizei* were several feet away from the gate. Anna continued to watch as paramedics pulled two bodies from the front seat of the Mercedes. It was too far for her to see their faces, but neither looked like Frederick by their physiques.

Two officers and two paramedics approached the house. Anna backed away from the window as Maria Arnett came to the door. Seconds later, the paramedics checked Anna's vitals and asked her questions to determine coherence.

"Are you sure you do not want to go to the emergency room?" the paramedic asked in accented English.

Anna shook her head. "I'm just shaken up. I need to lie down."

The two cops spoke to Maria Arnett, scribbled notes, and constantly looked in Anna's direction. A tall female officer in a black pantsuit came over and flashed her badge. *She must be the detective,* Anna assumed.

"Anna Venu?"

"Yes," she answered.

"Agent Vogt will be here momentarily."

Anna prepared herself for a wave of questions, but they did not come. The woman proceeded toward Maria Arnett.

Anna's voice stopped her. "What happened to the people in the car?"

The officer turned on her heels and stared at Anna firmly before responding. "The passenger is dead," she said. "The driver is in critical condition headed to the hospital."

The woman's eyes searched Anna's for a clue as to what had happened, but her expression remained blank until the detective walked away.

Anna kept her face buried, pressing on her eyes until she heard the doorbell ring. When Agent Vogt stepped into the room, he swiftly assessed the interior, quickly spotting Anna. Nodding in her direction, Vogt spoke to two officers and promptly made his way towards her.

"Ms. Venu, you did the right thing by calling me. Are you alright?"

"I'm not injured."

"Good. Good..."

Anna gave him a halfhearted look.

"Ms. Venu..." Vogt hesitated. "I do not mean to be callous, but we have a fatal crash outside this property. I will get to the bottom of this, but I need information from you, and I need it now. I am sure you understand the gravity of the situation, and I—"

Maria Arnett's heightened tone broke the agent's sentence. "Anna just escaped the grips of two killers, and *you* want answers? She's in shock! Anna needs to—"

Maria Arnett's voice faded to the background as Anna's mind left the present situation. The car crash she had witnessed in Phoenix had panicked her, but this—this felt different. Anna did not feel fear, stress, or anxiety. She felt nothing at all.

Her love for Frederick had been destroyed, mangled, and torn like the stripped Mercedes out front. There was nothing left of it. She was alone, yes, and she had been here before, but this time it felt different; she had become different. In its place bloomed an airy sense of freedom. She thought of Grandmother's perseverance. *I am a lot more like you now.*

Fatigue suddenly overcame her. Maria Arnett and Vogt kept arguing in German. Maria Arnett's arms flew around heatedly while Vogt attempted to calm her down. Anna stood from her crouched position, silencing Maria Arnett and Vogt, who turned to her with attention.

"My dear, are you alright?" Maria Arnett's hand was on her shoulder.

"Was Frederick Häuser in that car?" Anna's voice sounded unfamiliar to her; it was dead-cold.

Vogt's eyes narrowed, trying to assess the severity of Anna's state of mind.

"No."

"Maria, can you make us some strong coffee? We need to speak with Agent Vogt. Let's go to the kitchen."

"Ms. Venu…" Vogt began, "it would be best if you and I spoke alone."

Anna's face hardened. "Agent Vogt, *please,* it would be best if you let me say what I need to say, considering you're part of the reason I was almost killed."

She watched Vogt's face redden but couldn't extract any pleasure from it. Anna turned and walked toward the kitchen. She heard nothing but the footsteps of two people following closely behind.

Anna put a wet towel to her face while a Turkish pot filled with aromatic arabica coffee simmered on the stove. She slowly drank a glass of water, oblivious to the hawk-like eyes of the man across from her, impatiently waiting for her to begin.

Maria Arnett set three glass espresso cups on the table and scooped ice cream into Anna's. "You need the sugar."

Anna drank the sweet, rich concoction and closed her eyes. How strange it was for everything to change so drastically, yet her taste buds knew no difference. Coffee still tasted like coffee.

"Agent Vogt, the day we met changed the course of everything."

Anna began to retell the past month's events as Vogt furiously scribbled notes, while Maria Arnett simply stared in disbelief.

"It was a pure miracle that I flew through those gates and that the Mercedes crashed into them. It's hard to believe it even happened. It's harder to believe they tried to shoot me."

Maria Arnett's hand cupped over her mouth.

"You truly are Maria's granddaughter," said Maria Arnett with admiration.

They sat in silence until the agent cleared his throat. "Do you still possess the video recording from Kalkriese Hill?"

"Yes," Anna stated.

Vogt became visibly excited. "I'll need to see it immediately."

Anna retrieved her laptop and opened the file. He watched the video twice in full, and then paced the room as Anna pulled up the edited photographs of Walter Balke and Frederick's father.

"Ms. Venu…" the agent grabbed his chair and maneuvered it next to Anna. He leaned into her with gleaming dark eyes. "You have to make this video public. For the sake of Germany, you have to do it." Beads of sweat had formed at his brow line.

"I would rather turn it over to you and the police."

"That will do nothing. If I hand this over to my superiors, even with all the evidence I have accumulated, there is a good chance the entire case will be buried by Frederick's well-connected father, just as it had been before. Justice is nothing in the face of money and power."

"What are you suggesting?"

"We need to leak the video to the media first. That way, there can be no police intervention. Your statement to the detective outside will begin with the car chase, don't say anything else—not who you suspect the men to be, or why they were after you; nothing. Once the video is out, no one will be able to stop it, and my superiors will be forced to take action and start an official investigation. The German public will keep them accountable for it."

"Who do you plan to leak it to?"

"I have the perfect person," Maria Arnett interrupted, "Agent Vogt, I am sure you have heard of her, Kristina Kristof?"

The agent's eyes grew wider. "You have a direct connection to her?"

"Yes," Maria Arnett answered, "she is a friend."

Anna furrowed her brows in confusion.

"Anna, Kristina Kristof is one of the most respected investigative journalists in Germany, focusing on human rights issues. Having this story come from her will give it national exposure. I will make the call now."

"Alright," she said coolly. "Let's leak it."

"We need to do this as quickly as possible. No police will protect you as well as the media will."

Anna understood.

Agent Vogt looked her over for several seconds. It was as if he had just noticed that Anna was not basking in triumph. The man cleared his throat, making way for a voice that was calm and weighted with significance. "If I may, I can understand that the way this all unfolded is painful. I am sorry this happened the way that it did...." He paused but Anna did not react. "You made a personal sacrifice for Germany, and it is much appreciated.

"If you ever decide to work in criminal justice, I believe your analytical mind and incredible creativity will take you far. To be honest, your story left me speechless. I had completely underestimated you. Even with all of my experience, I still saw you as a young tourist caught up in something she knew nothing about. Of course, if you need my assistance in the future, I am in your debt."

Anna looked up into his dark eyes and said, "Thank you, Agent Vogt."

He nodded in response. "And, out of curiosity, where did you learn to drive like that?"

She felt the left side of her lip curl upward, the first smile in what felt like ages. "My father is quite overprotective. When I got my driver's license, he forced me to take months of defensive-driving courses until my response to danger became automatic. I thought he was crazy, but I took it as an opportunity for some fun. I guess everything does, in fact, happen for a reason."

Agent Vogt nodded as Maria Arnett burst through the door. "Kristina Kristof will be here within the hour. Anna, are you sure you have the energy for this?"

"I don't," Anna answered flatly, "but I don't see myself having the energy for it tomorrow, either."

Kristina Kristof asked complicated specific questions, many of which Anna didn't have the answers to. Exhaustion continued to drain her until there was virtually nothing left, and her answers began to blur together.

Anna's head did not hit the pillow till the early hours of the morning.

Agent Vogt stayed the night in case the police officers stationed around the house detected any threat.

When Anna awoke, it was 2:00 p.m. the next day. She had a limited recollection of the previous day. It felt like a series of events from someone else's life.

"I don't wanna do this anymore..." Anna lightly sang to the ceiling, "...it's so surreal."

The silence of the room seemed to acknowledge Lana Del Rey's lyrics. Outside, the perimeter of the property continued to be secured by police surveillance. Any lingering hope that this had all been a nightmare permanently erased itself. The only trace of the black Mercedes were the dented gates and the stiffness she felt throughout her body. Anna pulled the curtains closed and left the bedroom.

Agent Vogt had left, but would return once Anna was awake and feeling more like herself. That was what Maria Arnett explained to her while telling Anna it was not a good idea for her to leave yet.

"He insists on taking you to a remote hotel on the outskirts of Berlin under a false name. He says there will be undercover security for you the entire time, but I told him that there is security for you here, too, and you won't be alone."

Anna took a sip of tea and it scorched her throat. "Can't I just go home?" Anna asked sincerely.

Maria Arnett returned a knowing smile. "I wish you could, too. But Agent Vogt says you need to stay until the story goes public. They won't hurt you if the information you possess is no longer a secret. Even if they wanted to—the public would know who was behind it."

Following the agent's advice, Anna relocated to a small bed-and-breakfast checking in under the name Helga; a symbolic gesture for herself. She slept most of the days away, refusing to give herself conscious space to process what had happened.

After a few days had passed, Vogt made her re-enter reality.

"It's all over the news!" he announced. "Maria Arnett has already started receiving calls and messages from the media trying to locate you for interviews and such. I just want you to be prepared."

When Anna hung up the phone, for the first time in what seemed like weeks, she checked the news. Vogt was right. As she flipped through the channels, Anna saw that she was the top story. Accidently, she had exposed the true agenda and funding sources behind one of the most covert German extreme-right groups.

Vogt's name was everywhere, too. He was leading the criminal investigation. Anna watched as Vogt spoke to the media: "Ms. Venu's current location is not being released at this time for security reasons. Herr. J. Häuser, through his attorneys, refused to comment."

The news articles that followed described Anna's actions as heroic, just, and critical. Words like "cunning," and "skilled" were used to describe her. The headlines played heavily on Anna's bloodline and her great-grandfather, Lieutenant Commander Hans Ritter.

I guess in the end, you got what you wanted, Frederick—my bloodline associated with your cause.

Anna searched but was unable to find Frederick's name mentioned in any of the news articles she skimmed through.

Chapter 36

She skimmed through various airline flights immediately following Vogt's decision to permit Anna to leave the country.

Ironically, the decision to leave felt heavy because Anna knew that she would never return here, just like Grandmother. Germany had given her love, adventure, incredible life experience and most importantly, crucial answers, but it had also caused her much grief.

There was only one more thing that Anna did not yet have the chance to do. Something that Frederick had promised to show her himself. She had yet to see the war diaries of her great-grandfather, Lieutenant Commander Hans Ritter.

Both Karl and Frederick had referenced the commander's U-boat journal writings from the early months of World War II several times when describing how heroic, humorous, and talented Ritter was. Anna wanted to read them for herself to gain some sort of connection to the man that had had such a significant impact on her life.

The Department of Military Archives in the university city of Freiburg im Breisgau, stored the war diaries and log journals of German U-boat captains along with other records

Google let her know it would be an 8-hour drive from Berlin, much farther than she had expected. If she wanted to get to the archive before her trip home, she would need to take a plane.

Anna called Vogt.

"I will have an undercover car escort you to and from the airport," Vogt replied after hearing of Anna's plans. "And, Anna, please rent an unassuming car using your false identity when you get there. No more attention-grabbing BMWs."

Anna hung up the phone, booked the last hotel in Germany that she would stay at, and the last car she would rent.

The comfort of Berlin began to fade as her airplane climbed higher. The feeling of escape was intoxicatingly freeing. Anna focused her thoughts on her great-grandfather.

What kind of man was he really? She wondered what stories his journals would disclose from the time he was on war patrol in the Mediterranean Sea between 1939 and 1940. And there was the question of whether or not he ever pledged allegiance to the Nazi regime.

Anna landed at the EuroAirport Basel-Mulhouse Freiburg and picked up her unassuming mini Renault Twingo. As promised, she was accompanied by one of Vogt's men who tailed her from a distance up until she arrived at the Dorint An den Thermen Hotel. The resort was in a beautiful forest on the edge of the Mooswald conservation area.

Anna ordered room service in the luxurious room themed in whites, oranges, and warm woods; she thought it best to remain out of the public eye.

The German press had managed to steal a photograph of her from social media before she had deleted her accounts. Despite Vogt's efforts to have it removed for her safety, it was now all over German media. In bed, Anna read through the military archive website in more detail and immediately wanted to kick herself.

The website informed her that, "The U-boat war diaries of the Kriegsmarine are available at the Military Archives within our archival holding RM 98 (Unterseeboote der Kriegsmarine). You are welcome to attend our reading room in Freiburg. To get a reservation for a seat in the reading room, please announce your visit four weeks in advance directly to our staff. To prepare your visit, please fill in, sign, and return the enclosed form Benutzungsantrag."

"I can't wait that long!"

Another roadblock that she had to get out of her way.

Anna clicked through the military archive's employee profiles on LinkedIn until she found the Director, Alexa Koenig. Her contact information was unlisted. Anna would have to convince her to gain expedited access to the journal in person.

At 11:00 a.m., Anna parked in front of the Department of Military Archives, a white eight-story building that towered over the surrounding structures. She approached the man at the front desk and they exchanged greetings. A rolled-up newspaper with her photograph stuck out of her purse. As expected, her request to speak to Director Koenig was not possible.

Anna slid the newspaper clipping toward the receptionist as if it were a stack of hundreds.

"My situation is unique. I am leaving Germany and I am confident that Director Koenig would want to meet with me."

The man scanned the story with immediate recognition but remained stoic.

"Ms. Venu, yes, I see. Let me make a call."

Anna thanked him and breathed in a sense of optimism.

"Ms. Venu, Director Koenig will meet with you shortly. Please take a seat."

Anna closed her eyes until her ears picked up the sounds of heels hitting the parquet. A petite blonde woman with radiant, intelligent blue eyes and a strong presence walked toward her.

"Ms. Anna Venu? It is a pleasure." She reached for Anna's hand and shook it with firm warmth. "Please follow me to my office. I only wish I had known of your arrival sooner. Many of our researchers and visiting scholars would have enjoyed meeting you."

"It was a last-minute decision," Anna said honestly.

The director's heels continued to click down the hallway with an energetic rhythm. "I assume you are here to read your great-grandfather's war diaries?"

"Yes..." Anna answered with hesitation that the director immediately picked up on.

"I only assume so following your recent story in the press. You have become quite the sensation. Our archive has become very popular following your story. Suddenly, the general public and not just historians are making appointments to examine various war documents. We have been pleased to receive numerous descendants of U-boat captains requesting to read the war accounts of their grandfathers, great-grandfathers, great-uncles, and so forth. ARD News even did a piece on our preservation work."

Anna heard pride in Director Koenig's voice. She suddenly came to a halt in front of an office door and turned to face Anna.

"Thank you for sparking the public's interest in our history and, of course, for your fascinating investigative work."

The director's eyes sparkled with an excitement that Anna wished she could possess. *It all came at a price,* she wanted to add, but instead nodded with gratitude.

"We have one of Lieutenant Commander Ritter's war diaries from nineteen thirty-nine."

"Director Koenig, I know there's a review process to access the records, but I'm leaving Germany, and, due to recent events, I don't know when I will return here."

Anna heard her own voice crack. Director Koenig nodded empathetically. "I understand. We do not normally grant access so easily, but what you have accomplished makes your situation rather unique."

She picked up her office phone before Anna could respond. "Yes, Lieutenant Commander Ritter's journal... We are in my office. Thank you, Derik."

After a few minutes of conversation, there was a knock on the door. An archive assistant stepped into the Director's office. The young man shook Anna's hand and approached Director Koenig's desk with his back to Anna. He seemed nervous. Anna noticed that he discreetly placed two journals in front of Director Koenig. They exchanged dialogue in German as Director Koenig carefully inspected one of the journals. She glanced in Anna's direction several times as if weighing a decision.

"Is something the matter?" Anna finally voiced, breaking the lingering tension.

The archive assistant walked out of the office and left Anna and Director Koenig to focus on one another.

"Ms. Anna, I apologize for the secrecy, but a strange event just occurred."

"I see you have two of my great-grandfather's journals," Anna stated.

"Yes, precisely, but as long as I have been Director, we have only had one."

"How is this possible?" Anna asked.

"It appears that the second journal had been catalogued along with another U-boat commander, Captain Fritz Wolf. Captain Wolf's descendants had only gained interest and visited our archive yesterday following your news story. They were the ones who found your great-grandfather's misplaced journal."

Director Koenig tapped the cover with her perfectly manicured nail. "It is from nineteen forty-four."

"The year before Nazi surrender," Anna added.

"Correct," Director Koenig said gravely. "I imagine the difference between the two diaries will be significant."

She pushed both journals toward Anna.

"Please take as much time as you need." Director Koenig smiled and closed the door, leaving Anna alone with the two booklets.

A label across the top of the thin notebook's yellowed cover read 1939: LIEUTENANT COMMANDER HANS RITTER.

Nervously, Anna opened the first journal. It was written by hand in faded pencil. She studied the long looped cursive script that stretched elegantly across the page. Unable to translate every word, she began to decipher sentences using her now-intermediate German.

Amidst the technical details of warfare, Commander Ritter described his excitement of spotting a merchant ship to target—a wicked cat-and-mouse game. He wrote beautifully about the spray of the sea and the pungent aroma of coffee and mandarins that came from below the conning tower. Spirits were high and the crew had become a family, celebrating birthdays, fishing off the top of the U-boat, and taking swims in the Mediterranean Sea.

Frederick had been right: Ritter's descriptions were rich with detail and alive with humor. It felt odd to sympathize with the worries of great-grandfather and the U-boat crew.

Frederick, Karl, and Benedikt had said Lieutenant Commander Ritter was a nationalist, without any allegiance to the Nazi party, with only the safety of Germany on his mind. True to their words, the diary made no mention of the Führer, but nonetheless, Anna's great-grandfather served an inhumane regime.

Her grandmother had never had a chance to read her father's writings; she hadn't even known that they existed. Now, here was Anna, on the other side of her world, finding herself by uncovering the stories of her bloodline. Her grandmother had always been brave, determined, and strong-willed. Anna thought she had inherited these qualities from her, but maybe it was her great-grandfather who deserved the credit.

Anna picked up the second journal from 1944. The first few pages had the same romantic cursive, but the tone was much different. The language was technical and filled with coordinates, weather conditions, military interactions, and updates on the crew's well-being. Across the next several pages, her great-grandfather's beautiful writing became tight, rigid, and dry, as if the writer had no patience left, but things still had to be said. Anna held her breath as her great-grandfather detailed a near-fatal attack on his U-boat.

They had been cornered by two destroyers in relatively shallow water in the Caribbean Sea close to the Florida Straits. Bombs pillaged the waters closer and closer to their hidden location. Water began to seep into the submarine from the power of the blasts; panic overcame the crew.

"Immediately, I instructed our engineer to release oil to the surface to give the impression that we had been hit."

Anna read on, biting her bottom lip.

"My second command was for the crew to scream and strike our pipes creating the clanking sounds of destruction for a total of three minutes followed by complete silence."

As Anna later learned, her great-grandfather's trick was not uncommon and it was something the enemy watched out for.

"The risk was in those three minutes. Our screams and noise gave away our precise location to the acousticians on each enemy destroyer. Our immediate silence, combined with the floating oil, gave the appearance of our submarine's destruction. I counted on enemy destroyers refusing to waste ammunition on an already sunken U-boat, and miraculously I was right. We lay on the seafloor for twenty-four silent dark hours. Lack of oxygen forced us to surface the next day."

Completely engrossed in the story, Anna flipped to the next page and the next. Suddenly the air in Anna's lungs vanished. The word *Gettysburg* was written in the last line of the entry. She could hardly believe it. It was the name of Grandfather's tanker. Chills pricked up the back of her spine and neck as she read:

"June 10th. Identified tanker headed north in a zigzag course. Followed the tanker for two hours before securing an ideal position to attack. First torpedo missed. Fired second torpedo, hitting and disabling the target. A third torpedo sank the vessel. Remained silent for several hours and left the area of attack at 06:00, taking course back to Saint-Nazaire base. The tanker was identified as *Gettysburg* under the American flag, carrying approximately 120,000 tons of crude oil."

Anna sat frozen; the short entry left her completely dumbfounded. It completely lacked emotion, yet she knew the other side of this same story. Her grandfather, delusional and lost at sea, and hanging on to his best friend, was shot dead by the U-boat captain, who would later become his father-in-law and her great-grandfather.

A wave of emotion consumed her. She had grown partially attached to her great-grandfather; she had admired him alongside the rest of Germany, but now, she learned that he was responsible for an unjustified act of brutality. He had shot defenseless James while sparing the life of his future son-in-law, the man who would rescue his beloved daughter, Maria.

One more pull of that trigger and I wouldn't even exist!

Anna looked at the cover of the diary: 1944. She reread the year. Something felt wrong. *Great-grandfather wasn't on patrol in 1944. He was in charge of the 2nd Flotilla based in France....*

Immediately, she sat up and snapped out of her mesmerized state.

She distinctly remembered Frederick explaining that Commander Ritter's last patrol was in 1940.

Anna left the office and went across the hall to where Director Koenig said she would be.

"Ah, Ms. Venu. How was your reading?"

Anna's wide-eyed expression made Director Koenig raise an eyebrow. "Is everything alright?"

"Director Koenig, the entries in this diary are from nineteen forty-four, but I know for certain that my great-grandfather embarked on his last patrol in nineteen forty. He didn't go to sea during the Battle of the Atlantic but directed the U-boat campaign from France's shore. How is this possible?"

Director Koenig lit up. "You are absolutely right, Ms. Venu. Commander Ritter ceased U-boat operations in nineteen-forty and took command of the Second Flotilla; however, he embarked on the mission you just read about for reasons unknown. It is a mystery of sorts for why and how he did this. None of his other surviving records explain this sudden change in duty."

Unable to fully process the information, Anna thanked the director and left the archive. She sat in the parking lot for twenty minutes, thinking. Her great-grandfather, a man known to have high morals, decided to return to patrol and even kill a fellow mariner after already sinking their ship.

Why?

She started the car and immediately knew where she was headed. At 10:00 p.m. that night, Anna banged on the heavy oak front door until Benedikt opened it, dressed in a smoking jacket and slippers.

"Anna! Are you alright? What has happened?" He rushed her into the house.

Anna's lips parted and uncontrollably poured forth the words which had been building inside her head since Freiburg.

"In nineteen forty-four, your uncle and my great-grandfather Commander Ritter went on patrol in the Atlantic. During this patrol, his U-boat sank the *Gettysburg,* an American oil tanker. After the tanker went down, his U-boat surfaced next to two sailors gripping a floating buffet in the middle of the ocean. Instead of helping them, he shot one of the men, and left the other to die alone. Does any of this sound familiar to you?"

Benedikt's naturally red face lost its color until it was a sickly white.

"Does this sound familiar to you?" Anna repeated, still in Benedikt's front hallway.

"Anna, for God's sake, how did you get this information?"

He cleared his throat uncomfortably. "That old snake Gunter had something to do with this, didn't he? You found something of his? Read something of his?" Benedikt hissed.

"Gunter?" Perplexed, Anna stared at Benedikt until her brain made the connection.

"Oh, yes—the sailor your family has supported for years. Frederick told me all about him."

"My family?" Benedikt raised his voice, "Our family, Anna. It is *our* family!" He wiped building beads of sweat off his forehead.

Anna took a deep breath and tried to calm herself. She didn't want to cause Benedikt further distress.

"You're right; our family." She paused until Benedikt looked a bit more composed. "Benedikt, I need to tell you something else, something even crazier."

"Anna, your discoveries are more bizarre than those of all my clients," Benedikt said. With a tired expression, he led the way into his kitchen.

"Please, sit..."

Immediately Anna began explaining, "The second sailor, who was left at sea with his murdered friend and who witnessed Commander Ritter's war crime, is my grandfather, John Venu."

Benedikt's small round eyes dilated until they looked like perfectly round glossy marbles. Anna studied the silence on his face.

"You are saying…" Benedikt began with some difficulty, "that Maria married the surviving sailor?"

"That is *exactly* what I am saying," Anna replied firmly.

Benedikt rubbed his face until it returned to its natural red glow.

"God almighty… How? How is this possible? I just... I..." Benedikt threw his hands up in surrender. "I thought I had known everything... The years I spent pouring over details of our past. Then you appear and it is one shock after the next!"

Anna nodded. "I have come to realize that it is when you are most confident in something that the universe turns your world upside-down and humbles you."

"Anna, how do you know this? It is of the utmost importance that you tell me."

"From my great-grandfather's nineteen forty-four U-boat log journal."

"His journal from forty-four?" Benedikt's tone verged on the miraculous.

"It was recently discovered at the Department of Military Archives." Anna eyed him suspiciously. "And judging from your reaction, I gather that you knew about its existence?"

"I have never read it!"

"Benedikt, your choice of words is striking. You say you have never read it, but not that you have never known of its existence. It's just so curious that Ritter's nineteen forty-four journal wasn't discovered before. I have to ask: Did you have anything to do with its convenient misplacement?"

"I can never have my defenses down with you, can I?" Benedikt answered, amused. "I am not lying to you, Anna. I have not seen it, nor have I read it, but, yes, I knew of its existence. When the archives first opened to the public, my father was the first to look for all possible information regarding his brother. Apparently, the circumstances surrounding the nineteen forty-four patrol had been kept secret by Admiral Doenitz. When my father uncovered the journal, he was unable to steal it. The only thing he could think to do was to purposely misplace it into the file of a lesser-known captain by the name of Wolf, who had only gone on patrol once, having to turn back immediately when his U-boat malfunctioned. Wolf's journal was mostly blank, and my father searched for any living relatives and found only one descendant. The chances of Captain Wolf's journal being read were slim."

"I see..." Anna paused, going over the information. "Then can you explain to me why great-grandfather did this? Why did he act in cold blood?"

Benedikt exhaled a laborious sigh and began brewing a pot of tea. "According to my father, a problem developed when U-boat torpedo detonators began failing to detonate at impact with a targeted ship, exposing the U-boat's location. The morale of the entire U-boat fleet began to wane.

Admiral Doenitz worked tirelessly to get new detonators placed on all torpedoes, but he first wanted to test them out in battle. Purposely, Doenitz had kept my uncle away from sea patrol, considering his value as Commander of the Second Flotilla. However, Doenitz needed someone he could blindly trust to carry out his secret mission to test the new torpedoes. That is how your great-grandfather once again embarked on patrol on U 66, secretly replacing its captain just hours before departure.

"My uncle was excited to have this opportunity to return to the sea and to combat. Within a month of patrol, the new torpedoes proved to work correctly. During an arranged meeting with a U-boat tanker to refuel, the crew of U 66 got severely infected with some bacteria or virus. One sailor died from the infection, several men were in dire condition, and my uncle was verging on death.

"The U-boat had no choice but to head home to seek medical attention for the crew. In another week's time, uncle began showing signs of recovery, as did some crew members. As soon as he could stand, he was back at the conning tower, scanning the horizon.

"There were only three torpedoes left, and he wanted to make another kill before returning home. Soon enough, he spotted an American tanker and followed it for some time before sinking the ship. The crew celebrated, but for uncle, the victory would not last long. Silently, the U-boat waited for any further orders. Very late at night, their radio operator received a coded message which partly read, 'the lion cub is dead.'

"This was a personal message from Admiral Doenitz to Commander Ritter. It meant that Peter, the Admiral's son, had perished in the Atlantic Ocean with the rest of U 954. Ritter was Peter's mentor and saw him as a younger brother. The news truly devastated him.

"Early the next morning, before the U-boat surfaced, uncle's fever once again spiked in response to his desolate emotional state. His hallucinations returned and he ordered the U-boat to surface for fresh air. He climbed up and opened the conning tower. The rest of the story, you already know.

"Yes, he shot one sailor. Yes, he spared the life of the other merely because an alert sounded, signaling a large ship approaching. The U-boat submerged and that was the end of it."

"You knew all of this?" Anna questioned.

"Your great-grandfather was deeply ashamed of his actions. Killing a fellow seaman and leaving another man to die at sea lacked honor. My father noticed that his brother had become different after his return from patrol. Ritter confessed to my father that when he first entered the war, he had promised himself that he would never go against his morals—as much as a man could in war. He said that he would never unjustifiably kill anyone. He had been tested many times, but he had held onto his sanity with everything he had every day. Finally, after that last patrol, the war broke him. In his own eyes, he had become a war criminal just like so many others.

"Anna, our family went through hell, but we are not unique. Billions of people are subjected to this sort of unnecessary violence even today.

"Trauma surpasses time. Look at me or even yourself. We were not directly affected by the war, but it is in our DNA now. We still carry the fear and pain the war instilled in our ancestors."

Anna let Benedikt's words resonate. "And this is what you and your father have tried to cover up for years?"

"Yes, my father deeply loved his brother and was protective of his legacy. On his deathbed, I gave him my word that I would continue to guard it."

"How is it that none of the other crew members had repeated the story over the years? They must have heard and seen what had happened..."

"Of course, they knew of what happened, but my uncle was highly respected and loved by his men. The crew of U 66 made a pact to keep this secret with respect to their captain, who had secured their safe return home.

"As soon as the submarine got to the base at Saint-Nazaire, Ritter returned to his primary duty managing the Second Flotilla, and Oberleutnant G. Seehausen took on commanding duties of the U-boat. After repairs and the reloading of ammunition and torpedoes, the submarine and its crew left for the sea.

"That would be their last patrol, as U 66 was sunk on May 6, 1944, near the Cape Verde Islands. All hands were lost."

Benedikt remained silent for a minute before continuing with the rest of the story. "There was only one young sailor who did not return to the vessel before its departure due to sickness. The sailor's name was Gunter Krauss. Years after the war, he found my father and blackmailed him— threatened to reveal his brother's secret. In response, my father and I have been forced to support him for the rest of his life to keep his mouth shut.

"War ruins most people's sense of humanity, but your great-grandfather tried to hold onto his as best as he could. For that, I respect him, and so should you."

Benedikt slapped his thick hand onto the marble kitchen table, zapping Anna back to the present.

"Considering these new developments, which are as crazy as you promised them to be, you now have to decide what we should do next."

"I think the only person who can decide what to do next is my grandfather."

Benedikt nodded in agreement and lifted both of his pink palms as if he were in defeat. The weight of the promise Benedikt made to his father had burdened his life, but now, the burden dissipated. The secret was released to Anna, and she would share it with the only person who would genuinely value its truth, her grandfather.

Anna said her farewells and left Benedikt's home, realizing afterward that she had nowhere to go. She was too tired to drive back to Maria Arnett's and too emotionally drained to remain at Benedikt's. Anna sat behind the wheel of her car, deep in thought.

There were the obvious horrors of war: killing, destruction, and so forth, but Benedikt was right; the trauma didn't stop there; it forever affected the lives of survivors, their families and friends who are forced to carry on with the memories of unexplainable pain and grief.

How many people have to die on this planet before life gains value over power, greed, and ego?

The urge to see her family became overwhelming. Anna started the car and with nowhere else to go, she drove to the airport for her flight to the United States with a connecting stop in Paris, France.

BOOK III

THE WEB OF HUMANITY

Chapter 37

Her flight to the United States with a connecting stop in Paris, France, touched down at Charles De Gaulle Airport during the morning hours. Feeling Berlin minimize with every passing minute had a freeing effect on Anna. Worry, fear, sadness, anger—all of it shrunk until it completely disappeared underneath thick white clouds. For the first time in weeks, Anna felt she could take a full breath of air. She had started the journey back home.

Anna entered the airport and looked at her watch. She had an almost twenty-hour layover—just enough time to enjoy a day in a familiar city that held nothing but great memories of family vacations with her grandmother. A part of her understood that the stop in Paris was procrastination, but it also served a purpose.

According to Anna's mother, Grandfather was frail. She harbored an intense fear that the truth would end his will to live. However, now there was no way around it. Berlin was done with. Paris provided solace not only to her but to Grandfather. It was where her grandparents had met. The street where Grandfather had rescued Grandmother was what Anna was looking for. If Anna could show photographs of the place that changed the course of her grandparent's lives to Grandfather, maybe that would add comfort to the uneasy truth.

After dropping Calvin off in an airport locker, Anna traveled to the République Métro station. She walked out into the chilled sunshine of an early Parisian afternoon and breathed in the air of a different nation. Anna was in the Marais District, one of the oldest parts of Paris lined with shops, cafés, bars, narrow streets, and the homes of French aristocracy from a long time gone.

Anna walked down Rue du Temple, a central street, for about two blocks and made a left on Rue Dupetit-Thouars. The side street Cité Dupetit-Thouars was just ahead. The name of the street was fixed on a blue-and-white placard on the side of the brick building. Tracing her fingers along the rough exterior, Anna wondered if this was the same wall her grandmother had been held against or if that building was long gone. Anna got out her cell phone and began taking photos.

No one knew where she was, and this ability to be anonymous returned a sense of peace to Anna. An aroma of fresh bread whisked its way on the current of the wind. It guided Anna back to the corner café at the end of the street. Choosing an outdoor table, she ordered a cappuccino and a Brie-and-jam baguette.

Across the street stood an old church; its façade adorned with Doric and Ionic pillars and saints' statues. A small group of people sat on its steps and others assembled by the entrance. Melted Brie dripped onto the plate from her sandwich.

It must be a wedding... Anna sipped her cappuccino and watched the crowd. It continued to grow in size. *Were they waiting for mass?* It was already well into the afternoon. *Didn't mass already end?*

The crowd continued to expand until the entire street in front of the church was filled with Parisians and tourists. Curiosity made Anna cross the road and approach an older couple speaking English with an Irish accent.

"Excuse me, what is this crowd for?" she asked.

The older woman looked at her from behind bejeweled golden-framed glasses and said, "It is for Father Bernard!" She crossed herself three times. "He is a living saint; God bless his soul!"

Suddenly shrieks erupted from parts of the crowd and people in the front fell to their knees. The church doors had opened, and a small, frail man emerged. Surrounded by deacons, he walked with such slow, smooth movements that he appeared to be floating. The priest looked to be blind but walked with the confidence of knowing exactly where he was going.

Anna nudged her way closer to the front to get a better glimpse of the man who began to disappear into the crowd as he descended from the last step onto the sidewalk. People parted in front of him like a mythical sea. They tried to reach for his feet and brush their fingertips against his robe as he gave blessings to the right and left.

Anna moved her gaze to the old priest's face as he passed her and gasped. A large chunk of his right ear was missing as if a big dog had bitten most of it off. Without thinking, a desperate intuitive urge shot through Anna, compelling her to call out: "Spring nineteen forty-six, an American soldier saves a young woman from a street gang on Rue Dupetit-Thouars!"

The crowd's eyes stared her down as if she were mad; immediately, Anna felt like disappearing.

Why the hell did I just do that?

Her face flushed a deep red. The priest suddenly stopped, slowly turned around, and looked straight at Anna with his blind eyes. It felt as though he stared into her very existence. When his gaze left her, the surrounding air began to pump in and out of her chest feverishly. It felt as though someone had been gripping her lungs but then finally let go.

The priest whispered something to one of his assistants and continued to walk forward. The crowd's attention returned to the old man until a deacon made his way to Anna. Again, all eyes were on her.

The young man said something in French, but Anna shook her head in response. "No Français. Parlez-vous English?"

He tried again, this time using hand gestures, waving her over and asking her to follow. Around her, people gasped in shock and began to swarm Anna's legs, arms, and hair, trying to touch the girl who the holy priest wanted to see. The overzealous atmosphere made Anna incredibly nervous, but she continued to follow.

The deacon led her away from the crowd and into the church. The calming scent of frankincense and myrrh drew her into the beautiful atmosphere of the spiritual world.

The ribbed vaulted ceiling of the church drew Anna's eyes upward. Sunlight beamed through beautiful stained-glass windows that painted colorful reflections in the black-and-white marble floor. She was led past statues of saints and carved wooden reliefs into a small room, the priest's office. The deacon gestured for her to sit and wait. He closed the narrow wooden door and left Anna to wonder if this Father Bernard could be who she felt he was.

Anna was so deep in thought in the tiny room that she hardly noticed the door quietly open. The priest glided before her and took a weightless seat in the chair facing her.

"My child," the priest said in heavily accented English. "I am Father Bernard."

"My name is Anna," she said, placing her palm into his warm outstretched hand.

"I know who you are."

Anna's eyes grew wider. She looked into the closed lids of the man in front of her.

"May I touch your face?" he asked calmly.

Automatically, Anna came forward and knelt next to his chair. Soft wrinkled fingers began to glide over her face, but she did not feel their touch. Instead, Anna sensed lines of heat radiating from his fingertips as he traced the outline of her forehead, then down the middle of her nose, outward to her eyes and cheekbones and finally to her lips.

The priest smiled and said, "You look like your grandmother."

Anna felt her mouth drop open. She felt for the chair behind her. This was unreal.

"She was beautiful," Anna managed to mumble out, "...but she died."

The priest nodded with understanding. "Her physical body did, yes, but she remains with you and she will forever remain beautiful."

Father Bernard's blind eyes continued to focus on her as if they were open.

"It brings me great happiness to see you here. God used me as their matchmaker, you know. Here in Paris,"

Anna remained stunned.

"But you must already know the story."

The man touched the missing part of his ear and chuckled lightheartedly as if the memory brought him back to a joyful time.

"You were the man my grandfather shot?"

"Yes. Yes," the priest said with an ethereal smile. "I was lost back then, and I often think of how my life would have turned out if it had not been for your grandfather. God used him as a messenger. When I was lying on the street bleeding from my ear, I saw an angel. That image forever transformed me; it forced me to change my life."

"What do you mean you saw an angel?" Anna's voice felt hoarse.

"I would like you to tell this to your grandfather. He is ill right now, isn't he?

"Yes...but..."

"I know." The priest solemnly nodded and tented his fingertips together. For a moment, his face grimaced with sadness.

"I watched your grandfather walk away with your grandmother leaning on his arm. A beautiful silvery-white translucent figure followed her for several steps and then turned to look at me before vanishing in front of my very eyes. I have never forgotten that image."

Anna's stomach flipped. "Father, how is it that you knew my grandfather was sick?"

"My child..." An astute smile framed his pale lips. "God uses more sophisticated forms of communication than phones or the internet."

"You mean that you have been communicating with my grandparents telepathically?"

"I am just an observer." The elderly priest waved away her question. "It doesn't matter. What matters is that your grandfather is ill. His soul changed my own, which then allowed me to help thousands of people. I know that he doesn't believe in God, but I would like to give him something special. My only valuable possession."

The priest unbuttoned the top of his robe and removed a simple wooden cross on a leather string from around his neck. He kissed it, handed it to Anna, and closed his hands over hers. "Be sure that your grandfather has this when it is time for him to transition to the other side."

The thought of Grandfather dying brought a stream of tears to Anna's eyes.

"This cross was carved by St. Bernard of Clairvaux in the twelfth century. It will protect your grandfather on his journey home."

Anna thanked the old man and wiped away her tears, completely overwhelmed with emotion.

"I know you have a lot of questions, but it is not the right time for you to know the answers." The priest stood up, signaling that their conversation was at an end.

Anna bowed her head and the priest blessed her.

"Your soul is full of violet light. Soon you will begin a new path, but first, finish what you have been chosen to do."

A surge of heat traveled through Anna's body.

"One more thing, be careful when you meet the dragon man. He is dangerous."

"What does that mean?" Anna begged for clarity.

"You will know." The priest closed the door.

Somehow, without even thinking, Anna's legs carried her swiftly out of the side exit of the church and into a parked taxi.

"Bonjour. Charles De Gaulle Airport."

Chapter 38

Charles De Gaulle Airport soon turned into Sky Harbor airport, which welcomed her back to an oasis in the middle of the desert—the greater Phoenix metropolitan area. Anna picked up a cappuccino at Cartel Coffee Lab and watched a digital advertisement for Arizona State University flash overhead. If she had started law school, instead of picking up and flying to Europe, none of this would have happened.

Around her, passengers carried about their everyday lives, but Anna no longer felt like one of them. The feeling was both empowering and isolating.

Inside a ride-share, Anna texted her parents that she had arrived an hour early and had caught a car. The freeway took her past Dreamy Draw Park, the last place her life had remained unchanged before she got into her car and drove to the corner of Bell Road and Frank Lloyd Wright hearing Beethoven's Fifth Symphony.

I have come full circle.

Anna's mother was waiting outside as the car pulled up. Immediately, Anna was swept up in emotions. Her body began to loosen; it felt as though her mother's energy was removing the tension from her limbs.

"When can we see Grandpa?" Anna asked nervously.

Three days ago, Anna's grandfather had been admitted into the Mayo Clinic with severe cardiac arrhythmia. Her father had been at the hospital while her grandfather hung to life.

Her mother stroked her hair and said, "We'll go in the morning. The cardiologist's team was able to stabilize him. He's just sleeping now."

"Mom, can we go now? I *need* to see him. Please."

Her mother nodded and went inside for the car keys. Anna stepped into her house as if entering it would erase memories of the past months. Leaning against the wall to the right was a large rectangular package. The word FRAGILE was stamped across it. *It must be Grandmother's portrait that Maria Arnett shipped from Berlin.*

They entered the polished hospital and Anna's mind raced. *What if Grandfather had an attack—what if he would never know the truth?*

"I'm sure he's fine," her mother said sensing Anna's anxiety.

When they got to her grandfather's room, Anna gently pushed the door open and saw the smiling faces of her father and grandfather.

"Anna!"

Overwhelmed by emotions, Anna tasted tears at the corners of her mouth. She hugged her grandfather's fragile body.

When did he become so small?

"Anna, my dear, Anna! Welcome home."

She embraced her father and got ahold of herself. There was so much to say and yet she didn't know where or how to begin.

Grandfather's eyes were on her, communicating both his many questions and his inability to hear the answers just yet. This was going to be a battle her father would not win.

Immediately, Grandfather began, "Anna! How was your trip! How was Germany?"

The question seemed innocent enough, but everyone in the room knew that that was not the question at all.

"Grandpa, it was something I could have never imagined."

Her father cleared his throat and said, "Dad, Dr. Browning warned you not to get too excited. Let's save these questions for the morning. I'm sure Anna is tired, too."

Grandfather shot him a sharp look. "I may not have till morning!"

Anna's eyes grew big. "Grandpa!"

"My dear, I'm fine. I just can't wait any longer. Your emails about Helga... I have so many questions."

Her father cut in, "Anna, what emails?"

"Get Dr. Browning in here!" Grandfather bellowed.

"Calm down," Anna's dad whispered, "I'll call for her." He left the room and returned several minutes later with Dr. Browning.

"Doctor," John began, "my son needs your confirmation that I am well enough to hear about my granddaughter's trip to Germany. I might remind you that there is no guarantee I will live to see tomorrow and if that happens doctor, I will haunt you every night and I don't think you'll be happy."

No one in the room laughed except Dr. Browning, who quickly returned to a more solemn tone. "Mr. Venu, I try to leave my work at the office, and a haunting just won't do." Her large, knowing eyes gave John a mischievous look. "If John here can make such jokes, I think he's stable enough to make his own decisions."

"Ha!" John whooped the air triumphantly. "Anna! Start from the beginning!"

With all eyes on Anna, she began to tell her story to the person who needed to hear it most.

An hour and a half later, John Venu sat completely upright in his bed; his face drained of color.

"Pure fate stopped Commander Ritter from taking the life of his future son-in-law. That's you, Grandpa."

The family was stunned.

"Christ!" Grandfather exclaimed, "How is that even possible? It's miraculous!"

Anna shrugged her shoulders. "The truth wanted to be set free and it was just waiting for someone to go looking for it. I just happened to fall into that current."

"Do you have the portrait of Maria with you?"

For a moment, Anna didn't understand who her grandfather was referring to. It clicked an instant later; it was the first time he had used her grandmother's real name.

"Grandpa, yes. The package was delivered yesterday, but it's at home."

John leaned close to Anna's father and said, "Son, please bring me the portrait. I need to see it now, please."

Her father looked beaten down and suddenly much older. The deep lines in his face showed no signs of confrontation. "Of course," he said softly.

When Anna's parents left the room, John looked at her with an intensity she had never seen.

"I knew," John began, "all these years, I *knew* something wasn't right. I never pressed it because it upset your grandmother when I did. I let it be because that's what she had wanted, but I always knew."

"Are you upset?"

John shook his head. "No, I could never be truly upset. A well-intentioned reason backed every decision she ever made. I just wish she had had more trust in me. That is the only painful thing. It was her fear of my reaction that forced her into living this lie her whole life."

"Grandpa, I don't think it was you." Anna reached for his hand. It felt soft and light, as if it could merely float in the air like a feather if she let go.

"Admitting this lie meant admitting her entire past. I don't think Grandmother wanted to face it. Telling you would mean reliving the war and the pain of those years, and she probably just couldn't go through it again."

John nodded in agreement.

"She loved you, Grandpa. You know this. The war was a part of her that she needed to not bring into the future with you."

John looked into Anna's eyes. "When did you become so wise?"

A much-needed smile broke into both of their faces.

"You're taking an old man's only virtue. At least leave me my wisdom."

Anna burst into laughter just as her mother and father came through the door with the still-packaged portrait. With heavy-duty scissors, Anna's father began to tear at the cardboard packaging.

Anna heard a gasp from her father and turned to see her grandmother's serene face glowing through layers of clear wrapping. Carefully, her mother cut through the remaining packaging, freeing Maria from the final confines of Germany. Together they placed the portrait on top of the table facing John's bed and leaned it against the wall.

"She is perfect..." Grandfather's voice cracked.

The deep sense of loss Anna felt when Grandmother first died resurfaced. This very moment was what the last several months had been about; aligning the past with the present and bringing peace to those who loved her grandmother most.

A nurse knocked and peeked her head into the room. "I'm sorry to interrupt, but your father's sleeping medication should be taking effect shortly. You may want to say your goodbyes while he's still lucid."

Everyone looked at Grandfather.

"I'm fine," John said. "I have Maria with me now." His smile glowed with genuine happiness. "Everyone's tired. Go to bed and I will see everyone for breakfast."

Anna embraced her grandfather in silence before leaving the room. Then she and her parents walked outside into the cool desert air.

Above them, the stars shone brighter than they had under the lights of the Berlin skyline. In the desert, they glowed like planets.

Anna's head hit her pillow and heavy sleep overtook her. She had no dreams, just deep slumber. In the morning, her mother's voice woke her up. She was crying. Anna immediately knew the reason why.

"Grandfather?"

Her mother nodded and hugged her. In the kitchen, her father paced and appeared to be wiping his face.

"What happened?" Anna ran over to him.

"We just got a call from the hospital. Dad died in his sleep."

Bereft, Anna and her family went into her grandfather's hospital room. His eyes were closed, his face serene. In his right hand, Anna saw the wooden cross she had given him from Father Bernard.

Dr. Browning handed her father a slip of paper. "Your father was holding this in his left hand. He must have known…"

Anna's father took the paper and read it out loud, "I can't wait to see Maria." Anna's father turned to face them wide-eyed.

All three of them looked at Grandmother's portrait. She continued to smile, unchanged. Anna understood that Grandfather's desire to find the truth was what kept him hanging onto life. That gave Anna a profound sense of closure.

Chapter 39

A sense of closure came from returning to Phoenix itself. The desert air stroked Anna's cheeks and quickly dried any tears following her grandfather's death.

Had it been over a month now?

However, that same soft breeze that carried with it the scent of the Sonoran Desert no longer inspired her; thus, it no longer served her. All around, downtown Phoenix residents lounged on couches and clicked their fingertips on laptops inside the eclectic Lola Coffee Bar. The glass windows overlooked the tracks of the Phoenix light rail.

I can't stay here anymore, Anna thought. *It's all too familiar. I've outgrown you, Arizona.*

She already missed the spirited freedom of her life in Berlin. Anna browsed through images of San Francisco and Seattle.

Maybe that's what's next?

Anna took time to observe her new post-Berlin self and realized that investigative journalism would be her route. Filling the holes of people's stories excited her, and she missed the challenge of searching for clues.

After her grandfather's funeral, there had been several things to lay to rest. Anna was relieved to have had the help of her mother and father; she was tired of dealing with the past on her own.

Together, they had changed her grandmother's gravestone to her real name: Maria Ritter Venu. She packed a glass jar with earth from her grandmother's gravesite and shipped it to Benedikt Ritter in Berlin. When he received it, he spread the dirt on Helga's gravesite and changed her gravestone to read her real name: Helga Eckert. Anna contacted Inna in Austria and finally cleared up her family mystery. Inna cried over the phone, thanked Anna repeatedly, and began planning a trip to Berlin to visit Helga's grave.

Outside the café, an older man slowly made his way past the window on a shiny black sports bicycle. Anna was struck with the question of what had happened to Officer Razumov?

Anna wondered if he, too, had become someone's grandfather, perhaps cycling down the streets of Moscow. The urge for an answer pulled at her. At her fingertips, she had much of the world's information, records, and social connections. *Why haven't I looked for information about him before?*

She typed "Razumov" into Facebook. Only ten matches came up: the faceless profile of an online gamer, a young woman, a painter, and a few others. To each match, she typed a message explaining her search to find Razumov's descendants: "The man I am looking for was in his early thirties at the end of WWII; tall, had dark hair and was an officer in the Red Army's infantry. He fought in the Battle of Berlin and had a mother and younger sister in Moscow."

She would end the message with a request: "He also had a scar on his face. If everything is a match, please describe the scar."

Specifically, Anna was looking for the jagged scar on his left temple as the final identification marker. A few messages filtered into her inbox without any match.

The wheels in her investigative mind turned, and Anna decided that just Facebook wasn't enough. Since Razumov was Russian, there had to be a Russian platform that was more popular.

Anna did another search and came up with VKontakte, the largest Russian social networking site.

She easily made an account using their English version and again typed in the name Razumov.

"Shit!" Anna said out loud.

9,029 results showed up on her screen.

How am I going to go through all these people? This is impossible...

To the right of the screen were several filters prompting Anna to narrow her query to the city of Moscow. There were 961 Razumovs in Moscow. She exhaled a heavy sigh.

Here we go...

With the use of Google translate, Anna created a generic message in poorly translated Russian and added: "If this description does not match your relative, please do not respond to me. I'm sending out 961 individual messages. Have pity on my inbox."

For the next three weeks, Anna set to work messaging fifty matches a day. The process was grueling.

Several respondents wished her luck; some flirted, while others told stories of their relatives and their experiences in the Red Army. Clearly, her concluding sentence was getting lost in translation.

It was midnight and Anna's eyes were burning from fixating on her computer screen. She closed them and refocused on her window. Behind her golden curtains, a new moon contrasted sharply against the clear dark sky. A message popped into her VKontakte account and as Anna read the English words, her eyes grew wide with sheer excitement. *An answer—from the right person? Could it have finally arrived?* She reread the last line aloud.

"My grandfather had a scar that ran above his left ear; if this matches what you are looking for, message me right away."

Immediately, Anna clicked on the Razumov who had responded to her message. His first name was Dimitri; he was from Moscow but now lived in England while attending Oxford. Anna couldn't believe it. Could he really be the grandson of Officer Razumov? She began typing a response:

"Dimitri, I can't even believe this, but I think your grandfather is the man I've been searching for! I have so many questions—I hope you don't mind answering them."

For the next few days, Anna was attached to her computer and cell phone even more than she had been in the past few weeks. She and Dimitri had been texting each other through WhatsApp every other hour. Anna was caught in the whirlwind of yet another family and the ways in which their fates played out.

Georgiy Pavlovich Razumov was indeed the man grandmother had fallen for. But Dimitri didn't have the same connection to his grandfather as Anna had had with her grandmother. He had died in 1995 and Dimitri knew him more from the stories his family told of him rather than from Razumov himself. Dimitri sent Anna a photograph of his grandfather before WWII.

George P. Razumov

After the war, Razumov returned to Moscow and enrolled in medical school, motivated by his experiences in battle only to be arrested on false charges of conspiring against the Communist Party.

Razumov would spend the next four years in Siberian gulag camps surrounded by the horrible memories of war and by the men who also experienced them. He was released and rehabilitated after Stalin's death.

Given another chance at a life worth living, Razumov eventually became a nationally known orthopedic surgeon, got married, and had a son and daughter. Following Perestroika, Razumov's son found success in business and Dimitri planned to follow in his footsteps.

The more Anna spoke with Dimitri, the more she couldn't help but feel that same spark of interest she had once felt with Frederick. And yet, this felt different. From the beginning, Frederick was cold, closed off, and secretive—red flags Anna now realized she should have picked up on immediately. Dimitri was the opposite: He was open, honest, and warm with a great sense of humor.

Their conversations became more personal and more frequent. Somehow, she almost forgot why she had started speaking with Dimitri in the first place until he suggested they go on a trip together.

"From what I heard about my grandfather," Dimitri began, "he never liked vacations, but every July he would go to our dacha—our summer home, and completely go rogue."

"What do you mean?" asked Anna curiously.

"He said his best friend had died in July of nineteen forty-five. He went there to mourn his death."

"That's so sad," Anna responded, moved by the story.

"Yeah, but it was strange. He wouldn't take phone calls, and he wouldn't talk about it—I mean, nothing. I don't even know his friend's name!"

"War silences people in their pain," Anna responded.

They shared a moment of silence that Dimitri broke, "Anna, what I started saying earlier was, let's travel somewhere together. I want to see you in person."

A thousand miles away, Anna blushed into her cellphone; she, too, wanted to see him.

It wasn't until Anna lay in bed staring at the whiteness of her ceiling cast in the evening's shadow, excited about what could be between them, did the past truly dawn upon her.

She sat up in bed. By July, the war had already ended. Razumov was already with her grandmother. *That is what Razumov was mourning every July—the last day they were together!*

A great sadness suddenly overtook her. *Had Grandmother mourned him, too?*

Razumov must have searched for her, must have decided that she had died, and with her went a part of him. It didn't sound like he had found such love again while Grandmother had moved on.

Epilogue

Anna sat inside Cartel Coffee Lab at Sky Harbor Airport, waiting for her flight. With her feet resting on top of Calvin, she watched the flow of people coming and going through the terminal. *Souls passing one another without any knowledge if they were ever to meet.*

A sense of privilege came over her. She'd been able to uncover her own web of interconnection. Now here she was, flying to meet the grandson of a man her grandmother had loved until destiny had opened another door for her. Maybe that had been the point all along—for Anna to meet Dimitri two generations later.

Letting the philosophical mood envelop her, Anna removed a new Moleskine journal from her purse and began to write. Thoughts channeled through her pen in clear sentences as if they were coming from a source outside herself. Anna described the connection between all human beings that exists without their acknowledgment, like lines of energy that flow between people, uniting their worlds and pulling others into their spheres.

She thought back to the past year and found herself in the middle of a network of endless connections, some of which she discovered accidentally.

Before, Anna had her family and her friends, a small part of a much larger web that she now understood in one way or another, contributed to her existence and somehow continued to govern her life.

Helga, Ada, Inna, Razumov, Maria Arnett, Benedikt, Father Bernard, Vogt, and now Dimitri, among others. This was a web of connections that had started with her grandmother and those before her and continued onward through Anna and those in front of her.

Anna's thoughts paused on Frederick. He had been such a strong vibrant connection, but now the incredible energy she felt between them had diminished into a memory. Frederick had turned out to be weak and vulnerable, just like anyone who uses violence to solve problems.

Whether it was Frederick, a mass shooter, or a politician who starts another war, they share the same psychological traits: They are broken people trying to solve their insecurities, anxieties, and faults with violence or hate. However unfit they are to support the web of humanity; they remain a part of it.

"Flight forty-four twelve will now begin boarding..."

Anna noticed her untouched cappuccino and took a few sips. She picked up Calvin and headed toward the gate. Her lips formed a soft smile. She walked onward, feeling vibrant energy lines all around her, knowing she'd be forever supported by the universal web of humanity.

The End

Since the end of WWII, there have been roughly 353 wars and military conflicts across the world! How did we get here, yet again? The irony is that psychologically, war gives us a sense of meaning and belonging; united against the "other," we feel a collective purpose.

Exploiting this innate desire is simple, and throughout history, leaders of countries, ideologies, and religions have coerced us into killing each other while they profit from more land, more resources, and ultimately, more power.

As human beings, we will always have our differences, but shouldn't there be a far greater uniting force—our humanity and the sanctity of life? Why do some lives matter less and who gets to decide? Until we can value each other as we value ourselves, we will continue to lose to unnecessary violence.

I hope you can use the Web of Humanity as a tool to question the status quo with your friends, colleagues, and family. If we cannot stop human conflict ourselves, no one will do it for us.

Author's Note

Dear Reader.

As the characters in this book portrayed, ancestral pain impacts future generations' livelihoods, ultimately damaging the fragile web of humanity of which we are all a part. No matter where we come from, our lineage remains interconnected. This is especially true in the United States—a country built on both forced and voluntary migration.

Like Anna, I hope you are inspired to uncover and reclaim your own story, which may have started with one of the many immigrant waves:

*Please note that the following lists major immigrant waves in the history of the United States. It is in no way exhaustive and does not intend to discount the immigration of any other groups or peoples.

Indigenous peoples and tribes who guarded this land for millennia.

1600–1800

Africans who were inhumanely and unjustly brought to the U.S. as slaves.

Dutch explorers under the Dutch East India Company.

English Pilgrims and Puritans who sought religious and personal freedom.

French explorers of the Gulf of Mexico and Atlantic coast followed later by Protestants looking for religious freedom.

Germans seeking economic opportunity and freedom from government control.

Portuguese explorers of the California coast.

Russian explorers of Alaska and the Pacific Northwest.

Scottish who escaped religious persecution.

Spaniards who sailed to Florida to explore the Southwest.

1800–1850

Chinese who came to the U.S. to escape the economic downturn in China.

French immigrants fleeing France's 1848 Revolution.

Germans seeking agricultural and business opportunities.

Irish who escaped starvation during the Potato Famine.

Portuguese looking for economic opportunity.

Swedish, Danish, Norwegian, and Finnish who escaped poverty and religious oppression.

1850–1930

Armenians who escaped a methodical genocide by the Ottoman Empire.

Eastern European Jews who escaped antisemitism and the war in Europe.

Filipinos who sought work opportunities in Hawaii.

Greeks who escaped persecution under the Ottoman Empire.

Italians who escaped poverty and Mafia rule.

Japanese searching for economic opportunity following the political and social changes of the Meiji Restoration.

Koreans who escaped famine and political turmoil in Korea.

Lebanese and Syrian Christians who escaped religious persecution.

Mexican exiles and refugees who fled violence during the Mexican Revolution and later the Cristero War.

Molokans and followers of Leo Tolstoy who escaped persecution by the Russian Orthodox Church.

Polish who escaped the atrocities of the Franco-Prussian War and the partition of Poland.

Punjabi Sikhs who immigrated looking for work on the Western Pacific Railroad.

White Russians who escaped persecution under the Bolshevik Revolution.

Post World War II

Africans who escaped civil wars and communist regimes in different parts of the African continent.

Bosnians, Serbians, and Croatians who fled the Balkan War.

Cambodians who escaped the Cambodian genocide under the Khmer Rouge communist regime.

Chinese who faced economic pressure and political turmoil in China.

Cubans who escaped the Castro regime.

Czechs and Slovaks who fled the Soviet invasion.

Eastern European refugees of World War II.

Filipinos who fought alongside U.S. forces and immigrated following the war.

Followers of the Baha'i faith who escaped persecution in Persia and throughout the Middle East.

Hungarians who fled the Soviet invasion.

Iranians who fled the Islamic Revolution.

Koreans who escaped northern communism and the Korean War.

Mexicans lacking economic opportunity in Mexico.

Middle Easterners who were forced out of their countries by Islamic extremism and civil wars.

Puerto Ricans who left the ongoing depression in Puerto Rico and returning war veterans who served in the U.S. military.

South Americans who escaped narcotics-related violence, poverty, and government corruption.

Soviet Jews who escaped antisemitism.

Vietnamese refugees following the Vietnam War.

And to the millions of immigrants, past and present, who have overcome hardship, xenophobia, and harsh immigration policies to contribute their hard labor, talents, and souls to build the United States of America. No matter our origin or our identity, we all create the Web of Humanity.

References

The Web of Humanity is a work of fiction, but it is based on real historical events, the stories of my family, and the real experiences of others. Friends, family members, and colleagues were used as the basis for many of the characters to make them as authentic as possible, though names and personal details have been changed to protect their identities. For further reading, please explore the following works:

The historical events surrounding the sinking of the *Gettysburg* by the German U-boat, U 66, are accurate, aside from its two fictional characters that I placed amidst this tragedy.

Regarding the history of the Battle of the Atlantic, I sourced various documentaries, the powerful German movie *Das Boot,* as well as the following publications:

A Measureless Peril by Richard Snow

The Battle of the Atlantic, Volume I by Samuel Eliot Morison

Ten Years and Twenty Days by Karl Doenitz

Black Flag. The Surrender of Germany's U-Boat Forces by Lawrence Paterson

Iron Coffins by Herbert A. Werner

The historical background on pre-war Germany was sourced from:

In the Garden of Beasts by Erik Larson
Mussolini Segreto by Claretta Petacci

The historical information on WWII and the Battle of Berlin were sourced from:

The British documentary series: *World at War*
The American documentary series: *The Unknown War*
The German documentary: *The Unknown Soldier*

The scene Ada describes of the pregnant woman kneeling in front of Hitler's portrait was witnessed by Mussolini when he visited Berlin in 1937. Mussolini retold the account to his lover Claretta Petacci, who then captured it in her diary.

The scenes describing the events that took place in the zoo bunker, as well as the words of Dirk, the young SS officer, were cited from an excellent book:

The Fall of Berlin 1945 by Antony Beevor.

The scene of the American pilot impaled on a spiked fence was witnessed by Marie Vassiltchikov in Vienna and captured in her memoirs:

Berlin Diaries 1940–1945.

The events in Berlin after the end of WWII were based on the following sources:

> *A Woman in Berlin* by Anonymous (later discovered to be Marta Hillers).
> *After the Reich: The Brutal History of the Allied Occupation* by Giles MacDonogh.

Some eyewitness accounts were preserved in my family as events observed during the Battle of Berlin and after the war by my great-grandfather who was Chief Surgeon of the Russian Sector of Berlin after WWII and became the foundation for Razumov's character.

Regarding the Nazi occult connection, as well as its influence on young Hitler and the roots of the neo-Nazi movement after WWII, the following sources were used:

> *The Occult Roots of Nazism* by Nicholas Goodrick-Clarke
> *The Nazis Go Underground* by Curt Riess
> *Hitler's Priestess* by Nicholas Goodrick-Clarke

About the Author

Maria Turchin is a human rights researcher and advocate focused on violence against women. Born in Ukraine, Maria grew up in Brooklyn, New York hearing about her great grandfather's experience serving as the head of the Red Army's 47th division field hospital on the first Belarusian front during World War II, and later as the Chief Surgeon of the Soviet sector of occupied Berlin.

Maria currently lives in Santa Monica and holds a Master of Public Policy and a Master of Social Welfare from UC Berkeley. She would like to express deep gratitude to her family, her partner, friends and especially to her father, who served as her first reader, honest critic and who exhorted her to complete *The Web of Humanity*, her first novel.

Made in the USA
Las Vegas, NV
07 March 2022